MAROONED

A NOVEL BY MARTIN CAIDIN

*This low-priced Bantam Book
has been completely reset in a type face
designed for easy reading, and was printed
from new plates. It contains the complete
text of the original hard-cover edition.*
NOT ONE WORD HAS BEEN OMITTED.

MAROONED

*A Bantam Book / published by arrangement with
E. P. Dutton & Co., Inc.*

PRINTING HISTORY

*Dutton edition published February 1964
2nd printing . . . March 1964
Bantam edition published July 1965*

*Bantam Books are published by Bantam Books, Inc., a subsidiary
of Grossett & Dunlap, Inc. Its trade-mark, consisting of the words
"Bantam Books" and the portrayal of a bantam, is registered in the
United States Patent Office and in other countries. Marca Registrada.
Bantam Books, Inc., 271 Madison Avenue, New York, N. Y. 10016.*

PRINTED IN THE UNITED STATES OF AMERICA

for Tom Heinsheimer

Appendices describing technical details of the flights appear at the end of the book.

Chapter I

HE TRIED TO avoid thinking, to still his mind. Coming out of a deep sleep, he struggled to force himself back into its comfort.

He lay absolutely quiet, his eyes closed. But his mind was a persistent intruder which defied his attempts at silence. Yet, he tried.

In the stupor of grasping at sleep, his thoughts were hazy and muddled. For a long moment he did not know, could not remember where he was. How had he come to be in this incredibly soft and comfortable bed? He allowed his thoughts to trickle slowly upward from his mind like small bubbles rising in a pool. He permitted his senses almost one by one to pierce the haze and to become alert. Yet stubbornly, he kept his eyes closed.

He felt no pressure upon his body, so comfortable was his bed. He marveled at this, but even as he did so he strained to hear sounds about him. Slowly they pressed upon his mind. Yes, there *were* sounds.

For a moment he believed himself to be aboard a ship— a ship at sea, sliding effortlessly through a calm surface. The sounds . . . he listened to a subdued humming. It was a background noise. It did not intrude upon his thoughts, but when he listened for it carefully, it came to him clearly. Other sounds of machinery filtered into his thoughts. There was a vibration, so slight as almost to be more felt than heard. He sharpened his thoughts, forced away the cobwebs.

There—the humming separated into its own distinctive elements. He listened to a slow, easy wheezing. It merged with a steady but barely perceptible clicking. The sounds resembled those he might have heard aboard a ship at sea, yet they were also different, unlike any others.

And there was no motion. Not a shudder or a breath of motion. Every vessel has at least that much, every ship offers its signature in movement. So it couldn't be a ship.

1

He could hear more sounds now: a quiet hiss of air, like a breeze playing ever so gently across his face. It eluded him; it was close, yet he could not place it.

He forced his eyes open. Darkness. No, not really. He looked straight ahead, not moving, and stared at a glow. It was enough. In that instant, with stark and absolute clarity, he *knew* where he was, he knew everything that had preceded this moment.

He saw dim, glowing circles floating before him in the blackness—circles of red, fleckcd with touches of pale green. The glowing circles were dials. They contained letters and numbers and the tips of pointing needles that also glowed softly in the darkness. He had only to glance at the soft glow to know what they represented, what they meant.

The sounds—he had listened to the humming noise of the inverters, the subdued murmur of the blowers, passing oxygen through tubes and circuits and ducts. The hiss of air . . . he smiled to himself in the darkness, amused that he had failed to recognize the sound of his own breathing.

The flicker of mirth vanished as reality crowded into his mind. He understood now why he had struggled to reclaim the enveloping comfort of sleep, the sweet limbo of not thinking. Now that he was awake, and alert, his mind functioning with precision, he could remember everything. He preferred to forget. . . .

Abruptly he reached out with his right hand to grasp the edge of a long fabric strip. His gloved fingers closed around a tab, and his hand jerked suddenly toward his body. He listened to a sound like tearing linen as the strip of Velcro came loose. Then he closed his hand around a curtain edge and slid the curtain along guiding metal rods. In this motion he unveiled a wide, flat window.

He leaned forward to bring his face closer to the window, and looked out upon the naked universe.

Billions of suns blazed before his eyes. For eight hours his eyes had been closed. They had adapted to conditions of almost absolute darkness. Now, more than a hundred miles above the surface of the sleeping planet below, far above the mantle of thick and muddy atmosphere, he gazed in awe upon the unblinking heavens. The universe seethed with light. It teemed with great wheeling galaxies

2

and glowing nebulae and the uncountable billions upon billions of suns.

His practiced eyes separated the glints of red, the soft touch of yellow, the gleam of blue and white, and the blazing heart of colorless stellar fires. At the lower left of the spacecraft window there shone one sphere of exceptional brightness. But this was a world, not a star, and it reflected the light of the sun closest to the planet below. The bright sphere was Jupiter, the planetary giant of his own solar system. It seemed so unbelievably close. . . .

He relaxed his muscles, but his body did not move. He did not fall back against the surface of his couch, as he would have done at any time in his life until just a few days ago. He knew now, as he dragged himself awake slowly, why he had wondered at the softness and comfort of his "bed." What could be more gentle, more comforting, than a cushion of air itself?

Not an ounce of pressure pushed against any part of his body. Not an ounce of weight pressed against his skin, tested his sinews, alerted his muscles. He felt a comfort so luxurious as to be impossible on the surface of the world below, a relaxation of body so unreal as to be beyond description. Weightlessness . . . the result of falling around his native world with a speed so great as to be meaningless.

He floated inches off his contour couch, content for the moment to remain in the darkness of the spacecraft, bathed in the stellar glow of the universe. He floated without weight, without bodily sensation, lighter than the lightest of feathers—and plunged around the world at nearly five miles per second.

He stared vacantly upon the heavens, his eyes seeing the nuclear fires of space, while his mind drifted. He looked down upon himself; he observed his body and the bell-shaped capsule into which it was sealed—the capsule into which his body was woven, while the two, merged as one in a man-machine system, whipped through hard vacuum with a speed of nearly three hundred miles per minute.

He smiled without humor as he thought of plunging across the entire width of the United States in eight minutes. The figures meant nothing. His speed meant nothing, for there was no sensation of movement, no rush of flight. No, that was wrong. If he chose not to look through that window, if he excluded deliberately from his mind where he was, what he was doing, he then existed in a universe entirely apart from the world of men just below him.

His speed meant nothing, for he could not feel its effects. And yet, his speed meant everything, for it had passed sentence upon him. The instant that he thought consciously of this fact, his mind tried to shut it out, to throw up a wall that would keep out the dreadful reality.

But there could be no stopping these thoughts. A sentence of death had been passed upon him. How could he ignore that? When realization first came to him, when there could be no doubt of his predicament, he brushed away the tendrils of fear that snaked into his mind. He brushed away the fear because there was absolutely nothing he could do to save his life. He had tried everything, and it didn't work. Ergo: there was nothing left to fear. His razor-honed senses and reactions, which had more than once saved his life, could avail him no longer.

Now he knew a great sadness, moments of bitterness. But not fear. He had courage; he had learned that long ago, when he learned that every man who flew as he did always flew with fear. Courage was what enabled him to dampen the fear, to use it to sharpen his senses, to give him animal alertness. No one in test flying, or in combat, left the ground without fear as his companion. After a while you came to know fear, to accept it, and you tried to be shrewd and let fear become an advantage. When disaster loomed, adrenalin squirted into a man's system. Fear opened the valves, fear quickened the reactions, let a man's training and instinct operate his limbs faster than his mind could command their actions.

And now none of it was worth a damn. Since there was nothing he could do to change the facts, he—accepted them. He wasn't a hero. He was a realist.

But in two more days, give or take a few hours, *then* he would be a hero. Then he would be a martyr, the first man to be claimed by space, the first astronaut not to return alive to the earth which had spawned him.

They would make speeches, he knew. He couldn't repress the grin that came with the thought. Officials of the National Aeronautics and Space Administration would make speeches by the dozens. Senators and Congressmen would make speeches. The ladies in the hundreds of clubs

4

around the country would sniffle into their handkerchiefs, the editors would eulogize, his friends would curse angrily —but at least he wouldn't have to suffer the speeches that would come in just about two more days.

Sentence had been passed by—*what?* A wire? A relay? Beads of moisture in an electrical terminal? Unknown heat that caused wires or metal parts to flow just enough out of shape so as to be useless? An impossible chain of minute and unimportant failures? Minute and unimportant in themselves, but lethal in combination? He didn't know what had failed, but he dearly would like to know.

Behind him, only inches from his back, separated by thick insulated walls and a fiberglass shield, there was a rounded pack with stubby projections. This was the retropack, the canister of plasticized rocket power that was his return trip ticket from space back to earth. It clung to the gently rounded surface of the ablation heat shield by the pressure of three metal straps. A network of electrical lines ran from batteries, through switches and terminals, through relays. There were control switches behind the instrument panel less than two feet in front of his face. There were automatic controls that were operated by a timer. There were backup firing controls that were operated by an emergency manual switch. There were still more backup firing controls that could be triggered by radio signal command from the earth far below.

Inside that pack strapped to the base of his Mercury capsule were three small rocket motors. Each was about the size of a basketball. Each rounded motor contained exactly forty-eight pounds of rubbery chemical. Each motor, he knew, was tested and inspected a hundred times before it was mated to the bottom of his spacecraft. Each motor was X-rayed, vibrated, drop tested, and exposed to humidity, salt spray, aging, and dozens of other tests. They couldn't fail.

He needed those motors to change by only a fraction his tremendous velocity as he orbited the earth. Each motor kicked for ten seconds with a thousand pounds of push against his line of flight. Three thousand pounds of blazing fire, kicking in ripple fashion, would slow him down by just a little more than three hundred miles an hour. Not much—only one-fifth the speed of the jet fighters he had flown for years—but enough to start him curving back

5

toward that thick, muddy, wonderful blanket of air smeared around the surface of the earth.

If the three rockets didn't fire, two would do the job. If two didn't fire, one could bring him home. The ride would be long, and the heat pulse would—could—become savage. But it would bring him home.

The designers of that little package had left nothing to chance. Each motor had two igniters. It only needed one, but it had two for added safety. It took one squib to start an igniter. Each igniter had two squibs. And the wires that led from the batteries were routed in such a fashion that not even wire failure, or battery failure, or relay failure, or motor failure, could prevent the system from operating.

The system was foolproof. It had so many redundant features that even the backup systems had their own backup systems. It was foolproof.

It had only one weakness.

It had failed.

And so Major Richard J. Pruett of the United States Air Force, detached from active duty and assigned as an astronaut to Projects Mercury and Gemini of NASA, was a dead man. Or he would be in two more days, give or take those few hours that no one could judge with really true accuracy.

The fifth American to thunder into orbit looked through his capsule window as he rushed to meet the dawn. Many hundreds of miles away, obscured by the huge curving mass of the planet, the sun began to make its presence known. At nearly 18,000 miles per hour, Astronaut Pruett hurtled toward the exquisite beauty that was dawn as seen from space.

Through the window of the spacecraft, as he arced well over a hundred miles above the surface of the world below, it seemed to Pruett that it was not the capsule that moved —but the earth. He seemed to be suspended in space, hovering without movement in a star-studded bowl, while the massive sphere beneath rolled with ponderous swiftness toward him.

At the moment no moon was visible. Yet he could see clearly that there were many cloud formations, although their features merged into the night. Toward the distant horizon the earth was absolutely black. This very abyss of darkness revealed the rounded edge of the planet, creating

6

as it did a sweeping slice of stars that seemed to vanish impossibly at a lower point in the sky.

There came the first breath of light. It appeared as a whisper, the most gentle of touches to reveal the distant roll of the planetary surface. For the moment, Pruett forgot the death sentence under which he was flung through space. All his attention focused on the vivid, glowing crescent line that separated night from day. It was a crescent of rainbow hues, brilliant and gleaming. It glowed from within; it shone and radiated light and color, almost like a living band sliding along the spherical body of the planet. Ahead of the crescent line, even beyond the deep blood-red of its edges, light sped over the earth. In this twilight zone the surface lay in blackness, and the higher clouds were scalloped shells over which there was deposited a faint pink glow.

The speed of the dawn disturbed him. His tremendous velocity provided him a sunrise and sunset every ninety minutes. During his first orbits, Pruett had marvelled at this, and was even grateful that he would have the opportunity to see the succession of dazzling displays. It was a matter of time being compressed, being squeezed, accelerated enormously. Every ninety minutes he whirled through a day and night. He was in a time machine, as the entire world spun rapidly before his eyes.

Even as he watched, the earth turned. Beyond the crescent line he looked upon the velvet backdrop for the glowing dawn, the mantle of absolute black. It filled him with wonder. The endless black of space lay beyond the iridescent dawn, with countless, brilliant needle points of stars splashed against the velvet.

And then there were two worlds below, one blanketed in night, the other washed in the light of the star about to lift above the horizon. It came with shocking suddenness, catching him by surprise, as it had for the last three days. . . . No; he shook his head. Almost four days now. Each time the sun had burst from behind the edge of the globe. Each time the savage glare had stabbed into his eyes.

He winced with the pain and turned his head, cursing himself for his carelessness. He closed his eyes tightly, then opened them slowly. He was absolutely alert now; at least, he thought, the sun had jolted him back to some active thinking.

7

He touched the instrument panel with his fingertips, and pushed gently. The slight nudge moved his body securely into the couch. Pruett grasped his seat strap and secured it across his midriff.

He scanned the instruments, reached forward with his right hand and flicked a switch. His capsule had been modified to carry a separate source of battery power for minimum energy drain when he went into long drifting flight—as he had been through the period of sleep.

He twisted a dial and watched the brightness of the panel lights flood the instruments. For several moments he studied the satellite clock panel, noting the readings on the glowing dial, checking them off against numbers that glowed in small windows.

He had four clocks. The first was set at GMT—Greenwich Mean Time, or Zulu Time—which coordinated all time hacks for all tracking and communications stations around the world. The second clock showed his elapsed time in minutes and seconds from liftoff, with a window insert for single numbers. A glowing green 3 stared at him; soon the minutes would read 1,440 and the number 4 would pop into the window. Four days . . .

The third clock Pruett regarded with wry distaste. It ran backward and, until twelve hours ago, it had been a vital indicator. It showed exactly how many minutes, seconds, and fractions of a second were left from any particular moment until the instant of retrofire. The fourth clock was actually the retrotimer and control. Before launch from the Cape, he had set it exactly to the flight plan. But because there are always inconsistencies in any plan, because each orbit was very slightly but vitally different in its time period from the preceding orbit, it was necessary to reset the retrotimer during the flight.

He had done all this, of course. But he was still here, in orbit, and the backward clock and the retrotimer were just so much useless junk to him.

Pruett noted the time. He reached out to grasp a handle, twisted it to the left, and pulled open a small hatch door. From the storage space he withdrew his star chart and flight plan. The star chart had been prepared for him by astronomers before the flight, and was valid for a period plus or minus fifteen minutes from the scheduled moment of liftoff. Well, he'd gone on schedule, all right, and had good reason to wish that he hadn't. . . .

Angrily he dismissed the break in thought and concentrated on the chart. The stars were blocked out in intervals of thirty-minute periods. Carefully positioned on the chart were the major stars, the constellations, planets, and the moon—and exactly where they would be at any one time, in reference to his particular point as he sped around the earth. In addition to this reference, the astronomers had provided him with an accurate angular measurement of what celestial bodies he could use as reference to locate his earth position at any specific time.

He scanned the sky, cautious this time to keep the sun from his direct gaze. Off to his right, Jupiter gleamed against the blackness. The double stars of Grus formed an unmistakable line. Fomalhaut shone to the right of his flight path; it gave him an excellent crosscheck with Jupiter. As a clincher, he picked out Al Na'ir, and then Peacock.

Australia below . . .

The capsule was powered down to conserve the energy of the main batteries. His gyros were caged, the attitude control system switched off. He'd flicked the environmental control system to suit only, bypassing the cabin control, when he went to sleep, in order to conserve oxygen and power. The engineers had added some neat power-bypass controls since Gordon Cooper's flight in *Faith 7*. Pruett could switch on just enough power to bring the radio communications to function. He could block operation of the telemetry system, which transmitted data on capsule operation and on his own physiological processes. These *had* been important before; now, conserving power, fuel, oxygen, conserving everything was far more to the point.

He switched on the radio to call the Muchea tracking station in Australia. While he slept, computers at Goddard in Maryland had been working steadily on his unique problem—being marooned in space. At the same time the engineers at McDonnell's plant in St. Louis were tearing apart a capsule identical to his own. As were other engineers, he knew, in Hangar S at Cape Kennedy. They were going through every tiny fraction of an inch of the capsules, reviewing every line, every cable, every wire, trying to duplicate the condition that had blanked out and rendered useless his retrofire system.

The Goddard computers might have some more refined data on exactly how long he could remain in orbit. He knew that roughly, of course. The information from the tracking radar had flashed their reports to Goddard. The computers were chewing through the data bits: the exact weight of the capsule down to the last ounce, and just how rapidly it would continue to change weight as its living passenger breathed, perspired, urinated, gave off heat, and performed other bodily functions. They digested the hydrogen-peroxide fuel weights, the attitude of the capsule, its exact height in the looping orbit about the earth. The computers considered the rise and fall of the atmosphere by day and by night. They compared his capsule and its characteristics to other bodies that had been in orbit.

When they were all through, they would spit forth their answers. Answers? No—the *verdict*. They would issue streams of thin paper on which there would appear a series of numbers in code. When these came out of the decoding machines, a man would glance at them, and he would be able to tell exactly how long the capsule would remain in orbit before that orbit began to decay.

Pruett raced through a hard vacuum. But vacuum no longer meant what it once did. Space was a radiation environment. It also swarmed, at this distance, with stray molecules from the onionskin atmosphere far below him. He orbited just above a border. Scientists called it the aerothermodynamic border, and its upper edges lay a hundred miles above the planet's surface. If his spacecraft could dip into that border, it would encounter mounting resistance to its passage. Not much resistance. The finest machines on earth couldn't duplicate the hardness of that vacuum. But he was moving at nearly five miles every second, and at this velocity, impact with even sparse molecules has its effect.

The trouble was, his orbit was almost perfect. It lay just above the border. His orbit was decaying, but the key to that decay was *time*. It was a race—and only he could be the loser.

If the orbital path decayed before his oxygen ran out, chances are that he would come to enjoy the notoriety of a narrow escape from death in space. If the oxygen ran out before the orbit decayed enough to bring him lower into the atmosphere—well, he had one of the most expensive coffins ever known to man. He grimaced at the thought, then noted with some satisfaction that at least his sense of humor hadn't abandoned him.

While he slept, he knew that no one would try to call him. No tracking station would disturb his sleep. Sleep was precious to him, and it had nothing to do with being physically tired. Sleep meant time on his side. When he slept, his body slowed down its processes. It required less heat to operate; it cut down on its intake of fuel. In physiological terms, fuel meant *oxygen*. The longer he could stretch out his limited oxygen supply, the longer he would remain alive.

He needed . . . not so much extra time, really. He had run through some of the computations on his own. Twenty or twenty-four hours *after* the last of his oxygen was gone, he estimated, the capsule would start its re-entry. But it didn't matter. Only one hour—only a few minutes "over" the end of the oxygen supply would write *finis* to his flight, as far as he was concerned.

His chances did not look good. In fact, he mused, they were rather impossible. But one never could tell. The superfast IBM computers at Goddard might come up with something he had missed.

He flicked the radios to life.

"Muchea Cap Com, Muchea Cap Com. This is Mercury Seven. How do you read? Over."

They must have been hanging on the receivers in the station down below; the response was immediate.

"Mercury Seven, this is Muchea Cap Com. Read you loud and clear. How me? Over."

"Roger, Muchea, you're coming in five by five."

Pruett ran quickly through the reporting checklist; he reported on the spacecraft cabin temperature, suit inlet temperature, hydrogen-peroxide fuel supply for automatic and manual systems, primary and reserve battery power, temperature of instruments and various parts of the spacecraft, and its general condition. Not until he reached the end of the list did he realize that he had kept the reading of his oxygen reserve until the very last.

The Capsule Communicator at Muchea was judicious, to say the least.

11

"Mercury Seven, I seem to have lost the tail end of your transmission. Say again your oxygen supply, please. . . ."

Pruett studied the indicators. He had dispensed with the pressure readings of the oxygen system, and thought of it now only in terms of hours. And, possibly, even in minutes. At the moment that he passed over Muchea, he judged that under normal consumption rates, he had about forty-three hours of oxygen remaining.

But could he stretch this out? Could he lower his intake of oxygen, reduce the pressure in the cabin? Would this squeeze out additional hours and minutes? The more time he could drain from the limited oxygen supply, the better the chances he gave himself. They were bad to begin with, but quitting was out of the question. Time, time, *time*—he orbited the earth, and life orbited about time, until the oxygen hissed empty, and the story ended. He couldn't tell —no one could—what the engineers would find as they went without sleep in their attempts to track down the malfunction in the retrofire system.

Muchea Cap Com came on again: "Mercury Seven, you're fading out here. We're losing contact. Recommend you go over to Woomera."

"Roger, Muchea."

"Woomera Cap Com, this is Mercury Seven. Over."

"Mercury Seven from Woomera Cap Com. Loud and clear, Dick. How do you copy? Over."

"Read you loud and clear, Woomera. I am still in chimp mode, powered down and drifting, minimum call on batteries. You have my last report to Muchea?"

"Roger, Mercury Seven. We received your last reports from Muchea. Cape has a report for you through Goddard conference.[1] Are you ready to copy? Over."

"Roger, Cap Com. Go ahead."

"Message from Cape is as follows. . . ."

He listened in stony silence.

He had forty-three hours of oxygen remaining. It wouldn't matter if he could stretch it to forty-five or even fifty hours.

What did matter is that he wouldn't have enough oxygen to last him through. Hours before the spacecraft began to edge back into the atmosphere, he would be dead.

[1] Mercury world-wide communications network.

12

The computers at Goddard made it all very cut and dried. He carried enough oxygen for a total flight, including all emergencies, of no more than five days plus twelve hours. He could stretch out the oxygen supply by reducing his intake, by sleeping, by lowering the capsule pressure from its optimum level of 5.3 pounds per square inch. He might get perhaps another six hours at the very outside.

A shudder passed through him. So close; *so close!*

The computers had digested the raw data and spat out their answer. The Mercury Seven spacecraft, without retrofire thrust to decelerate its speed, would suffer orbital decay in approximately six and a third days after insertion into orbit.

It was very neat and specific. . . .

If he used every trick in the book and invented a few new ones, he could extend the lifetime of his oxygen supply system, from the moment of liftoff until it drained completely, to a total of 138 hours.

He had an emergency oxygen supply bottle in his survival kit. It contained enough oxygen to last exactly fifteen minutes. It wouldn't matter at all.

The capsule would drop back into the upper fringes of the atmosphere in approximately six and one-third days from the moment of insertion into orbit. That came to a total of 152 hours.

That was it, then. He would be dead for barely more than a half day—fourteen hours—when his coffin started its fiery plunge back to earth.

Chapter II

"MERCURY SEVEN, Mercury Seven, this is Canton Cap Com. Do you read? Over."

Silence.

The communications operator in the tracking station on Canton Island in the Pacific, a speck of land in the midst of a vast liquid nowhere, tried again.

"Mercury Seven, Mercury Seven, this is Canton Cap Com. This is Canton Cap Com. Do you read? Do you read? One two three four five five four three two one. Do you read, Mercury Seven? This is Canton Cap Com. Over."

The silence hung heavily in the room. The communications operator turned to a closed-circuit microphone.

"Radar, this is Cap Com. We do not get a response from Mercury Seven. Do you have positive acquisition on tracking? Over."

A panel speaker rasped. "Radar to Cap Com. That is affirmative. We have positive contact. The spacecraft transponder is not operating. Repeat, the spacecraft transponder is not operating. But we have positive contact, positive contact. Over."

"Roger, radar. Confirming that you have positive contact. Cap Com out."

The operator turned again to the transmitter. "Mercury Seven, Mercury Seven, this is Canton Cap Com. This is Canton Cap Com. Do you—?"

"Roger, Canton Cap Com. This is Mercury Seven, and I read you loud and clear. Sorry for the delay. Over."

The operator let out his breath in a grateful sigh. "Okay, Mercury Seven. You're coming in five by five."

"I have a message for you from Mercury Control through Goddard conference. Are you ready to copy? Over."

"Roger, Cap Com. Fire away. Over."

"Roger, Seven. Mercury Control will have specific data for you when you come over the Cape. I repeat, Mercury Control will have specific data for you when you come over the Cape. They have a request for you—"

"Cap Com from Seven. Say again that last part. You were garbled. Over."

"Roger, Mercury Seven. Cape Control has a request for you. They advise a complete review by you of all procedures and steps taken during your mission. Cape Control asks you to try to remember anything that may have happened during the flight that might give them a lead on the retro malfunction. Repeat, they desire that you try to recall anything, no matter what, that might have been out of the ordinary. Did you copy? Over."

"Roger, Cap Com. Let me check that back with you. Cape wants me to try to remember anything during the flight that may have been out of the ordinary. Is that correct? Over."

"That is affirmative, Seven."

"Seven to Cap Com. Well, I can give you one thing right away to pass on to Cape that's out of the ordinary. The damned retros don't work. How's that for a starter?"

The capsule communicator choked off his sudden laugh. For a moment he was unable to reply.

"Roger, Seven. I sort of have the idea that they are aware of that little problem. I—"

He stopped. He knew Dick Pruett. During the astronaut's training he had spent many hours with him in Houston, at the Manned Spacecraft Center. They had gone over the radio equipment in the capsule on several occasions. He liked Pruett; he was a great pilot and one hell of a man. He shook his head; Pruett had less than forty-eight hours to live and . . . and he was trying to be funny. The capsule communicator dropped the official tone of his transmission.

"Dick, how about a personal favor for me? Over."

"Anything to oblige, Cap Com. What gives?"

"Just between us, of course, Dick. Will you try to breathe *real* low and slow? Over."

Pruett's burst of laughter vibrated the speaker set into the radio console. "Okay, Cap C—okay, Sam. But it's just as a personal favor to you, understand? Seven over."

"Mercury Seven, you're fading out now. Advise you contact Hawaii. Over."

"Mercury Seven to Cap Com. Negative on that, Sam. Repeat—negative on contact with Hawaii. Tell Cape Control I'll call in to them when I come within range. I want to do some skull time on their request. Do you read? Over."

"Roger, Seven. I have your message, will pass it on to Cape Control. See you next time around, Dick. Canton Cap Com out."

Pruett eased the pressure on his restraining strap. His body floated upward gently from the couch, then stopped as the loose straps prevented further movement. He had developed in his brief time in space a great desire for completely unrestricted movement under weightlessness. Of course, there wasn't that much room in the spacecraft. In fact, it was an ingenious use of every cubic inch available.

15

The beautiful little machine had no more volume in its pilot compartment than he could find in a telephone booth. But it was utilized brilliantly. What would have been uncomfortable, even punishing, under terrestrial conditions, under zero gravity was not only endurable, but the greatest comfort he had ever known.

He thought back to his own choice of words with which he described the conditions in the spacecraft and his reaction to them. None of the other astronauts who preceded him had ever referred to the earth as "terrestrial." It was always earth, or the planet, the world, or the globe. They were the stock, normal, commonplace references. But ever since those first moments, many years back, when he thought in a serious vein of space and his possible participation in its exploration, Pruett had automatically adopted the uncommon expressions.

They were, to him, pertinent and meaningful. "Back on earth" and other such phrases had always seemed clumsy and awkward, and a tendency to cling to the familiar. Well, space wasn't familiar. It was anything but that. It was, in fact, a screaming contradiction of normal life. It defied prediction; it teemed with hidden but meaningful surprises. You couldn't tell their nature; some were delightful and others were lethal.

The one lesson above all others was that you couldn't go into space with hidebound, preconceived notions and not expect to have them blow up in your face. From the very beginning of the program, no one group of men had been more off the beaten path of reality than the top scientists of the country. It was an old story by now, of course, but how many people remembered just a few years back, when the scientists brushed off man as a helpless blob of blood and flesh who could never withstand the violent forces of flight into, through, and back from space? . . . The Black Box had reigned supreme for an uncomfortably long time, and pilots developed a hangdog expression as the Wizards of the shining ivory towers proclaimed the end of their usefulness. Electronics—ah, that was the answer. Electronics and solid-state gimmickry, and great electronic brains. They were better than man. Man was all used up when it came to space flight.

It was ridiculous from the beginning, of course. It had no more basis in reality than did a concept that rejected all machinery and electronic aids and proclaimed mind, muscle, and reflex as supreme.

The scientists had only to look directly in front of their noses to see the answer, but they didn't. They went at it the hard way. They ignored the man-machine system inherent in modern aircraft, in which the living creature and the machine merged into a single entity to attain the greatest performance, the greatest reliability—the *only* system with a built-in safety factor that could meet the unexpected and not fly to pieces like an alarm clock vomiting its parts in all directions.

Pruett bit his lip. He was snared by that unknown factor that could defy the best of the electronic sorcery and the best of man; one in fact, that defied the best of both. His spacecraft had performed flawlessly for its required time of almost forty-eight orbits. It was the best of Schirra's textbook flight and the cream of Gordon Cooper's great mission, all rolled together and with icing on the spacecraft. Nothing went wrong during the scheduled time of nearly seventy-six hours in orbit. The capsule was—well, she was a beautiful, responsive bird.

Until *that* moment, of course . . .

He had come up on the tail end of his final orbit in perfect condition, flashing across the northeastern coast of New Guinea, rapidly approaching the point in space and time where he would fire the three retrorockets. His command and check sequence would come from the *Radar Queen,* one of four tracking and communications ships that formed part of the global Mercury net. The *Rose Knot* cruised slowly in the Pacific to the west of South America, the *Range Tracker* lay off to the west of Midway Island, and the *Coastal Sentry* moved due south of Kyushu Island, Japan. The *Radar Queen* cruised just north of the New Guinea coastline.

The Mercury Seven spacecraft came looping up to pass along the northwest edge of Australia, arrowing in its final orbit toward New Guinea. He ran through a final checklist with Muchea Cap Com. Things could hardly have been better.

The satellite clock system was less than a half-second off, and he corrected this at once. He called off his checklist to Muchea Cap Com in rifle-fire order. He selected fly-by-wire low for his attitude control, using the one-pound thrusters for positioning the capsule in space. He went to retroattitude; the heat shield of the capsule pointed up at an angle of thirty-four degrees to the horizon. Yaw and roll were smack on the nose, the capsule behaving like a dream.

He shut down the light sources within the spacecraft cabin, stowed all his loose gear—cameras, flight plan, star charts, and other odd items in the cabin. He adjusted the suit coolant quantity setting to position number eight. His suit inlet temperature was down to a comfortable sixty-five degrees, and it would drop to between sixty and sixty-two by the time he was ready for retrofire. This would give him lower temperature levels than he had maintained for three days of orbital flight, and would provide additional cooling for the period of heat pulse when the capsule slammed back into the atmosphere.

He called in his checklist to Muchea Cap Com:

"Okay on the clock, and everything is set. Now for the thrusters. Roll left auto is one-one-eight degrees. Roll right auto is one-one-five. Roll left manual is one-oh-one. Cabin heat exchanger is at four-three. Pitch up auto is nine-five. Yaw left auto is eight-zero. Yaw right auto is right on at one-zero-zero. The two-fifty inverter is perfect, holding less than one-six-zero. The one-fifty inverter is at one-one-zero and I have the standby at one-two-five.

"How do you copy, Muchea?"

"Mercury Seven from Muchea Cap Com. Read you loud and clear, Seven. Go ahead. Over."

"Roger, Cap Com. I'm checking out d.c. volts right now. Main bus is two-four; isolated bus just above two-seven; and I've got a reading of two-five for numbers one, two, and three. They're all on the button. Standby one is two-five volts; standby two is also two-five; and isolated is two-eight. Back to main. ASCS and fans are both at one-one-five volts. Drawing . . . ah, two-zero amps."

"Roger, Seven. Do you want to go through your pre-retro-sequence checklist?"

"Affirmative, Cap Com. Let's wrap it all up right now. . . ."

Pruett checked the hydrogen-peroxide thrusters through low and high thrust, switching from the low control level of one-pound-thrust to the high mode at twenty-four-pounds thrust. He checked out the correction thrusters, went quickly through the different control settings—automatic, fly-by-wire high and low, manual proportional. He set up his radio systems, checked again the pressure seal on his visor, and all pressure and temperature levels of the cabin and suit controls. He flicked the control to warm up the gyros of his stabilization system, and set the squib switch to *Arm*.

Five minutes before retrofire time he eased the cabin pressure to four pounds per square inch. Suit pressure slid down the scale to just under five pounds per square inch. The cabin temperature held at eighty-six degrees, and the suit inlet was down, he noted with satisfaction, to sixty-two degrees.

The capsule rushed out of Muchea Cap Com range, and Pruett established contact with Cap Com on the *Radar Queen*. He rechecked to see that he was on UHF-high for his radio transceivers, and that the telemetry system was functioning. He scanned the fuse controls; everything was okay, with all except the landing switch fuses in their live positions.

He whipped over the northeastern coast of New Guinea, ready for retrofire. He went to ASCS RETRO on the attitude and stabilization control system, letting the automatic brain of the capsule do some work for a while to hold proper attitude. He called the *Radar Queen,* using the official communications signature.

"Pacific Command Ship, this is Mercury Seven. Do you read? Over."

"Mercury Seven, this is Pacific Command Ship. We read you five by, Dick. How you? Over."

"Loud and clear. You're coming in up here like you're on stereo."

"Roger, Seven. Understand that you've had enough roaring around the universe for a while. You ready to come on down?"

Pruett laughed aloud. Derek Larssen never had been one to stay within official communications signatures. Once he had positive identification and contact, he threw the rulebook out the nearest window.

"Roger, Derek. The long trip is just about over. I've got everything set here. Oh oh—I see I've already armed the squib switch. I'm a bit ahead of schedule on that."

"No sweat, Seven. We'll just carry it through the count

check." Larssen's voice changed very slightly; he had, without being aware of the transition, switched from the friend to the Pacific Command Ship Cap Com with a job to do.

"All right, Seven, I understand you are going to use ASCS retro, with manual proportional standby."

"That is affirmative, Cap Com. The handle is in right now, and I am pulling out the handle—*now*—for ASCS retro and manual proportional standby."

"Okay, Seven. We've got green lights for confirmation here. Your attitudes all look like they're right on the button."

"Right. She's holding attitude beautifully. This bird has written a whole new book on performance. She's been just perfect."

"Roger, I understand, Seven."

"Seven to Cap Com. I'm coming up now to . . . to thirty seconds to go. I'll call the light. Over."

"Roger, Seven. Standing by."

"The five-minute light is on. We should have the thirty-second light in just about—ah, five seconds—coming up . . . five, four, three, two, one, and *light*. There she is, pretty and on the nose. The warning tone just went out."

"Very, very good. Confirmation here by TM. Timing is perfect, Dick. I'll count down to retrosequence, and you'll call the squib arm at five. Over."

"Okay, Derek."

"Here we go, then. We've got, ah . . . ten, nine, eight, seven, six, five—"

"Squib arm."

"—three, two, one, SEQUENCE."

"Okay! We are in the groove, Derek. Green on the attitude. She's holding her position like we were in cement. How do your gauges read down there?"

"Roger, Seven. Your attitude looks perfect from here, Dick. Coming up soon to retrofire."

The Mercury spacecraft obeyed the electronically whispered command of its automatic brain. The computer balanced itself with its spinning gyros, scanned the horizon with infrared seekers, followed its orders to hold the capsule with the retropack end pitched up to thirty-four degrees, the centerline of the capsule exactly along the line

20

of flight, and roll motions dampened out. For these seconds Pruett was content to be a passenger.

Wally Schirra in *Sigma 7* had run through retrofire in beautiful fashion with the automatic stabilization and control system delivering its performance right on the nose. Gordon Cooper in *Faith 7* didn't have that luck, but he vindicated the astronauts and confounded the scientists by flying the spacecraft manually through retrofire and down to re-entry with a precision even the computer couldn't equal. But Pruett was more than satisfied with the automatic system, and was content to ride along as manual backup to the computer for retrofire.

He kept his left hand poised just above the manual override to fire the retrorockets. There was always the chance that the retros might delay in firing. There was also the chance that the retros would fire perfectly, but that the light would fail to flash on the control panel.

Scott Carpenter had run into a retrorocket firing problem with *Aurora 7,* and Pruett had studied every single detail of this phase in Carpenter's mission. Carpenter went through retrosequence right on the button, and California Cap Com counted down with him to retrorocket firing.

It was a neat count, but nothing happened when the numbers came down to zero. Two seconds after the zero count, the retrorockets still hadn't fired. Carpenter at that moment hit the manual retrofire button. Another second passed before he felt and heard the first of the three rockets ignite. Those three seconds alone meant an overshoot of the planned landing area of at least fifteen miles. No one could tell how much time would have passed before retrofire had not Carpenter stabbed the manual control. For that matter, it would he hard to tell if the retrotimer would have worked at all.

Remembering all this, Pruett kept his hand poised to hit the manual control to ignite his retros. He didn't want to go sailing out beyond the recovery area, and turn his planned recovery into a naval adventure. *That* he could do without . . .

"Mercury Seven, here we go. We're coming up on the five count to retrofire."

"Roger, Cap Com."

"Okay—coming up *now:* Five—four—three—two—one—*zero.*"

Pruett braced himself for the sudden deceleration.

Nothing happened.

Without any conscious command, almost of its own volition, his finger hit the manual retrofire control.

Nothing.

He ground his finger hard against the button.

Not a quiver from the rockets.

Instinctively he pulled back his finger, stabbed down savagely.

The capsule rushed through vacuum at 300 miles a minute.

"Damn!" It burst explosively from his lips.

"Mercury Seven! Do you have retrofire?"

"Negative! Negative on retrofire. I've just about mashed the control into the panel, but nothing happens. Over."

Derek Larssen's voice came to him stripped of all emotion. "Cap Com to Seven. Check your electrical system readings at once. Over."

"No good, Derek. I've already scanned the board. Everything is reading just as before. I've got full power, everything is in the green. I have no indicated malfunctions of any kind. I am still holding retrofire attitude. Everything is in the green. But I did not have retrofire. Repeat. I did not have retrofire. Over."

"Roger, Mercury Seven. Stand by one. . . ."

There wasn't much else he could do. Pruett stared at the control panel and its gleaming instruments, the colored lights, the numbers and meters. Everything showed as perfect! Nothing was awry. Not a single thing . . . fuses, lights, meters, dials, switches, controls, handles—they were all letter-perfect. He knew the control panel and every device inside that capsule with exacting, methodical thoroughness. There were nearly 140 different controls, toggles, and separate units of his control system.

Pruett virtually lived inside the Mercury procedures trainer, a complete duplicate of his capsule, during his training. He had spent the equivalent of several weeks inside the actual capsule prior to the flight. He tacked a duplicate of the control board onto the wall of his bedroom, in his living room, even in his bathroom.

Not until he was able to lay out a large sheet of drawing paper and sketch out the location, shape, size, and purpose of every item in the capsule did he consider himself ready

22

for the mission. He could find any switch or control in complete darkness, operating strictly from memory.

Still, he scanned and studied every square inch of his controls and instruments. He did it a dozen times, on the chance that he still *might* have missed something.

He hadn't. He was to have re-entered for splashdown near the end of his forty-eighth orbit. But the capsule, of course, swept inexorably on through space when the retro-rockets remained mute. Mercury 7 flashed back across the United States. When Pruett crossed the eastern coast of the country he was north of Cape Kennedy, which had been Cape Canaveral until its name was changed on Thanksgiving Day of 1963. Pruett's forty-ninth orbit would duplicate the ground track of orbits four, nineteen, and thirty-four. He had plenty of time, working with each capsule communicator, to recheck every last item in the spacecraft that could possibly have gone wrong.

When the retros failed to fire, he felt his blood shift suddenly to ice water. The long mental preparation for the deceleration effects of the retros, after more than three days of weightlessness, had primed his body and mind for the moment. The absence of deceleration came almost as a shock because of the anticlimax.

In that instant, Pruett knew he was in trouble—in deep trouble. A man could overcome all sorts of problems with the spacecraft. Lord knows the other astronauts had had more than their share. But if everything came unglued—hell, you could set up retroattitude and punch the retrofire button almost anywhere along the orbital route, and get down. Even if he splashed down in the middle of nowhere, the rescue teams located throughout the world could get to him in a matter of hours.

You could handle just about anything in the way of an emergency. Anything—except a failure with the retro-rockets.

Despite the enormity of the failure—and the immediate realization of its consequences—he wasn't licked *yet*. There was always that chance of the engineers coming up with the answer. . . .

No, he told himself. Even that might not help. Suppose the engineers tearing down a duplicate capsule *did* find the snag that had hung up his retros. That didn't mean that he could repair the failure. It didn't mean, not by a hell of a long shot, that he could do a thing about it. He might learn in painstaking detail exactly what had gone wrong, and the knowledge would be damned little comfort to him when the last of his oxygen finally hissed out of the tanks.

That last message from Canton Cap Com didn't do any good for his state of mind. If Mercury Control at the Cape wanted him to scour his memory for any detail, no matter how insignificant it might be, in terms of locating the cause of the failure . . . well, it held little promise for him.

It could mean only that the engineers couldn't find anything, that they *hadn't* found anything. It meant also that they were desperate and grabbing wildly for straws.

Suddenly the temperature in the capsule seemed much colder. . . .

Pruett stared at the oxygen indicators and at the sweep hand of his clocks. He could almost hear the ticking. Each little arc of movement meant that much more oxygen gone. Each time the second hand swept around it meant another minute of life gone, gone forever, never to be reclaimed. . . .

He saw things with a terrible sense of motion slowness, saw them in his mind. He saw the perfect harmony of his spacecraft as it swept around the planet, the wonderful harmony of balance between centrifugal force and gravity.

Everything in space occurred with a mathematical precision and order. Everything in space obeyed the commands of celestial mechanics, and sometimes it was so damnably a paradox. To return to earth, he must fall. To spill back into the waiting atmosphere, he must fall.

But that was exactly what was happening to him. He was weightless because he *was* falling. He was plunging in an infinite fall around the earth.

The commands of celestial mechanics were of the finest order and harmony. They were beautiful; they had always fascinated him. And they were also a beautiful, harmonious trap.

The spacecraft whipped through vacuum, falling in the most shallow of arcs. You can't repeal the law of gravity. But you can bend it, so to speak, and this is what he did with his capsule. Gravity tugged constantly at the machine. Responding to that tug, the capsule fell. Like all other objects it fell toward the center of the earth.

But it was plunging with great velocity through space. It sailed through the seas of vacuum high above the earth at nearly five miles a second. Its velocity gave it a great, outward, whip-cracking effect. Instead of falling steeply, it fell in that smooth, deceptively shallow arc.

But it did not approach the earth, and that was the wonder of it. For the shallow arc of the fall was a splendid mating to the shallow curvature of the planet itself.

As fast as the spacecraft fell, the surface of the earth curved away beneath its curving line of flight. So he fell in the Mercury spacecraft, and he would keep on falling until something could rearrange that harmony, that balance. He had to steepen the curve, to bend it a little tighter toward the earth.

That was where the retrorockets came in. When they fired—or were *supposed* to fire, he thought wryly—they would slow him down. His speed would drop to perhaps 17,250 miles per hour. More than enough!

Gravity would assert its sudden superiority to centrifugal force. The cracking whip of his velocity would be just a shade reduced. He would fall along a slightly steeper curve. And very soon he would slip back into the edges of the terrestrial border, the upper, extremely tenuous remnants of the ocean of air far below.

What's tenuous at a comfortable, slow speed can be a mass of sticky glue at three hundred miles a minute. The sparse molecules of air were a vacuum in terms of man and survival, but that's from a strictly relative viewpoint. The racing spacecraft would start to slap against the molecules. It would hit hundreds of them, and that wouldn't mean much. But the number would rush upward on an almost vertical scale, to the thousands, the millions, trillions, and uncountable numbers beyond.

Everything was so beautifully in balance. It takes kinetic energy—*heat*—to get a capsule into orbit. That energy comes from the howling fires of the big Atlas booster. The Atlas exchanges heat, its kinetic energy in the form of thrust, for velocity. Orbiting the earth, his capsule was a supercharged package of kinetic energy.

It didn't seem that way, but it would—it surely would—in re-entry. He would have to get rid of just as much energy as it had taken to get him into space—in order to

25

get down again. He would have to exchange heat for heat, energy value on an equal basis with the big push into flight through the seas that lie beyond the world of men.

He would yield that energy in the form of friction. The atmosphere would quickly become a seething furnace of heat. He would plunge earthward with a bow wave—a shock wave, actually—riding well ahead of his blunt heat shield. A bow wave of more than 11,000 degrees temperature, hotter than the surface of the sun. Barely a foot from his back the fiberglass and spun resin shield would soak up heat, would blaze at 3,000 degrees, and would spatter away the terrible temperatures in wisps of gases and flowing resin.

He would . . .

"Can that crap!" he commanded himself, in harsh tones. The explosive outburst took him by surprise. His years of experience, his training, his fine-edge of subconscious protection against a dangerous situation, came to his aid. He realized with distaste that he had allowed his mind to slide without control into a wishful state. He was startled at the clarity with which he imagined the re-entry through the atmosphere. He could understand the longing, but Pruett was himself his harshest critic.

Years of flying, much of it in experimental airplanes where mistakes and sloppiness brought only disaster, had created in him an unbending drive toward perfection. That this was a state unattainable did not in the least interfere with his drive for the impossible, for it promised, if nothing else, the highest possible level of skill and capability. Answerable only to himself, he regarded excuses as a weakness and alibis as worthy only of disgust.

He concentrated on Cape Control's request. Try to remember—anything. He realized that it was possible for him to have overlooked something, some small and, at the time, perhaps seemingly unimportant item. It had happened before in flying; it happened to pilots new to the game and to the old veterans with twenty and even thirty thousand hours of flying. That's why the market for printed checklists was just as good today as it had been for years, and why they still made pencils with erasers.

But he knew better than to wrack his brains to find the straw in the haystack of thousands of events these last days. There had been a constant, steady schedule for this flight. He had trained almost incessantly until he was like a skilled fighter about to enter the ring. And then . . . well, this was his first time in orbit. Only four Americans had ever gone the route before. He had exulted (and he still did) in the sensations and miraculous experience of it all.

Under the pressure of meeting his flight schedule, carrying out the scientific experiments, reporting on schedule to the capsule communicators around the world, drinking in the beauty of the heavens and the huge globe below him . . . yes, he could very well have missed up on something, somewhere, Not for a second did he believe that he *had* done so. But he had learned also, under the lash of past errors and accumulated experience, never to take anything for granted. He could permit himself the luxury of generalization. But Pruett had never been guilty of self-confidence to the extent of *knowing* that he might not slip in the meticulous schedule of his flight.

He knew, also, that it was important to approach the problem from an oblique angle, to enter it slowly, treading the mental pathways with caution. Any desperate attempt to discover the error, if indeed there had been one, would only fog his thinking. He had to go through a mental checklist. He had to unwind, to relax his body as well, to free himself from the tensions which had shouldered and pushed their way into his processes of thought. Only by complete objectiveness could he divorce himself from the chilling immediacy of the lethal end he faced. He *must* relax. For a little while, at the least, he must get his mind off the problem. He must step outside the arena for a mental moment, and then return slowly, fully in control of all his thoughts and senses.

He closed his eyes, oblivious to his plunge about the massive world. He drifted gently above his couch, sandwiched in between pressure bulkheads and humming machinery and his control panel, but absolutely free within his weightless state.

He let his thoughts drift, idly, washing gently to and fro in the memories he knew and cherished most of all. . . .

Chapter III

EARLY MORNING was the best time to thumb a ride from his home in Huntington, on Long Island's north shore, to Roosevelt Field. Twenty miles was a long haul on foot, and he learned to leave as early as possible. With the sun hardly over the horizon, the roads were fairly empty. Gasoline rationing kept many of the cars off the roads, but there were always plenty of trucks. Early in the day the drivers were willing enough to pick up a kid in his early teens with a grin on his face and a thumb raised in the time-honored gesture. He'd listen for the sharp hiss of air brakes and the welcome squeal of tires as the rigs slowed. He enjoyed running down the side strip, and swinging up into the big tractor-trailers with their wide, worn leather seats.

He'd tell the driver he was on his way to Roosevelt Field, near Mineola. He said that maybe he'd even get a chance to fly, if luck was with him. Handling a huge rig was a man-sized job, but the drivers were always interested, and the trips were short enough. He'd climb down, yell his thanks, and then take off in a trot for the airfield.

When he was fourteen, an older friend took Dick Pruett into the sky for his first flight. The airplane was old, its fabric a faded and splotched yellow, and the engine dripped oil on the ground. It reeked of gasoline in flight, and it shook horribly. But the pilot didn't care, and Pruett was madly in love with the clanking, wheezing machine.

He often thumbed his way to Roosevelt Field just to watch the planes. In the distance, fighters and bombers snarled into the sky from Mitchel Field. Sometimes he'd walk down to the road that crossed the end of the Mitchel runway and stand in awe as a fighter crashed its way scant feet over his head, tucking up its gear like a crippled bird and fleeing to the haven of the skies.

But at Roosevelt he could get close to the planes. He could watch the pilots shouting contact to the mechs, the wooden props swinging down suddenly and catching with a stuttering cough. He loved to stand behind the ships when the pilots revved them up for power checks. The air blast whipped back, throwing up dust, stinking of oil and gasoline. It flattened the grass down like the ears of a frightened dog, and it blew strong and heady into his face.

More than once he walked to the end of one particular runway. There was a marker at the site. Sometimes he would place his hand gently on the marker, sliding his fingers slowly over its surface. It was then that he would see in his mind a silver monoplane bouncing along the grass, moving with painful acceleration, bumping until the tail came up and the speed came. He listened in complete silence as the old-timers at the field recalled that great moment when Charles Lindbergh opened the throttle on his Ryan and launched himself on an incredible journey and into fame. From this runway, from this very spot, he thought, flushed with the wonder of being right here, at the very same place, where Lindbergh had passed.

But he didn't do any more flying himself. His friend with the clattering old airplane moved away, and Pruett had to settle for the smells and the roaring engines, and the wind blowing dust into his face. He'd stand near the hangars, just watching. One day a man rolled a gleaming new Luscombe out of the hangar. No one was around to help. When he saw Pruett, he called to him.

"Hey, kid! Give me a hand, willya!"

Pruett stumbled in his haste to get to the little two-place ship. He ran behind the right wing and pushed on the strut. The beautiful machine was light and easy to roll along the grass. The man said, "Thanks," and left for the flight line office.

When he returned Pruett was standing on a box by the nose, polishing madly with his handkerchief. He'd cleaned the cockpit glass and was working on the side windows. The man watched him in silence for a few moments.

"You like a ride, son?" he asked.

Pruett's broad grin was all the answer he needed. "Okay, then, hop in."

The boy breathed deeply to soak in the smell of the Luscombe. It was a new ship, everything clean and sparkling. The two seats were side by side, the instrument panel dazzled Pruett, and with great care he ran his fingers over the rubberized grip of the control stick on his side of the airplane.

Twenty minutes later they were at six thousand feet, drifting lazily above white puffs of clouds. Pruett hadn't said a word, but his eyes were glued to every movement the pilot made. He couldn't believe it when the man turned to him and said, "Want to try your hand at it?"

"Y—yes!"

The pilot laughed. "Okay. But remember, she's real light and sensitive on the controls. Handle her real gently."

His hand trembled slightly as he closed his fingers around the grip. The pilot grinned at him and held his hands up to signify passing the controls. Pruett swallowed hard, afraid to believe that he was really *flying* the airplane.

He wasn't. He was manhandling the Luscombe. You don't push one of those airplanes around; you breathe your wants and desires, and the silver machine responds with obedience. Ten minutes after he started, the pilot took back the controls from Pruett.

He landed at East Hampton, far out on the Island. "I'll be back in a little while," he said. "Stick with the airplane and don't let anyone fool around with it."

An hour later the man was back, and they were at the end of the runway. "Hang on to the stick lightly, and put your feet on the pedals," the pilot ordered. "Now, you can follow through with me on the controls, and really get the hang of it." Pruett nodded. The Luscombe bounced down the strip, and Pruett hardly noticed the slight nudge of the stick toward him. But the airplane responded and soared away from the ground.

They were thirty miles out of Roosevelt Field when the pilot told Pruett to be sure his seat belt was cinched tightly. "Ever do any aerobatics, son?"

"No—no, sir, never did anything like that."

"Okay, hang on. And tell me—right away—if your stomach starts to slosh around too much."

The sky vanished. Pruett stared at a vertical line where there had been sky, and realized with a start that the edge of the world, where there had been a horizon, now stood on its end. But not for long, as the Luscombe continued on over, rolling around the inside of an invisible barrel in the air, until the ground was up and the sky was down. He had just enough time to catch his breath when the nose went down and a hand pushed him gently into his seat and glued him there as the nose came up, and up. The horizon disappeared again and the engine screamed with the dive. Then the nose was coming up, higher and higher, and the engine began to protest the pull against it. The sun flashed in his eyes, and Pruett found himself on his back as the Luscombe soared up and over in a beautiful loop.

There was a lot more to it, and Pruett's eyes were glazed with delight and wonder when the silver airplane whispered onto the grass at Roosevelt.

There could be no stopping him after that delirious flight. He lived and slept flying, and drove his parents near distraction with his long absences from his home. He lugged home stacks of books from the library, and stayed up long hours into the night. In his reading he mixed adventures and dramas of pilots with serious studies of aerodynamics. He plunged into the world of flight with an exhilaration that ebbed slowly and only after he began to accumulate a growing number of hours at the controls. He replaced exhilaration with competence.

He worked every afternoon when he left school. He scrimped and saved, and he took a job on Saturday night in addition to his after-school work. He spent every weekend he could at Roosevelt Field, and did odd jobs there as well. He accepted his pay in flight time; as little as fifteen minutes made it worthwhile.

On his sixteenth birthday he had ninety hours logged in his book, and he almost flew home on his own private cloud. For he soloed that day, and there is only one first solo for any pilot, anywhere.

The war had almost dried up the supply of aviation gasoline. But by now Pruett had learned the ropes, and he made certain to form fast friendships with several pilots in the Civil Air Patrol. They flew anti-submarine patrol missions off the Atlantic coast. It was a tremendously brave and, many claimed, an incredibly ludicrous mission to carry out. Some of the pilots rigged crude shackles beneath their small airplanes and slung a fifty-pound bomb from the contraption. At best it was a hazardous thing to do, since the little airplanes bounced and rocked through takeoffs and landings, and what the hell was a man in a fabric putt-putt going to do against a submarine if he ever did run into one on the surface?

No one ever found the answer, because one day a Stinson hit a bad hole on takeoff, and the bomb jogged loose. It didn't dig much of a hole in the runway, but it tore the Stinson and its two pilots into very small fragments. That ended the armed patrol missions.

Pruett flew on every trip he could. It meant time in the air, time at the controls. He was sharp at it, he understood mechanically what the airplane did in flight, and he gradually added superb skill to his unflagging enthusiasm.

He graduated from Huntington High School in the summer of 1943, and went straight from the graduation ceremonies to the Army recruiting station where he volunteered for flight cadets. He had four hundred hours logged by then. . . .

Early in 1944 he pinned on his gold bars as a spanking-new second lieutenant, and wore with a deep pride the silver wings on his tunic. As quickly as he could he slipped back to his room and closed the door.

He stood before the full-length mirror. It didn't seem true, not really true.

"Richard John Pruett . . . fighter pilot," he breathed. He stared at the image for a long time.

The Army Air Forces sent him to an advanced training base for new fighter pilots. The biggest airplane he had flown yet was the AT-6 advanced trainer, a rugged and snarling brute with six hundred horsepower behind the prop. At the new school he stood before the gleaming nose of a Mustang. He ran his hand hesitantly along one of the four big propeller blades. He spent an hour with the sleek fighter, in love with its lines, burning with the desire to take it into the air.

He ran his instructors to exhaustion. He couldn't get enough of the Mustang. It howled with energy, it was lithe and tigerish and deadly, and it seemed a fulfillment of all the hours that had led to the airplane. He took to mock dogfights with a fury, and within several weeks had turned aggressor against his instructors, who discovered quickly that the young lieutenant seemed as much a part of his fighter as the engine.

Pruett was more than a natural pilot. He was a brilliant,

natural pilot who combined these characteristics with technical skill.

But he never had the opportunity to fire the Mustang's six heavy guns in combat. With the war coming to a close in Europe, the Army Air Forces released him from active duty to attend college. Pruett had seen the handwriting on the wall. When the war in the Pacific ended, there would be a flood of pilots all over the place. Tens of thousands of pilots, and they'd be so cheap in the flying game that their flight experience wouldn't be enough to make them stand out in any crowd. He'd heard of the new jets in European combat; he talked to pilots who had been bounced by the twin-engine Messerschmitts that flashed by them with a speed margin of more than a hundred and forty miles per hour.

Swept wings, mach numbers, compressibility, gas turbines . . . the lexicon of the budding new age was both exciting and a warning. Exciting because of the new dimensions of flight that lay just over the horizon; a warning because being a pilot wasn't enough. Not any more. You had to be strong in the brain department as well.

Pruett entered the University of Minnesota and cut himself a wicked schedule. Other pilots had done it; he could match any one of them. He took the full four-year course and doubled up on all his classes. The outside world seemed to merge into a fog that swirled around his new life, and he ignored it almost completely. Two years after signing up at the university, he graduated with a degree in aeronautical engineering.

He paused only to catch his breath, and signed up at once for additional work. A year later—and fifteen pounds lighter than when he first came to the university—he had his master's degree in aeronautical engineering.

The Air Force told him to wait for recall to active duty. The end of combat brought with it a dizzying downward spiral in flying activities, and the military was crawling with pilots hunting for airplanes to fly.

Pruett went home. It was the fall of 1947, and he was grateful for the respite from the grueling pace he had maintained for three full years. He was content to spend his days in lazy relaxation. There was plenty of fishing, and mild surprise at the way the girls he'd known in high school now filled their tight dresses. But there was one girl in

33

particular—Ann Fowler. She had been a person apart from the others he'd known and whom he had dated, and while neither of them ever had broached the subject directly, the assumption rested quietly between them that marriage waited at some time in their future. Ann had never pushed, and even in her unconcealed deep pleasure at greeting Pruett, she was certain, as always, to keep their relationship unstilted and undemanding.

Yet she was, as she had been, uninhibitedly frank with him. And it was at her open suggestion that Pruett borrowed a small cabin cruiser from a friend, and he and Ann Fowler disappeared for a week all to themselves.

When they returned, Pruett found a letter waiting for him. It was from the Pentagon; he was to report back for active duty on January 20, 1948. Pruett shouted for joy.

He decided to celebrate by—well, what else but flying? He drove south from Huntington to a small airport near Amityville. A friend of his father—Ed Lyons—had started the Lyons Flying School the year before.

Zahns Airport wasn't really an airport, Pruett thought. There were two grass strips, one about a half-mile in length and the other less than two thousand feet. After walking around the field for a while, he knew that this description wasn't really correct. The strips were grass *and* mud.

But the old hunger in his belly came back. The sight of small airplanes bouncing across the field reminded him of his own student days, and he grinned at the familiar stink of oil and gasoline. Ed Lyons had four new J-3 Cubs for student training, but Pruett paid them little attention. He walked into the one hangar at the field and stared at a gleaming red-and-white Stearman biplane. It was a pilot's dream. This was no ordinary Stearman; he could see that at a glance. The engine was bigger than he'd ever seen in one of these, and the entire airplane was waxed and glossy. He noticed immediately the structural beefing on the airplane; he could tell that this machine had been modified for a pilot who liked to throw it around the sky.

He heard footsteps behind him. He turned to meet a broad-shouldered man in greasy clothes. The man jerked a thumb at the Stearman.

"Like it?" he asked.

"Christ, yes. I've never seen a ship quite like this before."

34

The man laughed. "That's for sure, because there isn't anything else like it. I rebuilt this airplane right here, stressed it to take just about anything a pilot could do to it. It's one of the best aerobatic ships in existence. Say—" he looked at Pruett closely—"aren't you Bob Pruett's son?"

Pruett shook hands with Ed Lyons. "Your old man tells me that you're quite a pilot," Lyons said.

"No, I think that's going a bit too far," Pruett replied. "I can handle an airplane with a lot of them, but as far as I'm concerned, I've just about opened the door. But one good thing is in my favor," he grinned. "The Air Force trusts me with their iron birds."

They sat in Lyons' office, drinking coffee and discussing Pruett's flying background. Lyons stood up suddenly. "Want to go up with me in the Stearman? I'd like to see how you'll make out with her."

"You're *asking* me if I want to fly that airplane? Don't ask twice—let's go!"

Pruett knew that he was with one of the true "old-timers" of aviation. His father had told him about Lyons' background, how he had flown around much of the world as a soldier of fortune. No one really knew how many hours Lyons had spent in the air, and the pilot couldn't have cared less. He was rated for just about everything that could get off the ground.

In 1937 Lyons had flown Russian Katushka attack bombers in Spain and petrified a succession of rear gunners by flying below treetop height, screaming through narrow mountain passes in vertical banks, because there wasn't enough room to get the airplane through in level flight. He would bring the powerful Katushka to point-blank range when he went in after his targets, almost as if he were trying to decapitate enemy soldiers with the flashing propeller.

With four big guns firing forward in the Katushka, Lyons would grin when opposing fighters bounced him. The Russian biplane was considered duck soup by the enemy fighter pilots, for most of the Katushka crews would simply run for it when they were caught by the smaller, faster airplanes.

Lyons didn't know how to run, and he *did* know how pilots were prone to think. They got careless when they encountered the heavier and slower Katushkas. These facts all were weapons to Lyons. Also, he was one of the great masters at aerobatics, and he could do things with the Katushka that other pilots said were impossible.

He suckered in the opposition. He threw the Katushka into a dive when the fighters came roaring after him, but a dive that curved slightly in its path and that put him into position for a wild and skidding turn. He timed it with precision, skidding just beyond range of the enemy guns, bringing the nose of the Katushka around. Which brought the four heavy guns into position to lead a fighter. Lyons chewed the enemy airplane from nose to tail, walking the rudder pedals to get a buzz-saw effect from the guns. This also gave his rear gunner a chance to get in a few licks. Faced suddenly with a demon coming at them in fighter fashion, the enemy pilots almost always forgot about the man in the rear cockpit with his twin guns.

Before he left Spain, three fighters went down before his forward guns. His rear gunner flamed two more. Besides this astounding record, Lyons sometimes used the Katushka as a fighter by diving full speed into enemy bomber formations. He shot four twin-engine bombers to ribbons in the air.

And all this was back in 1937 when, Pruett realized, he was still dreaming about the sky. . . .

Pruett was better than good. Despite his disclaimers to Lyons, he had come out of light cadets as the head man in his class. He had everything going for him as a pilot. The Stearman wasn't new to him—he'd flown one in cadet primary training. Of course, it wasn't anything like this airplane, with all the extra work Lyons had done to it. Immediately he noticed the huskier cry from its engine. It was tougher and stronger, and rode the choppy turbulence at low altitude with a feeling of great solidity. It was spectacular in its response to the controls. The barest touch of the stick brought about an instant reaction with a wing snapping up or down. Pruett had never imagined such sensitivity.

As Lyons climbed away from the strip, Pruett adjusted his leather helmet and goggles and plugged in his intercom jack so that he could talk directly to the pilot behind him. They went to seven thousand feet over the island's south shore, and Lyons gave him the controls.

"Go through whatever you'd like," he said. "And don't worry about the stress loads with this airplane. Okay—" he held his hands above the cowl—"she's all yours."

Pruett was in heaven. He ran through the book—slow and barrel rolls, Immelmans, falling leafs, chandelles, snap rolls . . . he went through cloverleaf turns, figure eights, loops, everything he had ever known in the manual on aerobatics. He did it all with great precision, enough to satisfy the roughest instructor he'd ever known. And he had run more than one instructor ragged in mock dogfights.

"Not so bad, not so bad," Lyons commented as he took the controls.

"Whaddya mean, not so bad?" Pruett retorted. "Where did I drop the ball?" Lyons' remark irritated him. Hell, he'd flown that Stearman with absolute precision through *every* maneuver.

"Anyone can run with the ball, my friend," Lyons said quietly. "Anyone can do that. It's a matter of practice, that's all."

"Hey, now, I don't want to be hard-nosed about this, Lyons, and you are a friend of my old man—" he grinned to himself—"but if I'm such a slouch, why don't *you* show *me* how to fly?"

There was only silence from the rear cockpit. Pruett couldn't resist laughing aloud. After all, any man would be just a bit weary after all those maneuvers he'd flown, and Lyons was quite a few years older. But Lyons had stuck in the barb, and Pruett couldn't back off from rubbing things in a bit himself.

"C'mon, old man," he shouted, *"show* me!"

Lyons didn't reply. Instantly Pruett regretted his words, for they had been unkind, and the man had done him a favor by taking him up in the Stearman. He started to apologize.

He never said a word. He *couldn't*.

The world vanished explosively into a blurred streak of sky, sun, water, and earth. Pruett didn't even know what Lyons had done, but in an instant he transformed the Stearman into a living creature. He barely had time to whisper, *"Good God!"* to himself as Lyons blended his hands and feet and personality into that of the gleaming biplane, until man and machine were a single entity.

The airplane sang its cry of flight as Lyons flashed

through his maneuvers. He didn't fly through a transition of one maneuver to another; it was all a constant, fluid motion without a single instant of hesitation, a flowing movement of glimpses of the sun, streaks of blue water and green earth, and a steadily shifting series of pressure movements against his body.

The snap rolls were unbelievable. The Stearman plunged for the earth, then sailed up and around in a towering loop, wind sighing through the wires. She seemed to poise at the very top of the earth, bathed in sunshine and sprayed with cool air. She floated up and over on her back, contemptuous of all that lay far beneath her, and then the stick moved and the rudder pedals danced, and Pruett realized that Lyons was taking her—at the top of the loop!—through three consecutive, perfect, snap rolls. The Stearman came around through the third roll and the stick was coming back again and the airplane whistling earthward in its curving, inverted dive.

Then the earth returned to where it belonged, and the rising and falling keen of flight from the engine steadied down to its familiar drone. Pruett took a long and a deep breath, letting it out slowly. Never for a moment had he imagined that flying could be like *that*. Good Lord, why . . . why, compared to the skill in Lyons' hands and feet, Pruett was a stiff-limbed neophyte who could barely get off the ground.

And he had called him an "old man," and dared Lyons to show him—big-mouth Pruett—how to fly!

The gleaming wings eased over to the left into a turn. Lyons steepened the bank until the wings were almost vertical, the agile biplane clawing around tighter and tighter. Pruett glanced down and saw the mud-green lines of the little airfield. He—

His muscles tensed. The Stearman was starting to shudder—little motions, light slaps against the wings and body. The buffeting became more pronounced. Lyons was getting into a stall with a steepening bank, and he couldn't even feel it happening. Pruett started to shout a warning; any second now the higher wings would stall out and—

Too late! The Stearman tore herself out of her pilot's hands. With a wicked, jerking motion the biplane clawed up and over on her back, flipping around. The nose

38

plunged, and the earth whirled giddily as the Stearman fell toward it in a spin.

Lyons made no move to bring it out. . . .

The whirling earth rushed upward at them. They had only seconds before it would be too late to come out of the spin! Frantically he grasped for the stick, but it moved suddenly of its own accord. He felt the rudder slam hard over and the stick snapped forward. With the precision of a machine the Stearman cracked out of the spin and glided forward.

Pruett couldn't believe what he saw. The edge of the runway slipped beneath the wings, and the Stearman sighed gently, almost happily, as the wheels kissed the grass in a whispered landing.

"Hey, Hotshot!"

Pruett didn't answer. He was still too overwhelmed with the entry into the spin, the dizzying whirl earthward, his sudden moment of complete fright, and the unbelievable skill that Lyons demonstrated in snapping out of the spin and onto the runway. . . .

"Hey! You back there! Are you still alive?"

The stick banged violently from side to side, cracking against his knees. He grabbed for it to stop the beating.

"Well, well. It's good to have you back with me, Ace," Lyons rasped. "Do you think that with all your Air Force experience you might be able to taxi this thing back to the hangar?"

Pruett didn't answer. By way of reply he eased the throttle forward, taxiing in a weaving pattern to the gas pit. He locked the brakes, opened the mixture control until the engine starved for gas and coughed to a stop. He killed all the switches, pulled off his helmet, and climbed slowly to the ground.

Lyons waited for him, fists on his hips, and his head cocked to one side. Pruett, embarrassed, walked up to him.

Lyons shoved a thick finger into Pruett's chest. "*You*, my young Von Richthofen, are going to buy *me* the biggest steak dinner that it is possible to find anywhere on this island. Right?"

Pruett nodded quickly. Lyons roared with laughter, and spun on his heel. Pruett followed quietly into his office.

That evening—over the steaks and a tall bottle of wine—they talked flying. Pruett was shocked at his lack of knowledge. He had over a thousand hours logged, a master's degree in aeronautical engineering, he was an Air Force fighter pilot. . . . Lyons didn't wave all this away, Pruett noticed gratefully, but neither did he accord Pruett's background any special significance.

The older man tapped the table for added emphasis. "Dick, you're a good pilot. Really good." He smiled at Pruett's sudden glance.

"Never mind the ribbing you took in the airplane," Lyons explained. "You weren't the first and you won't be the last. But you *are* worth working on. You have excellent timing, you understand precision, and you have, above all else, what I call an identification with the airplane."

Pruett listened carefully. "Go on, Ed."

"But you have faults. Oh yes, you have faults. All that engineering is actually getting in your way."

"How?" He was puzzled; how could knowledge of aeronautical engineering interfere with his flying?

"Oh, it doesn't interfere with your flying an airplane in excellent fashion. No, you'd make any inspector a happy man. You fly that thing exactly as the book says it should be flown. *That's* your trouble, Dick. Flying by the book is fine, until you really start to learn how to fly. You can't be expected to notice the little things until you develop a special sense for them. When you're learning, you must concentrate upon the airplane, upon what it does, how it reacts. Sure, I know what they teach you. 'An airplane is a mechanical device, and it will always respond in a specific manner to mechanical laws.' Hell, boy, the Wright Brothers knew that, too.

"*But*—and this is a very big *but*—you must finally reach a point where you no longer think consciously of these things. I don't mean you are to forget them; that would be stupid, and you'll kill yourself one day.

"You've got to take all that fancy knowledge they crammed between your ears and make it second nature. You've got to stop flying with a slide rule. You can fly with great precision that way, but you're never going to get one inch away from the book. You're going to be a wonderful, excellent, by-the-book flier."

"And that's bad?" Pruett countered. "What's wrong with trying to be as perfect as possible with the controls? Hell,

Ed, it's guys like you who wrote the book. If the book isn't any good, how come we're paying so much attention to it?"

"And who says the book isn't good?"

"Why—*you* did, just now," Pruett said in surprise.

Lyons drained his wineglass and held it out for Pruett to fill. "You've got too much learning between the ears, boy, and you do *not* listen very carefully. I said the book was fine, but only up to a point. After that, well, then you've got to graduate into the next stage."

"Which is?"

"The book and everything in it must become second nature, just as I said. You don't think consciously about it; it becomes like—well, osmosis would be a good term for it. It must become as natural as walking. You don't think about balancing yourself when you walk; you just do it naturally. But every child must *learn* to walk. Right?"

Pruett nodded and remained silent.

"Good! We're getting through to you, then. Now, for the rest of his life, the child-boy-man no longer thinks directly about his balance when he walks or runs. Even when he's in trouble, everything is reflex action. When he's dizzy, for example. He doesn't try to keep his balance mechanically. It's a reflex, an instinct.

"And that is what flying must be to you, if you want to be something more than a mechanical pilot."

The wineglass waved in front of Pruett's nose. He emptied the bottle and signaled the waiter for another. "Well, I'm glad to see you've got good instincts when it comes to good wine, anyway," Lyons said.

"Now, we talked about the book, and you made nonsense about old-timers who wrote it. That's where you're making your mistake, Hotshot."

Pruett winced.

"Your mistake is that you're accepting the book as the final word. It's not. It's not the final word by a long shot, and it never will be. Because we're still rewriting it, we're changing it, and we're adding things to it. Because good pilots with twenty thousand hours are still getting killed, and the book doesn't help them at all. The book, my fine young friend, is a guideline. It goes only so far, and then— well, then you've got to carry on to the next step. And your classroom is in the cockpit." He pointed with his finger, and Pruett looked up. "That's right," Lyons said softly. "Up there—the only classroom that counts."

Later they drove back to the airfield so that Pruett could pick up his own car. He was closing the door when Lyons beckoned him closer.

"How long before you report back for active duty?" he asked.

"I've got about six or seven weeks left," Pruett said.

"Not much time, but maybe we can do something before you return to those iron monsters you kids are flying today." Lyons was silent for a few moments; Pruett waited, not interrupting his thoughts.

Lyons looked straight at him. "Be here tomorrow morning," he said. "And be here at six o'clock—*sharp*." He roared off before Pruett could say a word.

It had been a long day, he mused, as he drove home. Hotshot Pruett, and Lyons had made it all too clear that Pruett was still wet behind the ears. Damn, but that man could *fly*. . . .

The next morning he was at the field at five-thirty. Before Lyons drove up, Pruett had the Stearman out of the hangar. He'd drained the sumps and checked the airplane over carefully.

When Lyons walked to the hangar, Pruett bowed low and intoned: "Greetings, O Master! Thy pupil awaits thee."

Lyons grinned at him. "You learn fast, Hotshot. At least you've got the right attitude." He glanced at the Stearman. "All checked?"

"She's ready."

"Good. I'm not." He tossed a ring of keys at Pruett. "Open the office and make us some coffee. That's the first step in becoming a good pilot." He disappeared within the hangar.

During the next six weeks Lyons hammered at him. He gave Pruett no quarter, allowed him no excuses, shouted and cursed at him for the slightest infraction of Lyons' orders. He was merciless, and he knew how, with the barbed needle of the veteran, to bring Pruett's temper to the boiling point. Whenever that happened, and Pruett began to turn crimson in his rage, Lyons would shove his face against Pruett's nose and talk in a voice like sandpaper.

"What's the matter, Hotshot? Too much for you? You're a great big pilot who knows everything? Maybe," he sneered, "you want to teach me instead? How about it, Hotshot?"

And always in time Pruett cooled off and held his tongue. For this was as much an element of his maturing as anything else, he realized. Lyons needled him at every opportunity on the ground and in the air. Once, coming out of a series of maneuvers, he brought his pupil to the point of choking with his rage.

Immediately Lyons passed the controls to him. "Okay, Hotshot, since you're such a tiger today, let's see how you can . . ."

He rattled off a series of demanding aerobatic maneuvers and ordered Pruett to perform them with absolute precision. Pruett tried but failed, his body flushed with anger. He vented his rage on the airplane, and the airplane, of course, flew like a truck. To show his disgust, Lyons would grab the stick and bang it back and forth, pummeling Pruett's thighs and knees.

He had welts and bruises in profusion when the light dawned. Lyons was delighted when Pruett accosted him in the office and insisted on a blunt talk. He asked his tutor if the needling was intended to sweep him into anger.

"What ever gave you that idea?" Lyons queried, his voice suspiciously pleasant.

"Because, goddamn you, you always give me the stick whenever we have a fight, and you insist that I go through those maneuvers, and you know goddamned well that that's the worst time for . . ." His voice trailed off slowly.

"Oh. I see," he continued quietly.

"You see *what?*"

Pruett looked like a kid with his hand caught in the cookie jar. "You've worked that needling bit to a fine perfection, haven't you?"

"Who, *me?*" Lyons asked.

"Yes, you . . . you old reprobate. Now I see what you've been doing to me all this time. Why, you've been doing your best to get me mad!"

"And, if you will notice—" Lyons drove the needle in deeper—"I have been very successful. What else have you learned today, Hotshot?"

"You know damned well what I've learned."

43

"That's right, Hotshot. You've been letting your anger get the best of you. You've been a simple-minded ass who forgot he was a pilot who knew how to handle a plane. And you were flying that airplane like you were kicking a dog that had leaked all over your new pants.

"You ever do that in combat, Hotshot, and you're a dead man." He said it slowly, softly. "A very dead man."

Pruett asked him to continue.

"That part of your schoolwork is over," Lyons said. "But you had to learn it the hard way. There's nothing wrong with anger, or fear. They kick your glands in the slats and they shoot adrenalin into you like it was coming from a fire hose. It whips you into a fine pitch, if—and *only* if— you still stay in control."

Pruett slumped in his chair and waved an arm. "And all this time, when you stuck in the needle, I twitched, just like a Pavlovian dog." He screwed up his face. "Okay, Ed," he sighed, "I've learned my lesson."

"Mr. Pruett?"

"Yeah. What now?"

"*Mister* Pruett, I think you will be pleased to know that a certain Mr. Hotshot has departed these premises."

Pruett looked up, eyes wide. Lyons held out his hand and Pruett shook with him.

"Today is graduation day, young friend," Lyons said. "I don't think the needling is ever going to work again. Now, since you've proved you're so smart, go make us some coffee. . . ."

They had three weeks before Pruett was to leave, and they were in the air as often as the weather permitted. Lyons dropped the needle, and they settled down to hard, unremitting work. Pruett uttered silent thanks to the older man, for he realized the priceless gift that Lyons was bestowing on him. He was infusing Pruett with the best that he—Lyons—had to give. And it was a priceless gift that very few pilots ever earned for themselves.

Unlike many pilots, Pruett liked spins. He seemed to have no sensory endings in his stomach as he whirled and spun, rolled and dove, soared and skidded happily in the sky. If Lyons had been rough before, he was brutal now in his demands. But Pruett no longer took offense at the shouts and the profane cries that Pruett was a clumsy, ham-handed ox. Lyons was driving him as hard as he could, and this in itself was the greatest and most meaningful compliment that he could have paid the youngster. It could mean only that Lyons had judged him capable of trying for perfection, the never-attainable but always-sought level of skill. Judged him capable, but not yet there.

As an Air Force fighter pilot Pruett was fully qualified for instrument flight. Using the gauges for reference to an outside world blotted out by clouds and fog, he flew with skill and confidence. He had a flair for instrument flying; he was able to switch his senses almost instinctively from a view of the outside world to the universe enclosed within his cockpit and represented by the glowing dials and needles. In cadet training, his instructors had been visibly impressed by his obvious skill.

His instructors had been impressed, but Lyons wasn't. Before Pruett left for the Air Force, Lyons drove home another hard lesson that would prove invaluable for all the years to come. The Air Force trainers and fighters that Pruett had flown were extensively equipped with instruments; flying on the gauges was a snap once you got the hang of it.

Lyons put an opaque hood around the front cockpit of the Stearman, blocking out the world to his student. Pruett stared at the naked panel. Lyons had taped over the artificial horizon, the directional gyro, the navigational homing instruments. He left uncovered only the magnetic compass, the airspeed indicator, the altimeter, and the needle-and-ball for judging banks and turns. Nothing with gyroscopic action was left for him to scan.

The altimeter read 8,000 feet when Lyons passed the controls to him. Sealed beneath the hood, Pruett followed instructions to fly different courses, to make climbing and diving turns. Lyons ordered steeper and steeper turns. The course changes came more quickly, more demandingly, and Lyons began to mix the instructions into a batch, ordering changes even as Pruett was attempting to follow a previous command.

His temper grew, until he recognized the danger signs and forced it down again. He'd learned that Lyons never did anything without a reason. Twenty minutes later, Lyons drove home the lesson, leaving Pruett shaken badly.

For those twenty minutes he tried to follow Lyons' constantly changing orders. The minutes melted into a blur, and beads of sweat began to collect on his upper lip and on his forehead. It was difficult, almost impossible flying. And it was *hot;* he didn't know that Lyons had opened the blower that sent warm air across Pruett's feet. Lyons *wanted* Pruett to be hot, wanted him to sweat.

The perspiration dripped into his eyes, blurring his vision. Pruett kept his left hand around the throttle, released the stick for a moment to wipe away the sweat.

"Keep your goddamned hands on the controls, you young fool!" Lyons' voice crashed into his ears. "You idiot, you're on instruments, you're in trouble! *NEVER* take your hands off the stick, you stupid idiot! Fly your airplane!" The stick cracked hard against his knees. Pruett groaned, but grabbed the stick at once.

He couldn't see, of course, that Lyons had directed the Stearman into building cumulus clouds. He kept hammering his orders at Pruett, and the airplane began to rock and pitch wildly. The magnetic compass was useless as it bobbed and whirled in its cage. The needle moved from left to right as the wings rocked and the nose yawed wildly; the ball in its curving tube was a wild thing as the Stearman skidded, and slipped and Pruett fought desperately to fly according to Lyons' roared instructions. And it was *hot,* so damned hot! The instruments were useless to him, he had no conception of up or down, or right or left, and he never heard the warning sounds about him as the engine began to scream and the wires shrieked with the increasing wind.

The warnings came to him too late, for his head was spinning, and he knew, for the first time in his years of flying, the sickening maw of vertigo. His balance organs were all scrambled, his head spun, and he was drenched in his own perspiration. The sounds of engine and wind blended into a terrible high-pitched cry.

He jerked back on the throttle, for he knew that if nothing else the airplane was plunging earthward. He stared in disbelief at the airspeed indicator. The needle was far beyond the yellow caution line; it had swung through the red line of Never Exceed speed, and was beyond even that mark. *And he had never noticed it. . . .*

The stick slammed painfully against his knees and he relinquished the controls. Lyons ordered him to slide open the hood. He couldn't believe it. The Stearman was over on her back, howling earthward in a dive.

Pruett hardly spoke for two days. For the rest of the week a grim-faced Lyons made him fly on instruments, but on the old, classic panel of needle-ball-airspeed-altitude.

And one day, when Pruett eased the Stearman back to earth, he realized that something very special had happened. In the office he turned suddenly to Lyons.

"Ed, it's just come to me."

Lyons was busy devouring a doughnut. *"What's* just come to you?" he asked between bites.

"Today, Big Man Who Flies . . . today was the first time since we started this torture session that you didn't yell at me. My God, you were actually pleasant up there! You didn't defame my ancestry, or call me an idiot, and you didn't use even one little dirty word."

Lyons slurped coffee and raised his eyebrows. "So what?"

"Didn't you have anything to bitch about?"

Lyons tossed the empty cup into a basket. Very slowly he pulled the wrapper off a cigar. He bit the end, spat the tobacco in the direction of the discarded cup, lit the cigar, and slowly puffed clouds of blue smoke at Pruett.

"Nope."

Pruett's face split into a wide grin. "You mean—?"

"That's right, boy. Graduation day is here. You just might survive your next flight all alone. Welcome to the club, pup. You have just completed Lyons' kick-em-in-the-ass flying course."

They had a wild celebration that night. Lyons saved the best of it for the morning. When Pruett showed up at the field, he was surprised to see a second Stearman parked alongside the airplane he'd flown almost steadily for six weeks.

"Today we are through with instruction," Lyons explained. "Today is—well, today's the graduation ceremony. You are going up in Old Reliable—" he pointed to the familiar Stearman—"while I shall fly in the Yellow Peril, over here. And then we are going to have a fight. There's radio in both ships; we'll talk on unicom."

They squared off at six thousand feet. Both airplanes roared at each other, head-on. Then, Lyons' voice crackled in his earphones. "Okay, break to the right—*now.*"

Both Stearmans whipped around in vertical banks, the opening play in the dogfight to follow. Pruett knew he was truly on his own when Lyons flung after him a final gesture. "Let's see how you stack up against an old man, Hotshot."

Pruett chortled at the name Lyons hadn't used for weeks. "Okay, Pop," he shouted into the mike, "hang onto your cane. . . ."

It was the pinnacle of flight. Two men, each with an airplane strapped to his back, each instinctive in his reaction to his machine and the pressures of flight, each honed as near to perfection as a man can be. Only, one had a slight advantage over the other; Pruett knew all that Lyons could teach, except one thing—the *knowing*, deep inside the belly and far down in the skull, of what it feels to have enemy guns ripping up your own airplane.

They went wild for nearly an hour. People on the streets and the roads stopped to watch, staring into the sky as the two airplanes wove a tapestry of magic in their flight. They were like butterflies one moment and snarling dogs the next. The finale came when Lyons ordered Pruett to swing around to his tail. Could he stay with the other airplane? Lyons would use every trick he knew, and he might even invent a few, as he tried to shake his "pursuer."

He couldn't. Pruett clung grimly to the other airplane, never conscious of the movements of his hands and feet, flying instinctively, never allowing the other plane to get away from him, to escape his dogged pursuit. Whatever Lyons did, the pupil matched. Whatever Lyons planned, the pupil anticipated. It was almost as if the same man were flying both airplanes, so well matched were the skills of both pilots.

Suddenly the yellow Stearman staggered. Pruett stared in horror as the biplane flipped crazily, then tumbled in a wild cartwheeling motion, completely out of control.

"My God," Pruett whispered. The biplane tumbled helplessly. Pruett banged the throttle forward, diving after the other airplane. He didn't know that he was shouting Lyons' name, crying out to him.

And he was stunned when suddenly the other Stearman flashed upward, wheeled beautifully down and around in a wicked loop. Pruett turned around to see a biplane sitting only a few feet from him, propeller gleaming.

48

His radio came to life. "And that, young friend, was the final lesson. Never, never believe anything you see in a fight. The other guy is always dangerous until you see the airplane come apart in the air, or until it crashes, or you see the guy jump."

Lyons hesitated a moment. "Let's go home, Dick." Then, almost as an afterthought: "I hope you never have the need to remember . . . to use . . . what you just learned."

They sailed home, wing to wing, tucked in tight, and they were in the same position as four wheels whispered together onto the grass.

Ed Lyons proved to be wrong. There did come the need to remember that "final lesson." It saved his life.

It happened at 43,000 feet, and it was four years later. It was a lousy, cold place called Korea.

Pruett was Ass End Charlie in a flight of four sweptwing Sabres when a pack of MiG's came swooping down from high above the Yalu. They came out of the sun and they were on the Sabres before the pilots could do a thing about it. There were twelve of them, and they scissored the Sabres, eight from above and four coming up from below to gut the Sabres through the belly.

Pruett followed his leader as the other pilot took wild evasive action, breaking hard and swift to the right.

But at 43,000 feet the Sabre simply was no match for the MiG. The Russian fighter sliced its turns closer, it ran away from the Sabre in a climb, and it was faster. Pruett watched big glowing coals sailing into the fuselage of the other Sabre as the MiG's hammered away with their heavy cannon. Pruett pulled his fighter around desperately to force off the enemy planes, but it didn't help. The lead Sabre vanished in a great, angry, red splotch of fire. And the other two Sabres were nowhere to be seen.

He was . . . alone, in the midst of a hornet's nest.

He kept flicking away from the tracers. He abused his airplane, but it was meant to be abused, and it obeyed him in the punishing skids and rolls.

He brought the fight to below 30,000 feet, and the Sabre came more into its own element, and here it was just as good as the lighter, agile MiG. In the bitter fight he caught two Russian fighters in front of his guns, and he

49

watched the wing snap away from one and the pilot eject from the other.

The kills made him too eager, too anxious, and the reality turned him to ice when he realized that the two remaining MiG's had suckered him into a trap, closing from opposite sides at a moment when he had been climbing and his airspeed was low. They had him boxed, and he knew it.

Normally he would never have stood a chance. But he wasn't the normal fighter pilot; he had been shaped and formed by a great pilot, and he remembered, with amazing clarity, Ed Lyons' "final lesson."

He timed it with precision. He waited until the tracers flashed, waited until the MiG pilots were certain of their kill, and then his Sabre lurched, and tumbled out of control. It flipped onto its back and whirled crazily. The centrifugal force in the cockpit dug at him cruelly, but he kept his hands off the controls. One of the MiG's followed him down to watch the airplane and its dead pilot. And suddenly the Sabre was clawing around, reborn, and Pruett watched with satisfaction as his six heavy guns streamed lead into the MiG cockpit, and she saw a froth of red amidst the exploding glass before the fire blotted out all sight of the airplane.

Those were the first three of the eight kills he notched on the Sabre's guns.

He wrote to Ed Lyons that night. His letter was brief, but he didn't need many words to tell what had happened. He didn't use words that thanked Lyons—not in the usual way. He just told him how it went, and he related the episode of the "final lesson."

Years later, when he drove to the field to visit his old master and close friend, he stared for a long time at the wall over Ed's desk. He felt a lump in his throat.

There, in a simple frame, was his letter.

Chapter IV

Mercury Seven drifted in attitude-free flight. The machine remained powered down, almost in a state of mechanical suspended animation, its electrical pulse reduced to the barest level needed to sustain its human occupant with the essentials of survival. The reaction thrusters gaped cold and silent at vacuum, and the spacecraft with its single member of the human race fell around the massive world. The sun gleamed nakedly across half the capsule surface; the other half lay in shadow and the pale bluish-green reflections from the planet below.

The capsule was not alone. Drifting around the compact machine were thousands of tiny particles. Frost and ice, some shaped like terrestrial snowflakes, others looping in form as curlicues, and more, an infinite variety of forms, all sailing in a great swarm around the capsule. Mercury Seven in the miraculous web of interwoven forces existed as the hub of a limited universe, and the frosty shapes orbited slowly around the machine and its pilot.

From a vent in the side of the spacecraft, steam issued forth into vacuum. It did not emerge as steam; venting from the system that eliminated overboard the heat created by the man's body, it touched vacuum and instantly froze into frost and ice and added to the drifting swarm.

The man saw none of this, cared not at all for the process which he simply accepted in its mechanical functions. As the capsule drifted, rolling and turning with the slowest of motions, so his thoughts drifted. He was, he knew dimly, following the course that would bring him to the present. It was a circuitous route of the mind, but he did not object. He gave his thoughts free rein, and he recalled those initial steps that, through the ensuing years, had brought him here—in time and in space—and to the grim facts he must soon again face. . . .

He wanted to wash himself clean. It would not be easy, for Pruett could not escape the nagging conviction that he had prostituted the miracle of flight and the wonder of wings. He did not want to kill, but he had killed. Once in the grip of the high and mortal combat of jet against jet, he acted not as a man or as a pilot, but as a disembodied killer. There wasn't any choice, of course. He was a fighter pilot; in the air, behind his controls, such a man must slip into the skin of the killer or he will not survive.

Pruett and flight were as one. It was not so much that he "loved flying," as so many carelessly spilled the expression in their conversation. His was a kinship with the sky; he did not study or investigate his feelings. He accepted them; flying was as essential to his life as eating or breathing, and he never questioned the matter.

Not even the deaths of enemy pilots reached him; not the bloody froth he witnessed on his third kill, or the pilot who ejected from his MiG—and slammed into the sharp wing of another MiG directly behind him. It had not been a pleasant sight as the body ripped into several pieces, and a thin spray of pink appeared for a moment with the spinning chunks of what had an instant before been a man.

Such things were . . . well, Pruett didn't know what they were. He did know, however, that in the high arena, they met as gladiators once might have faced each other. It was man against man, skill pitted against skill, and it could become acceptable because, despite the momentary differences in the battles, the odds averaged out pretty much the same. You fought a man, and if he couldn't hack it, that was the end of that scene.

No, the fights in the cold and clean edge of the stratosphere he could accept. What ground deeply into his mind was another incident, only one out of the entire Korean War, and it was this he tried to wash off his body and out of his soul.

Eight Sabres were called down from their high patrol to assist a small American force along the western coast of Korea. The unit had struck deep into Chinese lines, and was working its way back when the Chinese cut them off with a surprising dash around the Americans. The Chinese sailed on ahead, out on the water, and then brought their barges in fast to the coast and went rushing ashore. The Americans had Chinese behind and in front of them, the ocean to their right and steep mountains to their left. They were boxed in, they were in trouble, and they yelled for fighters to come blow a hole in the Chinese line ahead of them.

Pruett's patrol answered the call. The Sabres whistled down from high altitude, directed by the fire controller on the ground. They saw the boats, and the doughboys lobbed smoke shells into the Chinese positions to mark them clearly. That was all they needed. . . .

They massacred the Chinese. The Sabres swept back and forth, each fighter hosing its terrible stream of slugs into the screaming soldiers. They had virtually no cover, they couldn't run, and the Americans were coming in behind them on the ground behind their own wall of fire. There were more than a thousand Chinese, and almost all of them met their ancestors in the few minutes of the carnage. The ground was splashed with red; bodies sprawled in every direction.

Pruett came in low and fast, walking the rudder gently from side to side, turning his nose-concentrated guns into a terrible scythe that slashed and ground the little figures into pulp. A Sabre was in front and to his left, the other pilot doing the same. Suddenly the other man hit an ammunition truck. A dazzling ball of fire mushroomed upward, hurling pieces of truck and a dozen Chinese soldiers into the air.

One of the bodies smashed against the gaping air intake of Pruett's fighter. The Sabre jerked madly. Pruett simultaneously hauled back on the stick and rammed the throttle to full military power. The Sabre shook off the effects of the blow and arrowed skyward—as its pilot stared unbelievingly at the angry red splotches and little pieces of flesh plastered against his front windscreen.

All the way home he tried to shut out the sight, and failed. He nearly wrecked the Sabre as he screeched to a landing. All he wanted was to get away from that airplane. When he parked the fighter and slid the canopy back, several small pieces of what had been a human being dripped onto his flying clothes. An icy shudder swept through his body. He dropped to the ground, stomach quivering.

"Hey, Captain! How the hell did you manage to get this bird home in one piece?" It was his line chief, who was busy working on something that had jammed the side of the air intake.

Pruett walked around the nose just as the sergeant tugged

53

hard, and stumbled backward. He crashed against the pilot, his hands gripping part of a foot. Pruett turned white. He gritted his teeth and walked rapidly away. Behind the nearest building, he was violently, wretchedly sick.

He had ten more missions to fly, and he was lucky. Each time he eased the fighter off the ground he uttered a silent prayer that there wouldn't be any calls for help from the ground. He wanted his fight eight miles high, if at all possible. There were two skirmishes in the air; he punctured the wings of a few MiG's, but scored no kills. He didn't care one way or the other. He came home to his base with one hundred and twenty missions behind him, made certain that he had been taken off combat flying status, and was drunk for the next two days.

It seemed to wash some of the . . . he didn't know, but he couldn't rid himself of the feeling that he was tainted. For two days and two nights he didn't have to think, and he lay in his room, secure in the all-pervading alcoholic mists. No one bothered him.

Then he couldn't take any more of that. He asked for three weeks' leave in Japan before returning to the States, and the group adjutant told him to pack and be back in an hour. He was ready in twenty minutes.

An hour later he sprawled in the bucket seat of a Gooney Bird headed for Honshu. The twin-engine transport crossed the spinal ridge of the Japanese mountains and descended in wide circles to a landing at Komaki Airdrome, south of Nagoya. There he hired a Japanese cab. The driver bumped his way forty miles more to the south, winding along a narrow dirt road ambulating along the coastline. Pruett's destination was a hotel few Americans knew about. Those that did know kept their mouths shut—and the hotel largely to themselves, and to the Japanese.

For three weeks he forgot that the outside world existed. He took a suite of rooms which were completely and unquestionably Japanese. The hotel assigned him two sixteen-year-old girls as maidservants, and he'd been told in no uncertain terms by his wingman (who sent him there) that the young girls were exactly that and nothing else.

"All bets are off with the kids, Dick," he explained. "I can see you don't believe me, but I really mean it. They're strictly for your needs and wants, short of crawling into the sack with you. They'll wash your clothes, cook only for you, scrub your back in the tub and be always at your command. But you've got to play the game that way. You want a broad to shack up with, just call the old momma-san who runs the place. She'll get you whatever you want and—" he grinned—"those two kids will be sitting at the other side of the room while you indulge, waiting to obey your every command. It's a weird one, but it's wonderful."

It wasn't weird, but it was more than wonderful. It was heaven. He slept late almost every morning. The girl servants spoke little English, and he was grateful for their long silence instead of idiot small-talk. He wore only Japanese clothes; he soaked every day for at least two hours in a great stone tub and water close to boiling. He fell asleep as the two girls bade him lie on a mat. They stripped him naked, and four hands slowly worked oil into his skin. Four hands with wisdom in their fingers. He hadn't known how tightly bunched and tensed his muscles had been.

He was . . . content. He didn't try to think, but drifted aimlessly in thought. There were long walks on the beach, where in the evening he watched great, long-legged sand crabs rear high, peer at him through beady eyes, and then clack fearfully back to the water.

A Japanese guide took him into the hills for two days, and this Pruett loved most of all. They went after the dangerous wild boar of Honshu's southern mountains, and Pruett's heart was in his mouth as a yellow-tusked bull charged straight at him across a clearing. He didn't move an inch, his sights lining up carefully, and he crashed a heavy slug clean through the right eye of the animal. It took four Japanese to get the boar back to the hotel, where the momma-san threw a party for all the guests, with Pruett the most honored of all.

He didn't realize until the three weeks regretfully slipped away that not once had he thought of his wingman's advice; not once had he asked, or even thought to ask, the momma-san for a woman to join his bed. He grinned sheepishly to himself, knowing full well he could never admit the incident, because no one would ever believe him . . .

Rested in body and mind, he left Japan for the United States, sleeping for most of the flight in a big transport. Once again he felt that strange and disquieting sense of not-belonging; he would never make a good passenger. He was too eager to have his own hands at the controls.

He came home into a new world. With a sense of joy that flamed deep within him, he rushed headlong into demands on his mind and body that, only a few short years before, he would have considered impossibly beyond his capabilities. The blood-letting of Korea had had an effect upon him even he could not realize, of which he knew little or nothing. The eager fighter pilot, the hawk so swift of wing and temperament, had evolved. Pruett was unaware that he had returned from Korea almost as a new man, with a maturity which, had it been described to him, he would have vehemently denied and rejected.

He received assignment to one of the most coveted installations in the Air Force—the sprawling research center of Edwards Air Force Base in California. Here was the home of the Air Force Flight Test Center, and the gateway to dazzling new worlds of flight, and what lay beyond even flight itself—the awesome reach into vacuum, into space.

Pruett was mildly—and pleasantly—surprised to see that he would have a friend with him at the California center. He was Jim Dougherty, a towheaded and freckle-faced pilot who looked out of place without a blade of grass jutting from between his teeth. They met unexpectedly on the C-47 shuttle from Los Angeles to Edwards, and were delighted to learn of their similar assignments. They'd flown several fighter-bomber missions together in Korea, and Pruett's opinion of Dougherty as a fighting man and skilled flier would have given immense pleasure to the red-headed captain.

Dougherty had been the son of a farmer, and he was a farmer still when he started flying from the back pasture of their sprawling acreage in Ohio. Dougherty's father still was inflamed with the spirit of being a World War I ace; he had never given a damn for regulations when he flew Nieuports and Spads, and he couldn't have cared less for government regulations when his son Jim was growing into long pants. The father bought a near-wreck of an old Fleet biplane, patched it up himself, and ran it with the same cheap gasoline he poured into his tractor. It was wild flying, the regulations were ignored, and if the boy didn't fly as his martinet old man told him to fly, he could expect to get the hell whopped out of him that same day.

"My old man had the strongest right arm you ever saw," Dougherty explained to Pruett. His face split into a grin. "You got whopped a few times by Pop, and I tell you, Mister, you flew that airplane like an angel."

Pruett had taken to Dougherty immediately, and the two at once became fast friends. Now their mutual skills and desires had made their paths cross once more—and to an extent in the future of which neither could have conceived.

They came to Edwards with their imagination afire, but each with the status of student. The category delighted Pruett and afforded him much pride, for the small group of fifteen men that made up the student body of the Experimental Flight Test Pilot School were considered the most skilled, talented, knowledgeable, and promising young pilots in the Air Force. Each school term lasted for six months, and they proved to be the most grueling, demanding, exhausting months he had ever spent in his life.

From the start he knew, beyond any question, that this constituted one of the major pivots of his life. Already Pruett could look back upon the accumulating years, and slice those years neatly into identifiable segments. It had taken him a long time to understand that becoming a pilot, even a fighter pilot, had not been enough to separate him from the great body of men who took to the air. It disturbed his pride, but there *were,* he admitted ruefully, a distressing number of veteran military pilots around. But those brief months with Lyons, and the manner in which the man in his wisdom had reshaped him and created a new Pruett, could easily be recognized as critical for what the future man—Pruett—would be. Vindication had come in telling fashion in the thin cold air over Korea.

The second time he realized that he had stepped irrevocably through another door came when he walked down the hallway of the main entrance to the test pilot school. He moved slowly between rows of pictures of the experimental craft that had sundered the barriers to new flight regimes. He scanned the pictures, and saw in those brief seconds the growing wave of a new world. The intensive tests of the recent decade had been, literally, the roaring wave that men were riding, eager for the wave to break upon the shores of new—vertical—frontiers.

At the end of the hallway, almost as if it were waiting at the edge of the rows of pictures, a sign had been hammered high above the floor, nailed solidly into the panels of knotty pine. It did not use, nor did it need, many words to tell of a vast and stirring adventure. The sign said, simply:

"Through these halls walk the world's best pilots and crews."

Pruett knew the meaning behind the words. They were more than a tribute to those who had hurdled the barriers and sometimes had smashed them down with brute force. They were also a remembrance. That the latter was starkly true, Pruett reaffirmed to himself when he walked through the streets of the test center.

Edwards Air Force Base . . . he stood at a corner, and the name came swimming up through his memory from five years past. His full name was Glen W. Edwards, and he was a captain, and he had been at the controls of an incredible bat-shaped wing, a monster that was a wing only. Pruett remembered the giant, the huge wing-shape without body, with nothing but that wing sliding eerily through the sky. But in June of 1948, as happens in the business of poking and prodding into unknown flight regimes, the monster took Glen Edwards to his death. And ever since, the sprawling gateway to the future had been known by the name of that young captain.

As he walked slowly, Pruett looked at the street signs. He read the names, and some of these, too, drifted from obscurity to recognition. Wolfe, Forbes, Popson, Gregorious, Seller, Payne, Bailey, Sparks, Methusa, Mortland, Lathrop . . . and many, many more.

And every one of them had died—here, at this base, or not so far out beyond the edge of the great concrete runways.

Out there . . . like the surface of another planet. Over all, in the far distance, brooded the naked hump of Soledad, the Lonely Mountain. It looked down blindly on the plateau that rested a half-mile above sea level, the plateau of the Mojave Desert that they called Rogers Dry Lake. Here was the greatest landing field in the world, absolutely flat, stone-hard, baked by a sun that snarled its heat against the flattened earth.

Pruett gazed upon the ridges and the stark peaks of the

mountains he would come to recognize almost instantly from the air. The Shadow Mountains, and then the San Gabriel and the San Bernardino Ranges . . . a strange world within a world, a monotony of flat, almost completely sterile, nothingness. Yet he would come to learn that even here, in the midst of savage conditions, life could struggle. Hugging the sand were sagebrush in coats of grayish green; looming upward were the uncaring and distorted forms of the Joshua trees. They were the giants of the Mojave, giants thirty feet tall, defying all the odds of survival.

When the wind came screaming down from the mountains, it lashed the desert and blew enormous clouds of swirling dust and sand into the air. Clumps of tumbleweed raced ahead of the blinding sand, like animals in terror fleeing a sea of fire. Sometimes their flight was arrested by the treacherous needles of the crooked cactus, and there ensued a grotesque scene of the tumbleweed struggling desperately with its strength of wind to escape before the wall of roaring sand engulfed and devoured it.

There were creatures of the sky that cast their shadows across the Mojave and rippled over the concrete runway and the structures that loomed up from the edge of the base. Creatures that cried out from steel-ringed throats and spat long streamers of flame studded with the diamonds of shock waves, that hurled thunderbolts down through the skies to crash against the ground. Creatures with razor wings slashing back at impossible angles, flung through the heavens much faster than sound, hammering the ground with the concussion waves of supersonic booms.

Pruett stood one night on the flight line as a shadowy form at the end of the runway gathered strength into its steel-hard body. The lurking giant hissed powerfully, and then—as a man moved a rounded knob forward, he knew—began to moan. A moan that grew in volume, expanding hollowly into an impossible roar as the fires within its long and deep gut burned brighter and more angrily. And then the form began to rush along the concrete expanse, still only a blur, but accelerating with breathless speed. An explosion shook the flight line as the man encased within the giant moved his throttle into afterburner, and the flames shrieked loudly. The creature sped past him, shaking his body with the terrible sound. A long streamer of violet fire, surrounding a core of blinding, thin flame, beat at the air behind the giant. Then the wings clutched at the air, the giant shook off its chains of gravity. The plume of violet fire sped straight back from the exploding orifice, and bent as it met concrete. A flame bending cleanly, sharply, impossibly. It vanished as the giant screamed its freedom in a final overpowering cry of thunder. The sound splashed hotly across the concrete and rushed far out across the desert, finally to whimper itself out of existence in the twisting ravines and canyons.

A sense of wonder filled Pruett as he lifted his gaze to the heavens. The fire that sent the giant hurtling through the night air was now a dwindling pinpoint of orange flame. No longer did it rush through the air; it drifted upward. The whisper of its passage sank slowly earthward as Pruett studied the firmament revealed in the cold clarity of the desert night. And it seemed that the pinpoint of orange flame had abandoned the earth and was drifting among the stars.

There was precious little time for such scenes, or for his reflections as to where they might lead. He was a student once again, and in the period of six months allotted to his class he and the fourteen other neophyte test pilots would equal two years of intensive, advanced studies. A full colonel commanded the school, and the instructors were five majors. Each instructor years before had earned his master's degree in aeronautical engineering. Each was a veteran test pilot. It did not escape their attention that the new student, Pruett, also had earned his master's, although no one commented directly to the newcomer.

Major Paul A. DeGroff initiated the class. DeGroff didn't bear the faintest resemblance to a man with a master's degree. He was unbelievably wide across the shoulders, a stocky, lumbering bear of a man, whose appearance was helped not at all by an angry scar that ran from behind his right ear to the side of his mouth. Pruett learned—not from DeGroff, but from one of the other pilots—that the instructor had bailed out over Japan in the last days of World War II, and that a Japanese kid in a uniform had run screaming at him with a long bayonet while DeGroff fought desperately to untangle himself from his parachute. The Japanese soldier, still in his teens and shrieking frightened hate, came close to fulfilling his wish to slice the American's head into small pieces. His face laid open, blood spurting wildly, DeGroff emptied his forty-five into the soldier, killing him on the spot, and then fell unconscious. Other Japanese, coming upon him, took the American for dead. DeGroff remembered nothing until he awoke in a prisoner-of-war camp, attended to by an American doctor.

He survived only because the war ended four days later, and he was rushed aboard an airplane and flown to a hospital on Saipan.

Normally, Pruett never pried into the background of the men with whom he flew or worked. But DeGroff jarred his sense of proportion. Only a man of towering strength and indomitable will could have emerged from that horrifying experience, could have endured five major operations on his face, earned his master's degree, and returned to rank among the most capable pilots in the world. Pruett resolved to pay the closest attention to the bearlike major, and he was gratified to note that he and two other pilots were placed under DeGroff's personal tutorship.

The major sat on the edge of his desk, lit a cigarette slowly, and introduced himself. He wasted no time in getting down to business.

"Within the next six months, gentlemen, you are going to absorb the equal of two years of intensive and advanced studies. You are going to perform one step short of being supermen. I'm sure you already know that, or you wouldn't be here. I just want to focus it once again in your minds. You will be required to have a thorough knowledge of the theory of flight, of aeronautical mechanics and aerodynamics, plane geometry, algebra, differential calculus, meteorology, astronomy, every type of navigation you have ever heard of—and then some we don't have names for yet. You will span the full gamut from aeronautics, to astronautics, and you will learn, intimately, the function and operation of piston, jet, ramjet, and rocket motors. You will become expert in the fields of electronics, metallurgy, celestial mechanics, and—well, in short, anything and everything that may remotely affect the work we do here at Edwards and other test centers around the country."

A groan issued from one of the desks. DeGroff smiled. "If it will make you happier, gentlemen, that is only the beginning. The classrooms will constitute a lesser part of the time you spend in this school. Your real work—the *hard* work— will take place in the cockpit."

DeGroff stood up and stubbed out the cigarette butt. "I hope you will enjoy your stay with us, gentlemen. You have—" he glanced at his watch—"exactly twelve minutes before your first class begins. Those twelve minutes will be the only relaxation you will have, I'm sure, for the next six months. So—enjoy them."

Pruett plunged into his work. He had no concern that he could meet and likely exceed any requirements made of him either in the brain department or as a pilot. He studied and flew with the assurance of the man who has already put behind him a series of acid tests of his capabilities. Yet he was surprised by the intensity of the demands placed upon himself and the other students. He came to surmise —and correctly—that they were being pushed deliberately, that each new class provided a guideline to the maximums of performance that might be extracted from any one individual.

Pruett had learned one lesson through the years that stood him well: generalize, but never dogmatize. The advanced technical courses of the school were unquestionably severe, but he knew that his success in this respect lay directly in proportion to his efforts. Despite his well-meaning intentions not to anticipate his degree of success in the cockpit, he was to find that even with his already extensive experience as a pilot he had much indeed to learn.

DeGroff flew with Pruett in the F-100F supersonic fighter, a powerful, shovel-nosed brute the pilots unkindly christened the *Lead Sled*, for it could be harshly unforgiving of pilot inexperience or overconfidence. Ensconced in the rear seat of the fighter, he rested on his lap a checklist of pilot requirements so thick and heavy that it startled even the veteran fliers. DeGroff exhibited infinite patience with his pilot charges, an attitude permitted, no doubt, by the fact that his students had to be both brilliant and outstanding before being accepted for the punishment that he, DeGroff, applied with exquisite manner.

Pruett's instructor abandoned quickly the training program in aerobatics and detailed maneuvers. It did not require more than a single flight for DeGroff to recognize the superb touch of his student at the controls, and De-

Groff admitted readily to himself—and then to Pruett—that the student was the master of the teacher in aerobatics.

The night after their first flight, DeGroff realized that he had found a tremendous potential in his student. He conferred with the school commander, and recommended that careful attention be paid to the progress the new pilot would exhibit. Pruett was not yet elevated to the exclusivity of the test pilot circle, for scholastic knowledge and the master's touch in aerobatics do not necessarily a test pilot make.

Testing was also a matter of infinite patience, of extraordinary skill in flying with hairline precision in level flight, of ferreting out data on temperatures and pressures under meticulously established conditions. And there are few things more difficult in flying than absolutely straight and level flight over a long distance, when the air is filled with the invisible rocks and reefs of turbulence.

DeGroff unkindly put the screws on Pruett. The modern jet fighter is a metal animal with hydraulic sinews. At supersonic speeds it is impossible for a human being to move the control surfaces against the terrible airblast and shock waves inherent in such flight. So the control system is rigged with an elaborate power boost. When the pilot moves the stick, an electronic system senses the movement as a demand for energy. Immediately it adds hydraulic muscle to the control system, and the result is that the strength of a dozen men is available to move the control surfaces of the wings or the tail.

This system in turn creates its own drawbacks, especially for the pilot who has spent years learning to feel and sense instinctively the moods of his airplanes. He comes to know the whispers of external forces as turbulence slaps against his airplane. He understands what the airplane means when it trembles slightly, or "talks" to him in yet other ways. When he moves into the machine with power-boosted controls, he loses these sensory connections between his body and the airplane. The substitute is mechanical and hydraulic.

He must learn to adapt to the new system, and he can do this only by modifying his own instincts. There are many pilots who do not care for the change, but it is inevitable and it is easily mastered.

Except when the instructor is a man like DeGroff, who

sees in a student like Pruett great possibilities for the future. DeGroff ordered the mechanics to roll out an F-100F which had been modified through its control system. Instead of the normal power boost, this airplane had the kind of control sensitivity one fears in a bottle of nitroglycerine bouncing about the floorboards of a truck speeding along a badly rutted road. She was a bitch to fly, for the fighter was so responsive to its controls that the barest pressure of a finger brought about an instant and often astonishing reaction from the airplane. DeGroff could do extensive aerobatics in the modified F-100F with two fingers held lightly at the stick.

Pruett couldn't keep the airplane flying straight and level. The fighter shied skittishly the instant his hand touched the stick. At first he was astonished at the machine. After attempting to hold level flight, while the airplane wallowed its wings from side to side despite his best efforts, he grew both bewildered and angry. He flew directly on course but could not keep the wings level. As the airplane started to roll to the left, he brought corrective action to the right. But no matter what he did he could not keep the wings exactly level, and his flight resembled a boat rolling slowly from side to side.

His anger grew—more at himself than at the mindless machine—and threatened to destroy his attempts at control when there flashed in his mind one biting word: *"Hotshot."* Pruett chuckled and relaxed his grip. He brought up one knee close to the stick, and carefully placed his right elbow on the knee. Then, extending his thumb and index finger, he tried not to touch, but to caress the baffling control stick. The rolling motion eased immediately, and within several minutes disappeared altogether.

DeGroff watched the proceedings through two mirrors placed in the front seat. He anticipated the rising frustration of the student pilot, and was pleased that the natural reaction to anger should be eliminated so quickly. None of his pleasure showed.

"Captain Pruett!"

"Sir?"

"Captain, that is a hell of a way to fly an airplane. Would you mind telling me what those physical contortions of yours are supposed to mean? Are you bringing something new and illuminating to the world of test flying?

Perhaps you have some revolutionary methods to replace our shopworn and antiquated procedures!"

"No, sir."

" 'No, sir,' *what?*"

"Major, if I don't keep my knee just so, and my fingers just so, I can't keep this piece of metal from rolling like a drunken sailor."

"You can't?"

"No, sir."

"Well, Captain, you're an honest beggar, anyway. What's wrong with this sled?"

"Nothing that's wrong . . . but this thing seems to respond to the controls even before I decide what I want to do myself."

"Give me a flick roll to the left, Pruett."

The fighter whipped hard over to the left, a spinning blur as the wings flashed around. Pruett worked the stick and rudder to snap out quickly and exactly on point, level with the horizon, but the supersensitive airplane didn't stay where he wanted it. Instead it rocked badly and went through several roller-coaster motions before Pruett could calm it down.

"Pretty good, Pruett, pretty good for a novice."

"What the hell was—sir—what the hell was good about *that!*"

DeGroff laughed. "The last guy we had in that seat, who tried a flick roll for the first time, managed to settle down after he'd rolled around four times. Okay, I've got it."

Pruett rubbed his aching arm; the task of holding the stick with the lightest touch possible was proving to be more demanding of him than strenuous aerobatics. He had unknowingly created a deep impression on DeGroff, for the instructor had not expected Pruett to adjust so quickly to the oversensitive control system.

And so began the intensive program of shaping Pruett into the skilled and brilliant test pilot he would become, the program that would open the doors for him to flight at speeds and heights remotely beyond the reach of even the most advanced machines at the test center. He roared into the cool desert air almost every morning at dawn, DeGroff pushing, demanding, and privately exulting in the progress of the student. Pruett learned to master scientifically demanding procedures in dives, climbs, and zooms; he learned to move an airplane through a checklist of flight maneuvers during which he was expected to execute changes of flight measured down to split-second timing so that the instruments aboard the airplane might be able to measure and record exactly the stresses and motions imposed upon the machine. He learned to use the trim controls of the airplanes with the same ingrained skill with which a bird adjusts its feathers for flight. He sat through hours of coldly analytical studies of his performance, as he—and DeGroff —examined on a large screen slow-motion films of his flight instruments during his time in the air. Frame by frame the camera revealed the hairline errors in a performance which, anywhere else in the world, would have been accepted as outstanding skill. But here, at the great flight test center, these minute errors were no more than the impetus to go up, again and again and again, until not even a shadow of the hairline of error remained.

He flew fighters and bombers, trainers and transports, liaison airplanes and experimental craft. He flew them to requirements and tolerances he would quickly have described as impossible only a few short months before. He walked in blistering heat to his airplanes while burdened with a heavy pressure suit and helmet, chafing from the bladdered undergarments of a g-suit that would squeeze and grasp his legs, thighs and stomach when he wracked the airplanes around in turns and other maneuvers, and his body weight shot from his normal hundred and eighty pounds to more than fifteen hundred pounds.

He learned to fly an enormous roller coaster in the sky with the F-100F; learned to slide over into a dive at an exact angle and with an exact speed, and to pull up at a precise point in the sky, with exactly the right level of centrifugal force, to pull up at a specific angle, and then carefully to push the stick forward and to hold it . . . ahhh, *just* so.

And when he flew the roller coaster, which is how the pilots described the precision parabolic arcs of their fighters, the airplanes soared up and over in a huge curve through the sky, and for as long as sixty seconds they were completely weightless. For a full minute the fighters hung in a perfect balance between gravity and centrifugal force, and the eerie world of zero gravity brought dust and dirt floating up from the floor and beneath the seats, and the pressurization system of the fighter went crazy and spewed snowflakes beneath the rounded plexiglas.

In the back seat of the airplane, DeGroff floated freely between his seat and the rounded clear canopy, and when Pruett was really good and the parabola was perfect, the instructor would reward the student with a rasping rendition of "Come, Josephine, in My Weightless Machine."

And then the six months were gone, and the fifteen students were reborn with skills and capabilities which were the respectful envy of all pilots who truly understood the obstacles these men had overcome. Of the graduating class, thirteen men were assigned to test centers throughout the United States. No better accolade could have been afforded to Pruett than his own assignment. He would be a test pilot, here—at Edwards.

He disliked breaking up with Jim Dougherty, but the red-headed pilot had proven himself just one step short of a genius in the technique of lobbing high explosives from low-flying bombers into any variety of difficult targets. The Air Force assigned Dougherty to weapons development at Eglin Air Force Base along the Florida Gulf Coast, where he would wage a hellish war with hundreds of tons of explosives, perfecting new weapons and combat techniques.

"We're bound to meet up again in this business, Dick," Dougherty said as the two friends parted after their graduation. "I don't know if you're going to end up as a supersonic hatchet man on the deck, but—well . . . hell, I'll be seeing you." He threw Pruett a departing salute and climbed into the cockpit of his fighter. Minutes later Pruett watched the machine dwindle to a dot and disappear.

The years that ensued formed a pattern. When scientists from the Air Force School of Aviation Medicine in Texas came to Edwards to carry out their experiments in weightlessness, Pruett requested—and received—the job of pushing the F-100F two-seat fighter into and through its precision parabolic arcs. Again and again he went through the zero-gravity maneuver, until he became so adept at slipping into weightlessness that the scientists requested his permanent assignment to their research activities. Pruett flew at Edwards Air Force Base; he spent months at Wright-Patterson in Ohio; there was a period of eight months in Texas, where German space-medicine specialists fairly lived in the back seat of the fighter.

Behind him, men floated freely and weightlessly while they operated control boards and performed a great variety of tests. They sent pilots up with Pruett, and he learned to expect globules of water quivering through the cockpit as the men tried drinking experiments while weightless, and more often than not squirted water all over themselves and Pruett. Pieces of bread and the crumbled remains of cookies joined the parade of items floating about, and Pruett came to accept even the yowling of kittens, which the scientists brought along to observe in the weightless state.

There were choice assignments to which most test pilots aspired. Pruett was flying advanced tests at maximum altitude—above one hundred thousand feet—with the bullet-shaped F-104 fighter when the X-15 program moved into high gear. One look at the long black body of the rocket airplane was enough; Pruett immediately requested a place in the small group selected to fly the "Beast." Engineers talked of hypersonic speeds, of rushing beyond mach five, pushing well beyond four thousand miles per hour. Pruett watched with consuming interest as technicians chained the X-15 to steel shackles in concrete, and then fired the howling volcano in the tail of the airplane. He looked with undisguised hunger at the huge B-52 bomber being modified as the aerial drop platform for the X-15.

He studied the projected flight plans . . . great arcs through the upper sky that would take the man in the X-15 to sixty miles and even higher, and when he thought of the machine slicing through air so thin that its controls were useless, and the pilot must use reaction thrusters, the desire to be an integral element of this upward push became a persistent ache within him.

He did not receive the assignment. Scott Crossfield of North American Aviation copped the job of breaking in the X-15. Crossfield was a civilian test pilot who had previously flown for the National Advisory Committee for Aeronautics, and he was better than fabulous. Crossfield had broken a book full of world records, and he was the first man ever to fly faster than twice the speed of sound. He also had the distinction of being the first test pilot ever to wear out a pressure suit.

Captain Iven Kincheloe, Jr., was named to take over where Crossfield would leave off. Kincheloe was one of the greatest of the test pilots. He'd come home from Korea with a string of kills. He waltzed through test pilot school, and he flew with a skill and precision that was unmatched by any other man. But he never did fly the X-15. He tried to save an F-104 that flamed out on him; he tried to bring in the short-winged machine without power, and he simply couldn't make the runway. The other pilot in the air in a second fighter was screaming at Kincheloe to get out, and Kincheloe finally did exactly that. But it was a matter of too low and too late, and the tall, blond, brilliant pilot smashed into the blazing wreckage of his exploding airplane. And died instantly.

Captain Bob White—shaken by the loss of Kincheloe—moved into the lead position for the X-15. Joe Walker of NACA joined him, as did other pilots, for there would be three of the black beasts for probing into space. Pruett wasn't among that very special group, for his assignment to the F-104 project was a long one, and he couldn't be removed from that job without throwing a snag into the time schedule.

All of a sudden, it seemed, they were pushing closer and closer to getting men far up and out—into space itself. The satellite programs proved that we were getting the booster push needed to kick the payloads into orbit, and it was only a matter of time before the big boosters moved out of experimental status and were started on the program to rate them as acceptable for pushing a manned vehicle away from the earth.

There were no sudden breakthroughs, no startling revelations. It was just that so many people had been moving along a broad front, and that they were getting closer and closer, almost as if they were inching their way up along the slope of a steep mountain that towered out of sight. Pruett was at Wright-Patterson when the Air Force received the secret authorization for Project 7969, the first effort to put an American into orbit. He studied pictures of the giant Atlas missile in its static firings, and he could hardly believe his eyes when he walked into a heavily guarded hangar and saw the mockup of the capsule that one man would ride into vacuum at nearly eighteen thousand miles per hour.

He made sure that he wouldn't miss out again, as he had with the X-15 and this time Pruett received what he wanted—assignment as a project officer for 7969. Engineers were working day and night in wind tunnels with models of the capsule, and Pruett became an active member of this work. He spent weeks with the engineers of North American Aviation, the company that received the contract to build the capsule. Scientists came in from General Electric; their job was to develop and produce the life environment system for the capsule. It was quite a job—keep a man alive in space for a flight of at least twenty-four hours.

Few people realized or believed it, but man had been in space. Not at the end of a screaming booster, but in the familiar metal shapes with wings on them. Kincheloe had soared to more than twenty-four miles in the sweptwing X-2; when the stainless steel airplane hung at the peak of its arc, Kincheloe had less than a tenth of one percent of the planet's atmosphere above him. The equipment necessary to keep him alive and breathing at his altitude would have worked just as well at one hundred miles. After a certain point was passed on the way out from the planet, it was all the same. Physiologically, that man was in space. He lacked the means of staying alive, and could exist only within the artificial environment they packaged for him. He needed oxygen and pressure; he needed temperature controls and all the other things necessary to keep the spark of life going. Whether the tin can in which he was riding was called a capsule, airplane, or spacecraft, if he lacked the protection, he would die. Quickly and, most likely, not painlessly.

News of the first Russian satellite in late 1957 fell in their midst like a bombshell, followed by the heavy Sputnik II a month later, with the dog sent into orbit. The effect was a psychological shock and an official spurt in the manned capsule program. For nearly a year following the initial satellites, Pruett alternated between the roles of test pilot and project engineer. He was in the right place at the right time; and in the military, that could prove tantamount to getting exactly what a man wanted. And Pruett wanted, urgently, to be the first man who would ride that Air Force capsule into orbit.

He visited dozens of installations throughout the country, from the sprawling production center for Atlas missiles in San Diego to the electronics laboratories at Rome, New

York. He flew to Cape Canaveral; to Huntsville, Alabama; to the General Electric laboratories in Philadelphia; to the howling wind tunnels at Tullahoma, in Tennessee. More than once he returned to the great flight test center in the California desert, and drove beyond the edge of Edwards Air Force Base, across the entire span of Rogers Dry Lake, and some miles beyond, to the huge granite outcroppings and massive walls of Leuhman Ridge. Here, anchored deep within the granite, chained to the substance of the earth itself, were enormous static test stands for new rocket engines. Leuhman Ridge itself suggested an outpost into tomorrow; some mysterious upheaval of the earth unnumbered millions of years past had thrust the rugged granite masses out of the desert to stand alone, far removed from the ranges of mountains.

The desert air, normally quiescent, was tortured shamelessly at Leuhman Ridge. From squat buildings that pockmarked the outcroppings, there issued a cacophony of clanging, hammering, shrieking sounds as men operated power equipment, readied machines for tests, sucked supercold liquid oxygen from the blistering air, and performed the myriad other rites and rituals of the new technology.

One night in the autumn of 1958, Pruett arrived at Leuhman Ridge for the static testing of a massive new propulsion system. Two flaring combustion chambers were mated as a single booster. Rocketdyne in California had moved far beyond the thrust chambers for the Atlas, and for a year they had conducted preliminary tests of the new chamber, which produced flaming gases issuing from the chamber with a thrust of 400,000 pounds. And now the Air Force was ready for the first full-scale tests of the two chambers in a single booster.

Pruett glanced at the very top of the granite ridge, where an incongruous traffic light shone balefully with a single eye of amber. This signaled Condition General Amber, during which the technicians fueled the thick tanks for the static test. Pruett prepared himself for the jangling onslaught of preliminary sounds, announced by a fire alarm bell that clanged stridently. The sound that alerted him as to the closeness of the test was the shrill and mounting cry of steel-toned pipes singing in a high-pitched torment as they were subjected to 300 degrees below zero from the liquid oxygen bubbling into the tanks.

Floodlights stripped the area naked of darkness as a siren began to scream, and the traffic light flashed from amber to red. Along with the other observers, Pruett moved into a thick blockhouse, from where he would observe the firing through a periscope. He rested his arms on the scope handle, turning slowly to survey the entire scene.

Red lights winked along different elevations of the test stand proper, a towering assembly of metal beams that loomed against the floodlights like the hulking skeleton of a dinosaur dredged from the desert bottom. Beyond, silhouetted in the light beams spraying the desert, the Joshua trees cast mile-long shadows across the naked surface. Pruett swung the scope around hurriedly when he heard the blockhouse talker intone: "Minus sixty seconds and counting. This is a live count. On my mark—fifty seconds, and counting."

Two bursts of pure-white smoke. The appearance of the smoke was so instantaneous, so sharp and defined, so clear that it was almost as if two powerful searchlight beams had snapped on in velvet blackness. The smoke stood etched like two angled pillars of white marble. But only for an instant.

Flame: pure, blinding, shocking. White streams of fire. Not red or yellow or orange. Intense, *white.* Flame that was alive, hard as steel, punctuated throughout with shock diamonds that danced and quivered in the river-wombs of flame.

The blinding white subsided abruptly, and two tongues snatched from deep in Hell, intolerably red and impossibly bright, leaped into existence. In the pit far beneath the flaring combustion chambers, the flames became a *thing* writhing in senseless agony, struggling to run amuck. Pruett gasped as the scene overwhelmed him, and the earth beneath his feet, under his hands, began to shake ever so gently. Rotating steel burrs appeared suddenly within his teeth and rattled his eyes in their sockets; men in the blockhouse looked up, startled at the effect of the ultrasonic lash from the engines, the tremendously deep, sonorous rumble of thunder mixing with the higher sound. From below the flame pit great chunks of granite were shattered and flung wildly through the air, still glowing cherry red from the caress of the flame.

A cataclysmic shriek tore the sky. It seemed impossible

that it could continue, but it did, and in his mind Pruett imagined that savage fire hurling a great spacecraft away from the earth, and . . . a momentary scream stabbed into his ears as the flame died.

The velvet dark beyond the atmosphere did not seem so very far any longer. . . .

He walked into the main offices of Project 7969 at Wright-Patterson Air Force Base, and knew instantly that something had gone . . . well, had gone bad with the project. The deep undercurrent of excitement that infused the close-knit group no longer was there. It had been stripped and pulled away. Pruett walked into the private office of the project director. "Mitch, what's going on out here? It looks like a wake."

Robert Mitchell, eighteen years an Air Force scientist, master in aviation and space medicine, a man who knew to the last cell the limitation and the capabilities of the human body, had worked on 7969 from its inception. He *was* the project, as much as any part of it.

"It *is* a wake."

"*What?*"

"You heard me," Mitchell glowered.

"Talk sense, man! What the hell is going on?"

Mitchell's face was purple fury. He ground out the words slowly, deliberately. "We've lost the project."

Pruett's voice was a whisper "Say that again."

"I said that we have *lost* the goddamned project."

"But . . . *how?* What happened?"

"Don't you read the papers?"

"No. I've been busy flying an airplane. Will you please stop screwing around the edges of this thing and tell me what's going on?"

Mitchell dragged deeply on a cigarette. Then, suddenly, his shoulders slumped. "Uncle Sam, my good Captain, has decided to form a new organization for space flight. They announced today that Congress is working on the new bill to create a separate space agency. It will knock the pins out from beneath the Advanced Research Projects Agency, and it will—it *has*—knocked the pins out from under *us*." He waved an arm in disgust. "Oh, nothing official yet, but I've been given the private word. We have had it."

"But *why,* for Christ's sake?"

"Because, my militant young friend, it has been decided that we in the Air Force have no need for a manned space program. It has been decided that our country stands for peace and goodness, and that if we paint our rockets with lollipop colors when we we go into orbit, this will convince the Russians that they should follow our good example. The new agency—it will be built on the skeleton of NACA —is to be strictly a peaceful, civilian, do-naught-but-good organization of jolly fellows. You and me, my friend, we're military, and that means we're *bad*.

"So, as I said, we have lost the project. Sometime in the next ninety days it is to be scrapped; the civilan do-gooders will take it over and start the whole thing again from scratch. And you and all your nasty little friends in uniform will be kept from contaminating the universe."

Pruett couldn't think. A sense of disappointment with the weight of the world descended on his back and drained his strength from his limbs. It wasn't, couldn't be. But it was; Mitchell could speak only in dead seriousness about a subject that meant more to him than anything else in life. He—his mind refused to focus.

Mitchell clumped around the desk and stood before him. "On your feet, young Captain, we have work to do."

Pruett glared up at him. "And what the hell might that be?"

The project director stared down at him with an expression of malignant pity. "You and I, sir, are going to get very, very drunk."

Pruett rose to his feet and looked Mitchell straight in the eye. *"Amen."*

Chapter V

In Hangar S at Cape Kennedy, a small band of McDonnell and NASA engineers worked feverishly. Floodlights washed across their bodies and their hands, reflecting spots of brilliance from metal tools. The men worked against time to disassemble the thick steel hide and the complex plumbing of a huge space environmental chamber. Within the chamber, where other men labored with the same feverish pace and concern in the fight against the inexorable passage of time, there rested a capsule. It looked, at first glance, like an identical vehicle to the machine even at that moment orbiting the planet. But only at first glance, and to the unpracticed eye. The capsule was spawned of Mercury, but it was not the same machine. It was wider, deeper, higher, with much more room within its bell-shaped contours.

There was so little time! To remove the machine from the environmental chamber, to ready it for a critical, emergency flight—it had never been done before, all the odds were against it, even the optimistic ones among the crews at Hangar S said it was doomed to failure. The technicians and the engineers threw away their elaborate checklists that dictated to them the slow and cautious ritual of exhaustive, painstaking checkout. If there was to be even a chance of success, if the man then rushing closer, to pass almost directly over them, was to have any hope, they must do the impossible. They must rid the spacecraft of its encumbrances, rush it across Cape Kennedy to Pad Nineteen, and perform even more impossible feats.

The spacecraft bore the name of Gemini, like the twin stars Castor and Pollux. It might, it barely, incredibly, just might enable a man named Richard J. Pruett to remain alive for a much longer time than he granted himself.

But the odds were . . . no one knew. And what they were trying to do was best reflected in the conversation that followed the strident clamor of a telephone within Hangar S.

"This is George Keith at Merc Control. Have you got that thing out of the chamber yet?"

"We should have it free any minute now."

"What the hell is taking you people so long?"

With careful patience: "You know damned well what's taking us so long. No one has ever pulled one of these things out this way before. We haven't got any guidelines, any experience at this. For Christ's sake, man, we need time to do this."

"We haven't got any time. We haven't got a second to spare! How much longer?"

"If you'll get off the goddamned phone and let us keep working, we'd get this thing done a whole lot sooner. Now,

75

*stay the hell out of our hair. We'll call you the moment we
have something to say. . . ."*

The telephone slammed down onto the receiver.

*Ten minutes later the big capsule swung around slowly
in the air beneath lifting cables.*

*Twenty seconds after that the telephone rang in Mercury
Control; the call was from the environmental chamber
room in Hangar S.*

*George Keith dropped the phone back onto its cradle
and studied the large clock on the wall of Mercury Control.
In fifteen minutes more he would be talking to Pruett as
the capsule rushed up within range. . . .*

He wondered just how he would break the news to him.

The month of October, 1958, marked the death knell
for Project 7969, and shattered the hopes nourished by
Pruett and the many other people involved in the Air Force
effort to send a man into orbit by early 1961. Their deep-
rooted anger at the abrupt cessation of their work, which
amounted essentially to having the rug pulled out from beneath their collective feet, received no balm in the press
releases issuing from the offices of the new National Aeronautics and Space Administration. Those releases reflected
enthusiasm and hope and even a sense of wonder which,
when considered, was completely understandable, since
they involved the nation's first manned space effort—
Project Mercury.

Robert D. Mitchell, ex-director of the now-defunct
Project 7969, read the press notices with mounting disbelief. He studied the reports of the blunt-faced capsule,
the use of the great Atlas rocket as a booster, the flight plan
of the capsule—all written in glowing terms and—his
temper reached the point of no-return. He grabbed the
nearest phone and shouted imprecations at the stunned
operator.

Pruett the next morning found an envelope waiting on
his desk from Mitchell. He had to read it several times
before the message sank in. Mitchell was gone.

". . . and I'm making this decision stick," his friend
had written. "Reading all that glorious nonsense in the
papers about this 'new' Project Mercury, which is nothing
more than our old 7969 dressed up in fancy clothes, is
more than I can take. I realize that I'm close to retirement

and some nice pay if I want it, but I simply can't hack this stuff any more.

"I'm out of it now; out for good. You know that aircraft company down in Fort Worth that's been badgering me for the last few months? Well, I called the president of the outfit at two in the morning. Dragged the man out of bed, asked him right out if he still wanted me and on *my* terms. He affirmed their earlier offer, and I told him to put it in writing and have the contract waiting for me.

"Designing airplanes, even the type they want, won't be nearly as glorious or as exciting as what we have been working on for the last couple of years. I had deeply and sincerely hoped to see you as the first American, quite possibly the first man, ever to go into orbit. You didn't know, did you, that we were unanimously agreed that you were the one to go!

"But the Air Force is out of that picture now, Dick, and we're going to stay out for a long time to come. This new civilian agency is going to pick up almost all of the marbles, and they're going to be the darlings of the Congress. Just read the reports—it's all in there, and crystal clear.

"So I'm out. I'm going to stick with things with wings that fly.

"But don't *you* quit. I don't know what the civilian agency is planning for its pilots, or how they're going to pick their crop of space cadets. But I can tell you definitely that they will be test pilots, and they will be military test pilots, because of the nature of experience of people like yourself.

"You're on top of the heap. You're as good as the very few who are great. You have every chance of still being there in front of the group when the first mission is flown. So—stick to it, and if you're ever down near Fort Worth, stop by the plant and come in for coffee with an old civilian type. . . ."

Two months later, back at Edwards Air Force Base, Pruett received another letter. His hands shook when he put it down.

It was his invitation from the new space agency, NASA, to attempt to qualify as an astronaut for Project Mercury. His spirits ballooned as he fired off a telegram of acceptance.

He didn't make it.

He never had a chance to try. A preliminary government survey of active test pilots indicated that well over one hundred men met the specifications laid down by the space agency for astronaut selection. Pruett studied the specifications and knew he was in by a mile. The astronaut needed a bachelor's degree or equivalent in engineering; he had his master's degree and attendance at four advanced technical schools in the Air Force as well, plus graduation from test pilot's school, equal to another two years. The other requirements were a snap. As it turned out, Pruett had more flying time, especially in jets, than any other member of the group selected for astronaut status.

NASA officials called sixty-nine of the qualified pilots to Washington for preliminary meetings and conferences. Nearly sixty of them volunteered immediately. NASA screened out half this number and ended up with thirty-two men for final selection, finally accepting seven of these as the nation's first astronauts.

Pruett read the acceptance notice with shocked disbelief —he'd never been called to Washington for the interviews! He discovered quickly enough that neither had other pilots, as anxious as he to participate in the program. The qualifications of the original group interviewed were so high that selection was made from that group—and NASA simply had no need to go any further.

A telegram of condolence from Bob Mitchell didn't help. It wouldn't have been so bad had he tried, and failed, running second to the fortunate seven who were placed on inactive duty and assigned to NASA. Every one of those seven—Shepard, Grissom, Cooper, Schirra, Glenn, Slayton, and Carpenter—was outstanding in the air. But Pruett and a hundred other pilots were equally capable! Realization of this fact didn't help at all.

He thought of more than 6,000 hours in the air, of which 4,000 were in jets. He thought of the test programs in which he'd been involved, the hundreds of parabolic zero-g flights, the years of studying and advanced schooling, his perfect physical shape, his well-known and extraordinary skill in aerobatic flight. . . .

He cursed. He vented the accumulating frustration and rage on his friends, and came to his senses sufficiently in time to request a month's leave so that he could allow his emotions to settle down. He and a friend from the emo-

78

tional graveyard that had been their most cherished hopes for getting into space rented an airplane for the month, and flew down to Guaymas, Mexico. Two weeks of deep-sea fishing, lazing in the sun, and accepting the willing attention of vacationing women didn't do their spirits any harm.

They rounded up the leave with a hunting trip in the mountains of Wyoming, flying northward from Guaymas to Jackson Hole, Wyoming. It proved a beautiful flight, and the return to the personal level of flying after the screaming jets proved a tonic to Pruett. They came into Jackson Hole after slipping through a sun-dazzled gap in storm clouds, and descended toward the valley airstrip through a running succession of cloudbursts and gleaming rainbows. Ten days more of going after elk and the bighorn brought Pruett back to a state of calm.

He had no choice, of course, his life had already been etched in its mold. He had only one way to go, and that was up. Every time he flew, every time he soared to above 100,000 feet in one of the jet fighters, every time he watched one of the huge rockets splash flame downward, or the B-52 rumble through the rippling desert air of California as it bore the X-15 away from earth . . . every time this happened, he knew that nothing else in life would do for him.

He stayed in test work, concentrating on the astronautics aspects of the new regime of flight that no longer was either purely aviation or purely space, but a strange mixture of the two. He followed the progress of Mercury in every detail. He received assignment to the evaluation board on the X-15 program, and this put him in closer touch with engineers and officials from NASA. The black-hued X-15's were actually a joint Air Force-NASA effort, and despite acrimony in other quarters the program went off smoothly and in well-coordinated fashion.

Out of the X-15 there grew the new concept known as Dyna-Soar. It was hoped then that this rugged winged vehicle might be ready to orbit men by 1966 or 1967. Pruett received first crack at Dyna-Soar, and surprised everyone by rejecting the offer. Dyna-Soar was not the horse he wanted to ride. The program waxed and waned according to the Air Force's political fortunes in Washington, and its state of grace with the unpredictable moods and whims of the Department of Defense. It might never get off the ground, Pruett felt. He was not surprised when the word finally came that the Dyna-Soar project was wiped off the boards.

Project Mercury was a program with a clearly defined ending. Test, and check out, the many systems for a manned space flight. That was it—pure and simple. But *beyond* Mercury . . . ah, they were already talking about a new effort called Apollo, and their sights had been set on the moon.

Whatever the program, there wasn't a doubt in anyone's mind but that NASA or the Air Force, or both, would soon have their backs against the wall. Pruett studied the Top Secret reports of astronautics activities in Russia. He whistled in surprise at the huge bulk and staggering thrust of the Russian boosters, and he knew, as did everyone else, that the Soviets were going to beat our brains out in the manned space flight department.

Again and again Pruett went through the parabolic flights that gave him the taste of weightlessness, and the ever-present craving for more. He went aloft in giant Boeing jets modified for the parabolic arcs, and on these missions he was able to float, spin, soar, glide, walk upside down . . . to do anything within the forty-second time span of weightlessness provided by the four-engine airplane.

When Shepard and Grissom made their suborbital flights atop their Redstone boosters and entered periods where each man attained some 300 *seconds* of zero-g, Pruett laughed. The papers filled their columns with nonsense about proof of man's ability to withstand weightlessness. Pruett had, all together in his parabolic flights, accumulated more than four hours of zero-g time. But none of this truly mattered, because a quick dash around the planet by a man named Yuri Alekseyevich Gagarin made his experience, and the flights of Shepard and Grissom, quite academic. In fact, to be downright rude about it, the Redstone missions of the first two astronauts were primitive, despite their wildly heralded "trail-blazing." It was like applauding Lindbergh for a test hop around Long Island, while the opposition roared all the way to Paris and continued nonstop on to Tokyo.

Depite the reports from Intelligence, and the normal rumor factories that spilled reports and counter-reports from within the Soviet Union, the flight of the diminutive Russia cosmonaut, Gherman Titov, caught everyone almost completely by surprise. Pruett and a small group of pilots gathered in the operations office at Edwards, listening to the tracking reports coming in from NORAD headquarters in Colorado. They had the second Vostok pinned down neatly on the tracking nets, and there wasn't a doubt as to the size or the performance, or the tremendous weight of nearly 11,000 pounds, of the Russian spacecraft.

They tuned in to the Vostok II transmitters. Tracking sites around the world picked up Titov as he established contact with Russian tracking ships, high-flying airplanes, and ground stations. Suddenly a young lieutenant spun the volume dial to loud, and, as a static-crackled voice filled the room, he cried out, not without admiration: "Listen to the little sonofabitch! He's *singing* up there in that goddamned ship!"

As indeed he was, Pruett and the others noted ruefully. But then, he had something to sing about.

Gherman Titov's seventeen orbits around the world, his descriptions of the dawns and sunsets in space, the manner in which he spoke of cities from nearly 200 miles high . . . left Pruett feeling caged and trapped. But then, he thought, if I feel this way, how about those poor guys down at the Cape? And Glenn . . . damn, but he must be clawing the sides of the walls by now.

Mercury-Atlas Six ebbed and flowed toward its countdown, but never quite came to the point where everyone *knew* it would go. The countdown remained maddeningly just beyond reach of the Mercury group. Television camera lenses seemed to peer over the shoulders of the technicians and the astronauts, and they felt as if they were tripping over a forest of radio microphones and cables, while in the background there grew a steady, tumultuous roar which sounded distressingly like the thunder produced by a thousand typewriters hammered upon by a thousand impatient, frustrated newsmen.

The prelude to the first American orbital flight should provide nightmares for future historians and psychiatrists, mused Pruett. The army of press at Canaveral made it seem as if the pending mission by John Glenn would smash open the barriers to manned orbital flight when, in reality, he would attempt but a fraction of the mission already committed to history by Titov. That the first Mercury flight was no less vital, Pruett knew only too well. Neither could he divorce from his thoughts the knowledge that he, personally, had once been slated for that same flight . . . the first American waiting to leave the earth and plunge at five miles per second into vacuum.

The weeks dragged on. The Russians chortled loudly through the international press at the nonsense perpetrated along Florida's coast. Tiring of press handouts with only weather reports and countdown delays, the home editors lashed their reporters with biting demands for *news*. Before Glenn finally did climb into the capsule for the actual flight, Cocoa Beach enlivened the wearisome succession of delays with the juicy murder of a waitress whose estranged husband allegedly ended her days by pumping seven bullets into her belly and head, and an uproarious and devastatingly wild pursuit by hundreds of police, military helicopters, and packs of howling dogs. . . . Pruett shook his head in disgust at the neon-sprayed background to the Great Moment.

It happened finally, on the morning of February 20, 1962. The Atlas defied its critics with a thundering shout of freedom and a cry of sweet power that sent the capsule and its human passenger spilling upward into the sky in a flight that was rich and beautiful every single foot of the way into the cold and waiting vacuum. And Glenn did a fabulous job; simply tremendous. Pruett knew. Enough for a man to perform in that solid, capable, steel-nerved manner where other men have gone before . . . but to be the first, to experience for the first time the gamut of a thousand possibilities of failure; *that* and his performance added up to a truly fabulous pilot. And then, to sustain that calm and the efficient manner of flight, when that triple-damned switch lit up Segment 51 on the monitoring board at Cape Canaveral, giving the spurious signal that the heat shield was loose . . . Pruett listened to the flight, later heard it all again on tape, and read the technical reports, and took off his hat to a Marine named John Glenn.

Three months later Scott Carpenter picked up the ball and carried it for three more orbits through the void. Once again Pruett made careful notes of the difficulties encountered, the solutions, the possibilities of trouble or even disaster. The overshoot during re-entry he dismissed as unimportant; Carpenter wasn't the only pilot to miss his landing point on the first try!

The nation was still basking in the thrills of Carpenter's "disappearance" and successful rescue when Pruett took off for Washington. For many months now there had been talk of the new manned orbital program—Gemini—and the capsule that would take two men into space. Apollo still overpowered all other efforts, but Apollo itself was overpowered by the sheer weight of work to be done, problems to overcome, and completely new equipment to be created.

NASA's decision to go the route of rendezvous in space in order to drop two men to the surface of the moon gave the Gemini program a sudden new importance. Before we could commit the Apollo spacecraft to rendezvous, someone would have to prove that it could be done. Men would have to go into space, rendezvous with another spacecraft, bring the two ships slowly together, and dock.

NASA scientists talked of two-week flights with Gemini, spoke in glowing terms of rendezvous and docking missions, orbital loops about the earth to heights of 500 and 600 miles. They talked also of the "second generation" of astronauts, and Pruett knew again the aching in his belly, and the sense of fear that once again he might be shunted aside. This time he took matters in his own hands, flew to Washington and saw a friend. He asked no special favors; only, when the requests for volunteers went out, "make goddamned sure that my name is somewhere near the top of the list, will you?"

Pruett flew back to Edwards. Taxiing along the flight line he spotted his commanding officer waiting for him; Pruett waved in return to the colonel's greeting.

"What's up, Charlie?" Pruett asked as he slid down the side of the fighter. The colonel remained silent for the few moments Pruett needed to divest himself of his pressure suit and gear. They started toward Flight Operations.

"Dick, how bad do you want that astronaut slot?" That was like Charlie Howard, all right. No leading up to anything; just spit it out.

Pruett stopped and looked at the colonel. "How bad you want your heart to keep beating, Charlie?"

His commander smiled. "Guess I knew the answer to that one before it came out," he admitted.

"Hell, you never ask a question unless you know the answer beforehand," Pruett said. "Now, level with me, Boss, because you wouldn't be here unless you had some news."

"First things first, Major," the colonel replied, starting up again for the Operations office.

Pruett stood rooted to the ground. *Major?*

"Sure! Your gold leaves are right here—" he patted his shirt pocket. "The word came in two days ago, while you were busy trying to cut some of that red tape back east." He jabbed a finger against Pruett's chest. "And don't forget —cigars all around, *Major.*"

"And what else did you have on your mind, Boss?"

"Oh, nothing very much," Howard said casually. "I just wanted to save you the trouble of unpacking."

Pruett kept his silence.

"While you were on the way back from Washington, *Major,* a telegram arrived for you. Naturally, I opened it. And that's the main reason why I'm here to greet you."

He laughed at the look on Pruett's face. "Okay, okay, here's the rest of it. NASA has just opened the competition for volunteers on the Gemini program, and—"

"And *I'm* in!"

The colonel nodded slowly; his mouth flew open in a gasp as the exuberant Pruett slammed a hand against his back.

"Charlie, you old bastard!" Pruett yelled happily. "You kept me hanging all this time, when you—" He spun on his heel and started running, calling back over his shoulder. "Thanks! And I'll see you later, Boss."

"Where the hell are *you* going?"

"No time to waste, Boss. Gotta pack right away."

"Pruett, you damned idiot, you *are* packed! Remember?"

Pruett skidded to a halt and came back slowly. "That's right, isn't it?" he said sheepishly. "How about that, Boss? I'm already packed."

"C'mon," his commander growled, "I'll buy you a drink. Maybe it will calm you down a little and— Say, wait a moment. Isn't Captain Dougherty a friend of yours?"

Pruett nodded. "Why?"

"He's on that list with you."

"*Jim* Dougherty?"

"Yeah, that's the name."

"Whaddya know. . . . Things are looking up all over." Pruett threw his arm around the colonel's shoulder. "Let's go, Charlie, and I'll buy *you* a drink."

They walked across the flight line, sharing the wonder they both knew would come for one of them.

They were in the midst of the competitive examinations among the astronaut hopefuls when the news broke about Vostok III. From the initial reports it was clear that the Russians were shooting for something special this time; the best consensus of opinion among the NASA engineers looked for a flight of at least seven days by the new cosmonaut, Nikolayev.

The next morning they realized all too well the Soviet intentions and how, once again, they had underestimated the steady drive of the Russians toward their stated goal of orbital manned stations and flights to the moon. Vostok IV with Pavel Popovich roared up from the Baikonur complex and slid into a beautiful matching orbital plane with Nikolayev's spacecraft. The astronaut candidates were hard put to concentrate on their experiments when word came in that the two spacecraft had closed to within less than two miles of each other, before starting to separate.

The enormity of the Russian accomplishment was displayed in dramatic fashion to Pruett and Dougherty. They completed their tests and examinations before the two cosmonauts returned triumphantly to earth.

There wasn't any doubt about Pruett's selection, but they sweated out his friend, for the competition was rough. And then the word came through, and they did a brief and wild impromptu dance when they learned that once again they would be together. NASA accepted nine test pilots, Pruett and Dougherty among them, to increase the number of astronaut flight crewmen to a total of sixteen.

No, Pruett thought, *make that fifteen. We're one short* . . . and every time he thought of Deke Slayton, and the orders grounding the solidly built pilot from space flight, he wanted to go somewhere and be sick. Deke could manhandle a fighter in a skilled fashion that few pilots in the world ever approached. When he flew as a test pilot at Edwards, the supply shop ran out of g-suits, which helped a man's body to fight off the punishing effect of plus-gravity forces. So Deke went ahead and flew anyway, and *without* the suit. And he built up a tolerance to plus-g that made even old-time veterans blink their eyes. He could pull more than nine g in a fighter, without that suit, and still not black out. He pulled more pressure on the centrifuge than any other member of the astronaut team. But he had something in his heart that kicked every now and then, and a panel of doctors knew fright and they grounded Slayton. Whenever his heart "acted up," Deke Slayton had the sure cure. Either he'd lift weights or run like hell for a couple of miles—and that put him back into perfect shape!

But they were keeping him on the ground, because no one *knew* what might happen to his heart under sustained weightlessness. He still flew as high as the wings and the blazing afterburner of an F-106 could take him. Once that had been high enough, but only once, and whenever Pruett thought of how close that man had come . . .

A sense of compassion filled him. They'd offered Slayton another world out there in space. They'd offered; he'd accepted eagerly. And he flew his heart out, and worked day and night, and he was scheduled to go next after Glenn. Everyone who knew or talked to Deke Slayton knew that MA-7 rode uppermost in his mind. And then the panel of doctors, arguing among themselves and the men closest to Slayton, grounded him. Deke Slayton didn't quit; *any other man, myself included,* Pruett thought, *would have walked straight out that goddamned door and never turned back.* But Slayton stayed, and it was he who shepherded around the "new crop," the second generation of American astronauts.

And the door to space wasn't locked tight on Deke Slayton. There would be recurring examinations, and tests, and redecisions, and perhaps one of the two seats in a Gemini might yet be occupied by him. Finally, to better his chances, Slayton resigned his commission, kissed the Air Force good-by, and began sweating out NASA's "hopeful promise" for that Gemini flight.

Pruett and Dougherty were together at a roadblock on Cape Canaveral when Wally Schirra was counting down for Mercury-Atlas Eight, the third Mercury manned orbital flight. Their positions as observers gave them the rare opportunity to cover almost every inch of the Cape and the Mercury network of installations. They rode the elevators to the different work levels of the great gantry tower at Pad Fourteen. They climbed metal stairs and swung out over machinery and equipment. Pruett caressed the sleek skin of the Atlas booster, and together they marveled at the incredibly thin texture of the metal, so thin that without internal pressurization it would collapse of its own weight, like a deflated and wrinkled balloon.

At two o'clock the morning of Schirra's scheduled lift-off, Pruett and Dougherty entered Hangar S on the Cape. Later, both men watched silently as the astronaut's flight surgeon and his assistant began the final medical examination of Schirra.

By four o'clock Pruett and Dougherty were in Mercury Control, where the mission director conferred with his staff prior to making his decision for GO or NO GO. Assistants spread before George Keith all data pertaining to the upcoming flight of six orbits; they studied weather charts for the immediate time and that predicted for launch, during the mission, and during planned recovery. Keith scanned the report status of the world-wide tracking net, the condition of the astronaut, the disposition of the recovery forces. Up at Goddard Center in Maryland, the hulking 7090 computers had digested every factor available to them, electronically chewed the bits of information, and spat out answers that, fortunately, satisfied the mission director. On the basis of all the tests, reports, predictions, and his own analysis of all the factors involved, Keith gave a green light to the countdown.

The mission was a very definite GO.

They had time for a fast visit to the squat, domed blockhouse of steel-reinforced concrete where a staff of more than a hundred skilled technicians worked in concert under the Test Conductor—the orchestra leader who blended the skills and talents of his men and the capabilities of his electronic robots into a flowing movement that carried the events of the morning closer and closer to the countdown's final gasp of zero.

Pruett and Dougherty watched, listened, and learned. At T minus 225 minutes the blockhouse rang with the calls of the launch crew checking out the Azusa system, the complicated electronic tracking station net that would provide to the 7090 computers the running reports of Schirra's Atlas booster—its position at any and all moments in flight.

The stations reported in; antennas were checked as "homing to the bird" and "ready to track." One more step in the thousands of checklist items was scrubbed off the countdown worksheets.

Pruett and Dougherty left the blockhouse. Only scattered clouds could be seen, and the stars sparkled brightly in the early Florida morning. At 0420 hours they watched Canaveral come alive; at Pad Fourteen, the launch-stand workmen were switching on the powerful floodlights.

The red-and-white gantry loomed twelve stories above the ground, its colors sharp and clear, the gantry tremendous and massive along its bottom, tapering slightly with height, in the form of a gigantic, thick A. The blue-white lights poured brilliance against the tower and splashed fingers of light onto the booster that it embraced; the light spilled away and tumbled across the launch stand, the concrete apron, the dozens of men working steadily. The lights crisscrossed and rushed across the night sky, creating glowing avenues of light that sped up and up until they vanished.

The two new astronauts looked across the Cape and shook their heads slowly in wonder at the awesome scene. "You know, Dick," Dougherty said quietly, "I've always tried to imagine just what this moment would be like. I suppose I dreamed a lot. But never, never did I realize it would be so *beautiful*. . . . It's—it's *unreal*."

Pruett looked at his friend and nodded. Words weren't necessary.

By six-thirty, as they stood at the roadblock only two thousand feet from Pad Fourteen, the sky was bright and clear. Voices shouting commands over the pad bullhorns drifted, tinny and faded, to them. They heard the groaning sound of the huge gantry rolling back from the launch stand, nearly five hundred tons moving in slow and ponderous fashion to the side, where it would wait, silent, marked by the clarity of the dawn.

They looked up when clattering drones filled the sky, and big Marine helicopters, with their five-bladed rotors blatting in the morning air, moved into position. These carried the emergency rescue teams, ready instantly to go swirling out over the water or across swamp, should there be an abort and the capsule came quickly back to the sea or the earth. Booming horns sounded their deep, rasping call, the warning horns that had cleared the gantry. Deep coughing sounds and rumbles announced the arrival at the roadblock of fire trucks, crash wagons, and ambulances. A dirty white truck rolled up and dropped its sides; photographers, firemen, crash-crew personnel, and others at the roadblock gravitated to the recent arrival to purchase containers of coffee and thick, greasy doughnuts.

And then there was the shrill, faint, high-pitched screaming, and both men turned to look at the complex. The launch crew was now pouring liquid oxygen through the plumbing system, chilling it down, and the hot pipes screamed in metallic agony at the savage touch of the liquid oxygen, nearly 300 degrees below zero. A hissing sound was added to the cry of the tormented pipes, and soon plumes of white vapor streamed from the vent valves in the side of the Atlas—bleeding pressure from the oxidizer tank to prevent undue pressure buildup.

They looked straight down the road at the launch stand, with the Atlas alone and naked except for its blanket of ice frost around the supercold liquid oxygen tank. They looked to the side, mentally marking the position of a heavy truck —under which they would fling their bodies if the tanks erupted and bright flame came spilling out; for they were close, much too close to escape the concussion wave and twisting showers of debris if the Atlas should, for some reason, destroy itself or have to be destroyed.

They looked at the giant standing on the metal ring, and abruptly the plumes of white vapor streaming from the vent valves vanished. The flow of liquid oxygen to top off the tanks had ended; in his mind Pruett scanned the countdown checklist, knew that the tank valves had sealed, and that the tanks were being pressurized rapidly to bring the booster to launch status.

He could feel a hush descending on the Cape. He watched thin black snakes writhing alongside the capsule; there went the spacecraft umbilicals.

The verniers and main engines came on almost simultaneously. There was a volcanic birth of golden flame beneath the huge rocket, and two thin, bright fire wasps snarled from her flanks as the verniers flashed brightly. The cataract of golden fire erupted downward, met a flow of cooling water; with a screaming roar flame shattered against liquid and produced a boiling cloud of steam.

Pruett identified himself with the man lying on his back on the contour couch and did not know that he had stopped breathing, that he did not release the pressure of his lungs as ice crystals and gleaming chunks broke off the sides of the Atlas, falling freely. They were still falling as the massive steel shackles pinioning the rocket slammed back, out of the way, and offered freedom to the giant.

From his position close to the launch stand, Pruett stared in wonder at the blinding ball of golden fire, intense, shimmering along its edges, bulging down into a teardrop at the bottom, pushing with terrible energy at the bulk of the Atlas. The fire washed down with dazzling force and splashed greedily across the launch stand. But only for the briefest of seconds, for the giant tasted her freedom and pushed mightily at the clutching gravity of the planet. The flame lengthened into a ragged spear and hazy flaming gases trailed beneath the golden fire and touched only . . . air.

The thunder pounded across the Cape and rolled against Pruett with a terrible crackling, booming roar, painful and yet sweet to his ears. It was a glorious and triumphant cry of a giant running loose, a creature tasting escape, springing eagerly to plunge into the depths for which it had been hopefully created, the depths of vacuum that lay along the uppermost edges of the planet, beyond the world of men.

Pruett stared as the golden color deepened and turned to orange; then red appeared along the edges of the booster flame. The great rocket bent over steadily in its flight, programming more and more from the vertical. Almost as if the voice came to him from a great distance he could hear Dougherty shouting, imploring the booster to "Go, go! You beautiful sonofabitch, GO!"

The Atlas rushed into the lower edges of the stratosphere, stabbing into the cold air with a thick white contrail, a brilliant white ribbon arrowing away from the earth.

The swath in the heavens vanished. Pruett strained his eyes to retain the shrinking dot in his vision. There was the tiniest puff in the sky; the Atlas had staged, jettisoned her flaring booster skirt. A thin, double-walled veil kept rising until even this final tenuous glimpse of the rocket faded into nothingness.

When the word came several minutes later that Schirra was in orbit, successful in his towering leap away from the lower regions of earth, there were still tears on the cheeks of Jim Dougherty. He didn't seem to mind when Pruett noticed him brushing them away; he didn't mind at all.

Pruett was Cap Com at Zanzibar for the last of the Mercury flights. On May 15, 1963, Gordo Cooper whipped into orbit atop an Atlas that was as near to perfection in its performance as any machine possibly could be. He threaded the narrow space needle with an aplomb that astounded all those except his close friends. In fact, several times during the mission Gordo fell asleep. Doctors watching the tele-metered flow of data on Cooper's medical status were stunned to note that during the countdown, the astronaut had unconcernedly dozed off. He went to sleep again shortly after he injected into orbit, dismaying all the doc-tors who for years had warned of the terrifying punishment that space flight would inflict upon a man.

Gordo flew his mission with a sensitivity and control that, impossibly, improved upon Schirra's textbook flight. The man who had flown six orbits in the mission before Cooper's noted wryly that Cooper had thrown away the textbook and was rewriting it from beginning to end.

And the finale was another cliff-hanger in the tradition established by Glenn. When the .05g light came on in the capsule, signifying—erroneously, of course—that the spacecraft was encountering resistance from the atmos-phere, Cooper had no choice but to kill his automatic pilot and prepare for the critical re-entry under manual control only.

The rest was history. The scientists trumpeting the su-periority of the black boxes over man slunk off to brood in obscure corners when Gordo Cooper rifled his spacecraft down a mathematically precise corridor that was far more accurate than the best of the re-entries flown to date by the electronic computers. Once again the black boxes had failed the man and the mission, and had the man not proven capable of overcoming the failure and performing in superior fashion, Gordon Cooper might well have ended his mission in a great flaming ball spitting out chunks of blazing debris.

His brilliantly executed re-entry and triumphant return to Washington and New York brought the nation to its feet and screaming wildly in praise of the astronaut.

But the cheers echoed dimly and the glowing words were hard to swallow.

Gordo Cooper's flight was the end of the line. Its very measure of success, dictated the NASA administrator, eliminated the need for further Mercury flights.

The group of original astronauts disagreed vehemently. They spoke out angrily—and *publicly,* everyone noted with astonishment—against cutting short the program. Mercury had been spectacular in its success, had achieved goals far beyond the wildest hopes of anyone concerned when the program began. Now, with the opportunity to stretch the twenty-two orbits of Cooper's flight into a mission lasting three full days, the astronauts raised absolute hell and even went directly to the President.

It did them little good. Neither could success be achieved by the leading personnel of Project Mercury. Christopher C. Kraft, Jr., the brilliant Program Flight Director for Mercury, stated flatly that there was "a lot to be gained" from a longer space journey. Speaking for the record, Kraft told newsmen that he thought that the next mission—Mercury-Atlas Ten—should be flown "with the idea that we will keep going as long as it is safe."

For a few weeks it seemed beyond question that there would be an MA-10 mission. NASA scientists spent six hundred thousand dollars studying the problem and running extensive tests on the feasibility of the mission. By adding three hundred pounds to the Mercury spacecraft, most of which would be batteries, they could stretch out the safe mission time to well over one hundred hours. The batteries, for power, could be lashed by titanium straps to the outside of the capsule heat shield. The astronaut would need additional food, water, and lithium hydroxide for the removal of carbon dioxide, but these were details. There wasn't any question but that the mission could be flown. It could run for just over three days, and leave a two-day safety margin still in the capsule.

The doctors added their voices to the uproar demanding the MA-10 mission. They insisted that the flight was vital; during the three days of orbiting they would gain badly needed information on the problems of food handling and digestion, body waste disposal, consumption of power supplies, effects of sustained weightlessness, and dozens of other factors. Even the physical scientists agreed to the mission, for Cooper's handling of scientific experiments in orbit had provided data never before attainable through the robot satellites.

The answer from Washington remained unchanged: *"No; there will not be another Mercury mission."*

Project Mercury scientists were not only worried; they were angry as well. During the same month that Cooper whirled through his twenty-two orbits, the Russians had performed a singularly impressive and ominous feat. The giant Cosmos XVIII satellite, roaring into orbit from Baikonur, along the same orbital plane flown by the Vostoks, looped around and around the earth for nine days. One month later Lieutenant Colonel Valery F. Bykovsky thundered into space aboard Vostok V. For two days the cosmonaut whirled around and around the earth. He woke from his second night's sleep shortly after whipping above the tip of South America, on his thirty-first orbit, and discovered that he had company.

The Soviets inundated the world with details of the new cosmonaut—a *woman*. Valentina Vladimirovna Tereshkova, twenty-six years old, and an expert parachutist with over a hundred and twenty jumps to her credit. While the astronauts of Project Mercury cursed the cessation of their flights—and looked gloomily to a complete blank in orbital missions for the next eighteen months—the Russian man and woman drifted to within three miles of each other and sang duets by radio as they looked out and saw the sun glittering off the rounded hulls of the big Russian spacecraft.

Bykovsky remained aloft for a flight of nearly five days and more than two million miles. The astronauts tasted sour bile when Tereshkova finally smashed through the atmosphere in re-entry, and then ejected from her spacecraft to land by personal parachute, northeast of Karaganda.

The diminutive female had circuited the globe forty-nine times. It added up to a flight of nearly seventy-one hours and a distance of one and a quarter million miles.

Valentina Tereshkova had been in orbit longer than the flights of Glenn, Carpenter, Schirra, and Cooper—*combined.*

"There will be no further flights in the Project Mercury program. . . ." The officials at NASA headquarters refused to budge from their stand.

Al Shepard made no attempt to disguise how badly he wanted MA-10; he would have been assigned to the mission. Shepard, the remaining astronauts and Mercury officials pleaded their case again and again. Gemini was suffering slowdowns from financial shortages and the normal delays of equipment development. The two-man spaceship wasn't scheduled for its orbital flights until late 1964, perhaps even later. That threatened a gap of a year and a half before another American would return to space. They argued their case with facts; there were several Atlas boosters available for the mission. There were three Mercury capsules ready and waiting, already modified for one-day missions, and it would be a simple matter to add the equipment and changes necessary for the planned three days of orbiting in MA-10.

The presentations broke up into argumentative sessions where tempers wore thin and patience went out the window. One Washington official sneered at the advantages of sustaining national prestige by another Mercury flight.

"Screw national prestige," one of the astronauts snarled at him. "You can shove that stuff as far up as it will go. Don't you understand English, goddamnit? We *need* this flight. We *need* more medical data, we *need* to test equipment for the Gemini, we *need* to carry out tests that can cut a few months off the Gemini *and* the Apollo. We're talking about facts, and you're giving us a line of crap about prestige. . . ."

NASA was adamant; *no* more Mercury flights. They issued public statements as to saving money, moving faster into Gemini, and shuffling the huge manned space program to adapt better to the needs of Gemini and Apollo. Project Mercury was committed to history, the MA-10 mission remained a dream, and the nation looked forward to the huge blank in American manned space flight while the Russians crowded the stage. A great many people suffered emotions compounded equally of dismay and disgust.

But the rumblings continued beneath the surface. The flight surgeons assigned to Mercury had troubled sleep. When Wally Schirra returned to earth after nine hours in his capsule, he suffered from orthostatic hypotension. This was unusual for a man of his superb physical condition, for this is an occurrence more common to sedentary people, and evidenced by an abrupt lowering of blood pressure, with feelings of dizziness and a racing pulse.

Schirra's condition was not serious and it was brief, but it was also completely unexpected. Cooper experienced momentary dizziness and some of the same effects felt by Schirra, but these also disappeared quickly.

Other murmurs that all might not be well physiologically with the men who had orbited the earth came from within the U.S.S.R. Soviet medical specialists revealed meager information, but there was no question that they too were studying with some concern the condition of their spacemen. Both Nikolayev and Popovich showed the symptoms of "calcium mobilization"—an abnormal loss of bone calcium. In extreme cases this can also produce a condition of bone softening. Did the cosmonauts have mild and transitory effects, or were they more serious? The United States didn't know, and the Russians wouldn't say.

What about the physiological effects of the missions on Bykovsky and Tereshkova? The Russians clamped the news lid on tight.

During the months following Cooper's final flight, medical tests revealed other minor but potentially significant problems. The doctors found it impossible to draw conclusions; they needed more experience, more time with a man in orbit to confirm or to deny their suspicions. A worried scientist went to Washington with his fears. He told the NASA officials that they might not have any choice in the matter, that they might be forced by medical needs alone to reinstate the MA-10 mission. For if serious problems showed up after Gemini was committed, that effort could be seriously delayed, and the long-range plans to land an Apollo spacecraft on the moon threatened by crippling postponements.

That might cause Congress to go through the roof, with the possibility that the maximum effort to push Apollo, costing many billions of dollars extra, could go down the drain. NASA pondered more and more carefully the matter of bringing MA-10 back to life.

The undercurrent grew in a subdued but nonetheless persistent manner. To wait for the Gemini flights while these possibly critical questions went unanswered was folly;

it meant that the second-generation manned space effort would remain chained to the limited bioastronautic knowledge of the four Mercury flights, when it should be moving swiftly into the advanced areas, as the Soviets were doing with extraordinary skill.

Late in 1963 the Russians put up their first Polyot unmanned spacecraft. *Flight I,* as Americans came to know the craft, was a grim harbinger of the future. The robot ship increased its altitude by more than five hundred miles after injecting into orbit. Then it shifted the plane of its orbit, changing the angle at which it crossed the equator. In rapid succession, a series of Cosmos and Polyot missions demonstrated spectacular capabilities on the part of the Soviets.

An event that lasted from April 19th through 28th, 1964, settled the matter once and for all. The Russian flight of two cosmonauts in two new spacecraft—two cosmonauts in *each* of the new Vostoks—brought the demands for MA-10 to a feverish pitch. Friedrich Rynin and Mikhail S. Danilov went into orbit first in Vostok VII. Twenty-three hours later Vostok VIII boomed its trail through the diminishing atmosphere into vacuum, manned by Vasily S. Borisov and Igor M. Pokrovskii.

The first manned Gemini flight was still seven to ten months in the future when the Russian spaceships slowly drew together, and then docked with one another. Live television broadcasts from the two Vostoks to all the world captured the imagination of those nations over which flashed the two great spacecraft.

The Academy of Sciences of the U.S.S.R. announced that the Soviet Union intended to land the first manned spaceships on the surface of the moon by early 1967 and, should progress continue as before, possibly sooner.

Scathing denunciations of the sea-level vacuum in American manned space flight blistered the walls of Congressional hearing rooms.

The Russians remained in space for eight days, with the two spacecraft joined together for five of those days.

In NASA headquarters at 400 Maryland Avenue, S.W., in Washington, D.C., the lights burned every night for a week. *Something* had to give—and soon.

Chapter VI

"*Keep the telephone lines open, then! I don't care how many people want to get through. I want these lines kept open, waiting for my use when I say so! Is that clear?*"

"*Yes, General. I understand.*"

"*Good! Now, have the scientists at the Moscow computer center brought in any more reports?*"

"*No, sir. But we are expecting to hear from them momentarily. They said that—excuse me, sir, Professor Ogorodnikov wishes to speak with you.*"

"*Hurry, man! Put him on at once.*"

"*General Karpenko?*"

"*Yes, Academician. What news have you?*"

"*It is as we expected, General. It seems we were correct all the time. There is no question but that the American cosmonaut is experiencing serious difficulties.*"

"*Is it the braking rockets, then, as we have suspected?*"

"*That is correct, General. The spacecraft was to have initiated retrofire just as it crossed over the northeast coast of the island of New Guinea. At that moment the cosmonaut would have been approaching the end of his orbit number forty-seven—*"

Impatiently: "*Yes, yes, I know!*"

"*Bear with me, General Karpenko. We wish to be certain that the data we give you is absolutely correct.*"

"*Forgive me, Academician Ogorodnikov. Please go on.*"

"*We have continued our study of the orbital parameters. The American spacecraft has an orbital lifetime, from the moment of insertion into orbit near Bermuda Island, of approximately six days and eight hours. At that time it will begin to encounter increasing resistance from the upper atmosphere, and deceleration will commence.*"

"*Six days and eight hours. But you said approximately. Can you not be more specific?*"

"*No, it is impossible. There are factors beyond our control, factors which do not come within our knowledge. But* they are unimportant. Our calculations are quite accurate, General Karpenko. The atmosphere is never quiescent, as you know. It breathes like a diaphragm, up and down. It depends to some extent upon solar activity. But even at the outside, we will not be wrong by more than a difference of one or two orbits."

"Academician, how much time remains for the cosmonaut?"

"Of this we cannot be positive, General. Much of our information depends upon what the Americans have said about the artificial environment within the spacecraft. But it is possible to reduce the ambient pressure within the machine, or even to resort to the pressure suit alone, without cabin pressure. He cannot reduce very greatly, however, for his arterial saturation will begin to suffer. We have, however, come to some conclusions."

"And—"

"Please, General. We believe that he will exhaust the last of his oxygen approximately six to twelve hours before the machine commences the first phases of re-entry."

"Then there is no chance of the cosmonaut surviving?"

"None, General. Or none that we are able to anticipate, based upon all the facts we have at our command."

"Umm . . . Academician Ogorodnikov, from this very moment, from right now . . . how much time is there before this American—Pruett—exhausts the last of his oxygen?"

"Approximately forty-two hours. Why, General? Does it really matter?"

"Oh, yes! Yes, indeed, it does matter! I am grateful to you, Academician, for all your excellent work. Thank you, thank you!"

General P. L. Karpenko, Master of Artillery Sciences, Command Pilot, Corresponding Member of the U.S.S.R. Academy of Sciences, and answerable only to Leonid Sedov of the Academy, spun on his heel and walked briskly into the radio communications room. The guard at the door snapped to attention as the general, ignoring him, strode across the room to a switchboard operator.

"Quickly! Get me Vanichev at Baikonur."

"Yes, sir."

Twenty-six seconds later . . .

"Vanichev?"

"Yes, General."

"Listen to me carefully. The Academy has confirmed our beliefs. Furthermore, there is a time of only forty-two hours from now, until the cosmonaut reaches the last of his oxygen. Can we proceed with our plan; is there enough time?"

"One moment, please, General . . ."

Fifty-two seconds more . . .

"Sir, there is no question. Since your call yesterday, the men have been working without a stop. The guidance system already has been adapted to the new flight plan, and we are working without any delays. Yes, sir, we can do it."

"Fine, fine! But remember, no one beside yourself and your assistant—what's his name? Merkulov—is to know anything about the changes. You are clear on that matter?"

"Yes, sir, I understand perfectly."

"Good. What is your estimate to launch?"

"We must be in the air no later than eighteen hours from now, General."

"Proceed with your operation, Vanichev. I am flying out immediately. I should be there in four hours or so. Good-by."

General Kurpenko rubbed his hands and frowned thoughtfully. All was going as planned. The Americans . . . ah, but what an opportunity! He turned to the switchboard operator.

"Call the airstrip. Tell them to have the engines running and the machine ready for immediate departure."

"Yes, sir."

General Karpenko never heard the reply. He was already running down the long hallway, to the sedan which would rush him to his jet transport, and which in turn would rush him to Baikonur, where hundreds of men were working, had been working since yesterday, without sleep.

General Karpenko leaned back in his seat as the sedan's red lights flashed and sirens wailed; he leaned back, and smiled. . . .

His name was Robert C. Henderson, and that was a big name in the manned space-flight business. Henderson was Director of the Manned Spacecraft Center at Houston, and he greeted Pruett with a smile as the astronaut entered his office.

"Sit down, Dick," he said. "The others will be here in just a moment."

The others? Pruett didn't know who they were, or why he had been summoned to Henderson's office. But his eyebrows lifted slightly, the only outward sign of his questioning thoughts, when Roger McClarren, Project Gemini Director, walked into the room. With McClarren were several assistants Pruett had seen in passing, and they nodded genially to him as they took seats around the large conference table.

George Keith, who ran the Mercury Control Mission Center at Canaveral for the four orbital flights, arrived, and shook hands warmly with Pruett. Andy Blake of the Mercury Project team walked in. Behind him several technicians filed to seats at the table.

Henderson nodded to his secretary, who rose and closed the door.

"All right," Henderson began, "let's get down to business."

He looked directly at Pruett. The astronaut kept his expression blank.

"Dick, do you know why we called you here?"

"No, sir, I don't."

Henderson leaned forward, his hands toying with a pencil. "We have decided to go ahead with the MA-10 mission."

That's all he said. It was enough. Pruett felt his body tighten. His mind leaped at conclusions and just as quickly shied away from the possibilities. But he couldn't help . . . He forced a lid shut on his burgeoning thoughts and kept his mind blank, his face a mask.

"You know all the background details, so I won't bother with them," Henderson continued. "The heart of the matter is that we must make this flight. Gemini is on schedule—I should say the revamped schedule—and we still plan to launch sometime late this winter."

He leaned back in his chair and sighed. "We've had the devil's own time in checking out the world-wide net, since so much has been done already to convert to the Gemini standards. But we're assured that the network will be more than ready in time for the MA-10 flight."

"When will that be?" Pruett asked.

Henderson nodded to George Keith, who picked up the conversation.

"Dick, we're shooting for a mission on July twenty-first," he said. "That doesn't give us as much time as we'd like, but we don't have any choice. Essentially this is going to be a medical experiment. We've got to find the answers to some of the questions that have been cropping up. I don't doubt that many of our fears are unfounded; this has been the history of the program as far as our people who make the flights are concerned."

Keith frowned unhappily. "But we don't *know* the answers. Not for sure. And the Russians are playing it close to the vest. Early in 1962, Gazenko and Yazdovsky—you've read their medical reports that were released by the Academy of Sciences—gave us a great deal of physiological information about Titov. They even advanced their own theories, which subsequently proved accurate, that the disturbed equilibrium Titov encountered was strictly subjective, that it wouldn't be repeated in future flights.

"They were a bit more reticent when it came to Nikolayev and Popovich. They let out some 'data on their calcium mobilization problems. But they pretty well closed the door with Bykovsky and Tereshkova, and as far as medical reports go for the double-team flight this spring . . . well, they've locked the door and thrown away the key. We can't find out a thing."

He looked ruefully at Henderson and around the table. "I do *not* like—I do not like one little bit—being forced to rely on the Russians for handouts about physiological reactions to extended orbital flights. *Nobody* likes it, as far as I know. We simply must get another flight, one that will last for three days. . . ."

Pruett appeared as if he would explode.

"What's the matter?" Keith asked.

"*Who* is going to make the MA-10 mission?"

"I suppose we have been keeping you on tenterhooks," interrupted Henderson. "*You* are."

Everyone grinned at the expression on Pruett's face. Pruett waved a hand weakly. "Just—just go on, George. I'll let it soak in while you fill in the rest of the details."

"That's the hard core of it, Dick," Keith continued. "The mission will aim for forty-eight orbits—retrofire in the southwest Pacific and splashdown north of Hawaii. That will give us almost three orbits more than three days—almost seventy-six hours—if we go the whole route."

Andy Blake broke in. "For the last two weeks, we've made a real nitpicking study of the capsule—we've selected Capsule Fifteen for the mission—to confirm what we'll need for the flight. We'll keep most of the changes that we made for Capsule No. Twenty—Cooper's spacecraft. We'll leave out the periscope, the backup telemetry recorder, the rate stabilization and control system. You'll likely have a total of the one battery at fifteen hundred watts and eight main batteries, including reserve, each at three thousand watts. We'll mount these extra batteries on the retropack with insulated shielding for thermal balance after injection into orbit."

Pruett listened carefully, absorbing the words. But in the back of his mind, not quite obscured by the need for close attention to the conversation in the room, there seemed to be a tiny figure of a man he recognized as himself, joyously doing capers and grinning madly. He suppressed a smile at the thought. . . .

"—and we needed only ten pounds more hydrogen peroxide for Gordo's flight," Andy Blake went on, "than we did for the nine hours flown by Wally. Staying in chimp mode, even powered down much of the time, will reduce greatly the demands on the power and reaction fuel supplies. Oh yes, there's a clear-cut definition of thruster levels; no question at all about staying on the one-pound thrusters instead of kicking in the big ones at twenty-four pounds. In fact, we may decide to go ahead with a modification, if there's time, of putting a bypass control on the ASCS to give you the one-pound thrusters in that particular mode. It could prove a great help for a long flight, and . . ."

The discussion passed neither slowly nor quickly; engrossed in the planning work, the men ignored the passage of hours. There were technical details that produced thick checksheets and manuals; the engineers undertook to explain only the major items, leaving the exhaustive breakdown to Pruett's own time schedule as worked out for the mission. The flight surgeons were having a major part in the planning; rather than attending to the needs and requirements of the astronaut, as in previous missions, the surgeons this time carried the greatest weight in experiments. Pruett learned that he would be required to test as many of the bioastronautics systems of the Gemini spacecraft as it would be possible to bring into his Mercury capsule.

The surgeons wanted urine specimens stored for the entire flight. After three days in orbit this could present a problem of space and storage, but the doctors had worked that out neatly. Each passage of urine would be noted as to quantity in centimeters, and a small amount of the liquid drawn into plastic flasks with snap-tight and non-leak covers. (I hope they work, Pruett thought.)

Storage of the solid body wastes was far more of a problem, and work had already begun to modify Mercury pressure suits with several of the advanced features of the suits that would be used for Gemini. "In fact," one of the technicians smiled, "you're going to be our guinea pig. We have a number of ideas as to how we're going to permit defecation and adapt the body-waste collection system to the personal suit. We'll fill you in on the details later, but you'll notice on your time scheduling that you're to meet with us about a week from now for your initial suit fittings. By then we should be pretty well along with the modifications. Oh yes, well before you're ready for your flight we will have had some practical experience with the collection system."

Pruett raised his eyebrows. "That interests the hell out of me, Sam. Did you get any volunteers for the job?"

"Well, not *really,*" the technician hedged. He laughed. "But we thought up a few other chores they liked even less than living in the new suit for three or four days at a stretch. . . ."

Two more hours passed, and the meeting drew to its close. Time schedules were established for various groups; Pruett could see that he would need three months to accomplish what he must do in only two, but it was always possible to double up on much of the work, and then, his backup could handle many of—

They hadn't mentioned the backup astronaut yet, Pruett realized. And while he was at it, there were some other matters that had to be cleared up. *Now,* not later, for they could grow into ugly sores unless they were exposed at once.

The meeting was over; all essential issues resolved.

Pruett looked at Henderson. "Bob, would it be all right if we kicked something around for a few moments—not as a part of the meeting, but it's important."

The director glanced at his watch. "Sure, Dick, no problem at all."

Pruett rose to his feet. "Uh, I'd like to have George Keith and Andy Blake sit in on this with us, if you don't mind."

Henderson nodded his assent; Keith and Blake remained at their seats as the room emptied of the NASA staff, and the door closed.

"All right, Dick," Henderson said, "it's all yours. What's on your mind?"

Pruett went right to the point. "Who comes in as backup?"

Henderson drove right back. "Who do you think should be backup?"

He hadn't expected this; it was better, far better, than he'd hoped for. He shot out the name immediately.

"Dougherty—Jim Dougherty. He's best for it."

"Why?"

"We've worked closely together. He's as good as they come. We've learned we can almost anticipate each other's thoughts and needs. He'll be a tremendous help in getting through all that work in the sixty days we've got for this job. There's no question of that; the other men are just as capable, of course, but we've already slipped into the kind of very close coordination you get, usually, only after you've worked together for a long time as a team."

Keith and Blake turned to Henderson. "It's a good choice," Keith added. "And it *will* cut corners."

Henderson looked at Blake. "Andy?"

"I agree. Dougherty drops neatly into place in the whole thing."

"All right, Dick," Henderson said amiably, "you've got Dougherty for backup."

"Thank you; it will help to smooth out a great many of the rough spots," Pruett replied.

Henderson began to slip papers from his desk into a briefcase.

"But there's one more thing," Pruett said.

The three men held their silence.

"Look, can I make this a family conversation?" Pruett

asked. "Strictly within this room, and outside that door, it just never took place?"

Henderson looked sharply at him. "Go ahead."

Pruett took a deep breath and plunged. "Look, Bob, I'm honored by this selection. Sure, I know you judge on the basis of whom you and other people consider the best qualified at that particular moment to handle the mission.

"But you and I, and George and Andy here, and—well, hell, just about everybody concerned knows that Al Shepard was slated to step into position for the next flight, if we'd decided upon one after Gordo's mission. It would save a lot of . . . a lot of idle thinking on my part if you could see your way clear to blow away the smoke about my stepping up for MA-10 instead of Shepard."

Henderson bit off the end of a cigar, spat the tobacco into his wastebasket. He leaned back in his chair, slowly lit the cigar, then pointed the glowing end at Pruett.

"*Who* said Al Shepard was picked for the next Mercury flight?" he asked softly.

"Hell, Bob, that's been common knowledge!"

"Oh, it has, has it? Let me tell you something, Dick, and I want you to hear me very clearly on this matter. At the time of Gordon Cooper's flight, *no one* had been selected for MA-10, *if* we decided at that time to fly the mission. Well, we didn't decide to fly then, and we never made any decision as to who would have gone.

"I want you to have it straight. We *might* have picked Shepard, or Carpenter, or any one person of the original group. But we didn't make the selection, because we didn't have to, and I'm fully aware of all the crap in the papers and the magazines about how we definitely had made up our minds. All those people out their with their crystal balls and hours to fill on television and in newspaper columns simply didn't know what the hell they were talking about. Those that did know were smart enough to realize we don't commit the mission to any one individual until we are unquestionably moving toward a specific date on the calendar. Now—"

"Come off it, Bob! There isn't any question but that Al Shepard is the sharpest man in the whole crowd of us. As good as anyone else is, no one quite steps into Shepard's shoes. And if—"

Henderson cut him short with a voice as cheerful as icy

glass. "Major Pruett," he said with undue quiet, "I do not have any intention to indulge in guessing games or picking names out of hats. Despite whatever feelings *you* may have in this matter—" he glared at Pruett—"you are not yet in a position—and I would question your qualifications in this particular area—to pass judgment upon yourself or any other member of the flight crew for our programs. I am far more aware than you of the outstanding capabilities of Commander Shepard, and I am *also* cognizant, it seems necessary to impress upon you, of the many multitudes of factors which play their roles in the selection of a flight crewman for an orbital mission. You do not have this cognizance, which is understandable, since it does not lie within your province.

"Does all this reach you in no uncertain terms, Major Pruett?"

The selectee for MA-10 slumped in his chair. "Talk about putting my big foot in my big mouth," he muttered.

Henderson and the room thawed visibly—and immediately. "No, you didn't do that," he said. "And it may surprise you, but I am most pleased with what you did say and the motivation behind those remarks."

Pruett rolled his eyes in mock dismay. "You are losing me, Big Chief."

Henderson laughed. "Dick, you asked that this conversation be strictly a family matter and that once we left this room, it was shoved out into limbo. I appreciate that and I have not forgotten it. Neither can I find any fault with your attempts to give credit to someone else. I fully agree with you about the qualifications of Al Shepard.

"But he *is* assigned to the first manned Gemini mission; Jerry Masters will ride as his copilot. Grissom is already well into the equipment tests for the Gemini rendezvous experiments, and we do not want to pull him away from that work. Glenn, Carpenter, Schirra, and Cooper are all known entities to us. We need as many yardsticks and values as we can get with which to draw certain conclusions physiologically.

"You have been assigned to MA-10 for one reason above all others: you are the most qualified to fly the mission."

Henderson glanced at his watch again. "And now get the hell out of my office and let me go home. Damnit, it's after eight o'clock already and my wife will be having nine fits and a house full of sympathetic, clucking company."

His eyes seemed to twinkle. "Oh yes. There's just one more thing, Dick. Congratulations. . . ."

Driving to the housing area, Pruett still couldn't accept the incredible news. He felt he would burst unless he told someone about the tremendous meeting in Henderson's office. Andy Blake said there wouldn't be any public announcement for another two weeks; but hell, he did say *public* announcement, didn't he?

He swung his car about sharply and gunned it for the club. Directly beneath the *Positively No Parking* sign he screeched to a halt, kicked on the parking brake, and ran up the steps three at a time.

Several minutes later he staggered down the steps, a case of champagne over his right shoulder and a box of expensive cigars clutched in one hand. He dumped the case onto the front seat and tossed the cigars after the champagne, and returned to the club. Seconds later he was dialing the telephone number of Jim Dougherty's home and struggling hopelessly to calm himself down.

Pamela answered the telephone. Still struggling to keep his buoyant spirits disguised, Pruett assumed a gruff voice and in his most officious tone demanded to speak to Captain Dougherty. Jim answered immediately; Pruett almost snickered into the mouthpiece when he noticed his friend's crisp military voice. But he gave up any further attempts to disguise his own voice; instead, he managed to get across the idea to Jim Dougherty that something grave and terribly important had come up, and that both Jim and Pamela must wait for him at their home. He slammed down the phone, laughing in his excitement.

He chuckled helplessly during the ten-minute ride to the Doughertys'. Jim and Pamela, concern mirrored on their faces, were waiting for him at the door, framed in light from their entranceway.

Pruett skidded wildly on the driveway gravel, and mumbled to himself as his front left wheel chewed up Pamela Dougherty's flower bed. The couple stared at him as he slammed the door on the driver's side and walked to the opposite side of the car.

"Jesus almighty, Jim," he shouted, "just don't stand there! Give me a hand with this stuff."

As Dougherty came up, Pruett wheeled and tossed the heavy champagne case into the arms of his startled friend. Clutching the cigar box, he rushed past Dougherty as the captain lurched and tried to regain his balance. Pamela was staring now with mouth open and Pruett grabbed her around the waist, swung her high and around, and kissed her with enough force to leave her ear ringing for a week.

Dougherty banged the case in exasperation on his living room floor. "What the hell is the matter with you, Dick?"

Pruett laughed gaily. Then he shouted: "I'm going! If I don't tell you I'll bust wide open. I'm going, you ugly, freckle-faced baboon, and *you're* going to be part of it with me!"

Dougherty's expression was a prize in perplexity. "Going? Going *where*, you idiot?"

Pruett spluttered and choked on air. Jim Dougherty pounded him fiercely on the back as Pruett's face turned red and he gasped. Pamela looked on with concern and an expression that told of many years of experience living with a fighter pilot for a husband, and learning *never* to be too surprised at anything that might happen.

Pruett caught his breath. "I—I've got a little secret to tell you," he wheezed.

They gave him their full attention, afraid he might start choking again.

Pruett grasped Dougherty's shirt to bring him even closer. "James, my fine, red-headed friend, today I had a long meeting with the Chief Honcho. It was a very interesting meeting. Oh, I can't begin to tell you how interesting. . . .

"They're going for MA-10," he said.

Dougherty stared at him. "Do you mean you're cutting up like this just because they're going to run another Mercury flight? Hell, Dick, we've pretty well suspected that—"

He broke off at the widening grin on Pruett's face.

"You?" Dougherty whispered the word.

Pruett nodded vigorously, motioning for Pamela to bring over a champagne bottle.

"And do you know who, carrot top, is going to be backup?"

Dougherty shook his head slowly, and suddenly his grin was as wide as that on Pruett's face. He pointed his finger at himself in a wordless query. Pruett's head bobbed up and down more vigorously than before.

"Well, whaddya know," Dougherty breathed in wonder. "What do you know about that!"

"Pam! Where the hell is that goddamned champagne?" Pruett roared.

But she was gone. She returned five minutes later, with Pete Russell and Harry Scanlon and their wives in tow. They stopped short at the doorway to stare at Pruett and Dougherty, each with an open champagne bottle in his hand, drinking and waving the bottles furiously, and splashing champagne from one end to the other of the living room couch.

Pamela moaned. Her husband and Dick Pruett chortled merrily and greeted their fellow astronauts.

The neighbors, all members of the NASA team at the Manned Spacecraft Center, didn't know what was going on.

All they knew was that the uproar from the Dougherty house made sleep impossible for the rest of the night.

Chapter VII

The man in the center of the table, placed at the edge of the stage in the wide and long conference room, hammered relentlessly with a gavel. Microphones jumped and papers flew unnoticed to the floor. The man's face was white with anger, and a cheek muscle twitched visibly, like a nerve reacting to electric shock.

Facing him were batteries of blinding floodlights, stabbing cruelly into eyes that already blinked from the pain of an agonizing headache. The lights accented thick clouds of smoke and, in between and at the bottom of the smoke, a sea of faces and gesticulating arms dissolved into a nightmarish bed of unreal creatures writhing about and pouring forth an avalanche of sound. The gavel snapped in two suddenly and Desmond J. Barnes, weary, frustrated, enraged, for the moment forgot the five hundred newsmen in the room, forgot his position as Public Affairs Officer for the orbital finale of Project Mercury, forgot even the live microphones on the table, forgot it all and roared, "GOD-DAMNITALLTOHELL!" and flung the useless shaft of the gavel wildly away from him.

The explosive outburst vibrated every loud-speaker in the conference room and brought sudden cries of pain from sound monitors unlucky enough to be wearing earphones at the moment; the outburst and the totally unexpected sight of the normally staid and cool Barnes worked the effect he had been unable to achieve until this moment. The five hundred newsmen and women began to ease their outraged, vocal impatience; the roar of several hundred voices began to fall away, like a locomotive disappearing around the side of a mountain.

Barnes drew several deep, shuddering breaths and fought to regain self-control. The anger remained, but he forced it into a mental cage, and his voice was cold and clear as he picked up the microphone.

"All right; all right! If there is another scene like we have just had—" he let out his breath slowly—"neither myself nor my staff will consider it necessary to suffer this kind of abuse any longer. And this conference will end here and now."

He glared as the murmuring began anew. "Hold it! It is impossible to understand or reply to a hundred questions at once! Can one or two of you speak for the group? We'll never get anything done this way!"

The uproar again, but this time directed within the audience, not at the head table where the NASA information staff grasped eagerly at the momentary respite. Tom Stinson, Barnes' assistant, cupped his hand over a telephone speaker and leaned toward Barnes, his mouth close to the other man's ear.

"Mercury Control on here," he said. "They're not of any help, Des."

Barnes' cheek muscle jerked. "Go on," he rasped.

"They won't give me much. They say we're to stick to the original story. We couldn't bring Pruett down as planned because of rough seas in the landing area. Same stuff; no change. Everything is fine with the man and the spacecraft; we're just taking advantage of the poor weather and excellent flight to grab more experience. They say that—"

110

"Cut it," Barnes grated. He ran an unsteady hand through sweat-soaked hair. "It's the same crap. Jesus Christ, Tom, we can't keep up this farce much longer. A couple of those people out there KNOW we're lying to them. They've played along with us for a while, but no—"

The room was silent. Three men stood in a group by the center aisle. Barnes squinted to make them out; he felt cold all over. It wasn't good. There was Greg Saunders; he was from the wire services, and, God, he was as smart as a whip, and dangerous. Jack Kirschbaum from the television pool stood by his left; to Saunders' right was Syd Price. Barnes knew he was from one of the big New York papers, but at that moment he couldn't remember if it was the Times or the Trib. It didn't matter.

Saunders began to talk, slowly, deliberately, his words chosen with exquisite care, and as the words came Barnes caught his breath. His anger burst out from its mental cage, then fluttered helplessly as the calculating accuracy of Saunders' remarks slashed through the deception. . . .

"—and while we sympathize with your feelings of abuse, Mr. Barnes, we are also sympathetic with the needs of ourselves as a group, and far more sympathetic to the millions of people who are waiting to hear what we have to say about what is going on inside that spacecraft, and what really is happening to Major Pruett."

The voice began to cut deeper and deeper, and Barnes knew what was coming, and there wasn't a damned thing he could do to stop it, even though he saw the roof caving in on them. . . .

"—that, never did we expect to be in this situation. Mr. Barnes, I am speaking now for all of us, and—"

Saunders' voice took on a note of contemptuous mockery. . . .

"—I want you to understand that we shall carry this story exactly as I am stating it to you now."

"Here it comes," Barnes thought, as he gripped the table, knuckles white. "Both barrels . . ."

"Mr. Barnes—you are a liar."

Absolute, frigid silence.

"We have known for some time that the NASA statements about continuing Pruett's flight beyond the forty-eighth orbit were simply a smokescreen. The weather in the splash area is perfect. There is no storm. Now, we *agreed to your request for this press conference to be held as a closed-door session. We didn't like it; we don't like it; it stinks. But we agreed to it, and we are still sticking to it.*

"Unless you level with us—right NOW—we will break the story as a deliberate lie, a sham, a conscienceless deception to disguise the truth that Pruett may be in serious danger.

"Now—do you level with us, or not?"

Barnes thought swiftly; thank God for Saunders; he could have been a lot rougher. His mind raced; he couldn't keep the official story any longer. They all knew he was lying; none of them would hold it against him personally. If they were standing in his shoes, they would—with all regrets—do exactly as he had been doing. Better to say anything for a while until Mercury Control found out what really was going on. He shook his head to focus his thoughts. To hell with orders; he had to lay this on the line. . . .

"All right, Saunders. But before I say anything, I want to tell you—all of you—something. What I say now is still said off the record."

He put up his hand at the shouts that met his statement. "Damnit, I'm speaking this way because I have to. I must stay off the record until we have confirmation of certain facts. However, if nothing happens in the next hour, I'll consider all bars down and everything goes. Do I have your word on honoring my confidence with you?"

Saunders, Kirschbaum, and Price looked around the room. There were angry mutterings, but no spoken objections. Barnes knew that if the three men standing accepted his offer, the rest would go along with them. This time Kirschbaum spoke.

"All right, Barnes. We'll buy it—but only for the one hour."

Barnes spaced his words deliberately, slowly, going for the shock effect:

"Coming up at the last part of his forty-eighth orbit, Major Pruett set up his retrosequence.

"All telemetry readings were normal until that point.

"Then . . ." He paused.

"Get to the point, damnit!" a face in the crowd yelled.

Barnes stared without seeing.

"The retrorockets have failed to fire."

112

He had never heard a verbal thunderbolt before; for the first time he saw its effect upon the men and women before him.

"We—we are trying to find out exactly what the situation is. I do not k-know any more than that at this time."

His legs went to pieces beneath him and he dropped gratefully into his chair. For some ten minutes the room was again a bedlam of sound, then order returned.

Saunders' face was white as he turned to address Barnes. He never had a chance to speak; a man burst through the conference hall door at the far end.

"It's on now!" the man gasped out. "They're carrying it live on television from New York! They s-say it's an exclusive from Cocoa Beach. They say that P-Pruett's rockets don't work! They say that he's marooned in space!"

Angry shouting . . . cursing . . . a wild scramble for the doors and emergency exits as the outraged newsmen ran for telephones. They poured out of the conference hall of the Cape Colony Inn on Highway A1A of Cocoa Beach in a flood, their anger an almost visible aura. They had been scooped, and badly, in the greatest story of space that ever broke. But who—?

Less than thirty people remained in the hall where there had been five hundred. The newscasters for two of the major TV nets held up their mikes and telephones to indicate the dead lines.

Barnes stared helplessly from the table on the stage. He saw Jack Kirschbaum walk across the room to a television reporter, a "name" in science reporting. Kirschbaum reached out suddenly, ripped the headset from the man, raking an ear with a bloody slash as he did so.

Kirschbaum listened to a voice in the earphone, and turned in disbelief to Saunders and Price. "It's live. God help us all, he's been giving out the whole thing just as it was happening here."

He dropped the headset and whirled suddenly, savagely. Two hundred and forty pounds of enraged ex-paratrooper were behind the fist that smashed into the face of the television reporter.

It didn't matter, really. Because all hell had broken loose around the country. . . .

Pruett moved through a world that had seven workdays

113

in every week, and in which every day was filled from beginning to end with more work than could possibly be done. He seemed to face a series of hurdles that reared suddenly before him, and which required all his effort to clear; over the obstacle, he could slow down to the normal, everyday, maddening pace. Jim Dougherty moved with him almost as his alter ego, accepting as much of the burden as possible, checking on the countless details that needed cold-eyed scrutiny, and leaving Pruett free to concentrate upon those tasks most directly related to the impending mission.

Pruett learned the world inside Capsule Fifteen far more intimately than he had ever known any airplane in which he flew. The spacecraft became the single dominating thing in his existence as he labored to know, instinctively as well as consciously, every square inch of its surface, every tiny detail of its equipment, every move its systems and subsystems made in their operation.

The McDonnell engineers had been hobbled from the start when they won the fiercely contested competition to build the first spacecraft that would carry Americans into orbit. They had been limited by the ability of the Atlas booster to carry a certain mass at rest on the surface of the earth to orbital speed through the narrow eye of the mathematical needle high above the planet. They were restricted in weight and in volume. It was a crudely humorous paradox that so little space was available to the man who would be rocketing into infinite space. . . .

They'd worked hard—and in brilliant fashion—to give the astronaut the most out of what little they were permitted to use. This was obvious from the start, Pruett realized. His spacecraft actually had no more room within its curving walls than he could find inside a telephone booth, and no man in his right mind wants to spend three days in one of *those*.

But within the capsule the available room, the volume, was shrewdly exploited. The engineers pinned everything down to a specific place. They squeezed from the capsule every cubic inch it was possible to utilize, and when they were through they hadn't left enough spare room for a gnat to hide itself in.

The spacecraft accepted the human body with far more comfort than a passing glance might reveal. You didn't lie

114

on your back, as most people assumed. The semi-supine position elevated the back at a slight angle above the horizontal, and the knees were at a level just slightly higher than the head, with the contour couch and its plasticized, rubberized surface accepting the body as gently as was possible.

Most important of all . . . well, even a telephone booth wouldn't be so bad if its edges and sides were cushioned and molded and, above all, if you could float freely in the middle of the thing. The analogy to the telephone booth, Pruett thought, was unfair and misleading, since a booth invariably was uncomfortable, hard, and required bone-rapping contortions with those accordion-type doors that folded in the middle—and always toward the poor slob who was trying to get out while the door pushed in. To him the comparison should have been made with a sleeping berth of a train. It involved almost the same cubic space. Spending the night in a phone booth people would regard as cruelty; spending the night stretched out on a mattress meant simply going to sleep. And if you could float in the sleeping berth, without a single pressure point anywhere on your body . . .

Pruett looked eagerly to his first moments under zero-g, when exactly this would be possible. Lying for several hours in the contour couch—either in the capsule itself or in the procedures trainer that duplicated faithfully the capsule interior—could be and usually did become a pain. Because in the semi-supine position and under normal gravity the blood tended to drain from the legs and pool in the body, and a small itch could become a waspish annoyance.

But in space . . . even the Vostok wasn't *that* big, when you got down to it. It was just that even a little more volume can be stretched a long way under conditions of weightlessness. Enough for the Russians to release their straps, to stretch the body out straight. It wasn't a matter of standing, because under zero-g there isn't any such thing as standing. It's an artificial concept then, without the existence of up or down. Nikolayev was the first to perform a space ballet. Floating in mid-air, completely weightless, he grasped a cabin projection with each hand, balanced his body carefully, and spun himself about. He kept whirling around and around in a delightfully free movement without any additional effort, and ended the motion only when he grasped something to end the spinning.

So even the Mercury capsule, this smallest of the cocoons which man wrapped about his body to venture into the void, loses its discomforts and becomes not only tolerable but, best of all, even quite comfortable.

Of course, getting into the spacecraft was a bitch. There wasn't any other way to describe it, Pruett thought, as again and again he squeezed and wriggled his way with assistance through the small hatch. He went in and out of the capsule at least a hundred times, practicing emergency egress procedures, crawling through the hatchway, or squeezing up through the narrow space of the capsule neck where the parachutes were stored. It was one occasion when his 180 pounds of hard muscle, topped by broad shoulders, didn't make him any happier.

Once in the couch he let all his muscles relax and chanted into the microphone: "And there I was at six hundred and ninety thousand feet, flat on my bare ass without a heat shield—"

Pruett could never lose the slight sense of wonder with which he thought of his spacecraft. In orbit the machine, including his body, would weigh just about 3,300 pounds. Hell, that was a thousand pounds *less* than the convertible he drove. Yet, with that lesser weight, he would plunge around the world at nearly 18,000 miles per hour; the spacecraft would endure temperatures from a few hundred degrees below to several thousand degrees above zero. And it would shrug off pressure variations extending from complete vacuum to loads great enough to squeeze anything less than the strongest metal into a pulp.

Pruett directed his thoughts and comprehension of the spacecraft into what he considered to be its only meaningful relationship—a symbiosis of the man and the machine. It was literally a matter of weaving the human system into a fluid mating with the electronic and mechanical life processes of the capsule.

He would exist, literally, within a womb, and only the man who has seen a capsule with its layers of skin peeled back can appreciate the awesome complexity and interwoven fibers of the spacecraft. Around Pruett's body,

116

below his feet, to his sides, above and behind and all about him, and even connected to him, there was a total of more than 35,000 feet of wires and cables. Seven *miles* of veinous and arterial loops and connections within that little space, pumping electrical forces, heat, cooling elements, liquids, radiations . . . oh, the symbiosis of it was real enough.

Pruett stared in unabated wonder at the naked capsules, stripped and with their innards exposed to him, open to the air. *The air,* he thought, *the normal, everyday air we never think of consciously, but take for granted, just as we do the heavy weight of gravity which nails us to the earth. But not so to the man-machine system, not so during that time of re-entry, when a piece of the sun itself is created. . . .*

He thought of the ablation heat shield at the base of the spacecraft, of its spun fiberglas and resin, which seemed more at home in the hull of a sailboat racing over blue water than as a battering ram against the shrieking fires of re-entry—a flaming bath like none other, pounding its way back deeper and deeper into the enraged and furiously resistant mass of air, scrubbing the shield with thermal claws, raking it with white-hot talons . . . the heat of 3,000 degrees dissolving and melting down the shield during the brief minutes of exposure. And the bow wave ahead of the shield, an arc of savage fire in the form of a shock wave heated to 11,000 degrees, hotter than the surface of the sun itself!

He thought of these forces with which he would become intimately familiar at the close of the shrinking interval of time before the flight, and he did not mind at all the sense of wonder that pervaded his thoughts. He considered the spacecraft as it really and truly was, to the man whose existence depended wholly and completely upon its performance. A womb-cocoon, with an outer shell of corrugated shingles—shingles of super-alloy metal in an overlapping pattern, fitted so cleverly they seemed a single continuous sheet; shingles of nickel-cobalt alloy so thin that a dime in comparison was thick metal. There were beryllium plates which could expand with heat; Pruett had listened to the other astronauts explaining how they heard the metal plates and elements popping and crackling from dissipating heat when the spacecraft descended finally beneath its main parachute, and the howl of re-entry was only a recent memory.

He thought of the shingles as the multiple layers of protection one might find in ancient armor; they constituted only the outer layers of skin. Wearing the white garb of the McDonnell and NASA engineers, Pruett watched his spacecraft during its modification work and servicing. Beneath the protective alloy there lay an inch and a half of insulating material, and then, a double sheet of titanium molded to form the heart and soul of his space-voyaging craft—the pressure cabin proper, the extension of the world of men.

On the inside—the artificial environment and . . . himself. Then the two thin sheets of titanium, the insulation, the armadillo hide of alloy plates and shingles, and —*vacuum*. Not an absence of something, as most people thought of it; that was, could be, an error. To the man who ventures from the earth, vacuum is not a *nothing;* it must be regarded as an enemy, a gas of poisonous and volatile nature which must be kept from the body of the man, kept out of the spacecraft.

Pruett gave the closest scrutiny to the air-blower system of the capsule, for air within the spacecraft is not the same as air breathed on the ground, and the difference has nothing to do with pure oxygen as compared to ambient, "dirty" air. A technician crawled with Pruett into a mockup of the capsule that accentuated the environmental control system elements.

"We've been asked to be sure you have all this down by heart, Dick," the technician explained, "because if you lose all electrical power when you're upstairs, we'd still like to have you come home without your nose all dirty. So we want—"

Pruett interrupted with a pained grunt. "It will be much easier if you will kindly get your knee the hell off my ribs," he complained.

The technician laughed and twisted out of the way. "Sure, I don't mind at all. It would be much easier if we didn't have to go poking around in here." He turned to face Pruett and shook his head sadly. "Especially with a man who's completely nuts, like you."

Pruett raised his eyebrows.

"Oh, nothing personal, Dick. I just can't see you running around the solar system in one of these when you could be fishing, or saying 'yes' to all those good-looking heads that follow you around with panting tongues and . . ."

"Jesus Christ, Mike, will you stay with me instead of going into orbit by yourself?"

"Sure, sure. Okay, flyboy, down to business." He pointed awkwardly with one hand. "See those fans? Good; I want you to fix them carefully in your mind until you know 'em by heart. And be sure that you become very fond of them. Know their location, know how they operate, and, above all, you've got to learn their emergency operation as well. Christ! Let's get the hell out of this thing so we can stand up straight. . . ."

They retreated awkwardly and climbed to the floor. The technician dragged on a cigarette and bent over blueprints spread across a table. "Now, bear with me. Comes a brief lecture. . . ."

It was simple enough once you accepted the strange world of zero-g. In orbit, Pruett must have a constant, forced-air draft and circulation, because there is a complete absence of the convection that exists all the time on the surface of the earth in the normal gravity field.

The best example was the burning candle. As the candle burns, it receives a constant supply of fresh oxygen; this is the result of its own updraft of warm exhaust air rising above the candle. The exhaust gases rise, there is a difference in pressure created by this movement, and fresh air flows in to fill the difference—to equalize the pressure. The process exists only because there is a difference in the weight of the warm and cold air.

"But under zero-g, the air in the cabin doesn't have any weight," the technician added with explanatory hand flourishes. "And so convection becomes only a memory. You need the forced-air circulation to prevent you from breathing in a cloud of your own exhaled respiratory gases. The water vapor and carbon dioxide would simply collect in a big cloud or mass in the immediate vicinity of your body. You won't like it, and neither will your body, because you won't be getting clean oxygen. It affects your other body processes as well; without convection, the heat exchange processes would have to be carried out solely by radiation

119

between your skin, clothing surfaces, and spacecraft interior walls. You'd be caught in a trap, a sealed environment that would tend to get hotter and hotter."

He smiled brightly. "We've tried to think of *anything* that could screw up the operation. You know that you can work the thrusters even if you lose *all* electrical power by reverting to the completely manual system. Ain't efficient, but it works as good for attitude control as the automatic system, and you can set up for re-entry attitude with no sweat. Gordo proved that once and for all, as far as manual thruster control was concerned.

"But if you lost power, you'd also lose the blower system, and without convection, that spells trouble. So what we have done is to give you a manual blower system. There's this little hand crank, see? You just turn it around and around to keep from breathing your own foul breath and stewing a bit in your own juices. . . ."

Pruett looked with distaste at the technician, who was obviously enjoying himself. But there was no question of his faith in the environmental control system which, should the spacecraft suffer the one-in-a-million chance of complete electrical failure, could still sustain his safety by virtue of oxygen under pressure and his own muscle power.

"Besides, there's also the question of how long you could stand having to smell yourself," the technician added with a smirk. "Did you ever realize how much you stink?"

Pruett's startled expression sent the technician into a gale of laughter.

"Gets 'em every time!" he roared. "Man, you should see your face!"

"What the hell are you talking about?" Pruett growled.

The technician wiped tears of mirth from his cheeks. "Well, it's like this, space cadet. We don't talk much about it in public—in fact, we don't talk about it at all, because it ain't polite, I guess—but you're going to be a floating bottle of gas up there. Hell, you know that already as a pilot. Boyle's Law, and that stuff. The higher you go, the greater the expansion of gas, and so on."

He chuckled in self-enjoyment of his explanation. "Look, it's the problem of evolved gases within the system. When you're here, at sea level, there's about a quart of gas within the gastrointestinal tract. It's mostly air you swallow, but it's also got a pretty good percentage of gases resulting

120

from body processes. You know, the methane and hydrogen sulfide that's produced by the ferment and decay of the food you ingest.

"Well, when you're at capsule altitude—cabin pressure, that is—you'll be at the equivalent of maybe twenty-seven or twenty-eight thousand feet. That one quart of gas expands to about three quarts; sometimes, depending upon what you eat, even more."

He looked quizzically at Pruett. "Where do you think all that gas goes, space cadet? You've got to pass it, of course."

"So?"

"Oh, I was just thinking, that's all," the technician said, as his grin widened. "Just thinking of how romantic all this space jazz is, but no one ever says anything about how you've got to fart in orbit—" he howled with glee—"unless you want to go around the earth being polite and having a bellyache!"

Pruett left him doubled over with laughter.

Pruett was to learn, as had the other astronauts before him, that the training and the long preparations would prove to be physically more demanding than any part of the actual mission away from the earth.

The training simulators and special devices were the modern scientific hoops through which he was forced to move with great alacrity, a path of deliberate punishment and tests of his capabilities, but always pointing toward that ultimate goal of maximum possible preparation for the flaming thrust upward which would climax his efforts. The NASA engineers produced several simulators which they said would duplicate many of the situations he would experience in spacecraft control under actual conditions in orbit, and ALFA—the Air Lubricated Free Attitude simulator—was one of their favorite gadgets.

Events finally proved them wrong. "Flying" the airlubricated simulator wasn't similar to operating reaction thrusters under weightlessness. It was worse; much worse. And the first time with ALFA caught Pruett by surprise.

He climbed onto the contour couch, and a technician strapped him down securely. The large training room faded into darkness, and he remembered abruptly that he was balanced on a great steel ball, with the cushion beneath him nothing more solid than compressed air. He heard the dull hissing roar of the air and, not thinking, shifted his body as he tried to settle down comfortably.

It was a bad mistake, because the world skidded wildly out from beneath him. The couch tilted sharply and careened about in a spin. All he had done was to move his butt a half inch or so! . . . Instinctively he tried to brace his body, to balance himself, but with that exceedingly fine balance of ALFA itself, it only spun him faster and with a new movement to confuse him further.

He cursed; in an instant black mood Pruett imagined the laughter of the other astronauts, but *he* cursed himself. He felt the first brush of dizziness, and instantly he reverted to his most effective weapon in this specific condition, one that had become as much a part of him as any conscious process of thought. He blended with the machine; he forced his instincts and senses to flow into a man-machine system.

Before his eyes was a lens, and through the glass he concentrated upon a map, an unusual map, spanning a stretch from horizon to horizon of nearly two thousand miles, and unreeling before him with a speed of almost five miles per second—precisely what he would see when finally he did enter orbit. As his concentration flowed to the map, he had a passing thought that he no longer consciously heard the noise of the compressed air; it had started with a room-shaking blast, but now his mind dismissed the roar as effectively as he had come to dismiss the sound of pounding engines. His concentration became total.

The sidearm controller on his right, gripped in his hand, triggered compressed air forces through small reaction jets—the equivalent of the thrusters built into the spacecraft. He could pitch up and down, raising and lowering the neck of the spacecraft (he smiled to himself; he had adapted so thoroughly he was thinking in spacecraft terms instead of the ALFA system into which he was strapped) by moving the controller forward and back. That figured neatly, of course, for movement in the same plane with an aircraft control stick also produced pitch maneuvers and reactions. Moving the hand controller to the left or right meant getting roll in these directions; once again, the similarity to the aircraft stick was obvious.

But yaw was something else again. You could kick a fighter through the nose-swinging yaw movements from side to side by kicking rudder. But neither ALFA nor the spacecraft had any rudder, or any airflow or aerodynamic forces, and something else was needed. So he had to twist the controller to swing the nose left or right.

The trick was to work the hand controller with short bursts of thrust. It *wasn't* exactly the same as an aircraft, he noted ruefully. With a plane you could follow through your control movements, get a beautifully flowing movement. With this monster it was a matter of trying to roll a fighter through eight points—roll over to an exact angle and *hold it*. Then, come in again with control movement; the plane responds—hold it again. And so on. Nothing constant and flowing, but a series of movements specific and limited. He found it necessary to do the same thing with the ALFA hand controller; otherwise, it reacted angrily and tried to get away from him.

The "earth" hung before Pruett's eyes and four lines sliced neatly across the face of the curving globe presentation.

Without conscious thought of the movement, he brought up his left hand to scratch his nose—and immediately regretted the move, because the "spacecraft" wobbled precariously and then began to tilt, and heel over to one side. Instinctively he tried to correct the movement with "body English," and at the same moment he realized his hopes for immediate counterbalance were worthless. It seemed in the scope that the world was swinging wildly away from him. . . .

Pruett shifted his body senses and reflexes. The reaction hand controller was entirely new to him, but balance was something else again. For years Pruett had insisted that man had six, *not* five, senses, and that the sixth was balance. Now he fully merged his senses and mind with the machine and quickly, very quickly, he caught the feel of the stimulator. It was a total transference for him; in his mind he *was* in space, he was under reaction conditions of weightlessness. Just as he once nudged a fighter in close, close, *closer* to others in formation, so that he could even slap a wingtip gently against another, and still swirl up and around in great soaring maneuvers, so he now nudged the controls.

(*Or maybe that's not it,* he thought. *Maybe the comparison isn't valid because I'm thinking in relationship to other aircraft. That's it; go it alone,* he said to himself. *Think of it as coming in fast and tight on another fighter in the air, and you've got him in your sights, and you've got to correct with the barest motions, so you nudge, you tease the controls. . . .*)

The trick was a series of compound motions; the trick was to make the wrist as flexible and as loosely jointed as possible. The wrist had to become an extension of the brain. It had to become a long arm of the brain and a whispering touch of the senses, and it had to act almost upon its own volition.

It works! he exulted to himself. It worked beautifully. He brought the trainer around to stability faster than anyone else had ever done before. He balanced and jiggled it, started spins, caught them in midstride, and whirled it back again. He played the hand controller as though it were a flute and his fingers were drumming out the motions.

The technician running the main control panel whistled softly when he cut the air and came down to talk to Pruett.

"Nice. *Very* nice, sir," he commented. "You're the first guy in here that ever could match Al. He was an absolute wizard on this thing. He caught on faster than anyone else. You hit those things like you were Al himself."

He looked up at Pruett, and a trace of a smile appeared on his face. "Major, would you, uh, like to try some emergency maneuvers?"

There were canary feathers starting to appear on the technician's chin, Pruett thought. He looked at the man, and asked, "Tell me more, friend; what kind of emergency maneuvers?"

"Oh, I forgot you haven't been in here before. Well, you get it stabilized, see? And then we start giving you trouble. We'll knock out some of the jets, or give you instability in them. Sort of scrung things up a bit, and see how fast you bring everything back to snuff. Of course, if you're too tired or worn out—"

He left the rest unsaid. Pruett glared at him, and knew that every man in the control room was hanging on their conversation. In a way, he realized, he was being tested. He'd completed the entire schedule. He'd met the requirements, and now the test crew were offering him their own hurdles to leap. He could quit for the day, and he'd done

124

far better than even the average of the other astronauts. But he would leave a lot of disappointed people with shaking heads behind him. . . .

He leaned back and relaxed. "Let's give it a whirl."

The technician's face lit up with a smile. "Real good, Major! I was betting on you to say that."

The fences were down now; this was straight-out competition between Pruett and the control group. They were going to do their best to drown him in oddball reactions of the trainer, and he was going to do his damnedest to stay just one jump ahead of them.

They threw the book at him. . . . Fifteen minutes later the roar of compressed air groaned to a shrieking hiss, and vanished. Pruett wiped the perspiration from his face as the men unstrapped him. They helped him to the floor, and he leaned weakly against the side of the simulator.

"Who won?" he asked.

Someone slapped him gently on the back. "It was a draw, Major." He hesitated. "And—well, Major Pruett, that's the first time we've ever had anybody in here for his baptismal ride that we couldn't get to yell uncle." There was frank admiration in his eyes. "You'll do real fine, Major; *real* fine."

Pruett walked out of the test chamber feeling nine feet tall.

Pruett spent uncounted hours and days in the procedures trainer, the mockup of the actual spacecraft that duplicated almost everything in its instruments and panels that the genuine article could do. It was also "loaded" with emergencies; connected to a fiendish electronic computer and a human controller with a mind twisted to conform to that of the computer, the trainer threw fire, thruster, pressure, electrical, and other emergencies at the astronaut through every possible phase of a mission. When you could handle the procedures trainer through the gamut of these deliberate emergencies, Pruett thought with a groan, you were ready to tackle a trip to Mars in a canoe with an outboard motor.

Pruett concentrated, as had the other astronauts, on the trainer's attitude indicators—the roll-pitch-yaw gauge atop the instrument panel—to signify tumbling, gyrating, and other out-of-control motions and maneuvers. There were four instruments that constituted complete reference to the world outside the spacecraft in orbit, and they had to be learned until they were as much a part of his thinking and reflexes as anything he had ever done in his life.

At the left of the attitude panel was a circular dial with a blue pointer that indicated motion in the roll maneuver. At the far right was the pitch indicator. A circular dial below and between these two instruments indicated yaw. And all three movements were simultaneously represented in a square-edged instrument mounted between the two upper dials and directly above the lower, yaw indicator. The square gauge looked astonishingly like the omni course navigation system of the airplane, tied in to an instrument landing system glide-slope receiver. The trick was to keep the three needle indicators all exactly aligned so that he had a perfect crossmark on the multiple-indicator gauge. Any deviation from this meant deviation from perfect attitude control when the astronaut, for example, wanted attitude to match exactly the surface of the earth below in "level flight."

Once Pruett got the hang of the thruster system—the results of which were shown on the attitude indicator panel—he discovered that it demanded much less of the precision movements of control than a fighter. In fact, there could be little comparison between the two, for the airplane was much more demanding, much more critical, and much less forgiving than the spacecraft.

The procedures trainer as a faithful reproduction of his spacecraft gave Pruett the equivalent of actually living in the machine within which he would venture into vacuum. Directly in front of his chest and face, only two feet away, there poised the instrument panel with more than 130 dials, switches, knobs, buttons, and other controls. Lights glowed or flashed more brightly in banks of coded colors.

Pruett had once believed that the minimum room within the spacecraft cabin might produce a claustrophobic feeling. He discovered to his pleasure that this wasn't the case at all; that the normal world of the fighter cockpit is simply a state of attitude and experience, and that "normal" was entirely relative.

Thinking of flying brought him to the inevitable comparison between flight, as so many thousands of men had known it, and the plunge through space, with weightlessness sustained by that exquisite balance between gravity and centrifugal force.

Not a writer he had ever read, Pruett recalled, had ever looked upon space without a shudder, but had conjured up the scene of a harsh and cruel vacuum, of alien and merciless space, eternally hostile, even savage in its utter change from the familiar world of men.

Yet . . . from the beginning of Mercury, long before any man had ventured into the velvety blackness so far above, Scott Carpenter had disagreed with this picturization. Carpenter had already made the transition to an opinion completely different from that held by so many. Carpenter had predicted that once a man reached the balance that permitted orbit, he would find space quiescent and peaceful.

Pruett mulled over that prediction, and he compared what was now known of orbital flight with atmospheric flight through turbulence and the many other barrier reefs in the sky. There was the need to fight the controls to meet and dampen out thermals and crosscurrents; there were ice and haze and fog that bellied down to the ground and made a runway a tossup between a landing and a blood-splashed impact with the unyielding concrete. Once you went through the needle in vacuum and separated from the booster, well . . . no more worries about maintaining that even keel and keeping your thrust going where it belonged. No more sweat about moving the throttle into cruise power or afterburner or compressor stalls; when you got into orbit, you could forget the flaps and the gear and the dive brakes. There weren't any mountains to run into. And those piston jobs . . . with propeller pitch and throttle and mixture control, and carburetor icing, and cowl flaps, and a hundred other things, multiplied by numbers of engines.

And there weren't clouds that were almost as bad as mountains; Pruett remembered all too vividly a thunderstorm into which he had flown and instantly regretted. His powerful fighter was a wisp, a wraith, as the storm sucked him into its maw and then closed its giant, grinding molars on the fragile steel of the machine. He'd suffered a deep and nasty gash from having his head slammed against a cockpit projection. The thunderstorm was a roaring genie of blackness and sudden, terrifying bolts of savage lightning, and the invisible sledge hammers of wind. It slowly and methodically began to grind and tear at the big delta jet he was flying; the talons of wind plucked and tore metal loose, and threw him out of the storm like a fruit pit spat with contemptuous ease from monstrous, puckered lips. To save his life he'd fired the ejection seat, blasted up and away from the disintegrating jet. Hail slashed at his face; he threw his arms around his head when fingers of wind ripped away his oxygen mask. Curled up into a ball, his body shaking from the thundering blows of nearby lightning, he fell freely for ten thousand feet. He gloried in the sudden slamming fist of the opening parachute, and all the way back to earth he sucked deeply and gratefully of the cool air, and watched the black, towering mass of the storm, already several miles away, bristling with tongues of lightning. Far below, there appeared a little flash of red— what was left of his proud, powerful fighter as it smashed against the earth.

How had Carpenter said it would be? Pruett remembered: Carpenter said that once a man got into orbit, he would find it a "very friendly neighborhood." He had called *that* one right on the nose, as the Americans and Russians who'd made the round trip were quick to confirm.

All the violence was . . . gone. The fuel problem was a simple one; you knew just what you had in the tanks. So much hydrogen peroxide, and that was it. And if you didn't want to use the go-juice for attitude control, why, you could shut it off, power down, and let the capsule drift. You didn't dare act in such casual fashion with the needle-nosed and razor-winged jets, because they would drop like a rock or might even nose up into a high-speed stall, and how often can you survive a violent, cartwheeling tumble at twice the speed of sound? Here you could make a slip, commit an error, and there would be no giant fist to pound you mercilessly for a human fault. Here—up there, flight was attended to for you by the sorcery of five miles every second matched precisely to the curvature of the earth and that splendid, unending fall around the planet.

All things considered, Pruett thought, once a man could accept the unreality of the environment, the knowledge that Earth was somewhere else, another *place* . . . why, the astronauts of the future would have good cause to look back and say that Scott Carpenter truly was the most prophetic of all when he described the black void as promising to be a "very friendly neighborhood."

How could Pruett know how deceiving, how sinister, that void would become to him? How could he know that even when he struggled against the worst of the violence of the atmosphere, he had the one thing a man needed most of all? He could *fight*—fight the controls, fight the turbulence, fight for his life.

He was yet to learn that the most maddening thing about the death sentence that would be passed upon him in orbit was that . . . you couldn't do anything about it. You couldn't fight, because there was nothing against which you could struggle.

You could only wait. Wait to die, while a hollow laugh boomed and echoed through the airlessness of space, a laugh that only he, Pruett, would hear, in the echoing chambers of his own mind.

Chapter VIII

The two newsmen walked slowly along the main street of Cocoa Beach. The sun weighed oppressively on the air, the sidewalk, on their bodies. It was a weight without importance, for their thoughts and their words were elsewhere. They thought and they talked about a man named Pruett, whose remaining hours and minutes grew steadily shorter.

Walking in the hot sun, watching women in shorts and halters doing their shopping, watching the big shiny cars driving by . . . none of it seemed real, if you thought hard enough and could transfer your thoughts above the hot, sweltering atmosphere, and try to imagine what it was like, all the way "up there."

One of the newsmen stopped. His friend looked at him, wondering about the sudden look on the man's face.

"John, you were here when Al Shepard made his flight, weren't you?"

The newsman nodded, and waited for his friend to continue.

"I was just thinking," he said, as he started to walk again. "I was thinking . . . that the most impressive thing

about that flight wasn't something that happened up at the Cape. It was here; right here, in this town. Right on these streets."

"I don't follow you. . . ."

. ."Ted McCoy didn't go to the Cape with us. He covered the shot from here, in Cocoa Beach. You know—the human interest angle. Talk to the local citizens, see what their reactions were, ask them what they thought about a man going into space. The first American. You know what I mean."

"Yeah, I know. So how—?"

"No, hold it a moment." He wiped the sweat from his face.

"Ted told us he'd never seen anything like it. Everyone had radios going, the television sets on. When the count got down to near liftoff, everything stopped. Everyone stopped walking, or talking. Even the people in cars stopped, listening, waiting for the count to reach zero, so they could be sure to look up to the north. They'd be able to see the Redstone lift over the horizon, only seconds after it left the pad.

"Ted told us . . . well, he saw people, women, men, even some kids. They looked up and they saw that rocket. And right there, right where they stood, they were praying for the guy in that rocket.

"Some—Ted said that some of them went to their knees and prayed. Right out on the sidewalk, and in the street. They didn't care about anything but that man and—and—praying for him. He . . ."

The two men looked at each other. Neither spoke any more as they turned the corner and walked toward the white spire of a church.

They found it impossible to enter. The people of the Florida town had filled all the seats and crowded the aisles, and those who couldn't find their way inside the church had knelt on the grass and the sand outside, by the steps. Some were leaving; more were coming.

The two newsmen silently joined them. . . .

The MASTIF was a giant abortion of a carnival-house torture assembly that could spin a man about its three axes in the wildest, weirdest tumbling and gyrating that Dick Pruett had ever known—and had good cause to dislike intensely. The air-bearing couch of ALFA had been new and different, and had caught him unawares, but he had mastered it quickly.

This monstrosity—the Multi-Axis Spin Test Inertia Facility at NASA's Lewis Research Center—was a different beast entirely. It brooded in the giant training chamber, and he thought immediately that some demented and frustrated erector-set throwbacks had put the thing together during a long and distressing alcoholic nightmare. Three giant wheels made up MASTIF—three frameworks, placed one inside the other. The outer cage rested on gimbals, and its twenty-foot circular form could tumble nastily end-over-end. Within this shell there awaited another gimbaled cage, only *this* one spun around and around in the form of a whirling dervish. Finally there came the innermost or third cage, which resembled a capsule assembled only to a certain point, at which time the construction crew became ill at the sight and went home, leaving the job unfinished. The cage would spin, as though you snapped some good wrist action to a football and sent the pigskin spiraling rapidly through the air.

Pruett's suspicions of the monster were confirmed when he first heard it complaining; the electric motors were prodding it into movement, producing a distinctive groaning and grinding sound. The great hoops of metal surrounded him in a crisscrossing web, and very quickly he knew why the technicians had strapped him down so tightly that he could barely move. The bizarre dance of MASTIF almost at once brought home the pressure of the straps that hugged his body so securely to the contour couch.

Jim Dougherty had come along on this trip, explaining cheerfully to Pruett that he—Dougherty—wanted personally to be on hand when Pruett's stomach violently rejected everything loose that was inside. "M'boy, you are no doubt going to lose your cookies on that three-way ferris wheel," Dougherty said, "and it will be a sight to tell my grandchildren. How the Great Pruett splashed vomit in three directions at once on the MASTIF, and how he spent the next couple of days cleaning it up with a rag—"

"Go screw," Pruett retorted. Dougherty grinned at him.

In the chamber, Joe Vitello waited for Pruett and Dougherty. Vitello was a NASA civilian test pilot to whom the MASTIF and all its unpleasantries had become a second home. Although he wasn't on the astronaut team, Vitello could just about play music with the big monster, and no one's advice to the newcomer meant more than the chunky Italian pilot's. In the control seat himself, Vitello could juggle the forces acting upon him with all the finesse of a high-wire acrobat in a howling wind—and lighting a pipe at the same time.

Pruett made every effort to relate what happened to him in the MASTIF to the sensations he knew from flight. Shortly before he left for the research center, he and Dougherty learned that the second generation of astronauts would never know the full touch of MASTIF. Orbital flight experience with the first four astronauts to circle the earth made it more than obvious than the abuse suffered in MASTIF simply wasn't related to actual conditions in flight. So Pruett had the distinction of being perhaps the last of the astronauts to subject himself to the weird capabilities of the three-ringed machine, but he found the distinction hardly cheering.

Even when MASTIF whirled him around and around in spiral movement, he didn't mind it too greatly. It was somewhat similar to a series of rapid aileron rolls in a jet fighter, although Pruett admitted to himself that he never remembered being able to do sustained aileron rolls at the rate of fifty per minute! There was, at the least, one spark of comfort in the recesses of his mind. He might lose control of a fighter, but the MASTIF would never crash; it would just continue to scramble up his insides.

The rapid spinning of MASTIF had proven the undoing of more than one volunteer on the carnival-like monster, who tried to scream to be let off, but usually could manage no more than a gurgling strangle as the bile came up and plastered itself along the insides of the throat walls. But Pruett *liked* spins; as a pilot who dearly loved aerobatics, he had hundreds of times whirled earthward in the spin— the rotary stall, nose down and tail high, and whipping around and around toward the uprushing earth. Indeed, Pruett liked to bring the spin as tight as he could, and even with the earth a flashing blur in front of his eyes, he could calmly tick off the spins one by one. He could stop the spin, snap the plane out right on point, and kick it right back into a spin in the other direction. His fellow pilots complained that Pruett had a stove filled with cast iron instead of a stomach with sensory endings.

When he completed the separate MASTIF runs, one in spiral motion and the other in spins, Pruett was all smiles. "Hey, Vitello!" he called to the NASA pilot as the machine groaned its way to a stop. "I thought this bear of yours just chewed up space cadets and spit them out in little balls of vomit."

"You enjoying yourself, Major?"

"Yeah. I think my mother might even like to take a ride on this thing if we can get it into the county fair."

"Hmmm, 'zat so?"

"C'mon, you hairy ape, let's wrap it up. Let's get into the finale."

"Sure. Sure, Major." Vitello reached up to grasp the control switch. "By the way, space cadet, I'm glad you're enjoying yourself."

His smile should have warned Pruett. But, unfortunately, it didn't, and the first sign that all was not well came when his stomach began to protest, not from nausea, but from the unaccustomed end-over-end violence he suffered suddenly. Tumbling faster and faster, torso whirling over and over in wild pitching movements—a complete tumble every two *seconds,* thirty times each minute—was more than enough to unsettle any man and engulf most men with a complete loss of balance, sense of direction . . . all the elements of a violent onset of vertigo.

"Y-you b-b-bastard!" Pruett grated through clenched teeth. "You h-hairy bab-*oops!*—baboon, why d'didn't you w-warn me!"

Vitello's voice crackled in his earphones. "Just relax, space cadet, so you can tell Mom what a thrill she can look forward to. *Haw!*"

Pruett groaned as the MASTIF seemed to take on humanly fiendish delight in flipping him over and over. He felt as if all the loose parts of his body were frightened at the unnatural forces and were doing their best to break loose of *him*—and rush off somewhere on their own. He could literally feel the liquids in his body sloshing about wildly. And in the background, through his earphones, he heard Vitello happily singing a ditty about astronauts who take their first space rides in the inside of a washing machine.

Pruett sighed gratefully when the MASTIF complained its way to a halt. He lay limp as a rag as Vitello walked across the catwalk from the control room, leaned an elbow casually on the couch, and smiled at the astronaut.

"Hey, Joe," Pruett belched.

"Yeah?"

"I just—*urp!*—got a telegram. It's from Mom."

"Oh?"

"Yeah. She said to—*baaarf!*—send you her love, and be sure to tell you to take good care of her—*gasp!*—little boy."

Vitello roared. "Okay, okay, Dick," he said when the laughter subsided, "just stay back in the couch and rest for a few minutes. We're going to go 'over the falls' on the next ride, and I want to be certain that you'll be ready for the forces that will hit you this time. They *can* be mean, and I'm not joking. If you're prepared for them, I'm sure you can hack it."

"Should I turn green now or later?"

"Later, later. Now, shaddup and listen. We're going to give you all three motions *at the same time*. This will be a full gyrating motion in the fullest sense of the word. And I do not want you to act like a hero."

Pruett turned to look at Vitello.

"I mean that," Vitello emphasized. "It's possible to have the gyros between your ears get pretty scrambled on this thing, when you're going at thirty RPM in three different directions at the same time. You may have only the touch of a cold, and if it affects your ear—why, *blooey!* You're in a mental tailspin just like that. So if that happens, *let me know*. Just gargle 'help' or something like that into the mike, and we'll cut the juice to this rodeo queen.

"Now, I want you to be especially alert for fencepost blur. When—"

"Hey, wait a minute. What the hell is fencepost blur?"

"The flight surgeons have a fancy handle for that; they call it vestibular nystagmus. It's the result of getting your insides sloshed around and all scrambled. Your body and your brain are working against each other. It's—it's like watching one TV channel with your eyes while you're listening to the sound from another channel, at the same time. The messages come in scrambled, and it's almost impossible, especially on the merry-go-around, to unscramble what you're receiving."

"*Baaarf!*"

"God, will you cut that out!"

"Can't—*urp!*—help it. What the hell, Joe, if I bring it up again we can all have—*braaack!*—a hot meal."

Vitello rolled his eyes and ignored him. "Now, when we get you going, I want you to particularly stay on that instrument panel. You *must* do this, or I can guarantee you'll really scramble your gyros and you'll have all the sense of balance of a wet rag.

"This is where that fence post blur hits you. With so many messages of *un*balance rushing to the brain, your eyes simply cannot handle the input. The instrument panel will become a blur, but don't let it throw you. It's normal. It's caused not by the motions, but by the accelerations and decelerations that are involved. You'll get the blur going into stabilization and coming out of it again."

He stared as Pruett hiccoughed. "Hey, are you *sure* you want to give this thing a whirl today?"

Pruett belched and waved a hand casually for Vitello to turn the MASTIF loose.

Vitello did just that.

Pruett's senses and mind were as alert as a wolf on the prowl for a kill. Yet he found it an incredible sensation when he realized he was spinning around and around rapidly, like being seated on a huge swivel chair that had been spun by a maniac of awesome strength; at the same time he was also tumbling head over heels and, as well, whirling sideways in that spiraling roll. He was gyrating in three different directions at the same time, completing a tumble-spin-roll movement every two seconds, and he realized with wild fluttering of his intestines that if ever there was a machine designed to froth up your insides and turn your thinking matter into a loosely jointed porridge, this son of a bitch was *it*.

It made him ill. He was stunned when he realized the fact. He let himself go for just a moment; he relaxed, and yielded to the triple motion of MASTIF, and instantly the machine grabbed for the uppermost hand, and Pruett's stomach protested with a soundless, quivering shriek. Bile began to crawl up in his throat; he wanted to vomit, to rid himself of whatever slime was splashing around in such fashion *inside* him. He tasted salt, and realized with a start that cold sweat had formed a film over his entire face and was running down to his lips.

MASTIF was now tumbling *violently* . . . and he knew that he *must* stop the insane gyrations or Dougherty surely would have that story about him cleaning up for a couple of days with a rag. . . . All he had was the now-familiar one-hand controller, the stick with its back-and-forth, side-to-side, and twisting motions. Without his realizing the motion, his left hand gripped an imaginary handle, the throttle to which he had become as accustomed as any part of his life.

While his right hand came alive, sinewy and dextrous through wrists and fingers, turning the control grip into a responsive, living thing—and the MASTIF gradually yielded its hysterical motions—his left hand continued to squeeze by reflex the throttle that was an integral part of flight and a vital key to aerobatic maneuvers. Any pilot caught in such violence and changing acceleration as Pruett now endured in the simulator knows that he must reduce his speed, chop power, lessen the forces on his machine as well as those on his body. Without conscious thought on his part, engrossed as he was in damping out the severe motions of MASTIF, Pruett's left hand was squeezing and pulling back on that imaginary throttle. Later he found that his nails had bitten so deeply into his palm that blood welled to the surface of his skin. In time— and a short time—he mastered the art of killing the tumbling and gyrating and spinning motions rapidly. He also came instinctively to command his left hand to disregard the normal reflex action; like anything else, it was simply a matter of adapting. But he also filed his fingernails down short.

Exactly as Vitello had warned him—and he *was* ready— he watched the instrument panel dissolve into a blur. It was like staring out of a car window at high speed and trying to count fenceposts that whizzed past with a visual clickety-clack sensation. The eyes simply cannot handle the overwhelming input of messages. The blurring that Pruett experienced in MASTIF came not so much from the varying motions, but from their onset—the acceleration of building up to the three-way, simultaneous speed of thirty revolutions per minute.

Finally, under his expert manipulations of the hand controller, the world floated down in its many pieces and began to reassemble before his eyes. Everything clicked back into its proper place, and he was again in full control.

When he stabilized the grinding beast, he was ready for the sudden return of nystagmus. Vitello had warned him that the deceleration of coming down into stabilization would create its own problems, just as had the acceleration. Wisely, he heeded Vitello's counsel, and entered the condition of stabilization in slow, specific stages. The blur left steadily, like water receding from a shore, until everything was rock steady, and his wrist and hand moved almost as a creature apart from his body and brain, handling the reaction jets with jewel-like precision.

He grinned at his success, and earned a greater measure of the same when Vitello's voice came suddenly in the earphones. "Stay with it, cowboy, and you're gonna break that hoss yet."

In subsequent training sessions, he climbed into MASTIF with full space-going regalia—twenty-five pounds of suit, gloves, boots, helmet, and assorted gear—in order to accustom himself to controlling the beast exactly as he would be dressed to control his spacecraft. There was nothing like being realistic, Vitello said, brushing off his complaints.

Relaxed in the contour couch, Pruett looked down (a subjective reference in orbit, he reminded himself deliberately) between his feet. There he observed both a reflection of his face and a simulated section of the earth's surface. He trained for endless hours with this mirror system, which represented the periscope that once had *been* in the capsule—and no longer was. Glenn and Carpenter had found the periscope system of spatial observation of little value, and Schirra called it a "blasted nuisance," especially when the scope caught the sun and stabbed dazzling light into one's eyes. The astronauts were convinced the periscope was just so much dead weight, and NASA engineers removed it from Gordo Cooper's spacecraft for his flight. Why bother with the periscope when it was so much easier, and clearer, to roll the capsule to a position where you were inverted in relation to the earth's surface, but perfectly comfortable as you looked down through a window?

Unfortunately, no one had ever gotten around to modifying the MASTIF, and it was with the periscope that Pruett trained. It did him no harm, for without the periscope, some other simulation would have been necessary, and this certainly did as well as anything that might be jury-rigged together in a hurry.

One thing was certain, Pruett concluded; the MASTIF pushed aside all doubts of his ability to handle the space-craft through any control maneuvers in orbit. Before the first man went up—and we didn't learn much in this respect from Gagarin's flight, because the Russians played their information cozy—there were fears that the capsule under zero-g might respond with great sensitivity to any small or undue forces, and would accelerate rapidly into uncontrolled gyrations. It was because of this fear that MASTIF came into being. Under the worst punishment imaginable, could the pilot of the capsule, using the automatic and manual thruster systems, bring the thing back to an even keel, regain full stabilization, and sustain his desired attitudes?

The automatic brain of the spacecraft was an integral element in the automatic stabilization and control system, the ASCS mode. If the capsule did gyrate, or perform any unexpected maneuver, the brain was to decide what was wrong. It would then use its gyroscopic balance, its infrared sensors that scanned the horizon, and its other electronic gimmickry to fire the steam reaction jets, or thrusters, and bring a quick end to the gyrating nonsense.

But gyros *do* tumble, and no one, except some of the engineers who still had their senses clogged by the clouds in which they steadfastly kept their heads, could fully trust the system of black boxes. Pruett didn't enjoy such blind trust; any machine can go wrong, and more than once a demented electronic mass had tried to kill him in a fighter, and he remembered, painfully, too many friends who *had* been killed by the compact creatures as they suffered whatever aberrations exist in the strange world of electronics.

So if the autopilot didn't work, then Pruett's task was to disengage the brain, to slip its clutches, so to speak, and grab for the controls himself. He could use the automatic system circuitry, but by his hand motions of the controller he would manually override the system, turning it into an unwilling but obedient slave.

Yet slaving the system wasn't too accurate as an analogy.

The electronic brain could without warning suffer from some abnormality brought on by nothing more than condensation along a critical point of its circuitry, and then, despite the manual override, it could become a treacherous adversary, recklessly spurting the limited supply of reaction fuel into vacuum, and ignoring the hellish problem of re-entry without thruster fuel for attitude control.

At this point Pruett could resort to a secondary electronic system—something of a moronic cousin to the more highly developed brain (the engineers wanted to weep when Pruett expounded *his* analogies and interpretations of the system; he didn't care, so long as he knew how it worked and he would always be in the position to exert absolute control over the spacecraft). The secondary, or fallback, automatic system had only one blind purpose in life: stop all movement through the axes of pitch, yaw, and roll. It didn't care about anything further than this goal so rigidly impressed upon its feeble mind.

Pruett looked with some misgivings upon this particular creature within the reaction control and stabilization system of his spacecraft. If the intelligent brain fell apart, he wondered, how the hell could the moron with the single-track electronic mind be expected to do better?

He regarded more kindly the manual control system which allowed him to work the steam jets through straightforward, old-fashioned electrical connections. When he moved the stick forward to pitch down, the movement triggered an electrical impulse which, in turn, fired a spurt from the reaction jets. Although the reactions of the vehicles were worlds apart, it was the closest thing to a power-boosted control system in an airplane he could imagine.

And finally, he had his last resort—if that million-to-one chance came and the electrical system failed entirely. Under a condition only one step away from hovering disaster, Pruett retained complete control of his spacecraft by going to a pure-and-simple mechanical system. When he moved the hand stick, the movement itself—mechanically, just as the control linkage worked in an airplane—fired off the blasts of hydrogen peroxide-turned-steam.

They hadn't left anything to chance, and that was a conclusion that contributed significantly to sound sleep.

The acceleration built up in a steady, relentless drive,

*like a great locomotive starting to roll down a steep incline
and gaining tremendous speed and mass. It pushed him
down deeper and deeper into the couch, a massive hand
squeezing, kneading his muscles and flesh. The meter read
eight, ten, eleven times the force of gravity, and it kept
climbing. Still the force of acceleration grew until he felt
as if he were being mashed into a shapeless blob, unable
to lift his head or even his arm a fraction of an inch. He
suffered drastically from tunnel vision as his angle of sight
narrowed alarmingly; somewhere he heard the thunder of
the booster pounding at him, and he hurt, but he kept his
eyes open, his right hand on the stick controller, and he
tightened his body and tensed his muscles until they
stretched like cords, and all through the grayness and the
punishment he kept grunting out "Okay! Climbing . . .
okay! Okay!" as the needle on the meter went to fourteen,
fifteen, sixteen times the force of gravity. From somewhere
unseen a black cloud began to swirl, faster and faster, rear-
ing up in a shrieking roar; the needle read seventeen, an
impossible eighteen, it was at nineteen times the force of
gravity! and the cloud began to engulf him and the roaring
in his ears drowned out everything else. . . .*

"He's had it—he's unconscious. Cut the power—
quick!"

The *swish-swish-swish* of air lessened in speed and volume as the giant centrifuge slowed rapidly and groaned its
way to a halt. A doctor hurried from a door high above
the floor of the centrifuge chamber, yanked open the hatch
to a great clam-shaped gondola, and peered anxiously
inside.

Pruett was just coming to his senses, his face and
clothes soaked with perspiration. For a moment his eyes
were glassy, then clarity returned to them and he looked
with full recognition at the astronauts' flight surgeon, Dr.
James Michaels. The doctor knelt and leaned inside the
hatch with a towel to wipe away the sweat from Pruett's
face. Then he crossed his legs and sat on the ramp.

"How do you feel?" he asked.

Pruett managed a wan smile. "As if a dinosaur had just
sat on me," he replied weakly.

"Small wonder. You went to nineteen point two before
the lights went out."

Pruett whistled. "Did I really take that much?"

Dr. Michaels nodded. "All right, Dick. I don't want you to talk any more for now. Stay right where you are until we complete our readings. We're still taping information from the sensors on your body. We want a full report coming back down through the peak, and how long it requires for your body to return to normal."

Pruett nodded and gratefully closed his eyes. That had been the worst one of all. Over nineteen g . . . He was amazed that he had managed to remain conscious that long.

Every pilot has been intimate with the squeeze of g forces. The jets are sleek and they're swift, and when a man pulls one of the iron birds around in a high-speed turn, the effect is akin to a dozen people jumping into the cockpit and stomping away with abandon. But the fighter jocks like Pruett become acclimated to this, and experience enables them to build resistance to the punishing forces. Instinctively they tense their bodies, because the more a man strains until his nerves and muscles are quivering-taut from the effort, the higher goes his blood pressure, and the better he can withstand the onslaught of many times his own weight.

Pruett never thought consciously of the g's he pulled in a fighter; it had become a way of life. With his own hand on the stick, he could pile on the force and ease it off with the most casual of commands. But the centrifuge was rugged; no two ways about it. The great whirligig with its torture-rack seat, and the faithful mockup of the capsule's instruments and controls, whirled him around and around, and . . . it wasn't the g's he minded so much, because of the semi-supine position you could really take the punishment. But he nourished a full-blown dislike of the centrifuge because it brought on some wildly unpleasant side-effects of acceleration.

Once—at 11.2 g—he made the mistake of forcing his head to the side to look at the wall of the gondola. Dr. Michaels had warned him *not* to do just that. But Pruett had made several centrifuge runs at better than fourteen times gravity, and he wasn't about to accept the admonition unless he knew *why,* and he knew it for himself.

So as the gondola flashed around, he turned his head to the side, and suddenly a huge hand leaped out of nowhere and flipped the gondola on its side and smacked it crazily

141

into a horrible careening motion. Calling on all his strength he fought his head back until his neck muscles ached hotly, but he managed once again to stare straight ahead.

He completed the centrifuge run without a word of complaint, but Dr. Michaels and the medical crew knew exactly what had happened. The biological sensors on Pruett's body ran reports of his physiological activities to monitoring instruments in the control cab, and Michaels smiled knowingly when several needles suddenly jerked in their gauges.

Pruett was a pasty white color when the gondola slid to a stop. He didn't realize yet that by turning his head under the circular acceleration and high g force he had severely abused the mechanism of his inner ear; his semicircular canals—his body gyros for balance—had tumbled. With his sensing facilities haywire, he lacked anything more than a pretense at orientation. He did not yet realize that it would take a while for the inner ear to calm down and slowly return to normal.

Dr. Michaels and an aide gripped him strongly by the arms and led him into the control cab, placing him in a chair. The doctor looked at him strangely, and said, "Dick, bend over and tie your shoelaces."

Without thinking, responding automatically to the request, Pruett leaned over—and promptly sprawled on his face. He swore he had *tumbled,* and his expression mirrored complete confusion as he was helped back to his feet and out of the testing chamber.

Two hours later, in Dr. Michaels' office, the world had settled down to normal. A chagrined astronaut offered the doctor his thanks for the solicitous attention.

"Why, think nothing of it, Dick," Michaels replied. "In fact, to be perfectly honest with you—"

Pruett waited for the worst—

"the same thing happened to me."

Pruett looked his surprise.

"Only I didn't get my gyros to normal again for nearly three weeks. Of course, I don't have the experience, the background of becoming acclimated to the forces that pilots find a natural part of their life."

He shook his head at the unpleasant memories. "You should have seen me, Dick. I didn't dare bend down to pick up a pencil, because I might end up sliding across the floor on the side of my face. My kids thought it was funny, and the dog thought I wanted to play, but *I* didn't appreciate getting into bed and tumbling out the other side, among other things. . . ."

He tapped Pruett's medical papers. "You snapped out of it considerably faster than the average for the astronaut group. Two hours is a rapid recovery for the punishment your inner ear had to take."

Pruett relaxed, and chuckled. "Y'know, Doc, I was just thinking. That peak at nineteen g?"

Michaels nodded.

"Hell, riding the booster into orbit is going to be a snap compared to that thing—" he jerked his thumb in the direction of the centrifuge—" in there. Seems like this is a ritual of manhood. It's almost like having to fly a trainer at mach four in order to qualify for a fighter at mach two."

The weeks melted into a blur of training, testing, flying. Hour after hour passed in the procedures trainer and in a capsule placed within a huge environmental chamber, where Pruett in a complete pressure suit went through the changes of pressure and temperature he would encounter in his actual orbital flight. Engineers threw a bewildering variety of emergencies at him, everything from loss of attitude control to pressure leakage within the capsule. He reacted to the visual scream of fire-warning lights by banging swiftly against the de-pressure handle, dumping the cabin pressure overboard and resorting fully to his suit. A spacecraft cabin with one-hundred-percent oxygen—and everything within the cabin soaked and permeated with that oxygen—was a potential bomb. The *only* was to fight a fire would be to deny the flames any possibility of fuel—venting every last vestige of the oxygen into space itself.

Pruett and Dougherty, in a two-seat F-106 fighter, raced from one end of the country to the other. They flew to the great Rocketdyne center in the boulder-strewn mountains north of Los Angeles, where they inspected at close range the plumbing systems of the Atlas booster. They stood on a low hill, forming the lip of a curving bowl in the earth, and opened their mouths to scream when huge engines in the static stands howled with devastating fury and assailed their bodies with thunderbolts of sound

143

and the insidious needles of ultrasonic waves. Screaming or shouting helped to equalize the pressure and alleviate the physical sensations, but at its best it was an overwhelming experience.

At San Diego they walked through the production lines where the Atlas boosters took their form. In St. Louis they worked with engineers who had produced and modified the capsule Pruett would fly; many of these same men would work with him at the Launch Operations Center at Cape Kennedy, where they would attend to the spacecraft's needs and preparations with consummate care.

Then there were no more missions assigned in the MASTIF, or the centrifuge, or ALFA. But there were other places to visit, for pressure-chamber tests and suit fittings. Because of the limited preparation time before the mission, a careful review was made of Pruett's requirements in survival training. He was able to slice a week from this anticipated training phase because of his extensive survival training with the Air Force, and met his needs through an accelerated but nevertheless exhaustive refresher course at one base in Florida and another in the Nevada desert country.

Navigation skills seemed incongruous to the pilot of a spacecraft that would be inserted into an orbit determined rigidly by the push of his booster and the play of gravitational forces—a craft whose course he could not change at all. He could change the attitude of the capsule, it was true, but the orbital mechanics of his flight were not at all affected by attitude. Yet there was the critical need to be able to identify his position at any time, especially in the event of communications failure, heavy cloud cover over the earth's surface, or other problems.

A thorough knowledge of the stars and constellations, carefully integrated with the star chart that would be prepared for him, would provide at all times of the day *or* night, the ability to recognize the celestial signposts and utilize these in reference to determining his position over the earth. Both Pruett and Dougherty went to the Morehead Planetarium at Chapel Hill, North Carolina, where they began their training with recognition of the primary constellations of the zodiac. A Link trainer body, normally used for instrument instruction, had been modified with a window and headrest to simulate the external viewing conditions as they would exist from the spacecraft in orbit. They practiced recognition of constellations and major celestial bodies as they would be seen along different points of the flight; the planetarium's programming provided simulated flight not only in reference to the heavens, but with a continuing cross-reference of the stars to earth terrain, earth horizon, and positions of the moon.

There were dozens of scientific experiments for which Pruett had to prepare, fitting the times for them into his exacting schedule, as well as learning the purpose of the tests and becoming adept in the use of the equipment with which they would be carried out. These experiments ran through a wide spectrum of scientific observations. They included observing a small satellite ejected from his spacecraft, and flashing rapidly with a xenon strobe light. There were to be dim-light-phenomenon photographs, horizon-definition experiments, radiation measurements, photographs of clouds taken in infrared for meteorological studies, television system operation, antenna tests for Gemini, a series of ground-light experiments, and others.

One of the most important tests in terms of its long-range value was the horizon-definition experiment requested by the Massachusetts Institute of Technology. MIT had the contract to produce and perfect the navigational and guidance systems for the Apollo spacecraft that would be sent to the moon; Pruett's tests would make possible a study of the earth's sunlit horizon and atmosphere to determine whether these could be used as a reliable sextant reference during the mid-course phase of the flight to the moon.

The depth of research for such future projects never failed to amaze Pruett, and he was more than pleased to realize through his preparations that the most elaborate instrument satellites sent into orbit could not define the information that MIT's Instrumentation Laboratory needed so urgently. The scientists were extremely anxious to learn if it was possible to define a suitably invariant horizon line in the earth's atmosphere, near the surface, that would remain completely independent of changing atmospheric conditions. There had been photographs taken by the other astronauts of the horizon and atmosphere, with blue and red filters, but the tests failed to confirm whether or not there was a point of sharp cutoff in either spectral

145

region of the horizon or the atmosphere, a cutoff the moon-bound astronauts could use for accurate navigation sightings.

Thus the MA-10 mission would bridge a gap from the present to the near future when Apollo and three men would depart from the home world of earth.

There remained, finally, only one major preparation phase for the mission prior to Pruett's departure for Cape Kennedy and the last two weeks there before the date scheduled for liftoff. Because of the intensive medical observations for the three-day flight—the underlying justification for its scheduling—Dr. Michaels and his staff subjected Pruett to medical examinations and tests so exhaustive that he found them to be more wearying than the centrifuge. It was one thing to endure the punishment of acceleration and deceleration, or even of being gyrated in MASTIF; there, at least, he could *try* to do something to alleviate the pressures thudding against and through his body. But the medical tests; he shook his head unhappily as he was led like a prize bull from one laboratory to another.

The analogy became painfully evident when the doctors told Pruett to deliver a sperm sample.

"What the hell for?" he asked, astonished. He leered at Dr. Michaels. "Or are you planning to surprise me by sending along one small-sized, fully developed, cooperative space-type, female stowaway?"

"No such luck, space cadet," replied Michaels. "This is for posterity, not pleasure."

"The hell you say!"

"No, I mean it." Michaels laughed. "We use the sperm cells to draw up fertility base lines. Years from now—we don't know exactly how long it will be—we'll take some more seminal samples for additional tests. This way we can determine whether or not there's a long-term threat of sterility from your sustained exposure to cosmic radiation. Or maybe we want to see if you're a good bet to turn out little men from Mars as offspring."

"Thanks a heap, Doc," Pruett said dryly. "You're sure I shouldn't use it while I know I've still got it?"

"Nothing so drastic as that," Michaels said, pushing him into the laboratory bathroom.

Pruett shoved the door open. "Hey, Doc!"

"What is it now?"

"Daddy said I should never do this sort of thing alone. Send in some well-built company, will you?"

Michaels threw an ashtray that slammed off the door as Pruett ducked hastily inside.

The technicians took a series of X-ray pictures to search out any air bubbles that might exist in the bend between his spinal cord and the so-called "tailbone." Such air pockets weren't uncommon, explained Michaels, and normally their presence was ignored. "But where you're going for a couple of days," the doctor added, "breathing pure oxygen under a pressure equal to five miles altitude, expansion of any such bubbles is almost a sure thing. The pain could be so excruciating that you might have to abort the mission and come down prematurely.

"And it wouldn't look too well—I'm sure you'll agree—that you had to blow a ten-million-dollar shot because of a pain in your tailbone."

They X-rayed almost every part of his body. They studied with the greatest care the extent to which any arteries had hardened. Pruett had an appendectomy scar, as well as the scar along his forehead suffered in the thunderstorm as his fighter tumbled out of control; the medical technicians poked and prodded and stretched to determine exactly how much stress the scar tissue and related skin could withstand. They left him with eyes watering and half-blind for nearly a day after nineteen different studies and tests of his eyes. He urinated and defecated in a variety of containers and at odd times of the day and night. The doctors took motion pictures of his heart arteries, and jiggled and joggled his body through a series of revolutionary "static and dynamic tests." To be absolutely certain of his levels of body efficiency they ran tests of pulmonary function, total body radiation count, specific gravity of the body, blood volume, water volume, lean body mass, and even detection of tiny congenital openings between the chambers of the heart.

He was overwhelmingly grateful when Dr. Michaels announced the close of the medical tests and evaluations, and invited Pruett to dinner at his home.

Pruett fell asleep at the table, much to the chagrin of his host and the astonishment of the children.

He stayed with the Michaels family that night; the

doctor brushed aside his objections with muttered imprecations that he was ordering Pruett into bed—and at once. He slept for fourteen blessed hours.

The next day Dr. Michaels ordered him home for the weekend.

"I want you completely away from your training program and everything else that's going on for your flight preparations," Michaels explained. "You're all through here at Houston, aren't you?"

Pruett nodded.

"Good. If I remember correctly," the doctor went on, "you're to report next to the Cape, and complete whatever training is left on the procedures trainer there. Now, nothing is going to happen over the weekend, and a few days at home, free of all this—this kind of schedule—will do you a world of good. Besides, it will undoubtedly be your last opportunity to be with your family before the flight."

Pruett left Houston that afternoon in the F-106 fighter, bound for Suffolk Air Force Base on the eastern end of Long Island. From there it was only a short drive to his home in Huntington.

Chapter IX

HE SUFFERED mixed feelings about his brief visit home. He wanted to see his parents, but there was Ann, and at this stage of the game, with the mission so close, he wanted also to block out the painful thoughts. For Ann would be in Huntington, and he much preferred not to think of her at all, because he . . . he had shut her out until now only by grimly determined will power.

Now, knowing she would be so close, only minutes away . . . He fought almost helplessly as the memories and the desire surged within him and filled his mind. *God, just thinking about her again is enough to drive me nuts. I can see every line of her face, I know the whisper of her hair, that fabulous body of hers, and, Jesus, but I want her! I'm a fool for coming home now, I can't shake it. How the hell can I stay for a couple of days with Ann so close and—?*

"Approach radar to Air Force Six Nine Three, you are positive contact. Maintain heading of zero four zero, and start your descent now from four three thousand. You are cleared your present position and heading to one five thousand. Report passing through three zero thousand and two zero thousand. . . ."

The radar controller jolted his thoughts back to the present and—gratefully—he returned his full attention to the powerful fighter under his hands. He eased back on the throttle and ghosted down from the stratosphere, calling the controller as the heavy airplane sliced through thirty thousand and then twenty thousand feet.

Three miles high he fed in power and called radar. The airbase controller picked him up on the Suffolk scope. Minutes later his wheels screeched on concrete, and he yanked the handle that sent a drag chute billowing out behind the airplane.

Taxiing along the flight line, he looked through the slab side glass. He could see his father waiting for him; tall and dignified with his shock of white hair, he was a picture of stately pride as he waited for his son.

They drove slowly on the way home. Pruett slumped gratefully in the right seat, enjoying the respite from slab-winged airplanes and electronic trainer labyrinths. *It will be good just to hang around loose for a couple of days. . . .*

"We're very pleased that you could make it home to be with us, Richard."

He smiled at his father. "I didn't think I could get even this much time. The schedules have been a day-and-night business. With the short time for this one, we've been pretty much on the go."

"How long will you be with us?"

Pruett lit a cigarette and dragged deeply. "Don't know. Maybe Sunday night. If I'm lucky, I can leap off Monday morning. I'll probably get a call from Jim; he's already at the Cape getting things in hand. There's still a lot to do—"

His father interrupted, frowning. "They're not cutting things short, are they? I mean, well . . . taking any short cuts that might . . ."

He left the rest unsaid. Pruett laughed. "Nothing like that, Dad. We play these things right down the middle of those big fat checklists."

His father questioned him with a puzzled stare.

"I mean it. I know it sounds like a speech, what with those same old statements by NASA that 'we don't go until we're ready.' But they mean it. I don't get one inch off the ground unless they're absolutely sure that everything is exactly where it's supposed to be. Besides, well—just look at the record. The old Atlas has belted them right into the middle of the ballpark every time."

He blew a cloud of smoke slowly, watching it curl and drift. "No sweat. They haven't scratched any fenders yet."

He studied the passing countryside. "Hey, I haven't even asked. How's Mom?"

It was his father's turn to laugh. "I'll give you three guesses."

Pruett grinned. "She still disappointed?"

"That's putting it mildly. Your mother had her heart set on throwing the grandaddy of all the wingdings she's ever planned in her life. You should have seen her, Richard. She made up a guest list that she kept secret and—well, I hate to say it, but I think your mother did some private exulting about who could and who couldn't come." He shook his head in wonder. "She's the social bigwig of the town because of you."

Pruett shuddered with the thought. "And all because her little boy is going to get shot out of a cannon." He sat straight up. "Say, you *did* manage to call off the dogs, didn't you?"

"Oh, yes, you're safe enough. There won't be any big dinner or even a small dinner. Your mother acted as if she'd suffered a mortal blow when I told her that you absolutely insisted on a quiet visit. You've ruined all those great social plans of hers." He sighed. "Thank the Lord for *that*, anyway."

His father slowed the car as they approached an entrance ramp to the Long Island Expressway. "Want to drive along that for a while? We'll get home somewhat faster."

Pruett shook his head. "Nope. Just continue the nice, slow tour of the back roads. I like looking at all those trees."

They drove in silence for several minutes.

"Richard?"

Here it comes, he thought. *I can tell just by the way he said my name. I guess there's no avoiding it; might as well have him drag it out now and get it over with. . . .*

150

He glanced at his father but did not respond. He watched the old man take a deep breath and then plunge into the matter about which they had never spoken aloud.

He asked it quietly. "Have you been in touch with Ann?"

His response came out flat. "No."

His father waited, silently begging his son to pick up the conversation and carry it on. Pruett flicked the cigarette butt out the window, lit another at once. He did not speak.

"Ann's mo—Mrs. Fowler—was by the house last week and . . ." His voice trailed off unhappily.

For God's sake, if you're going to drag it out—speak up!

"Son, can I level with you—stick my nose where it doesn't belong? Just between us," he added hastily, "only in this car. Just between the two of us." He stared ahead morosely. "If you'd rather not, I'll keep my silence."

Mom must have badgered him for weeks. Hell, the old man is even more unhappy about this than I am.

"No, Dad, I suppose it's better this way. Spit it out."

Tension spilled almost visibly from the white-haired man next to him. "I—don't want to meddle, Richard. But you and Ann . . . well, it's been almost accepted for years that you and she would—were . . . what I mean is—"

"I know, I know. The marriage bit?"

His father glanced sharply at him. "Yes. Yes, marriage, I suppose," he said. "After all, it's been more than just the two of you growing up together. You two seemed so perfectly suited and . . ."

Yes, we were; yes, we are, and, sweet Jesus, but I wish you hadn't said anything; I wish you had let me lock it up deep down in my mind. Yes, it was with the idea of marriage right from the start. That week we spent on the boat, just the two of us, all alone and unbelievably . . . well, unbelievably good. And we knew, alone, unhurried, loving one another, isolated within that little world for one whole marvelous, infinite week that we were for each other and . . .

"You needn't paint the picture," he interrupted harshly. "I'm well aware of the details. . . . Hell, I'm sorry. I didn't mean to be rude to you. It's just that I, well, I've managed to shut it out of my everyday thinking, and this sort of brings it up again where it hurts."

"We never did know . . . we still *don't* know what—what went wrong. Your mother and Mrs. Fowler, I know, have spent many an hour on this. Ann cuts her mother off short every time she approaches the subject, and I . . . well, I've tried never to push into your private life."

He rested his hand gently on his father's arm. "And don't think I haven't appreciated that. It's kind of hard to spell it out, because it came so sudden. One day everything was just perfect and—" He interrupted his line of thought. "Did you know that I had bought a ring for her?"

The old man shook his head slowly. "No. I had no idea." He lapsed into silence, waiting for his son to crack open the shell built tightly about his emotions.

. . . the ring. It was a beaut. A perfect blue-white to match her. She and the ring—they seemed to have been created with the same marvelous beauty. Ann never knew that I carried the ring around with me for a month, that I was just waiting for the moment that would really fit the occasion. I wanted us to have our own private little ceremony about placing that ring on her finger, because we'd known, without ever saying it aloud, that we were to be married. Sometimes there comes that wonderful relationship of two lovers—and that we were—who find that understanding without words. And then, just like that, it was all gone. It was over. Who the hell could have foreseen that Ann's coming out to Los Angeles would be the trigger to blow it all up? . . .

Through the years they had drifted slowly but surely closer together until finally both accepted, as Pruett remembered, that their marriage was only a matter of time. Ann Fowler had never written to Pruett of the sick feeling of fear every time she read his name in the town newspaper as it lauded one more kill in Korean skies for the favorite son of Huntington. She brooded under the conviction that he would never return alive, that in a spasm of gunfire the body to which she had clung in their fierce ecstasies would be torn and slashed. More than once she awoke screaming, face white with the horror of nightmare, dreams intensely and terribly real, dreams in which the thudding bullets ripped his smoothly muscled body from her arms and splashed his warm blood over her, and she tasted the salt against her lips and—

152

It was then she awoke, heart pounding madly, unaware that she had cried out, screamed his name.

And swore to herself that if by some miracle this should ever pass, that if the man she loved since he was a boy should survive what she sorrowfully *knew* was inevitable . . . that if Dick escaped the bullets destined for him, she would always be his, without any strings, without inhibition.

Her dreams alternated between garish nightmare and a physical longing for him that made her sleeping body writhe and low moans escape from her lips. She realized one night, awakening suddenly, that her body had arched to meet his in deep embrace, as she had done that incredible first time when they went away for that week, all to themselves.

He had anchored the cabin cruiser that night in a small and secluded cove. The air was warm and fresh from the sea, and the boat moved with a soft, sighing motion. Lying together on blankets, his arms around her, it was an idyl without a sense of time, without rush. All the clocks of the world came to a silent stop and waited upon them, waited while they held one another in timelessness, and looked out upon the stars and slowly began to find one another.

At some point in that evening Dick helped her to her feet. Without a word, unhurried, sure of himself and of her, he slowly removed her clothes. All at once she knew this was as it should be, that there would be no furtive movements of his hands, that . . . that it would be free on both their parts, and she knew, at that instant when his hands slipped her clothes down across her legs, that there was not even a breath of shame. She would be, she *was*, his.

That was enough.

He stepped back to look with open admiration at her supple young body, at the high, firm breasts. His eyes moved slowly down her body, gazing upon her flat belly, her thighs and her legs, and then back to her eyes. There was wonder and love in her face, and for several minutes she stood before him, naked. Then she moved to him, and silently took the clothes from his body.

She had never seen him, or any other man, naked before her. Her gaze was as frank and open and admiring as his had been. Gently they came to one another, and returned to lie together.

They remained there for several hours, luxuriating in the deliberate, gentle, unhurried quests of their hands across the two bodies, exploring tenderly, fingers caressing. And it was not until the first deep red of the dawn began to wash the darkness away from the skies that finally they moved their bodies into the inevitable climax.

They had learned much about each other that week, she thought. They had learned how to make love to one another, each trying to please, to bring wonder and pleasure to the other. And they had succeeded. *The delight and the wonder of experimenting in love, of searching for his moments of exquisite ecstasy so sweet it sometimes bordered on pain . . .*

And there was so much more for them! A week of love and fun and laughter in the sea and in themselves and the places they visited. They were taken almost always for honeymooners, and they shared their secret with the delight of children, and . . . the week fled.

Four years later . . . after four years of long absences, of weekends that came all too rarely, of never satiating her desires for him . . . the years passed, and he was gone, and she knew that where he was metal wings glittered in the high Sun and young bodies jerked and shuddered from the tearing metal, and the life vomited away in bright red chunks, and they were tearing *his* body from her arms and . . .

She came screaming out of the nightmares.

And then, by what miracle she knew not at all, the letter came. He had flown his last mission; he would be coming home. Relief flooded into and pounded through her body and mind. She cried almost hysterically, uncontrollably, her mother frantic. Her mother saw the letter crumpled on the edge of the bed, and gasped. For the news could be . . . could be only that the boy had been killed. With black fear she smoothed the paper, knowing in the back of her mind that as quickly as her daughter could calm herself, she must go at once to see Dick Pruett's mother; and then she saw that the letter was *from* the boy, and her heart almost stopped from the shock of . . .

They clung together, crying, until it washed itself away, and the cloud of nightmare fled for once and for all.

Another letter came soon afterward, filled with the excitement of his new assignment to the test pilot school in the California desert. Could she join him there; could she get a job in Los Angeles or a town nearby? Los Angeles was only a hundred miles away, and she found a job in Burbank, closer to Edwards. And as soon as she had an apartment, still without having told him of her arrival, she called him at the field. It was a brief conversation. She gave him the address and the apartment number; it was a Friday afternoon, and she wanted their first meeting after the years of her terror about Korea not to be short and hurried. She wanted the weekend to themselves.

He stood in the doorway and stared at her. She was more beautiful than he had remembered, and she stood tall and straight in the center of the room, and when he closed the door behind him she held out her arms and said quietly, "Undress me." She wanted it as much as possible like their first time, the moment they still remembered and still cherished.

She saw him mostly on weekends, for his daily schedules often meant his flying and working twelve and sixteen hours every day. She took at once to Pam Dougherty, and they spent many of their evenings together, while Dick and Jim studied and flew; and many of their weekends were spent as a foursome.

Pam Dougherty knew that Dick Pruett had bought the engagement ring for Ann. Since Dick had kept the matter quiet, she respected his silence and said nothing, either to Ann or her husband.

Four months after Ann's arrival in California, it happened. . . .

There was an open house day at Edwards, and Ann drove up from Burbank to be with them for the special flight demonstrations. All this time she had never seen a fighter except as a meaningless photograph or a shining dot in the sky. She did not look forward to the day; she had managed to blank out completely those nights of terror when she dreamed Dick was dying or dead in Korea. Now she would be face to face with the thundering machines which Dick respected and loved so deeply.

They were standing together, several hundred feet back from the runway, when two sweptwing fighters started their formation takeoff roll. She watched the clouds of black smoke billowing behind and above the airplanes, and then the first slow motions as the pilots released the brakes.

Thunder boomed anew as flame lashed the air behind the two fighters.

Dick leaned close to her. "You know Mike Bruno?" he shouted. She nodded; she had met Mike several times when he drove in with Dick and the Doughertys to meet a date in Los Angeles. "Mike's the lead pilot. He and his wingman are really good; they're going to do a formation takeoff and then they'll roll straight up before they break away! Keep your eyes close on them. . . ."

She watched the airplanes rushing faster and faster, the sound of their thunder swelling. The nosewheels came off the runway in matched movement, the fighters had empty space behind them, *and then there was a puff of black smoke behind the one to the right.*

It happened so quickly she was never sure of what her eyes, widening and painful, revealed to her. There was only that little puff of smoke, and the airplane seemed to stagger slightly, and to skid a bit through the air. She had seen the sharp wingtip stab into Mike's airplane, the one closer to them, and send the machine careening out of control. She thought it had tumbled, or cartwheeled, before it slammed belly down into the concrete, and began to come apart before their eyes, and the flame appeared sharp and scarlet for an instant before it blossomed up and outward and started to mushroom. There were pieces of metal in the air, and even as the airplane disintegrated it was still rushing forward, but now it was skidding and sliding off the runway, at an angle closer to them, and with unbelievable clarity they all saw the fire stab into the cockpit, and Mike's hands move frantically, like a little wax doll moving many times the normal speed of a human being. . . . She remembered Jim Dougherty's agonized cry. Just . . . *"MIKE!"* That's all, because the shining glass exploded upward, the body of the airplane broke into two, and ten, and a hundred pieces, just like that, and it was all of it washed with flame, scattering crazily in a wide path only fifty feet in front of them, and in the midst of the blazing sputum there was a *thing* that tumbled to a stop almost before their little group, and it was still alive, and the stumps of its legs twitched and jerked. . . .

And she saw it—him?—as Dick; and she didn't know that her fingernails were clawing deep into her scalp and she was screaming and screaming and screaming, and she didn't know that Dick was holding her, because she could see the hole where there had been a mouth and the twitching stumps and merciful blackness fell upon her.

It happened the next morning. White-faced, cold through her body and her mind, numb, she faced Dick in the living room of the Doughertys' home. She did not speak of the dreams (although Pam Dougherty knew) of Korea; she did not speak of much at all.

She stood before the man she loved more than her own life, and almost as if they were coming from a vast distance, she listened to her own incredible words. Her voice was an agonized whisper.

"I will . . . I could never go through that again," she said, her body trembling. *"Never!"*

Dick stared at her, compassionate, helpless, shut off from her by whatever stalked her mind.

"Every time you leave for an airplane, every time you fly . . . every time—" she spoke with pain— "that is what I will be seeing. That is what I must expect to see."

Her voice dropped so low they could barely hear her words. Except Pruett—they crashed through his brain.

"I—I could never live with that," she said.

He did not speak.

"There can never be the both of us . . . y-your flying and me." She forced out the words, knew she *must* say them now.

He spoke then, slowly and kindly, his face contorted. "Ann . . . please; please don't say that."

Her arms dropped limply to her sides. "I mean it. I . . ." Her voice trailed off.

"It hit you that bad, Ann?"

She nodded dumbly.

"But . . . but you've got to expect that sort of thing! Not often, but it happens every now and then, and . . ."

She shook her head sadly.

"And it will happen to you, too," she said. "I want you to . . . you must decide, *now,* Richard."

"Ann, please—"

"You *must!"*

Pain mirrored in his face as he stared at her. Neither of them heard Pam Dougherty's muffled sobs.

Pruett took a deep breath. With visible effort he forced out the words. "I love you, Ann. You . . . you know that."

"Please! *Now!*"

The compassion drained from his eyes and Ann Fowler knew a sudden stab of fear.

"All right, Ann. You must have known the answer all this time." He stopped for a moment. "You'll never have to ask me again."

He turned and walked out of the house.

He had never seen her since that moment.

That night, in his home, with Ann only those few minutes away, he found it impossible to sleep.

It was three o'clock in the morning when suddenly he threw aside his covers and dressed quickly.

He was on the phone to the airbase, requesting his fighter to be prepared for takeoff, when he noticed his father standing in the hall. He hung up slowly.

"I can't take it, Dad," he said simply. "It's too much with her so close. . . ."

His father nodded.

"I'm taking off immediately." He picked up his bag and turned for the door. "Explain to Mom, will you?"

"Of course."

They clasped hands.

"God be with you," his father whispered, then leaned forward suddenly and kissed his son on the cheek. He had not done that since the boy was nine years old.

By early dawn Pruett was pitching out in the big fighter over Patrick Air Force Base. Twenty miles to the north, a silver giant waited for him at Pad Fourteen.

Chapter X

HE STEPPED down from the transfer van and walked into another world.

He looked up, overwhelmed by the immensity of the scene that loomed and towered about him. It was a world of intensely bright blue-white lights, of a deep crackling and groaning sound of machinery; he heard the paper-rustling sound of hundreds of shoes scraping on concrete and metal; he listened to the night wind. And then, from out of the burning arc lights, the garish spots and the deep shadows, against the backdrop of a mountain of metal reaching into the darkness of the early morning, he heard the hands—the hundreds of hands as they were beaten and pounded together, growing in volume as voices swelled the sound. Hands applauding . . . the men of the launch crew roaring their approval and their friendship.

He choked back the words he wanted to say; and was instantly grateful that he couldn't, because he was afraid that he would stumble over his own thoughts, and that would be hardly the way to respond to this tremendous, spontaneous ovation from these men. He looked around at them all, and they knew that he was looking thus, that he saw in the sea of faces the men who had attended the giant that was embraced by the steel mountain directly behind their backs. The men who had given their all, worked day and night, to prepare the towering Atlas and its waiting capsule high above the ground.

He could not speak to them, but he could respond in kind. He stood there for those moments, the scene etching intself clearly, indelibly for as long as he would live, into his mind. He started to wave to them—a free, a casual and friendly wave. In his left hand he grasped the portable air conditioner that spewed cooling air into his pressure suit. His right arm came up and he started to wave, but almost of its own accord, without his consciously thinking of the desire, his gloved hand came to the helmet, where his forehead would be, and he . . . saluted them.

And then he walked quickly, Dr. Michaels to his right, Hans Buettner, the suit technician, to his left, the thirty feet to the steel-caged elevator. The bars clanged into position; motors whined deeply, and the elevator began its ascent to where the capsule awaited him, high above Cape Kennedy.

He had the fleeting thought, as the elevator rose the twelve stories above the ground, that they had made it, the whole works, dead on schedule. They had been aiming for this moment—the pre-dawn of July 21—and now the vastly complex and far-flung machinery that would precipitate the flame and the upward rush was in motion. Those men on the pad, they had been a reminder, too. There were more than ten thousand people like them, here on the Cape, at the tracking stations, on the ships, in planes, in the recovery fleet, at the computers . . . an army sprinkled around the middle belt of the planet, an army superbly integrated in the orchestration that would make all this possible for him.

No one spoke to him in the elevator. At this point they deferred any conversation not absolutely necessary to him. These precious moments, they felt—and for this he was grateful—belonged to him, and his mind moved rapidly through introspection enabling him to reach out and comprehend what was happening in so many places . . . then focusing down on this one place, this one moment, with himself at the center.

Clothed in white from head to foot, Jim Dougherty met him as he stepped from the elevator. Pruett shook hands with the McDonnell technicians who had lived, literally, with his spacecraft for months. Standing before the machine which would carry him through the sea of space beyond his planet, he studied the laboriously painted name on the side of the capsule. *Mercury Seven* . . .

His choice, one made unhesitatingly the moment they asked him for the name. There had been, before his spacecraft, the other *Sevens*—*Friendship, Liberty Bell, Freedom, Aurora, Sigma,* and *Faith.* Now, the last of the Mercury spacecraft. The name *Mercury Seven* was appropriate to the mission. This was the Seventh and final capsule that would carry a man into space in the program. There were seven pilots in the original selection of astronauts. He felt that the name *Mercury Seven* was a salute to them, to all the personnel of the long program, and a fitting sequel to bring it to a close.

Dr. Michaels disconnected the air conditioner. Pruett stepped up onto a cloth-covered stand where a technician removed the plastic bootees from around his silvered pressure-suit boots; better to leave the dust and dirt picked up walking here outside rather than in the capsule.

He placed both hands on the support rail above him, squatted down and lifted his feet to bring the boots to rest against the hatch bottom of the capsule. Thick nylon pads assured protection of the suit. Dougherty placed his hands beneath Pruett's body to support his weight and to guide him; a technician eased his feet into the capsule, and Pruett wriggled his way in. When his arms stretched out full, he relaxed his weight against Dougherty, then reached out to grasp the lip along the upper edge of the hatch. Seconds later he was in the seat. Dougherty leaned in after him and connected the capsule's air hose to the suit.

Pruett lay back and relaxed. Hans Buettner would replace Dougherty in a moment. Buettner and his skilled hands would check everything in the capsule, and personally attend to the electrical, oxygen and other umbilical connections linking the astronaut as a single entity with the spacecraft. Then would come several McDonnell technicians, Dr. Michaels, and, last of all, Jim Dougherty again.

Pruett glanced up at the instrument panel and broke into a sudden laugh. He read a neatly lettered card that swung from the panel:

PLEASE DO NOT THROW CIGARETTE BUTTS IN THE
URINALS, AS THEY GET SOGGY AND WET,
AND ARE HARD TO LIGHT.

There was also a going-away present from Dougherty. Pruett grinned ruefully as he reached out to touch the shining metal D-ring—from a parachute. It was Jim's crowning touch of irony, a token to recall that ejection in the thunderstorm and the descent by parachute that had saved his life. Now, he had another D-ring—and *no* parachute.

Buettner completed his checklist of the pressure suit and related equipment. A McDonnell technician leaned in through the hatch and handed Pruett another checklist on a clipboard. For nearly thirty minutes they went through the numbered items of capsule equipment, communications, pressures, electrical power flow—everything that assured perfect functioning of the compact spacecraft.

Cap Com in Mercury Control came in with assurance of continued good weather at the launch site and in the initial emergency splashdown areas at the Canary Islands and other sites along his route. The network was checking out beautifully, all tracking radar had called in; the Mercury organization was functioning in the manner of a well-oiled machine.

Then it was done; he was to be committed alone to the great rocket and the closing minutes of the countdown. Through the helmet earphones he heard the blockhouse talker: *"T minus one-forty-five and counting . . ."* Two hours and twenty-five minutes to go. This was the time hack for the technicians to fasten the hatch.

Pruett experienced an air of finality as the thick metal hatch was gingerly eased into place, and he switched to the spacecraft snorkels to bring in ambient air. The McDonnell crew paced their work as they inserted and secured seventy-two explosive bolts that sealed the capsule and, were it necessary, would blast the hatch free in a fraction of a second. For the next thirty minutes, as the work went on, Pruett talked to Dougherty and Mercury Control by radio. He knew the task was completed when a helmeted figure sprayed cleaning compound on the spacecraft window and rubbed briskly to clean off any marks or fingerprints.

"T minus one hundred and holding . . ."

No sweat, he thought. The hold was built into the count, a deliberate break in the preparations to allow a thorough nitpicking of any problems, to permit a general cleanup of the area and an unhurried final evaluation of the mission. Everything was in the green. *"Start helium pressurization. Start helium pressurization. We are at sixty minutes and counting; sixty minutes and counting."*

A moment later: *"Clear all tower workstands. Clear all tower workstands. Prepare to remove tower. Prepare to remove tower."*

A deep, mournful sound broke like a gentle wave against the spacecraft and faintly vibrated its way in to him—the warning horns that were booming their message at the launch complex and across the Cape, the signal that the towering gantry was about to be removed. Through his cabin mirrors and the spacecraft window he saw the men leaving for the elevator until only Jim Dougherty was left.

"Don't get any parking tickets up there," Dougherty cracked just before he broke his headset plug connection with the capsule. Pruett waved to him as Dougherty walked toward the waiting elevator. He stopped suddenly, remembering something, and moved quickly back to the spacecraft. Dougherty reached into a shirt pocket and brought out a folded sheet of yellow paper. He unfolded it carefully, smoothing out the creases, and held the paper close to the capsule window.

It was a telegram, brief and to the point. It was from Ann.

The words that stayed with him were simple: *"I love you."*

He closed his eyes for a long, long moment. The cloud deep in the back of his mind seemed to evaporate in those seconds. When he again opened his eyes, he was alone.

The great booster shook gently; the huge tower began to slide away from its position of embracing and surrounding the spacecraft. He had the strangest feeling that the tower actually was still, and that his spacecraft was sliding slowly to one side. Then the tower was gone, and he rested atop a thick needle, naked to the rich blue sky. He adjusted the capsule mirrors to study the Cape, the other gantries, the fleecy low clouds that drifted slowly overhead and to the side.

Vibration . . . the capsule shuddered. Far below his body, three flaring bell-shaped chambers moved on their gimbals as the blockhouse crew ran through a guidance-control check. Then silence again.

He felt the thick-bodied rocket sway slightly. It was the wind, blowing at twenty miles per hour against the Atlas. Superbly balanced on its launch ring, the booster accepted the side push of the wind and responded ever so slightly to the force. But enough to be noticed by Pruett.

He had considerable freedom within his confined space. The tightly restricting leg troughs and knee restraints employed for earlier flights had been removed. He could move his legs around through an unusually large arc. Pruett gripped the side of his couch and suddenly shoved his body back and forth with sharp movements. He grinned in delight as the great rocket beneath him swayed in response to his "body English."

"T minus thirty-five minutes and counting . . ."

A deep hissing sound carried to him; they were chilling down the plumbing with the supercold liquid oxygen. He knew precisely when the oxidizer began to pour into its tank. The capsule shuddered and vibrated as the thin metal skin of the Atlas flexed abruptly from the terrible cold of the liquid oxygen.

The minutes ticked away.

He heard the count moving progressively down, the men checking in, the great orchestra losing its preparatory discords and sliding neatly, expertly into position for the precise coordination needed to carry the mission to the point of ignition and the flight that he now anticipated with a sudden tremble of excitement.

He had wondered about this—what would be his emotions, his thoughts as he went right to the wire of the mission. He wondered if he would be calm, or if he would be awed and excited. Now he learned that he experienced all these emotions and feelings, but each observed by him, it seemed, as though they were on different planes. His voice as he responded to the countdown checks and even the banter from Cap Com and Dougherty, now in Mercury Control, was completely free of emotion. He might have been seated on a couch, engaged in idle conversation. Yet he felt . . . he *knew* that his senses were keyed to an extraordinarily fine pitch, that he scanned his controls and observed his instruments with startling clarity, that his mind encompassed all that was necessary for technical functioning and his duties . . . and yet, strangely, allowed him almost to look upon the entire scene as an outside observer, deeply emotional and excited at what was going on through every fleeing moment. He was grateful for this; he knew that his memories would not be obscured in the need for flawless performance on his part.

"T minus twenty-five minutes and counting . . . we are in a GO condition."

One by one they checked in. One by one they gave the anxiously awaited call in the new lexicon. Downrange weather was GO; optical tracking was GO; radar tracking —GO. They came in with their signals of "in the green" from Goddard, Bermuda, Zanzibar, Australia; from tracking ships and the recovery force at sea; they reported from aircraft flying at high altitude, from the Range Safety Officer's console in the Green Room at the Cape's Central Control. Emergency rescue forces stood by in the event of an abort; the forward medical area was GO. The red pencils ticked off item after item on the countdown checklists; the number of items remaining shrank, the number of

164

pages became smaller; the remaining minutes and seconds dribbled into nonexistence like grains of sand slipping through a crack in time.

"T minus fifteen minutes and counting . . ."

Pruett strained his body hard against the couch harness, tensed and untensed his limbs to assure that there would be no stiffening of his muscles, no unexpected, sudden body fatigue after the long wait on his back.

At thirteen minutes to liftoff the Marines fired up the engines of their big Sikorsky helicopters, ready to move out instantly, to go over the water or into the palmetto scrub or the swamps, to go after Pruett in the capsule if there should be an abort. The amphibious vehicles came alive, engines grumbling, crews prepared to button up their hatches. The fire trucks checked in with each other, with Cape Control. The Hot Papas pulled their heavy asbestos hoods over their asbestos-clad bodies, ready to walk directly into the midst of a screaming inferno, if necessary; ready to risk life itself to protect, to rescue the astronaut, a man they had never personally met, a man named Pruett.

At five minutes before GO they were playing for keeps. This was the final sweep through the last 300 seconds. The blockhouse crew sounded to Pruett like disembodied voices as he repeatedly scanned his instruments, checked for the hundredth time that his spacecraft also was in the green, ready to mesh into the coordination of the booster coming to life.

He heard the blockhouse commands to secure all air intakes.

Then, shockingly: *"Hold!"*

His breath exploded outward. The count was still perfect; the hold was built into the time frame. The test conductor in the blockhouse received a staccato string of *GO's* from each system controller. Then he heard the words that were music to his ears.

"We are in a GO condition . . ."

The seconds winked out of existence, one by one. He forced his mind into the count itself, became a part of the chanting ritual, checked off in his mind each item as it gained vocal substance and—gratefully—vanished off the checklists.

"Inverter switch to ON . . ." The internal AC power

system of the Atlas came alive to warm up the booster equipment.

"*Secure lox topping . . .*" The deep-bellied hiss close beneath him snapped off as the flow of liquid oxygen to its tank ended and the tank valves sealed tightly shut.

"*Start pressurization . . .*" Within the tanks, pressure built rapidly, waiting to ram the fuel and oxidizer down through the plumbing systems to the greedy engines.

"*Water systems to ON . . .*" A tumbling Niagara far below, beneath the Atlas itself. A deluge in the thick-ribbed, curving flame bucket.

"*Engine Arm Switch to ARM . . .*" His "bodacious afterburner"—the Atlas—was primed to fire, poised for flaming life.

"*Atlas to internal power . . .*" Electrical forces surged obediently through their channels within the rocket; the AC and DC internal power systems were alive and functioning. It was like listening to birth.

Only ninety seconds . . . Pruett lifted his left hand, firmly gripped the chicken switch, the abort handle, rescuer from distaster that could never be more than an instant away when a man lay atop a liquid volcano. One downward pull of his arm and the capsule would scream up and away from the Atlas, should the giant decide to tear out its bowels in a flaming eruption. He commanded the thought from his mind.

"*Systems Final Status Check . . .*" One by one, beautifully, the men at the consoles responded with that exultant, brief cry:

"*GO.*"

"*Mercury Seven?*"

Calmly, but with a feeling that quivered deep inside of him: "*All green—GO.*"

The final sequence rushed by . . .

"*T minus sixty seconds and counting . . .*"

He was astonished at the cold objectivity he felt.

"*Atlas helium to internal . . .*

"*Water to full flow . . .*

"*Autopilot to ARM position . . .*" The electronic brain to program and monitor the flight, to help the Atlas sling the spacecraft through the eye of the needle waiting in the sky, was alive.

"*Prestart . . .*"

166

And the response: *"GO!"*

"Minus fifty seconds . . ."

The range ready lights in the blockhouse flicked to green. The world-wide net stood ready to receive the spacecraft and the man.

"Thirty-five seconds . . ."

Almost simultaneously he heard and felt the next action. Even as the blockhouse talker cried, *"Eject spacecraft umbilicals,"* he felt the thump of their sudden push away from the side of the capsule. He snapped his eyes around the instruments; pressure, power, everything—in the green.

At eighteen seconds a hulking robot brain in the blockhouse, the Automatic Sequencer, assumed command. The count went to full automatic. An intricate array of robot sensors sniffed and listened for the signs and sounds of anything awry; they could automatically signal red lights to flash, stop the count at that same instant.

"Sixteen . . .

"Fifteen . . ."

A sudden squeeze of alarm within him; for an instant of unbelievable clarity, he thought of the retropack so close beneath his body; he saw in his mind the posigrades and the retros, six potential flaming spears. What if they should ignite prematurely, what if—*now,* what if they ignited now? They were alive, the spacecraft was alive, things—

"Fourteen . . ."

—were happening to it. My God, if those rockets ever fired, the flame would stab—

"Thirteen . . ."

—deeply, would rupture the thin curving upper dome of the Atlas; it could rip into the—

"Twelve . . ."

—liquid oxygen tank, and the whole goddamned Atlas would go up in a flaming, bloody—

. ."Eleven . . ."

—mess, and then—

. ."STOP IT!"

The soundless voice screamed in his mind—

"Ten . . ."

—and banished the unexpected stab of terror. He knew it had had to come sometime; he was grateful—

"Nine . . ."

—that it had come, and was—

"Eight . . ."
over and done—
"Seven . . ."
with.
"Six . . ."
Exultation swept through him—a fierce cry of joy and—
"Five . . ."
—wonder, the wonder of this, of *now;* the sudden realization that came rushing to—
"Four . . ."
—him, that truly this was the fulfillment of those dreams, of all the years; instantly he thought of the giant beneath him, he thought—
"Three . . ."
—of the terrible forces that might erupt and run amuck, that might tear him and the dream into little pieces that would blow away in the wind like the tattered—
"Two . . ."
—memories of a parade after the shiny uniforms and the trumpeting brass were gone, and the children laughing were only an echo, and even—
"One . . ."
—if that *did* happen, he knew it didn't matter at all any more, only the dream, the *chance* for the dream was what mattered, and of a sudden he hungered fiercely for what stretched impossibly high and above h—
"ZERO!"
It came in a rush of impressions to him, like a kid running along the sidewalk, dragging a stick against the side of an iron fence, and each time the stick banged against the metal, that was an event; and each event now came to him, flickers of events melting into here and now—
He heard and felt the vernier engines on the side of the Atlas snarl into life.
Before he could think about it, a dull roar boomed through the Atlas and swept into the capsule; hard on its heels came a continuing cannonade of thunder. His lips came back in an animal grin of triumph—
"Mainstage!"
They were all lit. He felt the tremendous power beneath him, the vibrating, shaking movement of the mountain— not harsh or overwhelming, not quiet or subdued, just . . . an authoritative movement and thunder and—

168

"FIRST MOTION!"

The spacecraft swayed; ever so slightly it moved. His heart pounded; he—

"LIFTOFF!"

"Roger, liftoff, and the clock is started. Mercury Seven is on her way. How do we look, you guys?"

That voice—it was *him!* Almost a voice disembodied, calm, relaxed, efficient, in absolute control; *his* voice; and he had punched the clock, almost automatically, his body moving with a machine precision. . . .

"Roger, Seven. You look very good, very good from here. Everything is go."

The roar swelled into an ocean of thunder; there came a deep, wonderful surge upward, unbelievably smooth. . . .

"Everything looking good, you're for the money. Did you remember to release the parking brake, Seven?"

He laughed, and his voice responded when necessary, his eyes scanned the instruments steadily, his mind ordered the voice to call out the readings of pressure, battery power, oxygen flow, temperature and the dozen other critical items, and it all seemed to take place apart from him, because he was filled with the wonder and it . . . he could not think deliberately of it any longer; he gave himself up to the miracle, became fully a part of it.

Almost as soon as the Atlas lifted, the booster began to roll. The horizon moved around as the rocket turned to ascend on a heading of seventy-two degrees, to rush upward in a direction north of east of Cape Kennedy. For fourteen seconds the booster turned, and he could feel the angular motion as well as see it, and through it all the Atlas kept hammering her way upward, pushing, rejecting the earth with all the disdain of her glorious thunder, sucking a ton of liquids through her chambers every one and a quarter seconds, and—

"*No!* Stay with it; stay with it, baby, hang onto it, don't let it go. Stay with it. . . ."

His voice, soundless, but clear in his mind. The Atlas was turning too rapidly in her roll. It might be engine misalignment, or unexpected thrust from the gas generator exhaust, or anything. She burned and roared with perfection, but a sensitive brain within the Atlas, the abort system, felt the unexpected roll. If the magnitude of the roll transient reached the abort threshold value, the abort sensor would react in gibbering electronic fear and fire the escape rocket, and the mission would be over right here and now. The verniers snapped over in their gimbals and thrust against the direction of roll; for a moment the Atlas shuddered and then obediently stopped exactly on her mark and pushed faster and faster, and Pruett suddenly yelled, "That's my girl! That's my baby! Go, baby. . . ."

In Cape Control, in the blockhouse, in the Green Room at Central Control, men felt, shared that enthusiastic cry, and some of them whispered the same yell with him, not knowing that the words were spilling rapidly, fervently, from their lips.

The roll motion stopped and the verniers locked her on her course, and the electronic brain commanded the great engines to swivel ever so slightly; Atlas obeyed. The shrieking flames behind the rocket seemed to whip back at a slight angle to the booster. The Atlas no longer pushed straight up, but began to bend away from the vertical, commencing the long, smooth curve that would lead to the eye of the needle so far above.

Faster and faster, the invisible hand of acceleration pushed him down, steadily, with an amazing gentleness, into the couch.

The Atlas shuddered and the roar of the engines suddenly increased. The booster plunged into Max Q; aerodynamic pressure built to its shuddering peak.

A thousand pounds of pressure slammed and pounded each square foot of the capsule; Pruett was surprised at the slight reaction to the pressure. He reported that through the vibration he could still scan and see the instruments with complete clarity: thirty seconds after it began the shuddering vanished.

Faster, higher, clawing away from the massive world below, almost as if answering a call, a demand . . .

The sky darkened with a rush. The clean, light blue coloration ebbed from existence, replaced by a constantly deepening shade of blue. Light poured in through the spacecraft window; it was clear and strong. Pruett was astonished at the amount of light reflected from the earth.

The ascent was not a constant, smooth push. The acceleration remained unchanged as the booster fled the world, but at moments she seemed to sway, a wide and gentle yawing motion, becoming more pronounced as the fuel gushed into the chambers, the rocket became lighter, the thin body became more and more resilient.

Acceleration kept increasing . . . six times the force of gravity. The man in the couch weighed nearly one ton as he rushed toward the first critical command of flight, for booster engine cutoff.

"Mercury Seven, coming up on BECO . . ."

"Roger, Cap Com. Confirm coming up on BECO. Acceleration is at six. Cabin pressure holding at . . ."

One hundred and thirty-one seconds. Speed: 7000 miles per hour. Altitude: thirty-nine miles. Range from Cape Kennedy: fifty-two miles.

An electronic command shot through the booster circuitry. Valves snapped shut; fuel diverted. Pruett's body pushed against the straps. He was delighted with the transition in acceleration. Instead of the abrupt move from six to only one-and-a-half g, the movement felt stretched out, lasting at least a half-second or more. . With acceleration changes of this magnitude, that can be a *long* time.

He heard the muffled thud of explosive bolts.

Light flared suddenly outside the capsule window— exhaust gases from the sustainer engine, splashing against the booster engine and skirt as the unit slid back on rails and dropped behind the Atlas. The blazing exhaust showered an iridescent spray in all directions; the astronaut saw the event only as a flash past the window.

He breathed deeply, enjoying the stretched-out respite from acceleration before the Atlas built up the forces once again.

One hundred fifty-four seconds . . .

Another thud, explosive, heavier this time.

The escape and ejection rockets of the tower above him, clasping the spacecraft, departed the scene with the slamming thud and a roar. Brilliant flame washed before his vision. More than a half-mile in the distance, the escape tower rotated slowly as it raced for the horizon. Wisps of smoke trailed in a weaving pattern from the exhaust nozzles of the spent escape rocket; then it was gone.

Green lights before his eyes . . . all landing systems of the spacecraft were now fully armed. No matter what happened now, Pruett was committed to Mercury Seven. No matter what went wrong, he would ride the capsule back to earth in a ballistic arc. He had made the transformation; he now was embraced by ballistic laws and demands.

One hundred sixty-two seconds . . .

He was on the end of an enormous springboard—slow but distinct side-to-side movements, gentle but definite oscillations. The earth and the blackness and then the horizon slid slowly through a pattern of shifting positions.

The flaming booster kept pitching its nose down, more and more, until, impossibly, Pruett in the spacecraft was lower than the fiery sustainer engine and was driving with constantly increasing speed *downward,* back toward the earth. It was impossible, it couldn't—

But it *was* possible, and it was also necessary. Correcting through its flight, prepared to thread the eye of the needle for orbit, the Atlas kept pitching over until the capsule dropped to a position fourteen degrees lower to the earth than the sustainer engine.

When the movement began in the opposite direction, the capsule steadily pitching upward, Pruett knew he was sensing the final corrections for orbital insertion, for the moment of SECO. At that instant, soon, the sustainer engine would cut off and he would know, quickly, how it had all gone.

The acceleration built to six again, and seven, and began to peak near eight. Events began to rush toward a single moment; the capsule yawed more and more from side to side. But the smoothness of the motion was gone. The electronic brain lashed the programmer; the sustainer engine and the verniers jerked in their gimbals, pushing and shoving the accelerating, blazing rocket closer to the eye of the needle. The noise increased.

". . . coming up on SECO. You look good, very good from here. Everything looks like it's directly in the center of the target. Stand by for SECO. . . ."

Three-hundred-six-point-four seconds . . .

Thunder ceased.

There was a crash of silence.

Acceleration vanished; weight fled.

He tumbled forward—*"No; not so,"* he told himself; just the expected sensation at the end of acceleration.

Wonder soared within him. *He was in orbit!* The silence; he—

BANG!

Explosive bolts fired. The clamp ring holding spacecraft and booster exploded apart, freeing the two.

Thunder.

Beneath him, muffled thunder and vibration. An easy push. Three posigrade rockets flaming briefly, shoving the capsule away from the now-lifeless booster. The brilliant, curving line of the terrestrial horizon swung suddenly as the spacecraft's thrusters fired and the automatic pilot turned the capsule around, moving it into retroattitude.

Confirmation of separation, turnaround, retroattitude, between astronaut and Cap Com.

Then *the* words, so anxiously awaited. The message spat from the Goddard computers, flashed to Cape Kennedy, sprayed in colored lights on the huge mission board, was read with delight and passed on with the same emotion to the man high above the planet.

"You are *GO* for at least thirty-two orbits. Everything looks like it's right on the money. . . ."

They would have exact details of his orbital parameters as he swung around the world and came into range again of Cape Control; for the moment, he knew the orbit was perfect, or as close to perfect as could be. He dismissed the matter from his mind and enjoyed the fruits of the miracle.

A miracle in comfort, a suit without any pressure points anywhere on his body. A sensation of deep silence, the thunder no longer permeating the spacecraft.

The incredible sight of the booster, five hundred feet away, turning and rotating very slowly, flashing in the sun, with the big bellyband of white frost around the liquid oxygen tank, now empty, glistening pinpoints of metal elsewhere. Crystals of white and green in lazy streams, wisping from the sustainer engine. He could see the booster, abandoned to a coming fiery embrace with the atmosphere, for six minutes, until it vanished from his sight.

He stared at the sharply curving horizon. For a moment he knew disappointment when the heavens seemed emptier of stars than he had expected; he remembered, then, his eyes were still light-struck from the sun and would require time for night adaptation.

He looked down upon Bermuda and the brilliantly blue ocean. He marveled at the sharp, tiny clarity of cumulus clouds over the water. Fifteen minutes after liftoff, he stared at the Canary Islands, then the Atlas Mountains of Africa and tendrils of smoke and dust across the desert. Delight in the sharpness of shadows beneath the clouds; the silent wonder, seen through a thick visor, of the great flaming star that men called the sun.

He looped around the earth, racing higher and higher as the spacecraft rushed upward and over and then beyond Australia, his high point of orbit.

As he came back around the planet, the army of newsmen at the press site on Cape Kennedy were flashing the results of the Atlas booster's incredible performance—as perfect as could possibly be achieved, exactly as hoped and planned.

"America's fifth astronaut to race around the world," reported an enthused and impressed radioman, "is now moving through space with the kind of precision that once seemed impossible in this game of tricky and sensitive rockets. For the fifth time in a row, the mighty Atlas has sent an American into an orbital path with amazing accuracy. We thought that the Atlas for Gordon Cooper's flight couldn't be bettered in performance, but today's rocket did the impossible. And it did the job with a capsule that is slightly heavier than any Mercury spacecraft in orbit, more than a hundred pounds heavier, at 3,089 pounds, than was John Glenn's *Friendship 7*."

His engineer gave him the thumbs-up signal, and he kept pacing his report. But the public really didn't care about the figures; you can listen to figures and numbers over a radio, and they mean little. You just want the results.

So the average person didn't care about the specifics, only that he was up, that the shot was good, that he was going for the full forty-eight orbits everyone was hoping for.

It didn't matter that the capsule swung around the earth at an inclination to the equator of exactly 32.55 degrees, or that its period in a Keplerian Orbit—which is space-referenced and not earth-based—was exactly 88.81 minutes, and that this figure would decrease slowly by fractions of a second per orbit.

The Mercury Seven spacecraft raced through the radiation environment of space with a velocity at perigee of 17.548 miles per hour, as the scientists measured its speed relative to the surface of the planet far below. At the moment of its maximum velocity—at its perigee, or low point of the looping orbit—the spacecraft dipped to 87.8 nautical miles; and the radio and television newsmen explained hastily that in terms of distances as measured on their roadmaps, this was just about 101 miles high.

At the point of apogee, the high reach of the orbit attained over Australia, the spacecraft soared to 154 miles. In landlubber terms, that came to 177 miles above sea level.

The public didn't care about the details, for they were, after all, the kind of specifics that were hard to grasp and might even give you a headache. When a man went out to buy a car, he wasn't interested in the cubic inches or compression ratio of the engine and that nonsense; he wanted to know how many horses there were under the hood, how fast it went, and how much?

But specifics in orbit are unbelievably critical.

In a few days more, after the mission was successfully under way, they would pay much more attention to the details.

After all, how many times can you read a death sentence imposed in mathematical terms?

Chapter XI

His flight was a significant milestone that bridged the gap from the present into the future. Some said that Astronaut Richard J. Pruett was the first American to participate in the routine of flight through space. Until this moment every step made by the nation had been an adventure into a new realm. Each man had delved into a new area for the first time. Each astronaut—Glenn, Carpenter, Schirra, Cooper —sliced through the jungle of precedence by conducting new tests, carrying out new orbital experiments.

Pruett was the first American to know repetition in space. He repeated his days and nights until in the number of hours they matched the passage of time on the world below. His body performed its biological functions through

175

cycles which could be studied and interpreted by doctors to establish the first really thorough guidelines for the future. He slept and awoke, and two more times he repeated this cycle as well.

The small television camera within Mercury Seven brought home the stark drama of an astronaut's voyage through space with an impact unprecedented since that first moment of liftoff with John Glenn. The camera was limited in performance and it weighed but ten pounds; it transmitted its pictures with a slow scan rate, and much was lacking in the way of clarity. But it didn't matter. Improved and sharpened over the camera used in Gordon Cooper's spacecraft, it held the fascination not only of almost every American, but of hundreds of millions of people throughout the world.

Several times during the mission Pruett went on camera "live." The hundreds of millions of people thrilled to the sight of the young American grinning and waving at them, flipping weightless objects about in mid-air. The telemetry transmissions of the television scenes beamed to earth were retransmitted back to the three Syncom communications satellites girdling the globe twenty-two thousand miles out. The sight of the astronaut shredded all concepts of time as people around the world, despite local day or night, simultaneously watched the miracle before their eyes.

Pruett performed scientific experiments, and he remained in space long enough to add new tests suddenly conceived by the excited men on the ground. Pruett's face changed; he became the first American who remained away from the earth long enough to need a shave when he was ready to return.

Above all, in terms of science, he scored a triumph for the United States. A sudden decision to show to the world a hurricane as it appeared from space stressed with tremendous impact the future of manned weather observations from orbit. Several times Pruett pitched the spacecraft down and aimed his television camera at a great circular mass spreading over the ocean. The films were relayed by Syncom throughout the world, and the hundreds of millions of people watching received a first-class demonstration of what future manned stations could bring to them in the way of space-observed meteorology.

He had time to spend, time to use. He was the first

American who had the time to perform all those experiments that only a man in orbit could provide. He had three days and more to carry out his tasks. And when the three days plus three orbits came to an end, he knew that time had also become his enemy. . . .

Pruett computed his time with a yardstick no man in space, American *or* Russian, had ever found necessary to employ: hours, minutes, and seconds remaining until the last invisible wisps of oxygen hissed from the storage flasks and were sucked into his lungs. Then the percentage of carbon dioxide and the water vapor would begin to increase. The foul mixture would crowd and shove within his body, in the limited volume of his helmet and his suit, and within the cabin itself.

His knowledge of the processes of life now was as much a curse as it had once been a blessing, for he knew only too well what would happen when the mixture of gases billowed through his lungs, and the warm and moist alveolar walls struggled with sad biological futility to find the oxygen for which his bloodstream waited . . . and for which his brain would very quickly starve.

The knowledge of his certain death no longer evoked the tendrils of panic that had twisted and writhed for release when he first realized the inevitable outcome. He could, he knew, end it quickly and painlessly. He could lower the flow of oxygen into his suit, reduce the cabin pressure until, before long, his brain succumbed to the effects of hypoxia. It would come with delusions, and a strange feeling, strangely similar to that of a mild drunk, that all was wonderful. He would slide, slowly and without a pang of remorse or fear, into unconsciousness. And while his oxygen-starved brain continued to fail, cells dying like rows of wheat falling beneath a scythe, he would sleep his way into the eternal sleep of death.

He knew that this could be done, that it required only the twisting of one or two dials; and, knowing this, he knew also that he could not do it—not while there still remained the remotest ghost of a chance that something might happen. He no longer believed that he would find that miracle, or one of several possible miracles, to sustain his life; that he could stretch out the oxygen, or that the retrorockets would mysteriously come once again to life.

But anything was possible, no matter how implausible, and while he had accepted without further struggle the inevitability of his death, he was not about to yield a single second of the time remaining to him.

He had last spoken to the Mercury network as he flashed over Canton Island; there the Cap Com had requested—had passed on the request from Cape Control—that he review every possible event and step taken within the spacecraft. It was almost funny, he thought; the capsule had functioned flawlessly for more than three days, and sprung its most devastating failure at the last possible instant of his mission. And still it functioned as its engineers had intended; still it continued its perfect internal motions.

Except, of course, that mysterious failure in the electrical system that stayed the retros from their brief, flaming life.

The human body, he mused, is an engine. It is a mechanical device that requires certain metabolic supplies, as much as any combustion engine requires those same supplies to produce the heat that men tap for power. It had long before been worked out neatly.

If you weighed 180 pounds, as he did, then your body demanded just over two pounds of oxygen per day. A normal, healthy man needed along with these two pounds of atmospheric fuel a total of five pounds of water and one pound of solid fuel. Every twenty days, that man—his body—would consume nearly its own weight in fuel. Actually, he needed less than normal; weightless, free of running, walking, working, his fuel requirements were less than his needs on the surface of the planet Earth, which now seemed a billion miles away.

Disregarding the small fractions and percentages, he knew that in response to his intake, his body would yield every day about two pounds of carbon dioxide and water vapor, some six pounds of water, and a small amount of solids, urea, and minerals.

His was a need never imagined by the isolated castaway, no matter how fierce and hostile the desert within which he was marooned. For Pruett had more than enough water and food, the ingredients that men invariably need in their struggle to survive. They, in turn, had all the air necessary to sustain a population of billions, which the earth supplied so freely through its deep, heaving ocean of air.

The engineers and doctors who produced the environmental control system of his spacecraft had done their work with extensive experience behind them in aviation and space medicine. Adding to this the experience of the four Mercury orbital flights, they incorporated into Pruett's capsule three oxygen storage vessels, each containing four pounds of oxygen kept under a pressure of 7,500 pounds per square inch. This constituted his normal and emergency reserve supply. Included in the system were pressure transducers that lowered the primary supply to one hundred, and the emergency supply to eighty pounds per square inch, squeezing down the flow to that needed by his body and the spacecraft system.

He pictured the system in his mind, searching for the hundredth time the impossible possibility that perhaps he could find some means of stretching out that oxygen supply. He was so close to the time of orbital decay from the wisps of upper atmosphere that even a slight gain, an unexpected advantage, might tip the scales in his favor.

The precious oxygen fed into his pressure suit through a trilock adapter at his left waist. From here it flowed along the suit's arterial network of hoses to his arms and legs, fulfilling a dual purpose by cooling his limbs before moving to his helmet for breathing. His exhaled air, heavy in carbon dioxide and water vapor, exhausted from his body by a helmet vent close to his right ear. The discarded air then flowed into the capsule environmental system, running the gauntlet of filters and coolers.

Here the system scrubbed out the carbon dioxide. An electric fan pushed the exhaled air so that it flowed across a bed of activated charcoal and several open containers of lithium hydroxide. By now that waste air already was greatly cleansed of its impurities; it was ready for the next step.

The air flowed into a special exchanger which used nothing more exotic than water to remove from his body the excess heat—which had been transferred, during his respiration, to the air. The process of heat removal was quite ingenious and also productive for him. As the heat was removed, condensing droplets of water were soaked up by a sponge. Every thirty minutes a small metal piston squeezed the sponge dry of its liquid burden. As the water drained off it was sucked into a collection tank. While all this went on, the excess heat vented outboard from the spacecraft as steam and instantly, in the harshness of vacuum, was transformed into the white-green iceflakes that drifted from the capsule, mixing with the flakes from the thrusters.

For Pruett's mission, the water collection system had been modified. If his regular water supply ran short, he would be able to utilize the liquid by-products of his respiratory processes and perspiration by drawing upon the collection tanks. It was a simple and beautiful system for an emergency but, he noted wryly, in this respect he didn't have any emergency.

The environmental control system was not yet done with his exhaled gases, and it continued the process of scrubbing and cleansing. Special filters strained out his more unpleasant and noticeable body odors and whatever dust-sized debris had clogged the air. Only after all this had been done was the air considered sufficiently cleansed and purified to re-enter the suit inlet and to repeat the process of cooling the heat from his body, beginning anew the cycle.

It was all very neat and—goddamnit!—*too* efficient. He could see nothing in the system or its operation that would permit of any modification or action on his part that would aid him.

You figure out a man's needs by numbers, he mused. Normally, he recalled again, the adult male—"Example, *me*," he muttered—requires 2.2 pounds of oxygen every twenty-four hours. Okay, then, the three storage vessels, each about the size of a volley ball, added up to a supply of twelve pounds of oxygen.

Next: at a rate of 2.2 pounds of oxygen consumed each full day, he would breathe his entire oxygen supply in exactly five days and twelve hours—a period almost two and a half days beyond his expected time in orbit.

That, of course, was where the rub came in. He was going to double, and then some, his "expected" time in orbit.

The Atlas booster had operated to perfection. Its flight profile included consideration for the slight extra weight of his spacecraft. It had injected him into an orbit that was precisely what the engineers had demanded. That same orbit meant racing around the world for six and a third days, if the retros did not fire and orbital decay took place from atmospheric resistance.

Couldn't they have cut the orbit some in their original calculations? The question came to Pruett (and had been voiced by several thousand newsmen and editors), and almost immediately he rejected it. Not without a possible compromise of the mission, he knew. After all, the atmospheric ocean wasn't that much of a known quantity, what with its response to gravitational and solar forces. They had to be certain that he would be in an orbit high enough to complete the three full days, plus three orbits, without any danger of premature orbital decay. Bykovsky had run into exactly that problem with Vostok V. Scheduled for a mission of eight days (the big Russian spaceship could keep him alive for twelve days), he was forced to fire his retros prematurely—three days ahead of schedule— when the Vostok at perigee kept dipping precariously low into the atmospheric fringes.

No, there was no fault with the orbit or even the intended orbit. He wished, uselessly, he knew, that the Atlas had *not* performed to perfection, that it had failed to deliver all the thrust demanded of it. Wishful thinking of hindsight . . . After all, the booster had done almost the same thing with Gordo Cooper's flight.

Mercury Seven would slip earthward six days and eight hours after insertion into orbit over Bermuda, and—he shook his head, clearing his mind of the repetitive thoughts. The end result was that no matter how much he stretched out his oxygen, he would still be missing a half-day's supply of oxygen to breathe before re-entry began.

And no matter how earnestly he wracked his brain, he could not find *anything* during his orbital flight that provided a clue to explain the failure of the retros to fire.

He flicked the switches to feed power into his communications system and to warm up the radios. In a few minutes he would be within transceiving range of Cape Kennedy. Canton Cap Com had told him only that Cape Control would have "specific data" when he established contact.

Despite his own instinctive caution his heart pounded faster. Was it possible that they *had* found something?

Could they reach deeply into the grab bag of technological happenstance and come up with the solution that meant life?

"You're just dreaming, space cadet," a voice said, and he winced as he recognized his own practical, sarcastic self.

Chapter XII

Deep in the steel bellies of the ships, in the greyhound destroyers and the fat-bottomed supply vessels, within the cruisers and far into the nuclear gut of the huge carrier Enterprise, energy pulsed at its minimum. The vast Mercury recovery force cruised slowly, a pattern of shapes painting soft wakes on the ocean surface—a vast and powerful fleet of the Navy, its guns forgotten for this mission of recovering a man from the sea, as other men had been recovered after their voyages through the sea of space.

It was, in the rippling reflections of the moon, a fleet of frustration, an armada of helplessness, of more than twenty thousand men sick inside themselves, grim, some bitter, others angry, still others wishing and hoping that crying might help . . . but whatever their play of emotion, for each man it was his own brand of compassion.

There is among the vessels of the recovery force a fierce and vibrant competition. This is the world's greatest sweepstakes—to snatch from the liquid sea the man returned from that alien world beyond the ocean of air. It is fierce and proud competition, and when the great moment would come, the men would crowd and jostle on the decks, anxious to be first to see the telltale swath of contrail as the superheated capsule hissed and plunged earthward, and the small drogue parachute came out, and two miles high the big orange-and-white canopy blossomed. . . .

When a man came home from his voyage "out there," and the men crowded onto the decks raised their heads and pointed their fingers, the shout was one that could be heard far across the waves, that rolled in throated thunder from vessel to vessel, and swept up in its own emotional tides the wonder and joy of it all.

Except that the tides of emotion now brooded and sulked in the dark corners of despair that each man felt in his own helplessness. The decision had been made—the fleet will stay, turning its vast, slow, and rhythmic circle, the procession of frustration. Where was there to go? Who could leave?

They would stay . . . until the last breath of cool oxygen had been consumed, and the man in their thoughts strangled and drowned just as much as any one of them would strangle and choke liquidly to death were they rammed deep into the world of inner space beneath the heaving steel flanks of the ships.

They cast their moon-bathed silhouettes on the water, and the men stared moodily at the swirling green phosphorescence pulsing on the sides and behind the great metal shapes. On the seemingly endless deck of the Enterprise, winged shapes hulked in their impotence, and the carrier superstructure pushed up from the sea like a monstrous squid trapped and chained by gravity.

The man far above them was dying. And each one of them seemed to feel, in some degree, the weight of death pressing in upon him.

Snap!

George Keith looked down in surprise as the pencil halves jutted awkwardly in his fingers. Annoyed, he flung them away.

Behind him, tired and drawn men in shirtsleeves and with stubble on their faces evinced no surprise at this action of the usually imperturbable mission control director. In the shocked aftermath of the retrorocket failure of Mercury Seven, Keith had functioned as a bedrock of strength, in full command of his emotions, and a whipsaw to any man in the Mission Control Center who moved even an inch out of line.

A man would die unless Keith and the men who worked with and for him could pull a miracle from the failure that was both unprecedented and completely baffling to them. And time was running out. Time . . .

Keith glanced at the large wall clock, the red second hand turning inexorably, a pointer of failure and condemnation—at no one in particular and, at the same time, at all of them—here in the Control Center, in Hangar S, in St. Louis and in Houston. It didn't matter that almost everything was perfect about the flight; it was that tiny, insignificant thing that wasn't perfect that could kill.

Like a long drop through the air without a parachute, Keith reflected. The fall never hurt you. What killed a man was that sudden stop.

What was going to kill Pruett was something tiny, unseen, unknown. . . .

He would be within radio contact range shortly. Keith couldn't tell him that they had found the answer. Pruett knew they were looking for it; no one had to tell the man a hundred miles high that they were going without sleep and whipping themselves on, that there were curses of self-recrimination. . . . What the hell good would saying this do Pruett? He knew it; that was enough.

George Keith looked slowly around the Control Center, the heart and soul of the orbital mission, the nerve center on the surface of the planet for the machine and the man about to rush by overhead. Every man within his sight in the huge Operations Room, a sprawling nerve cell fifty by sixty feet where men and electronics merged in a strange, wonderful partnership . . . every man here felt as he did —trapped, helpless, infuriated at his inability to help the man who needed them and counted upon them, and—

"That's not altogether true," Keith chided himself. *"You know Dick Pruett better than that. He may not like it, he may be—and certainly should be—damned unhappy about all of this, but he's not going to brood about miracles. He'll count on all of us until the last brain cell winks out, and he'll buy the farm without a single thought that any man here would be ashamed to know. . . ."*

Keith sat in the center of the Operations Room, toward the rear. To his right, face buried in his arms (but not asleep, Keith knew) was the launch facility director. On Keith's left was the recovery operations director, a man with a white face and a feeling of stupid uselessness because he had a vast force directly under his control and couldn't do a damned thing with them.

Directly in front of Keith was John Novak, flight director for MA-10. Novak in turn was flanked by the network status monitor and the launch vehicle telemetry monitor. Neither man could fulfill his schedule now, for Pruett wasn't wasting battery power on his radar transponder or the telemetry transmitters. But there might come, at any moment, the need for immediate action; none of these men, or the others, would leave the building. They slept at their desks or passed out on canvas cots brought into the hallways.

The third tier—moving from the rear of the room forward—in front of Novak, included the support control coordinator, flight surgeon (Michaels had been without sleep for more than two days, Keith knew), capsule environment monitor, the capsule communicator, and the capsule systems monitor (and didn't *that* poor bastard feel, and look, miserable).

Keith turned slowly to survey the enclosed domain. Along the right wall of the room were the flight dynamics officer and the retrofire controller; the latter had been in constant touch with anybody—and by anybody he meant only the skilled and knowledgeable—who might know anything that would provide a clue to the failure in Mercury Seven.

Before the two men spread a display of four flight recorders. Here in the technical jargon of the computers and the engineers could be found the mission story; the first recorder plotted the launch path as the inertial flight path angle, juggling this against the velocity ratio. It also plotted the orbital path as altitude above a spherical (slightly bending the facts) earth, versus velocity. If you could read the language displayed and presented, you saw unfolding the picture of Pruett's dilemma. It was all there in the recorders—cross-range deviation and altitude versus range; orbital path as semi-major axis deviation and altitude versus ground elapsed time; insertion velocity and longitudinal acceleration versus elapsed time and yaw error and . . . hell. Keith closed his eyes for a moment and with his fingers kneaded the bridge of his nose. No matter how you sliced and dissected the technicalities, it all came down to the blunt but distressingly accurate words of the newscasters.

He's going to die before his orbit decays unless those people in that Control Center, and all the other people with whom they're talking, can pull off the biggest miracle ever known in the space-flight business. (*And the newsmen*

185

were already writing the glowing eulogies and the obituaries; the television directors were frantically piecing together every scrap of film on Pruett; radio stations the country over were snipping and connecting tapes of his voice; and Keith hoped that the police had cordoned off the Pruett home, or that his folks had slipped away somewhere, because the army of pencils-and-pads would descend upon them like the plague. The whole thing saddened Keith, but nothing could be done about that. Keith had never heard of a man named Ed Lyons, who had shaped a kid named Pruett into a pilot; nor did he know that at this same moment an enraged Lyons had pitched a loudmouthed reporter through his front window. . . .)

Stretching in front of the tiers of controllers was a world map eight feet high by nearly thirty feet wide. Along its multicolored and glowing surface wound the orbital paths of the spacecraft and the locations of all the world tracking and communications stations. Colored rings flashed with light whenever the capsule rushed to within range of a station's radar and radio beams, showing everyone in the center instantly, and at all times, where the capsule was in relationship to ground contact and tracking.

The colors of individual rings indicated the operational status of each station, degrees of malfunction . . . but there was only one malfunction that mattered now, and it was in the capsule that this elaborate rigging pursued with its electronic eyes.

Keith stared at the glowing ring showing the capsule's present position. Pruett would come within range in the next minute or two; Harold Spencer, the Center Cap Com, was already trying to establish the voice contact.

Keith shuffled the papers on his desk. Two engineers from McDonnell waited with several of his own staff immediately behind him. Those men were—and had been for many, many hours—in direct touch with groups of men in Hangar S, at the McDonnell plant in St. Louis, and the spacecraft assembly and checkout building at the Manned Spacecraft Center in Houston. They had accomplished through exhaustive efforts nothing more than confirmation of the fact that the failure in Spacecraft Number Fifteen was an enigmatic now as it had been. The papers spread before Keith were reports and studies which he had probed in the hope that *something* might break in trying to crack the failure.

And what the hell do we mean by failure? he asked himself in a snarling, angry voice. . . . A rocket with more than 300,000 parts had performed flawlessly. For more than three days a small spacecraft with over 10,000 parts had functioned in unprecedented, perfect fashion. Hundreds of millions of components of the vast global net had matched that performance. Yet, no matter what extent and breadth of success, he knew, all that fabulous performance wouldn't do a man named Pruett a damn bit of good.

What—*what* could it be! The failure was a wraith that danced just beyond their reach, just at the edge of their fingertips, and they couldn't touch it. But they had known bewildering problems before, much more complicated, sometimes in components even simpler than the retro system, and they had whipped those problems through scientific sleuthing that staggered the imagination and defied all the odds and carried Mercury through its trail-blazing efforts with a perfect safety— He stopped the thought sharply.

But it was all *true,* damn it! They had worked against and overcome problems that seemed impossible of solution within the time frames allotted them. They took absolutely nothing for granted—nothing, that is, except the inevitability of problems and troubles.

Capsule Thirteen, the spacecraft flown by Glenn, waited at Cape Canaveral for 166 days before it left the earth. The engineers subjected the machine to no less than 255 changes and modifications. That was the key to their operation: be always on the alert for the needed change, and be prepared to make that change—for the better—whenever necessary, no matter when.

The standing joke about Glenn's flight had been "around the world in ninety minutes after eighty-two days on the pad." Sure, it was funny in a dry sort of way. And there had been that heart-squeezing signal on Segment 51, when it appeared that Glenn's heat shield had jogged loose and there was the terrifying possibility that the man would come back to earth only as ashes sifting slowly down through the atmosphere. But it was one more step in the learning.

During the early days of Mercury, Keith recalled, there was one vital part of the capsule electrical power system that drove them wild. The system had passed every qualification test; it worked perfectly. Yet when it went into the capsule it failed. Again and again it failed, until the engineers started to look over their shoulders at all the eyes staring coldly at them. They subjected the system not only to every test known, but also to new ones they had to create themselves. And they found it—the trouble. There were certain components that no one knew were temperature-critical. When they were placed in the capsule, they failed. Taken out and tested—they worked. But back into the capsule—failure!

A heat source in the spacecraft, close to the electrical system, was the problem. All they needed to do was to move the electrical system a bit, get it away from the direct heat, and it worked perfectly. But it was only one indication of the infinite range of possibilities that could create failures. And if it had happened in orbit *before* it took place in the test chamber . . . well, cliff-hanging was a part of this game.

Like now.

Could something in the retropack, in the electrical system, have been installed improperly? The engineers swore that this was impossible. If they could have staked *their* lives on it, Keith knew, they would gladly exchange places with Dick Pruett, so certain were they of their systems. Of course, their willingness to do so didn't *help* Pruett. . . .

It was possible for electrical connectors to be unintentionally interchanged in the spacecraft. It *could* happen; that sort of thing had happened in the past. Once, here at the Cape, the Air Force had lost a Thor missile. And the missile was perfect. A technician in wiring the display panel for the Range Safety Officer had *crossed two wires*. The panel worked perfectly, except that the reversed wires gave the indication that the Thor was tearing out of its assigned missile corridor.

The rocket boomed spaceward in a flawless launch, but the Range Safety Officer had no choice. He pressed a button, and several million dollars' worth of rocket vanished in the deliberate explosion.

And there was the bitter, classic case of Mariner I, the first shot at Venus. A brilliant scientist, in preparing the taped flight plan for the computer that directed the Venus-bound spacecraft, really screwed that one up. His mistake was minor, it was insignificant. All he did was to leave out a hyphen in the coded instructions, and the towering Atlas Agena-B moved in the wrong direction, and the Range Safety Officer cursed bitterly, because he had to press that button again, and eighteen million dollars went up in smoke. All because of that hyphen. . . .

A great, sleek jet airliner plunged into the unyielding earth once because a little bolt, only three inches long, had been mounted in improper fashion. But that small bolt jammed a servomotor, and the towering rudder slammed hard over. The silver giant rolled over on her back and rushed into an inverted, suicidal plunge. Do you rate this as a failure of the airplane itself? (*"Yes!" screamed the 114 dead voices.*)

The special room where the capsules were built in the McDonnell plant was the most sterile chamber Keith had ever seen. The average room for surgery in a hospital could never pass the unbelievable requirements for cleanliness enforced by McDonnell in fabricating the different spacecraft. The room was absolutely white, it was sealed, and the air conditioning labored through a labyrinth of filter after filter. No one entered the room without a thorough inspection, or without first donning a surgical smock, white socks, white plastic shoes . . . and even then, he had to look at a spacecraft through protective sheets of clear plastic.

Even fingerprints were potential trouble in this business. The moisture contained in the process of pressing down a finger could cause the slow, insidious rust of a vital part. And with more than seven miles of wiring and 10,000 interrelated parts, you just *know* that the odds are that there will be, somewhere, the finger of trouble.

Gus Grissom went to St. Louis to observe his capsule under construction. Every possible precaution, as always, had been taken with the multi-million-dollar spacecraft. Yet Grissom received a surprise when he tested the reaction-control thrusters.

They had been reversed.

The capsule yawed to the left instead of to the right when he worked the hand controller. It was like crossing the aileron controls in an airplane; the pilot wants to bank to the left, but the airplane banks to the right, and if he's low, he hasn't time to figure out what the hell is wrong before the sudden meeting between the airplane and the ground solves his dilemma for him.

But in the Mercury spacecraft? . . . Sure, it was impossible! But still it happened.

Trouble came from sources no one could imagine. Grissom made a capsule inspection at Cape Canaveral before his flight. Keith tried to imagine the astronaut's reaction when he discovered that the eight-day clock in the spacecraft had *rusted*. It wasn't an experimental piece of equipment. It was the ordinary, reliable, aircraft-type clock which had been produced by the hundreds of thousands, and was in use around the world. Keith had never heard of one that rusted—except for the clock in Grissom's spacecraft.

You couldn't even use normal lubricants within the capsule. If you used oil—well, the fire would be spectacular. The spacecraft in flight has an atmosphere of one hundred percent pure oxygen, and pure oxygen and oil mean instant pyrotechnics.

So you use special lubricants, and you *must* use them with exacting care. For a brief and ugly period in Schirra's mission, there was the chance that they would have to abort the flight and bring Schirra down prematurely. The temperature of his pressure suit kept rising despite all efforts at control, and only because Schirra was so swift and sharp in handling the system was it possible for him to bring down the temperature and wrap up that mission in the classic "textbook flight."

What caused the trouble? There were some red faces about *that* one. In the control system there was a sensitive valve. The checklist called for that valve to have just three drops of lubricant and no more. A zealous technician used something like six to ten drops—*drops,* mind you. But it was enough to contaminate the valve and nearly wreck the intended mission.

Glenn, Carpenter, Schirra, and even Cooper had troubles with their suit temperature controls. Glenn also had to resort to manual thruster control because one of his one-pound yaw thrusters went on the blink. *Why* did that happen?

190

Again it was the case of learning through trial-by-error in the unprecedented environments of weightlessness and flight in orbit, and with all the other new factors to multiply the problems.

Any dirt or debris, any foreign object within a spacecraft is something that can't be tolerated. Before a capsule is mated to the Atlas, it is shaken, inverted, and probed with microscopic care to get rid of any debris. But still the astronauts found washers and other stuff floating freely in their cabins, and this can mean serious trouble—as Glenn discovered. The absence of gravity doesn't change one iota the electromagnetic force fields around equipment and the metal skin of a capsule. These forces eagerly pull in anything that is floating about loosely. The result of this little game is that you can whip up a hell of a short in the electrical systems, or jam a mechanical or flow system. On one test flight, the cabin fan jammed completely because something floated into the mechanism; they had to add a protective screen about it. During Glenn's flight, the floating debris neatly clogged the channels of his capsule's low thrusters. The fix? Just a screen; enough, however, to assure success instead of courting failure.

Carpenter had a few cute ones, Keith remembered only too well. His control system ticked off beautifully in its operation, that is, until the horizon scanners went psycho and triggered an intermittent error in his pitch attitude. He had to abandon automatic stabilization through retrofire and go to manual control. Then a yaw error crept in to screw up his exact attitude, the retros fired late, they *thought* there might have been a very slight loss of retrorocket thrust . . . but what it all added up to was an overshoot of 250 miles in landing.

There didn't seem to be much question that the problem in Pruett's spacecraft lay somewhere in the electrical system. Yet it was this system precisely that had received the greatest scrutiny and umpteenth-time checking. And it was also the electrical system that had put Gordo Cooper to the test of proving what a truly great pilot he was.

When the .05g panel light came on during Cooper's nineteenth orbit, everyone knew that *trouble* had come storming into the mission. The long and short of it was that the activation of that light eliminated part of the automatic re-entry control programming and forced him into manual control for retrofire *and* starting into re-entry. The *why* of that one caught them all by surprise.

Keith had been one of the investigation group. The trouble came in two connectors to an electrical amplifier—the amp cal. The two connectors were located in the amp cal where electrical signals of various spacecraft systems were converted into commands; the commands caused activation of the hydrogen peroxide thrusters in the automatic control system. It was a critical area in the system; it could hardly have been more critical.

They went after the source by examining Cooper's spacecraft with extraordinary and meticulous probing. They knew that the first evidence of failure had been the sudden appearance of the .05g panel light. But just as significant was the fact that, subsequently, there was failure of the AC power from the spacecraft inverter.

They traced the inverter trouble to the electrical power connector which, among other functions, passes the AC output from the inverter buss of the automatic control system into the amp cal. They discovered that the insulating qualities of the connector had failed. This permitted the AC power line to find a ground in the spacecraft and . . . short-circuit.

The inverters were designed *not* to operate in event of such a malfunction in the circuit. When this type of electrical fault occurred, the capsule automatically bypassed the sequence of events that were to take place with the faulty system. The engineers confirmed the working condition of the inverters—on the ground, hooked up to test equipment, they were perfect.

Then they discovered corrosion in and around another electrical connector, through which passed some of the circuitry to the .05g signal light. But where the hell could this corrosion come from?

Moisture.

Moisture? *In space?*

Certainly; why not?

There was a man inside that cabin. A man who drank water—and spilled some of it. A man who perspired, and whose perspiration, like the drinking water, drifted through the cabin in the form of quivering globules.

Several of these fascinating little spheres had drifted

192

about and touched a connection on the electronic box that made up the amp cal. The water globules spread over the equipment and corroded the connection. Very quickly the globules wiped out all automatic controls through much of the retro and re-entry sequences.

Because of a few, lousy, floating drops of water . . .

Few people were aware, Keith recalled, that Cooper had suffered another and equally serious electrical failure. The *Faith 7* spacecraft used five titanium straps to secure the retropack to the heat shield (the other capsules had only three straps). It was normal for the retropack to be jettisoned, after retrofire, in two steps. First a spring-actuated release separated at a point halfway between the retropack connection and the spacecraft connection. Then an explosive bolt fired, cracking free the remaining portion of the strap and the umbilical connections between the retropack and the spacecraft. It was neat, simple, and virtually foolproof.

Ah—*virtually.*

The explosive disconnection of that second step of retropack jettison very neatly failed on Cooper's spacecraft. In fact, only *one* of the five retrostraps exploded free. They checked that one out thoroughly, and they discovered the fault quickly enough. It was the igniter charge in the umbilical. Keith remembered the cool, cutting touch of the official report:

". . . analysis traces the cause of this malfunction to the igniter charge in the umbilical. Four out of five explosive disconnects were all from the same lot, and had been inspected. Four out of five did not have the main charge which would separate the straps and umbilicals. The fifth was from a different lot and functioned perfectly. . . ."

One disgusted engineer had some profane comments to make about "built-in cliff-hangers."

Keith lit a cigarette and—

"George! We have Mercury Seven now." It was Spencer at the Cap Com desk.

But Keith had the sudden germ of an idea. "Spence, talk to him for a while. Get the full status report, and anything he has to give us—*anything,* any ideas—on the failure. I'll be on in a few moments."

He cut the direct connection, stabbed another button. "Johnson? Keith here. Are we set up on that communications relay? Good! It will carry all the way through Zanzibar? Direct communications? *Very* good."

He switched again, this time to Hangar S.

"Scotty? Yes, this is Keith. What? No, never mind that. I want to ask you something, and I'll need a fast answer. We've contact with Seven now. No! Now, hear me out."

He forced his words to come slower, to be clear the first time.

"I want to ask you about the attitude-safety switch. You know, the new safety-interrupt for retrosequence and fire. Let me review it quickly and correct me if I'm wrong. The system is so set up as to block firing of the retros if the capsule fails to hold the proper retrofire attitude. Right?

"Good so far. Now, is it possible that there could be a snarl between the gyro sensors and the safety switch?

"What? No, no! If he brings the capsule to proper attitude, but there is an error in the sensing system, is it possible that the retros won't fire? Even if he holds it right on the nose, the sensors can misinterpret the attitude. Can that happen?" . . .

"It *is* possible?" . . .

"No, hold on for a moment. . . ."

They had installed the safety device after the incident with Carpenter's spacecraft. With incorrect yaw attitude-hold as he fired the retros, *Aurora 7* lost the effectiveness of some of the retrothrust; the force was at an angle to the flight path. So they put in the safety. Gyro sensors would note the exact attitude through pitch and yaw of the capsule. If the attitude wasn't right on the button through these two axes, the sensors would block the electrical current to fire the retros and . . . the retros would not fire.

But what if something were wrong *with the sensors themselves?* What if they weren't functioning properly, or they had jammed the circuit? . . . It *could* be the answer.

"Scotty? Suppose that this is the trouble. No, man, I know we're not certain! But it's the only lead we've had so far. Just suppose that this was it.

"If this is the case, can Pruett check out the sensor system?" . . .

"I know that, Scotty. But if this is the answer, can Pruett get to the system itself, the wiring? Can he bypass the sensors, eliminate the safety switching?"

194

The answer took less than a minute. Scotty was still talking when, with an infinite sadness, Keith cut the line.

It was possible, the engineer admitted. It was possible that this might be one of a hundred things. It was also *possible* for Pruett to get to the wires, but so implausible and impractical as to bring the odds of success to astronomical figures. And even then, it was only one chance in —what? Scotty had said one in a million, and even that might be optimistic.

Scotty was right, Keith knew. It was extremely difficult to get to the wiring system even when the spacecraft was on the ground and rigged up on its inspection stand. The capsule was built with systems piled atop systems in a layer-cake design. You had to remove ten things just to get to one, and you needed help, and everyone concerned had to be a top expert, with the proper tools, and working under excellent conditions.

Pruett was shut within his pressure suit. He was bound through his umbilical cords to his spacecraft. *How* could he operate under these restrictions? And if he lost cabin pressure, the suit would inflate with all the gentleness of a maddened boa constrictor, making it extremely difficult to do any work, let alone clumsily dig his way through rats' nests of wires. Even if he could overcome all these obstacles, would he be sufficiently aware of the details of the system to work on it, to correct the trouble, even to bypass it?

Under those conditions in the spacecraft, and wearing the thick-fingered gloves of the suit?

"Sure, and I can fly to the moon in a canoe," Keith muttered to himself.

He looked up; Spencer was signaling frantically, pointing to the headset speaker and microphone. Keith slipped on the set; Pruett's voice came in loud and clear. Strange, he seemed the only person who was calm. Keith took a deep breath and switched his line to transceive, and broke into the conversation.

"Dick, this is George Keith on the line."

"Greetings, amigo! You got any good words for me?"

"Yes and no, Seven. I—"

"Spill it quick, George; it comes a lot easier that way."

"Roger, Seven. First, we'll be able to keep this hookup for quite a while; we've got ships and planes in position to keep boosting our transmissions all the way to Zanzibar. Be prepared to stay with us on your present frequency."

"Roger."

"All right, Seven. We have not been able to determine the cause of the malfunction. I repeat, nothing we have found gives us any definite information to explain or to eliminate the malfunction of the retros."

Keith paused. There was only static on the radio line.

"Cape Control to Mercury Seven. Do you read, Seven? Over."

Several seconds passed.

"Yeah, Cape. Read you five by. Just took a moment to digest that jolt. It's pretty hopeless, then, isn't it?"

"Negative, Seven. Repeat—*negative*. We—"

"You got an ace up your sleeve, George?"

Keith smiled. "That is affirmative, Dick. This show isn't over yet—not by a long shot. Now, here is what we are going to do."

Instinctively he glanced at the wall clock and the red pointer sweeping away the remaining seconds. The sands of time, he thought. . . .

"We are preparing to launch a Gemini in approximately another fiften orbits. I'll repeat that. We are going to launch Gemini with one pilot aboard in just about twenty-four hours from now, and—"

"You're kidding!"

"Stay with me, Seven. The McDonnell crew has already pulled the unmanned spacecraft from the booster now on the pad, and are completing the mating of the manned spacecraft with the Titan. In fact, it should be—" Spencer was nodding vigorously—"disregard that; mating is completed. Confirming that the Gemini is successfully mated with the Titan, and—"

"But you can't get that thing ready in only twenty-four hours! It's impossible! It—it sounds wonderful, I admit, but you haven't a chance in a thousand of pulling off a stunt like that."

"Cape to Seven. We *can* pull it off, and we are going to be ready for launch in twenty-four hours from—"

"Who's the pilot?"

"Dougherty."

"You can't send him up on this, Keith! It won't work; you haven't got enough time to get everything set. You're

196

only going to kill Jim. He's not ready to handle that ship; it's a two-man job, and you damn well know it. Of all the hare-brained—"

Keith interrupted quickly, and his voice dropped. "Cape to Seven. You are directed to avoid all conversation from this point on except that relating to the rendezvous mission now in the count." He was crisp and cold in his tone, his words cutting. But it was the best way to end the confusion he knew must be swamping Pruett. And the man in the Mercury spacecraft must be ready and waiting for Dougherty in Gemini. . . .

He said a silent prayer. He knew only too well the odds against what they were attemping—were going to attempt. Despite the fact that Pruett was beyond question lost to all help through his own facilities, or those on the ground, many of the NASA engineers and officials were against the emergency step with the Gemini.

Keith had moved quickly and entirely on his own the moment he confirmed the full extent of the problem that had marooned Pruett in orbit. He knew that unless action were precipitated, and at once, the terribly thin chance that they might be able to snatch Pruett from a death that was otherwise inevitable might be lost forever by default. He had called the Gemini project officer—Roger McClarren—then at the Center in Houston. When he ended the call fifteen minutes later, the wheels were already turning.

There might not be the chance to fire the Titan II booster with the new spacecraft. But theirs was a heaven-sent opportunity, and he could do no less than to play it out to the full. The Titan II already stood on its launch ring at Pad Nineteen. Atop the rocket rested an unmanned Gemini spacecraft—the GT-2, for the second orbital test of the two-man capsule.

But there was also at the Cape the first Gemini intended for a manned orbital flight, and it was undergoing a full environmental test in the big chamber in Hangar S. McClarren admitted that there was a chance that they could yank the unmanned capsule from the rocket, and get the other vehicle out to the pad as its replacement.

He also warned Keith that they would have to throw away just about every precaution they had ever built into the system. Keith had responded unkindly; he wasn't interested now in checklists that took days and precautions that were part of any normal operation, because, god-damnit, this *wasn't* a normal operation, but a classic instance of life-or-death riding on the outcome.

And hadn't they learned their lesson *yet?* From its very beginning the engineers had designed the Mercury spacecraft and all its supporting systems on the inevitability of failure. It was almost as if success was something that *could* happen, if the capsule survived the gauntlet of imminent disasters. Well, screw that stuff, Keith thought. Glenn had said it best of all when he stated flatly that at long last they had piped man aboard as the master, instead of the passive passenger, of his spacecraft.

That was the whole philosophy of Gemini: *manned* control, decision by the two people in the spacecraft. Even the abort-system philosophy of Mercury had been tossed out the nearest window; the electronic wizardry of the super-sensitive black boxes simply wasn't needed.

We've gone back to the original concept of the pilot, Keith mused, and thank God for that. The engineers had been astounded when the Gemini astronauts in simulated flight disasters reacted to emergencies and initiated their escape sequence in an average time of just above four-tenths of a second. These boys aren't just good, or great; damnit, they're the *best* that ever walked or flew, and it's about time we threw our complete confidence into what we've been preaching for years. Keith's attitude left no room for doubts.

Dougherty could handle the Gemini; Keith didn't doubt for a moment that the man had the stuff. It wouldn't, of course, be a matter of walking into a successful rendezvous, because there was so little margin for error.

But by all that's holy, he swore, we've been given a chance, *and we're going to take it!*

And as for Pruett, Keith thought . . . well, he wasn't even aware that he had accepted beyond any question that he was committed to dying. It had to come; it was a conviction that would creep stealthily into his mind. It was time to jar Pruett, to bring him around again to full acuity, to get him working *with* the world-wide system, to grasp hungrily for that chance that he could have. And Keith believed he knew just the words to do that.

"Mercury Seven, this is Cape Control."

"Roger . . . yeah, Cape. Go ahead."

Cold, officious: "If you're through trying to meddle in our decisions here, Pruett, we'll start with—"

He reacted. *"Why, you son of a bitch, I—"*

"Watch it, space cadet," Keith interrupted with a broad grin. "You're going to make all the little old ladies in the country turn off their radios."

"I'll—" A sudden peal of laughter, then: "Okay, you win, George. What's on the agenda? Over."

Relief flooded Keith's mind. "Roger, Seven. Prepare to copy. . . ."

Chapter XIII

THE DOCTORS were doing a landslide business with dexadrine and the bottles of pep pills. There was too much to do in too little time, and sleep was a nagging biological necessity that simply must be shunted aside . . . for just a little while longer. Those men who found it possible to drop away from their work did so with catnaps, on benches and on floors behind desks, in cars, anywhere.

The job of preparing a new spacecraft for its mission into orbit once took anywhere from six to ten weeks. But that was Project Mercury. The new Gemini program slashed the time requirements. Gemini used a spacecraft built according to the modular and the plug-in concepts. You didn't stack things into the ship in the layer-cake design as with Mercury. Everything was "plugged in," with receptacles ready and waiting. If a particular electronic unit didn't work, you didn't spend weeks making repairs. You yanked it out, pulled a replacement from the shelf; you took only minutes to connect the replacement to the checkout equipment, and the prepared circuitry did whatever joggling and tracing its electronic components needed, and you found out quickly if the unit was ready to go. If so, the technicians opened the Gemini access doors, carefully slid in the replacement, and hooked it up securely. They ran a fast power check, assured that it tied into the vehicle circuitry, and went on to other business. There would be a final checkout of the Gemini vehicle and its systems and subsystems as a single package, but the point was that you didn't spend all that time. What required weeks in Mercury could be done now in hours which, when you thought about it, was the way it should be—since Gemini was the direct offspring of the original Mercury spacecraft.

Even the booster represented a quantum jump forward in ease, reliability, and speed of checkout time. No more shrieking, supercold liquid oxygen to freeze the plumbing and jam valves, and keep everybody on hair-trigger tension during the loxing. The great Titan II booster is paradoxical in the familiar scene of the Cape Kennedy countdown. It is a greatly subdued scene, for the booster receives its fuel several days before the mission, and the fuel is ready and waiting. So there is no loxing, and no vent-valves operation to worry about, and no chilling of the plumbing lines; there is just a separation of the hypergolic fuel. When it is time to GO, the two combustion chambers at the base of the Titan II receive the flow of dimethylhydrazine and hydrazine and nitrogen tetroxide, and because this is hypergolic fuel—self-igniting—the fire is instantaneous and Titan II is ready to lift almost as quickly as the flame gushes downward. And that means really slicing the fat off the count, and, above all, being ready to commence first motion on the *second*. This is a system intended from the start for split-second scheduling, and the rocket standing a hundred and ten feet tall is the answer to the need for rendezvous maneuvers.

The whole purpose of Gemini is to pave the way for Apollo to its long-range goal of having two men drag their boots through the surface dust of the moon. Gemini is the proving ground for the rendezvous of two or more spaceships in the silence of orbit. It is designed to carry two men, and its bedrock philosophy is that man is a hell of a lot more versatile than we ever believed, and that the crew of two must be an integral part of the machinery and the operation.

And it was just because of this factor that even the men who knew Dick Pruett as well as they did raised grave doubts and objections to the proposal that would send Jim Dougherty into space in the Gemini—*alone*. It's a two-man ship, they insisted, and we have from the very start predicated the success of the operation on each man supporting the other. Their major objections came not in the need for performance *after* orbit was achieved, but in the critical time of the long ascent into orbit.

If something went wrong here . . . it was their opinion that Jim Dougherty wouldn't be able to handle the spacecraft flight controls, to monitor his instruments, coordinate with the ground controllers, *and* be able to blow himself free of the booster should the law of averages bring about that great blossoming eye of flame that every so often claimed the great rockets.

And that would mean *two* men gone. . . .

They argued that the Titan II booster had only been man-rated on the basis of one flight. In March, the booster had kicked an unmanned Gemini—the GT-1 mission—into orbit. The booster now waiting at Pad Nineteen was intended to fire GT-2, the second and final unmanned spacecraft, into orbit for one week. Then, in late 1964, GT-3—the spacecraft which had been in the environmental chamber in Hangar S when Pruett lifted for MA-10—would have been ready to go with Shepard and Masters.

Simply to wipe out all the preliminary and proving steps was to court disaster, they insisted.

They quoted chapter and verse to back up their arguments to Keith. They emphasized the most critical danger points. The McDonnell technicians and the NASA engineers found a common agreement in this area, for a disaster in the rescue attempt could do far more harm than even the loss of Pruett. They pointed to the flight program of the Titan II. If control failure came under the time of maximum aerodynamic pressure during ascent, the aerodynamic instability created by sudden variations in the flight would cause the great booster to tear itself apart within *one second*. There were other problems, they insisted, that were equally critical.

George Keith didn't exactly shrug off their objections, because they were good men, honest in their convictions, and equally as concerned as he for the life of Dick Pruett. But somewhere along the line, Keith realized, you had to take the plunge. You had no choice but to gamble with the intrinsic values the engineers had designed and built into the equipment and the systems. With this behind him, a man could only make the decision to go with what he had.

George Keith believed with full conviction that a failure —even the catastrophe of an exploding booster—didn't signal the demise of one Jim Dougherty. What the hell were all their safety systems for, he muttered angrily to himself, if not to assure the greatest possible chances of survival in the event of just such a failure!

The very nature of the Titan-Gemini system could lead only to Keith's decision to attempt the rendezvous mission. The booster-spacecraft combination represented the shining white hope of many of the Mercury engineers; it was the vindication of their efforts to eliminate past restrictions and built-in errors, and it was rife with redundancy throughout its guidance, autopilot, and hydraulic control systems.

Assume the worst, he ordered himself—what happens then? Well, from his position on the launch pad until he reached a height of seventy thousand feet, Dougherty could blast himself away from an exploding or disintegrating booster by yanking hard on a D-ring in the front of his seat, between his legs. Hauling back on the ring would blow the hatch from his spacecraft, and a powerful rocket would kick the man and his seat far away from the Gemini. Even if Dougherty ejected on the ground, he would be safe. The seat would explode away from Gemini at a rising slant angle, and automatic systems would then snap his body away from the seat and deploy his parachute. The system was no more exotic than the thousands of seat ejection systems in the fighters and bombers flown by every nation in the world, and there *were* thousands of pilots walking around who had escaped from emergencies far more critical than anything Dougherty was likely to get into. Including a pilot named Pruett, Keith noted.

Keith reviewed the ascent flight profile: once the Titan II lifted above seventy thousand feet, it was free of the really dense atmosphere, and it wasn't climbing so fast at this point that it moved into problems of high aerodynamic pressure. The spacecraft drag at this point was reduced so much, in fact, that to escape a booster failure Dougherty had only to hit the switch that would salvo-fire his retro-rockets. The Gemini would rip up and away from the Titan II, and it would do so in a configuration that was aerodynamically stable and that would permit Dougherty to return to the surface by the Gemini landing system. And even if *that* failed, he could always eject with the seat and come down by personal parachute.

At long last, Keith reminded the dissenters, we had reached a point where we had safety systems equal to those enjoyed by the Russians in their Vostoks. Gemini escape provided several times the survival opportunities that a man had with Mercury.

Roger McClarren flew in from Houston, and Keith directed him to spell out the results of the simulated emergency runs that the astronauts had made. It was an illuminating conversation, and it eased the stiffness of the men who had recommended thumbs down on Dougherty's rescue mission.

"We set up every possible simulation of the launch," McClarren explained to the group meeting. "The whole bit —digital computers, full instrumentation, reproduction of sound cues, and so forth. Simulation was as close to the real thing as it's possible to make it, and we've got enough experience behind us to know that our guidelines were accurate. We recorded the pilot's response to each run, as well as getting exhaustive postflight assessments from engineers and the astronauts.

"It became obvious, very quickly, that the most critical malfunctions we were likely to run into were engine failures, or tank pressure losses immediately after liftoff or immediately after staging. Each pilot found that he could detect, very readily, a critical engine failure through redundant cues. He had a sharp decrease in sound level, a decrease in acceleration, and, of course, the warning lights and warning horns. We were getting pilot reaction to emergencies in times that went down to well below a half-second.

"But what really mattered was that the reaction times needed to counter an emergency—to eject, if necessary— never went above the absolute minimum of one second. Most emergencies, because of the nature of hypergolic fuel, ran well over this figure, and gave the pilot more than enough time to handle anything that happened. Some emergency situations that require abort gave the pilot as much as two and a half minutes."

McClarren paused and studied the simulated mission sheets on the table before him. "It's important to stress that except for a very few moments of the entire booster ascent, the pilot in Gemini enjoys the advantages of time in which to make decisions and initiate actions in event of failures. The pilot can live for a while with sensor failures and gradual tank pressure losses, and so forth. The best example I can give you is that of tank pressure losses—these are sensed by redundant transducers driven by redundant power sources and presented on redundant meters. And tank pressure losses involve a decay rate that is relatively slow. We found that the pilot was able to let the pressure graze the structural limit or, if he wanted, he could wait until the pressure dropped to within one psi of the structural margin *before* initiating abort action. . . ."

Keith ordered a special meeting of the project supervisors and key personnel from the small army laboring feverishly to prepare the Titan II and the Gemini for its rescue mission. Dougherty had been going through run after repeated run in the Gemini procedures trainer, for Keith had ordered a minor but extremely important change in the original Gemini launch plans. This time there was . . . well, this was the *first* time, and the flight program for the Gemini was going to be considerably different than the basic mission of rendezvous with an unmanned Agena satellite. Dougherty had already made more than a dozen simulated flights, and the most critical part of those simulations came *not* during the launch phase, but at the tail end of the powered flight.

Keith was, in short, betting Pruett's rescue on the adaptability of Jim Dougherty in manually controlling the final phase of the Titan's upper stage—the instant of engine cutoff—in order to slide as close as possible to the orbital path and position of Mercury Seven.

Thirty-four men assembled in the cafeteria with Keith for the impromptu session. Keith went right to the business at hand.

"We have little enough time as it is," he began, "so we won't waste any of it with preliminaries or talking about things with which we're all familiar. But let it be understood that it is my decision behind the flight with the Gemini. I want you all to know that the Administrator has backed me up one hundred percent, but that I am the one who has recommended that we go for this chance. If I didn't believe that Dougherty had every safety margin going for him, well . . . hell, we wouldn't even be here discussing this.

"However, I want to review with you just what our procedures and our flight plan will be. If there are any objections, comments, criticisms, recommendations—*anything*—for God's sake, let's have it *now*. You may be able to spot something that we've overlooked in the haste with which we've got to move. You may have an idea or two which will help. So break in at any time if you feel you have something important to say. . . ."

That there were definite limitations to Dougherty's capability of monitoring and reacting to emergencies was, despite McClarren's report, only too true. But as Keith pointed out in the discussion that followed, there was a way to overcome this, to back up Dougherty. The truly critical phase of the ascent would end after the first stage was jettisoned and the upper stage of the Titan booster successfully ignited with full thrust. Once this rocket was moving along its intended flight path, the worst of the ascent portion of the mission would be past.

It was during the preceding time that Dougherty would need help, and Keith knew that he would have it. For in the Gemini-Titan system there was a completely redundant or backup guidance setup with automatic and manual switchover. Keith had already ordered the mission profile to lean toward maximum use of automatic equipment, with ground monitoring as a backup, through most of the booster flight. The Malfunction Detection System of Gemini was manual—not automatic—and this was the loophole that might cut away much of the safety margin. But with a Ground Flight Controller right on top of the mission, maintaining constant communications with Dougherty, the astronaut would be prepared, during the few times when critical malfunction was possible, to abort the mission. At all other times, during the remainder of the boosted flight, Dougherty could concentrate on the performance of the vehicle and, above all, upon sliding into the orbital groove with Mercury Seven. Malfunctions which occurred at a slower rate could be monitored by the Ground Flight Controller, with voice communications warnings if something errant showed up on the monitoring panels.

George Keith felt weary. For the moment, and in the hours to come, there was little he could do himself. He would need a clear and sharp mind when Dougherty was committed to flight, and in the hours ensuing. He pushed against the table and his chair scraped the floor as he stood.

"Gentlemen, if I am to be worth anything to any of you in the coming hours, I realize I must get some sleep—even a few hours," he said. "Novak, McClarren, and my immediate staff will take over at this point. They know my decisions, as do all of you." He smiled tiredly. "I'm sure there aren't going to be any major disagreements among you."

Five minutes later, in his small, private office, he was sound asleep on a cot. Sleeping nearby, barely a foot away, was Dr. Michaels; he, too, had realized the absolute necessity of rest while there was time.

John Novak dragged several tables together. He spread flight profile sheets out in front of him. "These are the profiles we have been working out with the Goddard computers," he began. "They've worked out the precise orbital parameters of the Mercury spacecraft at our expected time of launch. They have prepared, as well, for any subsequent times . . . the figures, ah, to allow us to match any changing orbital parameters within the needs of guidance-control of the Titan.

"Now, what we've—"

An engineer broke in. "Excuse me, John, but what's the mission profile? Do we have time for setting Gemini up first in orbit, and then going through the slow-catchup phase?

Novak shook his head. "Can't do that, Harry. We're working much too close as it is. If Dougherty doesn't slide into the groove within the first twelve hours after insertion, he's going to have a dead man in the other spacecraft for company."

The men waited for him to continue.

"We can't use the technique of variable-azimuth launch. It saves fuel, but it's too costly in time.

"There's only one possibility. We've got to be ready to fire the booster for optimum launch. We're working on the basis of liftoff when the phase relationship between the target vehicle and the launch site is optimum. In other words, gentlemen, the mission sequence will be to go directly from the launch phase into the terminal phase. We're going to shoot for a bull's-eye from the opening gun. We *must* do it this way."

"How does the pilot fit into terminal guidance of the booster, John? Keith said that Dougherty would have some control over the second stage."

"Well, not in the sense of *flying* the booster as a pilot. That stretches things just a bit too far for our capabilities at this point.

"We're going to shoot for parallel-azimuth launch, because it doesn't require anything exceptional from the booster. We're going to try to slap the Gemini right into the same orbital groove as Mercury. If anything, we want to get the same perigee as Mercury, but a slightly lower apogee. This allows us to have a built-in catchup rate.

"We want Dougherty to be able to chase the Mercury capsule. What we'll do is try for direct, or immediate, rendezvous, by slinging the Gemini into the same orbit—or close to the same orbit—as Mercury. Both the perigee and the orbital plane will, we *hope,* be identical. Since the apogee is lower, this means a shorter period. Gemini will orbit the earth in slightly less time than Mercury.

"If Dougherty is trailing the Mercury after injection, he is going to be catching up with him. Now, because we've got the maneuverability of Gemini in our favor, Dougherty can add a kick to his spacecraft, or he can thrust in retro-attitude, and drop his apogee. But we don't want to mess with this if at all possible, because of the margin for error. We want the pursuit technique. Charlie?"

"John, how are you going to handle azimuth error? It seems to me that we're counting on too much when we expect the Gemini to slide right into the same orbital plane."

"We're programming—in the event of trouble in azimuth—launch-vehicle guidance in yaw. This is for the second stage of the booster only, of course. We do this by varying the launch azimuth of the spacecraft so that the azimuth becomes an optimum angle directed toward the target's plane. In this way we hope to reduce the out-of-plane distance *prior* to initiation of booster law guidance. This cuts down the work load of the booster in correcting for yaw discrepancies, and gives us the best chance to slide into the same plane—or close enough to get to that immediate rendezvous.

"Goddard tells us that they can track with sufficient accuracy to pick a prime booster cutoff moment. This is where Dougherty comes in. We have already started a tracking and communications vessel on its way, to take up a position between here and Bermuda. It's communications insurance. Goddard will be picking up the track data from the Bermuda radars, and correlating that with the ascent of the Gemini vehicle. The seven-oh-nine-oh computers are fast enough to run a constant prediction for us—they'll be receiving radar tracks of both the target vehicle and the chaser, the Gemini. From this data, they can give us a warning about five seconds ahead of the best moment for cutoff—the moment that places the Gemini as close as possible to Mercury, and in the best condition to effect closing in for the rendezvous. Now, we—"

"But where does Dougherty fit in with the manual control? I still don't see—"

Novak held up his hand. "Bear with me for a moment. The Goddard computers will be getting their track of both the Gemini and the Mercury from Bermuda radar. As you know, the FPS-16 at Bermuda is ten times as sensitive and accurate as the Verlort radars we have at most of the tracking sites. It can separate two targets differing as little as twenty yards in azimuth at a range of a hundred miles.

"Now, if we had plenty of time to fool around—which we don't—we'd go for a slow rendezvous. We'd start with a phase angle of two-seven-zero degrees. We'd launch Gemini—when Pruett was over the South Pacific, and we could spend the next day or two using orbital mechanics to let Gemini catch up. But we don't have that time, and we've got to make up for time with some sharpshooting in the Gemini launch, and then a really good visual close-in by Dougherty.

"We'll count down for a Gemini liftoff when Pruett is over south Texas. Assuming three hundred seconds for Gemini climb to injection, that should put both spacecraft close together near Bermuda at Gemini burnout. And this is where Dougherty comes in.

"The people at Goddard tell us they can utilize the impact-predictor system with their computers to help us in getting immediate rendezvous. The Titan booster has both radio command guidance from the Ground Flight Controller here at the Cape, as well as inertial guidance in case radio command is lost. We will use inertial guidance—with radio command standing by strictly as a backup—

through first-stage burnout and jettison, and successful staging and ignition of the second stage.

"Once we've got the second stage moving out, we switch from inertial to ground command guidance. The ground controller here at the Cape will have a display readout from Goddard of both the Titan, as it climbs, and the Mercury, as the target. He will be able to feed in yaw corrections directly to the autopilot in the booster stage. It will be a sort of continuing correction. We have a little more push to play with than would be normal, because the spacecraft itself is going to be lighter. There's only one man aboard, and we aren't bothering with the consumables that would normally be included. All told, we will use the several seconds extra from this lesser weight by trying to squeeze out greater accuracy from the booster.

"We've had some difficulty in the Titan shots with getting cutoff exactly where and when we've wanted it. We don't know if it's in the engine, but our suspicions lead toward ionization interference from the exhaust gases; they're blocking or distorting the cutoff signal.

"Dougherty will be getting a readout on the onboard computer on his visual display panel. As fast as ground control feeds corrections to the computer on board the spacecraft, the computer issues steering commands. The system is so set up that the ground controller modifies the preprogramming of the computer's flight plan. The computer in turn adapts its new information to the flight plan. Since the autopilot is slaved to the computer, it obeys the changes in command. At the same time, the computer is giving Dougherty a constant readout of the changes.

"Dougherty will be watching that display, and in one of the display panels he will see a retrotime signal come alive. He'll have to be fast; the best we can do is to give him first indication of prime—or optimum—cutoff at five seconds to go. He'll get a warning light and a numeral five on his panel. When the thing reads zero, that's the time to cut the engine, and get his orbital insertion."

Novak rolled a cigar in his mouth and clamped down with his teeth. "I admit we're playing this thing down to the wire. But suppose Dougherty gets some other information that shows him that he's *not* in the prime position for booster cutoff? He's got his onboard radar which will be feeding him distance *and* closure rates to the Mercury. The

Mercury transponder will operate with the Gemini radar—we've checked that one out already—and Dougherty will be getting strong signals. He may even get some good visual cues, although this one is sticky, because we don't have any really good lights with Mercury. In fact," he said unhappily, "we don't have any at all, and visual sighting by solar reflection is hardly anything to go by. We're still playing that one by ear.

"The whole point in this operation is that Dougherty will initiate the cutoff by manual control, and then separate from the booster. *If* he gets some visual indication, and a radar indication, or both, he can either cut the booster engine before the prime moment indicated on the computer panel, or he can extend it one, two, or more seconds.

"And then, being as sharp as he is, he's going to move in as quickly as it's possible to effect rendezvous. If everything works up to this point, we know that Dougherty should have visual contact with Mercury, and he'll try for the close-in on visual maneuvering. Of course, if—"

"Hey, hold on, John! How are you going to gamble closing in by *visual* cues? We haven't any basis for that sort of judgment. That's why we've always planned on the slow catchup procedure. It looks like you're pinning a hell of a lot on Dougherty pulling off the neatest trick of the year!"

Novak smiled. "This time I think we're one jump ahead. Have you seen the reports from the Boeing Company on their space-docking tests?"

"Boeing? Where do they fit into this?"

"We gave the Boeing people a research contract, completely aside from the other work being done on rendezvous and docking. You know—the Martin Company in Baltimore have had a docking simulator for a long time. Ling-Temco in Texas have an elaborate facility, as does McDonnell, and NASA itself in Houston. But we wanted completely independent research and results, and—"

McClarren broke in. "Let me pick up that one, John." Novak nodded and sat back in his chair.

"Boeing's aerospace division," continued McClarren, "has pretty well proved that a complete rendezvous and docking can be done under zero-g with little, if any help, from instruments. We consider these results—confirmed by the other contractors, I might add—as extremely significant. The Boeing people used a simulator floating on compressed air, oh, something like a bastardization of the ALFA simulator. It's free to roll, pitch, and yaw through reaction jets controlled by the pilot.

"The target satellite is suspended by cables from an overhead crane, and it can be moved up and down, sideways, and forward and backward. In the case of Dougherty and Pruett, of course, we're not too concerned with the Mercury capsule wandering off somewhere.

"But the key to the tests was in the spacecraft control by the pilot, especially when he had control through all three axes. Boeing ran eighty-seven complete rendezvous tests with the pilot using the three axes—*and eighty-six of those tests were completely successful.* And when only two axes of control were used—they got a hundred-percent success in forty-six out of fifty-two tries.

"They ran enough tests to get some guidelines on closure rates and fuel expenditure—basing the simulator thrusters on the push from the actual Gemini thrusters. Starting out with a separation distance between the two vehicles of eighty feet, their docking times ranged from fifty to four hundred seconds. And that is for actually snubbing the connectors and getting full docking.

"When you consider that Dougherty isn't going for hard docking—for direct contact between the two ships—the margin for success is enhanced even more. With the soft docking technique, coming alongside, so to speak, but through a three-hundred-sixty-degree circle, we think he's going to be able to hack this job without too much sweat."

"Man, you're sure doing a heap of hoping!"

"Don't you think we know that?" McClarren snapped.

"Yeah, I know, but—"

"You have any better ideas? I *mean* that."

"No."

"Okay, let's get back to work."

Chapter XIV

THEY WERE tired and unshaven, and their interest in the poker they played was desultory at best. The card room in the Press Club of the Cape Colony Inn held perhaps twenty newsmen. In the conference hall building adjoining the motel a skeleton staff of the NASA information office whiled away the time.

Nothing had happened, nothing was happening, but the hard core of the Cape Kennedy press gang wouldn't leave the room. They had a direct line to the NASA conference hall, but *those* poor bastards knew less than anyone else, it seemed. Several men sprawled awkwardly in their sleep in the club chairs, and the dining room kept up a steady flow of coffee to the Press Club. The more realistic of the group had brought along a liberal supply of scotch, and they nursed the dragging hours with drinks and weary profanity.

The telephone rang, the outside line. Bill Nowaslowski of the Dallas *Times* groaned with the effort and lifted the phone to his ear.

"This's Press Club. Whodya want?"

His expression froze and he sat bolt upright in his seat.

The movement was enough to command attention. The poker dealer sat rock still, and the sleepers were rudely shoved awake. Everyone looked at Nowaslowski.

"*Slower,* goddamnit!"

He listened carefully and his mouth worked as he started to speak, but waited.

"Give that to me again—wait, hold it just a second. . . ." Nowaslowski cupped his hand over the speaker and turned to the room. "There's another ship in orbit! Another ship . . . it's up now, in orbit with Pruett!"

Chairs were overturned in the rush to the telephone, and voices rose in a babel.

"Shut up, for chrissakes, so I can hear the rest!"

Instant silence.

"Yeah—go ahead." His eyes opened wide. "It's moving

in? Rendezvous? When?" He came slowly to his feet.

"Yeah, yeah, I've got it. You'll call with anything else, won't you? Yeah, thanks." He replaced the telephone slowly.

"Well, c'mon! What the hell's going on?"

"There's another ship up. Radar reports starting to come in from all over the world. I—I think he said they were getting closer, the two ships, I mean, and that they were talking about a rendezvous . . . a docking, I think."

"Goddamn! I *told* you they were working up at Pad Nineteen. Christ, what a story! I knew, I just knew those bastards down at the NASA office were giving us a line of crap. Hey, Bill. *Bill!* When do they think the Gemini will be able to get close to him?"

"Gemini?"

"Yes, you silly ass! When will the Gemini be able to close in to Pruett?"

"Who said anything about Gemini?"

"But you just—"

"It's a Russian ship. . . ."

Chapter XV

Two events, each separated by distance, and each bound inexorably by the forces of space and time . . .

A land of gently rolling hills and sweeping fields of tall birch and stately fir may be found on the surface of the earth at 47 degrees 22 minutes north latitude and 65 degrees 25 minutes east longitude. Here in this rich land of the farmer is the place called Baikonur. In the midst of the hills and the forests a four-lane highway slashes its naked path. Other roads finger out from the highway, and some of these lead to huge concrete humps that brood in the earth and, when the sun is right on the horizon, bear the mottled shadows of enormous steel towers that jut ponderously into the sky.

On July 25, nearly five days after a man called Richard

J. Pruett departed the planet earth from a tower-studded sandpit on the shores of the Atlantic Ocean, a man deep within one of the concrete humps in the rolling country of Baikonur was chanting the reverse numerology of an elaborate and exhaustive ritual.

At the precise moment that the man in Baikonur approached the emotional climax of his song-talk monotone, Major Pruett lay within the bowels of his small spaceship, placed exactly at 32 degrees north latitude and 48 degrees east longitude. The spacecraft and its faithful clouds of swirling iceflakes rushed silently through vacuum high over Iran. At that moment Major Pruett was some 300 miles east-southwest of Baghdad, 350 miles southwest of Tehran, and moving in a direction just slightly north of east.

It was at this juncture in time that the man in Baikonur toned—

"Tri

"Dva

"Odin . . ."

And cried out—

"NATCHINAI ZHAR!"

At that same instant a bank of relays snapped against waiting connectors. Electrical currents surged through cables and initiated harsh and screaming activity. Eight hundred feet away from where violence erupted, men in the concrete hump peered through optical lenses and electronic eyes and collectively held their breath. They studied the first laboring movement of a great vessel nearly twenty feet thick through its belly and standing more than 200 feet high, a machine ponderous in girth and volcanic in voice. It erupted downward a savage gush of green-red flame; it groaned through its structure and hurled its strength against the earth.

And then it rose in stately and majestic ascent, cracking the flame-seared lash of four giant chambers, combining their strength to howl with two million pounds of fiery thrust. Flame reflected in garish and flickering tones against metal, licked hungrily at the structure of the launch table, and then, seconds later, cried out in a shrieking frustration when it touched only air.

Each and every *second* that the flaming thing roared, each one of its four engines ingested, ignited, flamed, and spat away as exhaust gases more than 2,000 pounds of chemicals. Each and every second the creature consumed nearly 9,000 pounds of propellant and oxidizer, trading this greedy consumption for the favor of speed and steadily increasing height.

High atop the assemblies of metal and fuels, a great spacecraft lay beneath its protecting shroud of heat-resistant ceramic. Buttressed against the steadily increasing hammer blows of tumbling, complaining air and the touch of glowing fingers of friction, Vostok IX bore within its sealed cabin a man who would soon be known to many people other than the select group who knew his background and the many steps leading to this particular, unprecedented assignment. Cosmonaut-Colonel Andrei Yakovlev had begun the critical phase of his ascent upward from the earth, into a mathematically precise balance of gravity, centrifugal force, space, and time—and a rendezvous yet believed impossible by almost all those who thought seriously of the attempt.

Comrade Yakovlev perhaps did not extend his thoughts beyond his immediate orders, beyond the extremely fine maneuvers which he and his spacecraft would be required to execute; but if the eleventh cosmonaut of the U.S.S.R. had taken the trouble to extend his imagination, then he might have smiled to himself and thought of the incredible shock he was soon to impart to many, many Americans. But at the moment, as the hand of acceleration squeezed him deeper into his white plastic contour couch, he functioned in the superb manner of his predecessors, and steadily called off the readings of his instruments.

In sum, they were what they had been in the previous ascents of the Vostoks, and what they were supposed to be now.

"Zarya Odin, Zarya Odin. . . . machina rabotayet kharasho!"

Spring One, Spring One . . . the machine works perfectly!

Of course, Cosmonaut Yakovlev could not see the ashen face nor hear the hysterical curses of the Launch Safety Monitor in his glassed-in cubicle within the blockhouse.

Friedrich Rynin and Vasily S. Borisov, cosmonaut-pilots of Vostoks VII and VIII, the two spacecraft that early in 1964 had completed the first (and still the only) rendezvous-and-docking maneuvers in orbit, sat together at a radio console in the Baikonur blockhouse. Their experience in orbital maneuvers made them unquestionably the choice for the job of Spacecraft Communications Officers for the Vostok IX mission; the two men through surface-vessel and airborne communications links would maintain close running contact with Andrei Yakovlev.

They were also two of the five men in the blockhouse who were aware of the secret modifications to the flight plan of Vostok IX. Which is why they were unperturbed when the Launch Safety Monitor turned white as a ghost several seconds after the great booster rocket lifted from its launch ring.

All Vostok missions were flown along an orbital inclination to the equator of approximately 65 degrees, just as the Americans always flew their Mercury missions at an orbital inclination of 32½ degrees. To climb into orbital-injection position for the standard flight, the Vostok booster lifted vertically, rolled, and then began to pitch over via a curving ascent, on an azimuth, or horizontal bearing from the north, of 48 degrees.

Five unmanned spacecraft, eight manned Vostoks, fourteen unmanned Cosmos satellites, and four maneuverable, unmanned Polyot spacecraft had been launched from this same Baikonur complex, and all had faithfully followed flight along the heading of 48 degrees.

Vostok IX did *not* follow the prescribed path, and the Safety Monitor nearly threw a fit.

Instantly he hit the alarm button. Red light flashed throughout the blockhouse, in the emergency abort hangars, at the medical aid stations. Helicopters with rotors flicking slowly roared with power and shot into the air, starting to follow the anticipated flight line of the booster. All of these men knew nothing alarming about the ascent except that the abort alarm had suddenly—for the first time—clamored.

"Flight Control! Flight Control! The booster is rolling beyond the safety line! Correct! *Correct at once!*"

N. D. Merkulov, Launch Conductor of the Vostok IX mission, sat at his control console. His solid bulk rested with the impassivity of granite as he stared at the flight display readings on the electronic screen before him. The screen showed the great booster rocket continuing to roll.

It had passed the desired azimuth of 48 degrees, and it continued to roll, swinging around more and more. Merkulov did nothing to override the guidance system.

His assistant blanched as the Launch Safety Monitor raised his voice to a higher crescendo: "Correct at once! Correct at once, or I must initiate destruct!"

Merkulov did not move. His assistant leaned forward. "Comrade Merkulov!" he breathed. "Sir—the controls . . . aren't you—?"

He reached out a hand to the control panel, bypassing his superior. Instantly steel-hard fingers clamped about his wrist, sending pain shooting through his arm. His eyes opened wide as Merkulov, still unmoving, barked out: *"Sit down!"*

Behind the Launch Conductor, General P. L. Karpenko stood with arms folded, eyes following every movement, missing nothing. The trace of a smile appeared on his lips.

Friedrich Rynin maintained a running conversation with Cosmonaut Yakovlev in the accelerating spacecraft; Vasily Borisov sat alongside Rynin, methodically checking off items on a list.

In the glassed-in cubicle, the Launch Safety Monitor shuddered as a sob burst from his lips. With a convulsive effort his right hand shot down on the control console before him, snapped a bright red switch down to the position marked *Destruct*.

He closed his eyes and swayed. It had never happened before; they had never aborted a manned flight, they had never had to blow the explosives in the Vostok booster. And now, *now* he had to be *the* one who had triggered the nitro blocks and the primer cords strategically placed by the propellant tanks. Eyes still shut tightly, he implored whatever deities he remembered that the abort system of the spacecraft would bring Comrade Yakovlev safely back to earth.

"Still climbing . . . it's going well, very well . . . acceleration and programming are optimum. . . . We have positive performance all the way. . . . We are optimum condition . . . going very, very well. . . ."

The Launch Safety Monitor snapped open his eyes and stared in disbelief at the loud-speaker. . . . The rocket was *still climbing!* But . . . but . . . it could *not* be! Had he not triggered the destruct switch himself? He stared down in horror at the switch, leaning far over into the *Destruct* position.

He moaned. Abruptly he slammed his open hand violently against the switch. Again! And again! The switch sliced into his palm and blood sprayed on the gleaming console. He brought his hand down once more.

Ivan Vanichev, Baikonur Director, burst into the room. *"Oleg! Stop!"* he shouted.

He rushed forward to grasp the bloody hand of the Launch Safety Monitor. Slowly he brought the man's arm down.

"It is all right, Oleg," Vanichev said softly. "It is all right." He reached out and snapped the control console to its *Off* position.

His assistant looked up, his eyes begging the answer. "We could not tell you before, Oleg," Vanichev began, "that your lines are dead. There is no time to explain more to you now. Here, wrap a handkerchief around your hand. Then come with me."

Vanichev started back for the main control room. "Do not ask any more for the moment, Oleg. In a few minutes you will understand. Just come with me and . . . and watch."

On an exact azimuth of 90 degrees, rocketing upward in the curving line that led due east from Baikonur, the great booster split the stratosphere with its thick contrail and pushed eagerly into the swiftly thinning remnants of atmosphere. The booster continued to bend more and more to the horizontal, and from the four blazing chambers there flowed back a glowing, double-walled plume of ionized gases, spreading and swirling outward in a phantom teardrop a hundred miles across.

"Still going . . . going *very* well. . . ."

"Spring One to East Nine. You are approaching initial BECO. You are coming up on initial cutoff. On my mark, it will be ten seconds remaining to initial BECO. Counting now, ten seconds to go for initial BECO. Four—three—two—one—*MARK*. Counting down for initial BECO . . . at seven—six—five—four—"

Time from liftoff: 136.8 seconds. First-stage booster thrust in near-vacuum now registers 2,400,000 pounds.

"three—two—one—BECO *NOW*."

Time: 137 seconds. An acceleration force of 7.75 g weighs heavily on Andrei Yakovlev. Thrust and acceleration will continue to increase to unacceptable limits. To reduce structural rebound, Engines One and Three plunge into silence.

"East Nine to Spring One. Initial BECO exactly at one three seven. G down from seven seven five peak. Steady acceleration continues. All goes well. All readings are excellent. Over."

"Spring One to East Nine. Excellent, Andrei! Telemetry confirmation is complete. Stand by for final BECO. Stand by for final BECO. On my mark it will be five seconds remaining to . . ."

Time: 160.5 seconds. Engines Two and Four flash into cutoff. Final BECO comes with a mild 5.7 g. At this instant the powerful first-stage booster has consumed 1,303,000 pounds of fuel and oxidizer.

Time: 161 seconds. Explosive bolts fire and sever the connections of the empty booster stage. Simultaneously with the sudden cracking sound of the bolts, four solid-propellant retrorockets attached to the outer skin of Stage One ignite, and burn for exactly one second. The empty booster—75,000 pounds of useless structural weight— drops back from the upper stage.

Time: 162 seconds. Four ullage rockets burning hypergolic fuel at low thrust, attached to the frame of Stage Two, snap out brilliant spears of fire. They will burn for four seconds and impart a low acceleration to Stage Two. The acceleration will assure that the fuel settles properly in the tanks for ignition of the Stage-Two engines.

Time: 165 seconds. One second burning time left for the ullage rockets. A muted shriek resounds in the aft section of Stage Two. In his contour couch within the sloping walls of Vostok IX, Andrei Yakovlev hears the sudden roar of thunder, and grins happily.

"Spring One from East Nine. Staging successful. Ullage rocket burn successful. Stage Two ignition complete. Ignition g is one one four. Acceleration building. All goes well with . . ."

"Confirming sequencing and ignition of Stage Two by TM. Repeat—we have full TM confirmation of all sequencing and ignition. How do you like the view, Andrei?"

"It's wonderful! The mountains are very clear, and the plowed fields stand out as very dark in color. I can see the wheat fields—they are the color of lemons, and very bright in the sun. The forests are a deep smoke-green and the contrast with the wheat fields is very sharp. There are scattered clouds. . . . It is beautiful, incredible. . . . I am getting very bright sunlight through the port. I can feel its warmth even though the suit. The booster is very smooth, very smooth. . . ."

Time: 182 seconds. The two engines of the upper stage burn with a combined thrust of 150,000 pounds. At ignition the stage contains slightly more than 101,000 pounds of fuel and oxidizer. Rate of consumption is 500 pounds per second. Total burning time is programmed for 202.6 seconds. The booster at liftoff weighed 1,510,000 pounds. At ignition of State Two, the stage and payload weight total 131,700 pounds.

Time: 185 seconds. The ceramic heat protector around the forward end of the Vostok IX spacecraft separates from the connecting clamps. Two small solid-propellant rockets fire briefly; the ceramic shield darts upward and sharply to the side, away from the path of the climbing accelerating booster.

"East Nine to Spring One. Confirming jettison of nose shield. The shield departed in sight of the port mirrors. I could see a momentary flash as the rockets fired. The vessel is now clear. Posigrades are armed. Acceleration building slowly. Cabin pressure holding steady at one five exactly. I am very comfortable. . . ."

Corresponding to the terrain that unreeled faster and faster beneath the onrushing booster, the maps of men showed that the border of China was now in the near distance.

"Spring One to East Nine. Coming up on three zero seconds to stage cutoff. On my mark it will be three zero seconds remaining to final cutoff. Starting the count now to mark. Five—four—three—two—one—MARK. Counting down now to cutoff. Counting now at twenty-four—twenty-three . . ."

Time: 368 seconds. The twin-chambered booster leaps into the abrupt silence of cutoff. Yakovlev's body strains against the couch straps. Acceleration at cutoff is a mild 4.95 g, and the sensation of translating from acceleration to weightlessness is pleasant. The cues of separation come clearly—dull thuds as explosive bolts separate the clamp rings, then a surge forward and a muted thunder from the posigrades as Vostok IX slides ahead of the inert machinery of the empty, discarded stage.

"Spring One from East Nine. Everything goes according to plan. Separation sequence from booster completed. Posigrade ignition and cutoff as scheduled. Autopilot has damped out all spacecraft motions. Now stabilized to horizon reference. Cabin pressure, temperature, power readings, fuel are all proper. All goes well. My condition is excellent. Over."

"East Nine from Spring One. Congratulations, Andrei! We have full confirmation of all sequences. Good news—your initial orbital parameters appear good for at least one hundred orbits. We will have refined parameters for you on your first pass. General Karpenko sends you his congratulations and his best wishes. We will have—"

"Spring One. Spring One. You are fading rapidly. Repeat—you are fading rapidly. East Nine is switching to Station Alpha. Switching to Station Alpha. East Nine out.

"East Nine to Station Alpha. Come in, Alpha. . . ."

Vostok IX and its massive transstage rocket assembly joined to the manned spacecraft slide into a precisely calculated and superbly attained elliptical orbit of the earth. Unlike all the previous Soviet spacecraft, Vostok IX is now orbiting the planet along an orbital inclination of 47.3 degrees. There is a reason for this inclination, but it will become clearly evident only after the passage of the near hours to come.

The total weight in the 47.3 degree orbit is 30,400 pounds, easily within the capability of the second-generation booster of the U.S.S.R. manned space program and approximately of the same capability as the Saturn IB the United States has scheduled for launch in late 1965 or early 1966.

The disposition of this weight in the 47.3-degree orbit is extremely critical to the mission as planned by General Karpenko and his staff. The empty—or dry—weight of Vostok IV is 9,800 pounds. Within the spacecraft are a translational thruster system and 2,000 pounds of hypergolic fuel. It is this total weight of 11,800 pounds which will soon come to have full meaning.

The remaining weight is taken up, first, by the 2,000-pound structure of a rocket transstage. The transstage has a single engine of 75,000 pounds thrust, and during its brief period of life (when the moment is at hand) it will consume a total of 12,600 pounds of hypergolic fuel. The working weight of the payload in orbit, then, is 26,400 pounds; the remaining 4,000 pounds are made up by the empty weight of the upper booster-stage rockets, which was summarily discarded upon injection into orbit.

The orbit . . . its significance will appear slowly.

The looping ellipse of the orbit brings Vostok IX down to within 101 statute miles of the earth. At the top of the elliptical swing, the apogee, the spacecraft is well above 260 statute miles. That is unimportant. What matters is that the perigee, or bottom swing of the orbit, is less than one-tenth of a mile within the perigee of the spacecraft called Mercury Seven.

At the moment that Andrei Yakovlev in Vostok IX injects into his orbit, Richard J. Pruett in Mercury Seven is at 27 degrees north latitude and 74 degrees east longitude, over Jodhpur, India, and moving in the direction of east-southeast.

If all goes with the precision which the Russians have so meticulously planned—and which the daring mission requires—Major Pruett is in for a surprise, and Mercury Control is in for a severe shock.

But in the Baikonur blockhouse-flight control room, there is bedlam. General Karpenko and Merkulov roar with the flush of success as the control crews cheer. Karpenko slaps the other man enthusiastically on the back. "Comrade! It is time. Have the call to the Premier put through at once!"

Hundreds of people milled about in the enormous room, talking with animation or extreme care, depending upon their company and their listeners. They were of many nationalities and from many governments, and in the rites of international relations they had come to bear patient witness to the celebration of the latest triumph of the U.S.S.R. The United States and the Soviet governments, after years of negotiations, had agreed on the international airline route to run between Washington and Moscow, with twice-weekly commercial service.

And the Russians made the most of their initial flight. Instead of the huge Tupolev Tu-114 turboprop that everyone expected on the route, a new silver giant roared aloft from Tsushino Airdrome in Moscow. The Ilyushin IL-62, sleek and graceful, with four mighty engines grouped near the tail, carried more than one hundred passengers and the crew of eight to more than 40,000 feet.

Set at its cruising altitude, the sweptwing giant raced for the United States in a flight that swept the attention of the world and shook American aviation circles to the core. Inside the tanks of the new airliner a boron derivative mixed with the kerosene fuel and the engines rammed the Ilyushin through the lower stratosphere with astonishing speed.

Nonstop from Moscow to Washington . . . at an average speed of nearly 700 miles per hour. The Russian passengers beamed with smiles as they waved at the cameramen. Two days later the Ilyushin sped home, and beats its own record. The gala party in Moscow, attended by Khrushchev himself, was to lend proper weight to the occasion.

It was during the party that a straight-faced aide moved to the side of the Soviet Premier and spoke to him in hushed tones. A smile played on the round face, and Khrushchev turned suddenly to leave the room. He was gone for five minutes, and while the hundreds of guests wondered, the Premier listened to a crisply speaking but obviously enthusiastic General Karpenko.

Premier Khrushchev returned to his guests, knowing the unspoken questions that whirled through the minds of those who had seen, or had heard, of his brief absence. He smiled to himself and waited. *Let them puzzle and wonder. The bait is always more the succulent when they must hunger for it.*

For another hour he remained the congenial host. During a moment of conversation with his aide he learned that full confirmation had been received of the orbits. *Ah! Very good! If it continues this way, we shall snatch the cosmonaut from the very jaws of death. And how shall we treat our American friend when we bring him so unexpectedly to earth? Perhaps . . . perhaps it will be most effective if we give him the red carpet tour of the cosmonaut training center. Yes, yes, that would be good! We will have Nikolayev and Valentina as his guides, and we shall make his head swim with all that he sees when—*

"—do you think of that unfortunate fellow—the American? It seems a terrible way for a man to die. And so young! To be marooned in space like that—it is tragic."

The Soviet Premier looked blandly at the man speaking to him. *Ah, yes; from Italy, from that newspaper chain. And—good—newsmen from France, and that little one, from the Japanese news agency. The timing is good.*

"But you are too pessimistic! You talk as though the young American were already dead. It is too early, I think, to be already writing the obituary of that young fellow."

He sipped at his drink. The Italian snatched eagerly at the bait.

"Do you think it possible that he can be saved? There is nothing, really, that they can do to help him!"

The Premier laughed. "You are so sure, are you not!"

"No—no, it is not that, my dear sir. But—" the Italian spread wide his hands and shrugged—"without air, one cannot breathe. And it is only a matter of time before his air is gone. And then—*poof!* his life will go out like a candle."

The Russian leader cocked his head to one side. "Ah, but there are ways of getting more air. There is always hope. You give up on the life of this American too easily, I think."

Look at them—the newsmen are almost trembling, they are trying so hard not to miss a word. Good, good; come even closer, for it is better than my talking loudly.

The Italian belatedly came to his senses. He looked sharply at Khrushchev.

"Do you think it possible that he can be saved?" he asked.

The Premier smiled at him. "All things are possible.

224

And you know that our Vostoks are very big—well, who can tell! We shall have to listen to the news reports. Maybe they will have some interesting things to tell us soon. But, now! There is the designer of our wonderful new airliner. Perhaps he can tell us what are his plans for the future. . . ."

Twenty minutes later, in their respective offices, the newsmen were hurriedly preparing their stories to be cabled to their home offices.

And Khrushchev smiled. . . .

Chapter XVI

Def: TIME HACK *A coordination of timing devices by the personnel of one or more ground reference and command facilities, sometimes with the personnel of an airborne or orbiting vehicle or vehicles; usually made to assure split-second precision timing of separate events at the exact same anticipated moment. Normally this leads to an event at this future instant in time among two or more objects and/or personnel. The activities leading up to the coordinated event are not necessarily related until the future anticipated moment comes to pass.*

Seven hundred miles from Baikonur, Cosmonaut-Colonel Andrei Yakovlev looked down at the town of Panfilov, in the Sinkiang Province of Communist China. Vostok IX hurtled through space, and less than four minutes and 1,100 miles later the Soviet spaceman stared down and to the north at a serpentine line crawling across the surface of the planet—the Great Wall of China.

Fifteen minutes and thirty-one seconds exactly from the moment of liftoff at Baikonur, the spacecraft whipped high over the unsuspecting Chinese garrison burrowed deeply within the tunnel fortresses of Quemoy.

Sixteen minutes . . . The orbital line of Vostok IX sliced neatly along the northern edge of Formosa.

Twenty-six minutes . . . Yakovlev slid across the equator for the first time. The massive spacecraft pushed north of New Guinea, then north of New Zealand.

Sixty-one minutes . . . Swinging northeast, across the west coast of South America. Vostok raced up across Chile, Argentina, and Brazil. Yakovlev studied the massive spread of green on the earth, noted a line of thunderstorms, and watched in wonder as a tiny **v** stood out against the Atlantic, the mark of an ocean-going vessel so far below.

Seventy-five minutes . . . In the radar tracking rooms at the Canary Islands, Mercury network personnel marked charts, changed tape reels, and readjusted their radar and communications equipment. The supersensitive Verlort radar antenna made no move to track the thirteen-ton spacecraft that slipped overhead in silence; the Mercury crews knew nothing of Vostok IX or Andrei Yakovlev.

Thousands of miles from the Canaries, deep within garishly lit rooms burrowed from the solid rock of a Colorado mountain, American and Canadian officers of Headquarters, North American Air Defense Command (NORAD), studied a series of flash radar reports. The SPADATS radar fence system had reported several passes by an unknown vehicle which, from initial reports, was in orbital configuration.

The men were puzzled. The orbit seemed to lie along an inclination of 47.3 degrees. What the devil could it be? Nothing ever sent into orbit by the United States or the Soviet Union had ever made *that* kind of track.

And whatever it was—it was *big*. Bigger than anything ever tracked before.

The Canadian officer turned to an American colonel. "Should we notify NASA? They might be interested in this thing."

"Um, I don't think so. Not yet, anyway. We don't have enough data to firm up any conclusions with meaning to them." The colonel looked at the Canadian officer. "Besides, they've got their hands full right now, anyway."

The Canadian shrugged and scanned the reports. "You're probably right. We'd better not bother them at a time like this. I'm glad *I'm* not in that bloody tin can. . . ." He shuddered.

Seventy-seven minutes . . . Across the Spanish part of the Sahara Desert.

226

Eighty-two minutes . . . Algiers below. Yakovlev wrote carefully in his log, describing a tremendous sandstorm in the distance that blotted out much of the earth and edged over the deep, blue Mediterranean.

Eighty-six minutes . . . Vostok IX hurtled across southeastern Europe, bending in its orbital curve toward the east. In the cities and the towns below, people listened to announcers in different languages giving reports of the hours and minutes of life remaining for the American astronaut marooned in his spacecraft.

Ninety-six minutes . . . The first orbit ended and Yakovlev marked the log with the appropriate entry. The spacecraft moved on, faster and faster at perigee, and raced across the northern rim of the Aral Sea.

". . . Borisov speaking, East Nine. Come in please. Over."

"Hello, Vasily! East Nine reporting to Spring One. Everything is going beautifully. Temperature is comfortable, cabin at one-four-point-six, and I have perfect readings for fuel, power. . . . It is wonderful up here."

"Spring One to East Nine. Greetings to you, Andrei, from Premier Khrushchev, and all your fellow cosmonauts. Tracking has confirmed the accuracy of your orbital parameters. Prepare to copy all details when you contact Alpha. Repeat—prepare to copy all details when you contact Alpha. Over."

"Very good, Spring One."

"East Nine from Spring One. Your schedule calls for you to test the manual control system on this orbit. Do you understand? Over."

"You are very clear, Spring One. I understand. I am to test the manual control system on this orbit. Affirmative. I have just switched on the power system to the transstage. Over."

"East Nine. Very good, Andrei. You will give a complete verbal report into your recorder, and initiate telemetry transmission of the tape to Ocean Vessel Thursday. Over."

Ninety-nine minutes . . . Vostok IX sailed across the edge of China.

One hundred ten minutes . . . Just south of the main body of the Philippines, Yakovlev studied the islands large and small. He noted the dots and V's that marked ships at sea. The cloud cover had become heavier, and seeing was more difficult. The cosmonaut prepared to control his spaceship manually.

Yakovlev scanned his control panel and instruments; he reached out to flick a switch and instantly heard a humming sound from the control mechanism. He looked at a rotating globe five inches in diameter, a gold-black representation of the earth below. A crosshair target presentation and a small circle showed him precisely his position at that moment over the planet; the globe turned slowly, in perfect coordination with the sweep of the heavy spacecraft in its unending fall around the world.

To the right of the globe there was a unique speedometer. Yakovlev studied its figures—not in miles or kilometers per hour, but rather in the numbers of orbits and fractions of orbits already completed by Vostok IX.

He closed the gloved fingers of his right hand over a gleaming black handle. It accepted his fingers and his hand with the same sure grip he had known in his fighter airplanes. No, this was better, for it had been made expressly for him, after he had gripped soft clay, and an impression was made of his hand within his pressure-suit glove. For each finger there was a form-fitting groove and beneath his thumb was a glowing red button.

This was all he needed to control absolutely the attitude of the spaceship. He rested his hand about the control stick and leaned forward for a clearer view of the optical orientation instrument with which he would determine the spacecraft's attitude in relation to the earth. The optical sight was braced securely in a porthole. It consisted of two annular mirror-reflectors, a light-filter, and a latticed glass. The rays traveled from the line of the horizon to strike the first reflector. They passed through the glass of the port, reached the second reflector, and were directed through the latticed glass to the eyes of Yakovlev. When the ship's bearing in relation to its vertical axis was correct, the cosmonaut studied the horizon in the form of a circle in his field of vision.

Through the central part of the porthole Yakovlev saw the part of the earth's surface directly beneath him. He determined the position of the spaceship's longitudinal axis in relation to the direction of flight by watching the "run" of the earth's surface within his field of vision.

He moved the black handle and the spacecraft responded instantly.

Studying the optical lens by the port, he rolled the spacecraft from left to right, then pitched down, continuing through an arc of 360 degrees, snapping the ship to a stop exactly on his original heading. The Vostok was like a thoroughbred, unbelievably sensitive and steady. Then he turned the spacecraft again, keeping the line of the horizon visible in the orientation system. He flew entirely by feel, studying intently the concentric circle of the orientation system, matching his yaw with the plotting on the latticed glass, which served as a chart for his control and orientation.

One hundred eighteen minutes . . . As Yakovlev moved simultaneously through yaw and pitch axes in his control tests, Vostok IX eased south of New Guinea, running to the southwest. The spaceship crossed over Cape York Peninsula, Australia. For a period of seconds it slipped within the arc of effective range of the Mercury network tracking station at Woomera, then ran along the northeastern coast of Australia. The NASA technician in the Woomera station stared at his scope. "I would have *sworn* I had a positive target," he complained to a friend.

"Ahh, you're just getting blips on your eyeballs. Go get some coffee."

One hundred twenty-eight minutes . . . Yakovlev began a slow, spiraling motion of his spacecraft. The ship crossed the northern part of New Zealand. Directly ahead lay the southernmost part of the Pacific orbital track.

One hundred thirty-two minutes . . . Well satisfied, even delighted, with the sensational response of his machine, Yakovlev spoke steadily into the tape recorder in his cabin, and switched the telemetry transmitter to *Standby*.

One hundred forty-seven minutes . . . In its northeast run across the Pacific Ocean, the spaceship passed north of Woomera. Mercury Seven, unknown to its pilot, had begun to parallel the Vostok orbit, but the American capsule moved far to the northwest, sliding up for a pass across the Panama Canal area.

One hundred fifty-three minutes . . . Below stretched the Peruvian coast; Yakovlev shook his head at the thick cloud cover extending far out to sea.

One hundred fifty-seven minutes . . . Vostok IX crossed

the equator over northern Brazil and swung northeast over the Atlantic.

One hundred seventy-five minutes . . . Porto, Portugal.

One hundred seventy-six minutes . . . Across northern Spain. Yakovlev completed another entry in his log, after cross-checking the navigation globe with reference to constellations. Everything moved with extraordinary precision.

One hundred seventy-seven minutes . . . The rush into France.

One hundred eighty-five minutes . . . The German border passed; Vostok bends eastward in its orbit before commencing the swing to the southeast.

One hundred eighty-eight minutes . . . Caspian Sea.

One hundred eighty-nine minutes . . . Iran.

One hundred ninety-one minutes . . . Pakistan.

One hundred ninety-three minutes . . . White-streaked, stark and mighty, the Himalayas loomed upward from swirling beds of gray storm clouds.

One hundred ninety-four minutes . . . Moving southeast, toward the northeast coastline of India. At this moment the Mercury spacecraft has begun to slide across the earth at a slight angle to the Vostok orbit; the path is more easterly, but roughly parallel to that of Vostok. The Mercury spacecraft will make its pass directly beneath the southern tip of India.

One hundred ninety-six minutes . . . Bay of Bengal.

Two hundred five minutes . . . Over Derby on the northern coast of Australia. Vostok pushed over the Woomera tracking station. Tracking personnel, having received a flash alert from NORAD headquarters, were ready and waiting. The orbital paths of both spacecraft—(there is no longer any question that there is now a second satellite orbiting the earth)—crossed directly over Woomera.

"Got 'em! Clean as a whistle on the scope!" shouted the radar operator. *"No transponder, but look at the goddam bounce from that thing. What the hell is up there—?"*

Two hundred seven minutes . . . The word flashed out from the Woomera station with charged excitement. Men in Cape Control in Florida jumped to their feet; the Goddard center in Maryland came alive with sudden, intense activity. Even as the telephone in the White House rang, the Woomera Cap Com broke into his planned message exchange with the pilot of Mercury Seven.

"Woomera Cap Com to Seven. I think you've got some company up there with you. Disregard previous request. We have celestial coordinates for you to try to visually sight the bogey. Radar has definite confirmation of second spacecraft now parallel to your orbit—"

"Stand by one, Woomera. Still powering up from chimp mode. Just hang on. . . ."

Pruett had begun to bring Mercury Seven out of drifting flight. It was necessary to freeze and then release the gyros. He realigned them by looking through his window for earth reference, switched to fly-by-wire low, and received a close alignment with them and the horizon scanners. It took two tries to get everything set with accuracy. One time he discovered an error in yaw, but referred immediately to a bright star to come around to his proper heading.

He moved swiftly and expertly. His first step had been to cage and uncage the gyros in minus 34 degrees in pitch attitude, and dead-center on target with roll and yaw. Then he pitched up to an indicated attitude of plus 34 degrees, simultaneously holding the spacecraft at zero degrees in roll and yaw attitudes, and again locked and freed the gyros.

Finally he linked the gyros by slaving them to the horizon infrared scanners, wrapping up the job with his gyro alignment exactly as required. He had a bad moment when one of the twenty-four-pound thrusters inadvertently kicked in, but he snapped in corrective action and dampened out the abrupt movement.

"Okay, Woomera, let's have the rest of it. . . ."

He listened carefully. "Roger, Woomera. I'm on ASCS and holding in re-entry attitude. Think I'll feed in some roll for better positioning. There, that's got it . . . back to autopilot mode. . . ."

The seconds ticked away. Pruett could not actually sight the other spacecraft. He pulled open the latch to his equipment locker, withdrew a pair of Bushnell binoculars, small but powerful. The glasses were 6 X 25 power with a field of 11.0 degrees; if there were something out there reflecting the sun, he should be able to see it moving against the star field. He checked the coordinates once again, pushed up his helmet faceplate, and . . ."

231

"I've got him!" Excitement rang in his voice. "I can see the whatever-it-is clearly against the star field. Who . . . *what* is out there? I thought Gemini wouldn't be ready to go for a couple more hours. . . . Has Cape informed you of the Gemini flight? Over."

"Negative, Seven. Woomera Cap Com repeats negative on Gemini flight as yet. Can you see any details? Over."

"No. It seems . . . it looks *big*, whatever it is. Any ideas? Over."

"Mercury Seven, you're fading rapidly. Repeat your last transmission, please. Over."

Silence.

"Mercury Seven from Woomera Cap Com. Do you read? Over."

Static.

"Seven from Woomera. Do you read? Do you—?"

Crackling static; silence.

"We've lost him. Next station will have to pick him up. Hey, Fats! Get that report of his visual sighting and the radar plots to Cape Control *at once!*"

Two hundred fifteen minutes . . . Woomera radar has lost contact with the unknown spacecraft.

Two hundred sixteen minutes . . . The reaction began to set in. During direct contact with Woomera, and even as he studied the unknown through the binoculars, Pruett's mind had ticked away with automatic efficiency. But suddenly the tremendous impact of what was happening slammed home, jolting his senses, seeping through him like a cold shock pushing and sliding to every nerve. Without conscious thought his gloved hand released its grip on the binoculars; he did not even see them floating, tumbling in a slow and lazy end-over-end motion in mid-air before his eyes.

There's only one answer. . . . Of course! The Russians have put one up! I'll be damned. . . . That can only mean they're going to try a rescue and that . . . that . . .

"Well—whaddya' know!" he shouted in an outburst of joy to himself. "Maybe that final curtain won't come down, not yet, not yet anyway. But . . ." His voice and spoken self-conversation died out and his thoughts whirled. *But how can they shift over? How can they?* . . . He thought furiously of orbital mechanics, of the sudden possibilities, and even as hope flamed, he forced himself to temper his leaping enthusiasm at life with the realization that almost impossible odds still had to be overcome. *And maybe, space cadet, you're just grabbing at dreams, you're just hoping and praying that a rescue has been stacked into these cards. . . .*

Two hundred nineteen minutes . . . The small group of men rose to their feet as the President entered. He waved a hand casually. "Sit down, sit down."

He took his own seat and glanced quickly at each man. "We'll dispense with the formalities and get right down to business. From what Marvin has already told me by phone, we're in a serious mess with this one." He turned to Marvin Phillips, the official from NASA. "How do we stand now?"

"Sir, there's no change with Astronaut Pruett. Our original calculations are still the same. The, ah, probable time for re-entry . . . and the time when his oxygen runs out—" The NASA man shook his head in frustration. "We can't do a thing to extend his time—his time for oxygen, that is. And we've done everything possible to try to find that fault in the spacecraft, whatever it is, but . . ."

"Are they still trying?"

"Yes, sir, and they'll stay with it until they do drag it out."

The President raised his eyebrows.

"That is, sir, *if* it's possible to find it."

The President scanned a report in front of him. He leaned back and gestured with a pencil.

"Short and sweet, Marvin, what are the chances with the Gemini?"

"I think we're better than fifty-fifty."

"That's all?"

"Yes. As you said, Mr. President, short and sweet. It's all new. We haven't written off the premature cutoff with the upper stage and some other problems. But Cape thinks we've got a better chance than even I do."

"Well, that's a good sign. I—no, wait just a moment, Marvin." The President turned to the other side of the table, looking at the Assistant Secretary of Defense. "Moore, is there anything further on the Russian?"

"Yes, sir, there is. I've just received another track from SPADATS, and the pattern becomes very significant. We've

233

been feeding to Goddard, and we've alerted all their world-wide stations. Also, we—"

"Let's cut through the details of the routine, Moore!" The President gestured impatiently and reached for the tracking plot. He looked up suddenly. "What are the conclusions?"

"Sir, they're going to try to pick up our man."

"When?"

"We believe the attempt will come in a few more hours."

"Umm. Now, Marvin, I'd like your judgment on another question."

"Yes, sir."

"What are the odds for the Reds to pull this off?"

The NASA Administrator looked unhappy. "Better than they are for us, Mr. President. *Much* better. Their ship is *already* up there. They've got experience at this sort of thing. They've never translated fifteen degrees or more to another plane, but it's a matter of push, and there isn't any question but that they have a transstage up there for the attempt." He rubbed his hand against his jaw and said glumly, "I think they're going to do it. I don't like it, but that's the way it looks."

The President clasped his fingers together and leaned forward, scanning their faces. "Any other new developments?"

"Yes, sir." It was Thomason from State. "We've had word that Khrushchev is playing footsie with the newsmen at the reception now going on in Moscow."

"Go on."

"Well, it's difficult to pin these things down, but he chided an Italian reporter for accepting Pruett's d— ah, loss—as inevitable. He definitely hinted that something was in the works. We checked back. Khrushchev received a telephone call and left the main room at just about the time we estimate the Russian spacecraft was confirmed as in orbit. We believe it all fits."

"Well . . . but nothing official has come in from them?"

"No, sir."

The President looked around the table. "Well, gentlemen, obviously the question is whether we invoke the Pact and ask for help."

The men seated at the table with him fidgeted uncomfortably. "By God, but I hope we don't have to do that!"

ried the NASA Administrator. "At the same time, I—the devil of it is, Mr. President, that this might be our only chance to save Pruett and—" He hesitated.

"Yes, go ahead," the President urged.

"Well, sir, the Pact we signed last year specifies mutual assistance and cooperation, as you know, in many areas. That includes astronaut recovery and rescue. But they haven't released a word yet about their new shot. We absolutely believe they will attempt to shift orbits, but we don't *know*. And even if they do, there's no guarantee that they can pull it off.

"But the big sweat is whether, no matter how much is at stake—and I know Dick Pruett very well, Mr. President—we're justified in asking the Russians for help until, first, they do shift orbits, and, second, we *know* that they're in a position to have a chance at success. Bad as this is now—and it's going to be—if we ask them for help, it's going to break all over the world. And if—"

"I know only too well about that *if*," interrupted the President. "If we go begging for help and they do not shift over to the Mercury orbit, we not only lose the first man in space anyway, but we also end up with our national prestige in sorry state. That's about it?"

"Yes, sir," nodded the NASA Administrator, visibly unhappy.

The President addressed the group. "Gentlemen, I think you're all aware of the tremendous implications. Aside from our immediate concern for the life of that man, we cannot ignore the picture as it will be presented to the world. So I want us to have some line of procedure to follow. Now, hear me out on this carefully.

"First—we shall continue to do everything possible toward discovering and correcting the failure in the capsule." He looked at the NASA official, who reaffirmed his statement.

"All right, then," the President went on, "the second thing is that we are going to go all the way with the Gemini. I assume that no matter what happens, the backup, ah—"

"James Dougherty, sir."

"Thank you. . . . Dougherty will have every chance for his own survival, if we should prove too premature in risking his life with the Titan booster at this time. That is the other horn of this dilemma, gentlemen. We're on the edge of losing one man, and we're risking the life of a second man. If it should turn out that we lose both lives, the consequences will be . . ."

He drummed his fingers on the table. "And yet, if we *don't* try to save Pruett, that will be even worse. Much worse, in fact. It's not so bad to be damned for failing, but it is inexcusable not to try.

"So we're committed, then, in this area, at least. We will go with the Gemini. Marvin, I want all your people to know through a statement from me that I am fully aware of their effort to get Gemini off the ground in time. . . . I want, ah, something told to them as soon as possible."

"Yes, sir, we'll take care of that immediately."

"Good. Now . . . Pruett isn't married—*that* helps, even if only a little, but, ah, what about his parents?" He looked toward the end of the table at the Air Force Chief of Staff. "General?"

"There's little we can do for them, sir, as you know. We do not want to make this a visible move if at all possible. The base chaplain from Suffolk, the airbase on the island, sir, is already at the Pruett home.

"But there is—well . . . We have moved in another area, Mr. President. We have had our aircraft make contact with every Soviet trawler, tracking vessel, and anything else that's tied in to their electronic network. We are confirmed on their direct tie-in to their new ship. We have contacted them, and officially requested that they be alert for a call for assistance from us. You see, sir, there are several storms in the possible recovery areas, just in case we do get those retros back to life. The storms will make it extremely difficult for the world-wide rescue service to move in quickly, *if* we get a break with the Mercury. I know it's not much, Mr. President, but it's the *only* area of movement we have."

The President moved aside the papers before him. "That's the only way we can play it, then. We know where we're going with the Gemini—and that is strictly playing it by ear. Oh, yes, Marvin, if the Russian does move in next to the Mercury and he looks good for a pickup, are you still planning the Gemini launch?"

"Yes, sir. We've no choice. The Russian could be sitting on top of him and still not be able to carry out the transfer between the two spacecraft. No matter what happens, short of an actual rescue, of course, we will go with the mission."

"All right, gentlemen. You will keep me informed, day or night, of any major change in the picture, good or bad. You will be prepared to adapt to any situation. And I also want you all to keep your fingers on the public pulse. If we come out of this with a black eye, we can undo years of bringing people around. That can mean an uproar that no representative on the Hill would dare to ignore, and we could well wake up one morning and find the entire space program crumbling around us. There's really no way to tell.

"I want statements going out to the people. I want them to *know* we're doing everything possible to—well, you know the rest.

"That's it, then. Thank you for coming here so quickly."

They rose to their feet as the President turned and walked toward the door.

He stopped suddenly, and turned again to look at them.

"There *is* one more thing that might help our friend up in space."

They looked blankly at him.

"We could also try prayer. It might well be all that we have left."

Two hundred thirty-two minutes . . . The military Space Direction and Tracking System (SPADATS) net and NASA's SPASUR Space Surveillance Net have confirmed radio frequencies of the unknown spacecraft as voice transmissions on 20.006 MC and 143.625 MC, plus an intermittent "signal" transmitter at 19.948 MC. These are frequencies used often by the U.S.S.R. for its manned spacecraft. The Goddard computers have ingested tracking data reports and extrapolated in reverse, pinpointing the exact geographic coordinates and the moment of launch.

Orders have gone out from Cape Control to tracking stations around the world, and technicians have been working feverishly. The standard Minitrack Telemetry frequency is 136-137 MC. These receivers could not be used for the mystery—i.e., unidentified Russian—spacecraft. But the directional antennas usually used with these receivers have been hurriedly patched into the R-220 receivers for reception at either 20.006 or 143.625, on FM or AM, or in some cases, patched into the R-390 receivers for 19.948 MC on AM only. Signals from the spacecraft picked up on these receivers are being recorded on half-inch magnetic tape, using FR-100 or FR-600 recorders.

Technicians manning the stations have been making attempts to use the directional antennas for orbital path plots, and succeeding. The directional antennas have given excellent azimuth and elevation reports of the spacecraft, but not its range.

A steady stream of data have been transmitted to the Goddard computers.

Two hundred forty-one minutes . . . Vostok IX has rushed northeast, moved along a path taking it south of Central America and west of South America. Mercury Seven has swung well to the north, positioned west-north-west of the Russian spacecraft and due south of California.

Two hundred forty-three minutes . . . American reporters in Moscow have received uncounted shrugs of official Russian shoulders, complete with blank expressions and the repetitive monotone that, "We know nothing of any Soviet spacecraft in orbit."

No one believed them. The truth was, strangely, that they did *not* know, because General Karpenko had ordered a strict blackout on any public news about Vostok IX or Andrei Yakovlev.

Colonel Harrison R. Townsend, Information Officer for NORAD, North American Air Defense Command, had been shouting into telephones. He interrupted another shrill ring almost as quickly as it started, listened for only a moment.

"No!" he shouted again. "I tell you that NORAD does not and *cannot,* by DOD order, give out any information on tracking. *No!* I'm sorry, but those are our orders. All information must come from NASA in Washington.

"What? How the hell do I know?

"Mister, I can't help it if they insist they don't know anything about a Russian spaceship that's orbiting right now. *Officially,* we don't know a damn thing either!"

He slammed down the phone, cursing as he pinched a finger against his desk.

In the Cape Colony Inn, Tom Stinson wrote furiously

on a lined pad. "Yes, yes, I've got it so far. Okay, go ahead. . . ."

He continued to listen and to write as Desmond Barnes looked over his shoulder. The call was from the NASA office in Washington; reading the latest report rushed to his desk, the President had done little to conceal his growing anger with the situation. He concealed it even less when he personally called the NASA office in the capital and demanded to know why NASA had not announced the countdown under way at Pad Nineteen for the Gemini. He had cut his call short, but the inference was as plain as flaming letters each ten feet high. Get out the news about Gemini—*at once*.

NASA was releasing a statement from Washington within ten minutes. The press centers on Cape Kennedy and at the NASA information office in the Cape Colony Inn would be like an exploding ammunition dump if release wasn't made simultaneously to that group. As quickly as Stinson finished writing, a secretary started to click away on a mimeograph form, and two men stood by to rush the form into a reproducing machine for immediate copies.

Eighty newsmen and women stood behind a long white table in the conference room, murmuring like a colony of bees about to swarm.

Two hundred forty-eight minutes . . . Vostok IX's orbital path brought the spacecraft just south of the Panama Canal.

Two hundred fifty-one minutes . . . Puerto Rico lay to the east of Vostok IX as it rushed along in a northeast direction.

Two hundred sixty-five minutes . . . Pamela Dougherty dropped a tray of dishes and cups. For a long moment the breaking china rattled on the floor as her hand flew to her mouth and she gasped. She rushed to the radio and turned up the volume:

". . . —*etin has just been released by the national space agency. Astronaut James Dougherty, backup space pilot to Richard Pruett, at this moment marooned in his small spacecraft in orbit, will soon attempt a dramatic rescue of his friend. NASA revealed that within minutes of the failure of the retrorockets aboard Mercury Seven, an*

239

all-out attempt to prepare a Titan booster rocket with the new Gemini spacecraft was begun. Time is running out for Major Pruett, and Dougherty has only a slim chance to accomplish what would be the most sensational mercy mission in history. The launching is expected in less than twenty-four hours. If the tremendous odds can be overcome, then James Dougherty will bring Major Pruett back to earth inside the two-man Gemini spaceship. Rumors are still flying thick and fast about that mysterious giant spaceship that went into orbit only a few hours ago. There is no question but that . . ."

She sagged weakly against a wall. Jim was going to— But the Gemini wouldn't be ready for months! He had told her so himself; he had shouted angrily about the program delays and . . . and now he was going to ride that thing after Dick, and . . .

"Mother of God," she whispered, *"it's too soon, too soon, it's all coming so suddenly—"*

The telephone rang shrilly. She jerked upright, startled by the sudden sound. She started across the room when a screech of tires and brakes sounded almost outside her door.

The telephone kept ringing. She hurried over and picked it up. "Hello?"

"Mrs. Dougherty? This is the Houston *Times* press desk. Have you—? Good, then you've heard the news flash. We think it's terrific news, and it will make a wonderful story, you know, how one friend is risking his life to try and save his best buddy, and we want to ask you—"

There was a pounding at the front door and the doorbell rang steadily.

"I'm sorry, Mr. ah—oh, I didn't get your name. Please hold on. My doorbell, and . . . just hold on for a moment!"

"But, Mrs. Dougherty, you don't understand. We have a deadline and we want a statement and . . ."

A whisper of hysteria drifted into her mind.

She rushed to the door and pulled it open—and something savage exploded in her eyes. A shriek burst from her lips as she flung an arm before her face.

"What-what is it?"

"We'd like a statement from you about your husband and—"

A face with glasses pushed closer, loomed over her. "What do you think of your husband's chances, huh? Are you worried that he'll be——?"

A microphone smacked against her cheek. "Tell us what you think about the daring rescue, Mrs. Dougherty! Just say anything at all into the mike. Anything at all will do fine! How well do you know Pruett? Was he——"

They surged in through the door with flashing, eye-stabbing cameras, with microphones and pads; they shouted at her and jostled and pushed. She jumped frantically when a voice shouted at her from behind, a hand grabbed her shoulder, and she heard a woman's voice and turned to see a wide-eyed creature, and: "——Benson; Lorrie Benson, y'know, from the Woman's Page? We'd like you to tell all the girls about how famous your husbin' suddenly is, y'now? And——"

The flashes of light made her cringe. She gasped as a man leaped suddenly to her living room table, sweeping off the vase and ashtrays as he tried for a higher shot, to look down over the heads of the mob that had exploded into the house.

"Thassa girl! Just look up here, baby!"

The light stabbed again. She heard herself moan.

There were hands and the lights and voices shouting and yelling and she saw two men standing on the couch, waving cameras at her. Somehow she pushed her way through the mob; they poured around and after her like water being sucked into sand. She made it to the door and stopped short, mouth agape.

A huge truck had driven onto her lawn, and there were people all over the truck with huge television cameras, and a flashing red sign slammed into her eyes—YOUR FRIENDLY HOME TV STATION!—and an enormous lens suddenly swooped down toward her, and there were more cars coming, and people trampling through the flowers and——

Arms flailing, she made it back inside the house, and suddenly she knew she was screaming at them to get out, and they grinned and: *Get a shot of her, quick, you jerk! Man, talk about human interest, oh baby, get her when her eyes are shut and she screams again, whooee, what a picture!*

There was someone next to her, and she huddled against

241

the man's shoulder; *thank God, maybe he can get them out of here!* It was their neighbor, fury on his face; he had seen the near-assault into the house. He'd snatched up a shotgun and come running. But he couldn't get into the front door. Over the shouting he'd heard Pam scream, and he and his wife came through the back door and he bulled his way into the living room and next to the wide-eyed, white-faced woman.

"*Out!*" he roared. "Get out of here! Get out of here now!"

"F'r chrissakes, Mac, we got a story to—"

"Who the hell is he?"

"Getoutatheway, you're blocking the cameras!"

He lifted the shotgun and pointed it at the ceiling over their heads and pulled the trigger. The sound in the room was staggering, a tremendous blast of thunder. White plaster and dust spilled down onto the mob, and they drew back. He leveled the gun directly at them, and while his wife drew the sobbing woman away into the bedroom, he said very quietly that he would empty the other barrel straight at them. When they were gone and the truck had left its deep ruts in the lawn, he came back and looked at the wreckage of the room and sadly shook his head.

He opened the bedroom door. His wife was holding Pam in her arms. Grimly he closed the door and slipped a shell into the empty chamber, and sat down to wait as a one-man unwelcoming committee. . . .

Roger McClarren silently handed a wire story from the teletype machine to George Keith. The Mercury Control Mission Director quickly scanned the page, and angrily crumpled the paper into a ball.

"Those stupid bastards! We don't even *know* if we can get that thing off the ground in time, and they're already turning it into the biggest—Ah, *shit!* Forget it, Mac, we've got work to do."

Two hundred seventy minutes . . . Vostok IX crossed the French coast at Normandy, moving east.

Two hundred seventy-four minutes . . . Over central Europe.

Two hundred seventy-six minutes . . . The Black Sea below.

242

Two hundred eighty-three minutes . . . Persian Gulf.

Two hundred eighty-five minutes . . . Moving southeast, over the Arabian Sea.

Two hundred eighty-eight minutes . . . Vostok crossed the equator south of Ceylon. Mercury Seven is directly southwest of Vostok; orbits start to converge as they move rapidly toward Australia. It is the fourth orbit for Vostok IX.

General Karpenko, Vanichev, and Merkulov listened to the representative from Tass, who had just spoken to his office in Moscow. The four men burst into laughter. Merkulov gasped for breath and roared. *"They—they are going to send up an inv—an invalid to rescue a cripple!"* He howled and leaned on Vanichev for support.

Two hundred ninety-five minutes . . . Muchea radar in Australia reported an extremely clear pickup of the mysterious Russian spacecraft. Based on the radar echo and previous optical trackings, plus computer evaluations of orbital parameter changes from the known apogee and perigee, scientists at the Goddard center in Maryland concluded that the Russian craft must be at least forty to fifty feet in length, and that it weighed somewhere between 24,000 and 30,000 pounds.

Three hundred one minutes . . . Russian ship has been fading on Muchea radar.

Three hundred three minutes . . . Muchea radar scopes have lost the mystery spaceship.

Three hundred eight minutes . . . Woomera radar lost the "bogey" as it swung south of New Zealand, curving into an east heading before beginning the orbital run to the northeast.

"George, this is Halliday at Goddard. I—"

"Can it wait, Phil? We're running out of time here, and—"

"No, it can't wait. We thought you should have our consensus of opinion right away. I'm sure that your own suspicions will lead to the same conclusions, but we couldn't afford not to call direct."

"Go ahead, Phil."

"The long and short of it, George, is that we are con-

243

vinced the Russians are about to make their play. Forget the processes of our conclusions, but there seems little question that the Bolshies have put up a regular Vostok along with a transstage of some sort or another.

"We've let the computers run ahead with orbital extrapolations. We're convinced that unless they—wait, let me back up a moment. Based on the weight of the manned vehicle, they have enough fuel in the weight remaining to effect a change in the line of nodes. We're convinced that they are going to make a planc change and try to come out of it on the Mercury plane, and—"

"When?"

A moment's hesitation.

"When, Phil!"

"On the pass coming up."

"That's less than thirty minutes from now!"

"I know. That's why this couldn't wait any longer."

"Phil . . . um, how sure are you of this?"

"Sure? Hell, George, we aren't *sure* of anything! But those people have got to operate within the framework of the same physical laws that we do. And the pass over the Cape that's coming up now simply works out to the most efficient point in space and time to effect the plane transfer. They won't have this opportunity again for a while and . . ."

"Go ahead!"

"Well, Pruett's time is running so short now . . . and everything points to their shooting the works on this pass. . . . George?"

"Yes. I'm still here."

"George, it's our opinion that they are going to attempt a rescue. We think it would be wise if you passed this on to Pruett at once."

"Damn! And we're so close ourselves. The count is right on the button, Phil. But—we can't tell Pruett *not* to cooperate with the Russians! Jesus Christ, they're the ones who have experience at this, not *us.* . . . Phil, put someone on this line and keep it open. I'll do the same here. . ."

Keith spun on his heel. "Novak! Mac—and you, too, Blake. Over here by my desk—hurry."

Three hundred thirteen minutes . . . Vostok IX has

passed the tip of New Zealand. It rushes over the planet to the northeast.

Three hundred sixteen minutes . . . "East Nine to Ocean Vessel *Lenin*. You are coming in very clear. My condition is excellent and the spacecraft is functioning perfectly. I am ready now to begin the checklist countdown for the transfer maneuver. Repeat—ready for the checklist countdown for the transfer maneuver. Estimate transfer in twenty-seven minutes. Over."

"*Lenin* to East Nine. Very good, Comrade! We are ready for the checklist. Transstage pressure switch to . . ."

Three hundred twenty-two minutes . . . ". . . and this station has learned exclusively from its reporters at Cape Kennedy and in other vital space centers that the Russian ship now rushing through space is definitely carrying at least one and perhaps two cosmonauts. They may even be the same men who performed the sensational rendezvous and docking maneuver in space earlier this year.

"There seems to be no question but that the Russian spaceman, or spacemen, are going to try an amazing rescue of our own astronaut. Major Richard J. Pruett, who has been marooned in orbit for the last several days, now is nearing the end of his oxygen supply. If nothing happens in his favor, and quickly, then Pruett is a goner. The Russians seem to be ready to pull off the greatest rescue in history, and with the whole world watching and listening, success in this venture would do more than to bring Dick Pruett back to us, alive and sound. It will be the greatest coup the world has ever known, and a staggering demonstration of the superiority of Russian space science.

"As far as this reporter is concerned—and I'm sure you all share my opinion—I don't care who's winning the space race. Nothing is more important now than the life of a wonderful American, Astronaut Richard J. . . ."

Three hundred thirty-five minutes . . . Vostok IX is west of Panama, over the Pacific. Mercury Seven at this moment is almost due west of the Russian spacecraft. On a plotting board showing the present orbits and positions, drawing the orbital lines ahead in space and time, it is clear that the two spaceships will come very close together during their pass over Cape Kennedy. Vostok IX begins its run directly over Guatemala and Yucatán, moving northeast.

". . . and I say that's a lotta crap!" He slammed the beer can angrily onto the bar. "You don't think we'd let them lousy Russians just move in like that—" he snapped his fingers—"and pick up our boy, do you? Well?"

"What the hell do you expect them to do? Let the poor bastard die up there, when the Russians maybe can save him?"

"And *who* sez anything about him going to kick off, huh?"

"Whaddya talking about, Jake! The guy is running out of oxygen *right now*. The Russians don't pull him in like a fish, into their ship, he's a goner."

"*Bull*shit. Why, they probably give this Pruett orders not to have anything to do with them creepy Reds up there. You know what? You're a stupid jerk, *that's* what. Whaddya think we're gonna look like if we can't save our own boy, huh? If we let them lousy Commies move in, and they snatch the guy into their own ship, that means they take him back to Russia, to Moscow—right?"

"How the hell do I know?"

"That's just it, y'jerk! *You* don't know *nuttin'!*" He shoved a hairy paw into his friend's chest. "Let me tell you, *let me tell you,* chum, they ever get our boy back inside Commie land, they'll probably pull off all his clothes, stick 'im in a big cage, and parade the poor bastard up and down Bolshevik Square, or whatever the hell they call that place they make their parades." He waved an arm wildly. "Up and down, up and down, naked as a goddam jaybird, while the Commies all crowd around and make jokes about the poor slob.

"Nahhh . . . let me tell you, Jake, we're too smart for them Red creeps. That Pruett, he ain't goin' nowhere except wit' one of our own guys. Why, we'd rather have him *dead,* the poor bastard, than be dragged back to Moscow and get his naked ass froze in that cage they got waiting for him!"

"How come you're so sure they got this cage, and all?"

"Christ on a pogo stick, but you're a dumb one! Didn't I just explain the whole thing to ya?"

Three hundred thirty-nine minutes . . . Cape Kennedy radar picks up the Russian spacecraft. Empty coffee containers litter the tables, and the ashtrays overflow with crumpled butts.

Three hundred forty minutes . . . Andrei Yakovlev glances down at the edge of Cuba. *There is America, only seconds away. Soon we shall see* . . .

Three hundred forty-one minutes . . . Vostok IX reaches the southwestern coast of Florida. It starts a run over the Okefenokee Swamp.

The enormous area is hushed. There are thousands of people, of every description, standing crowded into the huge structure. The waiting room of Grand Central Station has been transformed. It is almost like a cathedral.

They stand in a great mass throughout the high-roofed room. They stand on the marble stairs leading to the upper levels and Vanderbilt Avenue. They stand in the entranceways to the train platforms, they are crowded onto the space where a new car is on exhibit, and they sit and stand on the shiny metal without knowing or caring that they do so. The newstands are still and they do no business, for the men behind the racks of papers and magazines, like everyone else in that vast space, are staring at a great screen, staring at a picture that is shadowy and that could be clearer.

They stand and they look at the face of the man who is uppermost in their thoughts. They look at the helmet and the face within the helmet and at the silvery spacesuit. They are looking at a scene flashed to an electronic station on the Pacific coast, and transmitted instantly to the great screen. Beneath the picture of the man named Pruett glowing letters slide silently from left to right, a continuing series of bulletins on the grim drama being played in the unimaginable vacuum so far above them.

They see his lips move, and each in his own way finds identification with the man whose face is on that screen. None of these people knows him, and yet, strangely, each feels, with full conviction, that he does.

A woman, young and attractive, holding a small child by the hand, is the first. Standing in a small space, uncaring about those about her, she kneels. The floor is hard and it is cold, but it does not matter. She kneels, and she bows her head, while the child stares at her in wonder.

A man watches her. His lips are pressed tightly together, almost white. He removes his hat, and then, too, kneels.

A porter holds his red cap in his hands and moves to one knee.

A man in an expensive suit kneels alongside him.

A small group stands with heads bowed.

A hundred . . . then six hundred . . . and a thousand, and hundreds more, and still more—pray.

A distant rumble of thunder moves beneath them as a subway train groans into life.

No one hears it.

Three hundred forty-two minutes . . . Vostok IX passes the east coast of Florida, just south of Cape Kennedy.

"Well, the pattern is getting clear now. See those tracks?"

Two intersecting lines, two glowing dots on a screen in Mercury Control.

"You can just about see it happening. The Russian *must* make his move any moment now. Their ship is only several minutes ahead of Pruett. . . . If they're going to play the game, now's the time for it."

Three hundred forty-two minutes forty-five seconds . . .

The mission control crew in the great room at Baikonur is silent. The men are frozen into their seats or where they stand. All eyes are turned to a large sweep-second hand.

General Karpenko murmurs, "Fifteen more seconds . . ." His voice is a whisper; he does not realize he is counting aloud. "Fourteen—thirteen—twelve . . ."

Three hundred forty-two minutes fifty-six seconds . . .

"Bermuda radar has a definite return on the Russian ship. . . ."

Three hundred forty-three minutes . . .

Andrei Yakovlev watches the numbers flashing in reverse in his instrument panel timer. At *three* he tenses; at *two* he holds his breath; at *one* his hand starts to move; at *zero* he makes the move for which he has waited these 343 minutes.

248

The spacecraft communicator aboard Ocean Vessel Lenin, *working swiftly as Cosmonaut-Colonel Andrei Yakovlev rushed overhead in Vostok IX, checked off several dozen items on the countdown list for the critical plane-change maneuver. As the huge ship plunged with increasing speed toward the Atlantic to the east of the Cape Kennedy missile site, Yakovlev ended his communications and once again rechecked the countdown list.*

Right fist gripping the black handle, he nudged the spacecraft about until the Vostok pointed along a new heading. The blunt nose of the ship now was locked to an azimuth of exactly 130 degrees. In effect, he was flying sideways, as much as 83.2 degrees from the angle at which his vessel had sliced across the equator.

The proper heading assured, he locked in the autopilot for his yaw mode. The electronic brain would now hold the new heading, while he continued the remaining steps and preparations. Again the gleaming black handle moved beneath his skilled hand. Open ports in the nose of Vostok spat exhaust gases into vacuum and the gases changed instantly to swirls of glowing iceflakes that drifted away from the ship. He overshot; the nose of the spacecraft dipped seven degrees lower than the setting he desired. More carefully now, he brought the nose up until it hung several degrees below the horizontal plane reference of the earth. Quickly he activated the autopilot mode for pitch, effectively slaving the yaw and pitch axes of his spaceship to the electronic brain and its attitude sensors. From this point on Yakovlev would function as a human backup to automatic control; he would interfere with the robot sequences only in the event of any discrepancy.

With minutes to go, he scanned the instrument panel once again. The igniters for the ullage rockets were at their proper temperature and were alive and armed. Transstage temperatures were exactly on point. Transstage tanks were pressurized and ready for operation. Combustion chamber lines had been flushed and triple-checked for freedom of fuel flow and ignition of the hypergolic fuel. Battery power registered exactly as required on the ammeter dials. His cabin pressure held at 14.9 pounds per square inch. Temperature, humidity, oxygen percentage, inert gases . . . everything was exactly as it should be.

He had checked his spacecraft clock with Ocean Vessel Lenin, and activated the backup firing timer as well. The timer would explode the spacecraft transstage into life; if it failed to do so, he personally would hit the manual ignition switch.

His eyes flicked over the controls and gauges. He made a minute adjustment to the master control for the ullage rockets, and readjusted the timer for the transstage engine. The ullages would burn for four seconds; one second exactly before they cut out, the big transstage engine with its 75,000 pounds thrust would roar into life.

The minutes fled; seconds remained. Aloud, he counted the fleeing of time. A red light gleamed brightly and his lips moved:

"Dye'syat
"Dye'vyat
"Vo'syem
"Syem
"Shyest
"Pyat
"Chyety'rye . . ."
More red lights snapped on. . . .
"Tri
"Dva
"Odin!"

He was ready and waiting; Yakovlev snapped the switch hard over to the left. He heard a low sound, almost like the whisper of very distant thunder. Far behind two ullage rockets flared, nudging the transstage and the Vostok gently ahead. The mild acceleration pulled the hypergolic fuel back in its tanks to settle properly and assure smooth feed to the engine. Three seconds after the ullages fired, a tremendous blossom of flame erupted behind the Russian spacecraft.

A huge fist slammed against Yakovlev. From near-weightlessness of the ullages he was crashed violently to an acceleration force of 2.88g; his body weight shot painfully to nearly 500 pounds. A crashing waterfall pounded against his ears; he smiled with the sound of the big transstage engine. He tasted salt; surprised, he licked his lips with his tongue, and discovered that in the sudden onset of the acceleration he had bitten deeply enough to draw a trickle of blood.

Pushed back into his couch, he kept his left hand ready to snap down against a button that would cut off the transstage engine. His right fist gripped the black control handle, and his thumb was ready to hit the glowing red button on the handle to switch over instantly from automatic to manual control. In front of him seconds flickered and snapped into and out of sight on the transstage engine timer, counting backward. When the time moved through a total of exactly 50.5 seconds, the engine should cut off. If it did not, he knew that he could hit the manual cutoff within two- to four-tenths of a second longer, an error completely acceptable to his mission.

The automatic pilot functioned with perfection itself, holding the spacecraft exactly on its programmed levels of pitch, yaw, and roll. He noticed the fuel flow needles flicker as the electronic brain fired the thrusters to compensate for the changing mass of his spacecraft, for its acceleration and the changing center of gravity as the fuel gushed through the thundering combustion chamber far behind him.

Everything now must happen within exacting requirements of celestial and orbital mechanics. The Vostok must sustain the precise azimuth and pitch, with any rolling tendencies immediately damped out. As it maintained these axes of control, the spacecraft must be provided a total velocity change of 6,500 feet per second. The latter performance must come, of course, from the transstage engine.

The engine ingested its hypergolic fuel with a consumption of 250 pounds per second. If everything functioned exactly as planned, the engine would shut itself down after two things were accomplished—the burning of just over 12,500 pounds of fuel, within the allotted time period of 50.5 seconds. At that moment the acceleration gauge would show a reading of not quite five and a half times normal earth surface gravity.

The clock came around to 50.5 seconds; the reverse

timer flicked to zero; the accelerometer nudged a reading of 5.43 g . . . and Yakovlev was abruptly hurled back into total weightlessness.

His body trembled from the rapid onset and decrease of forces. He sucked in deeply of air and blinked his eyes. His finger flicked toward him. Once again he felt and heard the cues of activity: popping sounds as explosive bolts cracked free the connections of his spacecraft to the now empty transstage; then, a crackling roar from four small posigrade rockets that pushed the Vostok away from the useless shell behind him. Quickly he stabbed down with his thumb to regain manual control, pitching up and bringing in roll so that he could visually follow the receding transstage. He counted to himself.

Eight seconds later he watched a small blossom of flame appear along the shell of the empty rocket. The transstage moved rapidly away, sliding off at an angle that would take it well clear of his own path—and that of the American, he reminded himself—in the coming orbits.

The radarman breathed slowly. Almost in awe he whispered, "Did you see that change? Good God, he's DONE IT! He's shifted completely to the Mercury plane . . . and he's right on the button!"

The antenna of the FPS-16 radar on Bermuda scanned the black heavens. The invisible beams flashed out and back with the speed of light and . . .

"We're getting a split on the scope! That's right, that's right. . . . We can get separation between twenty and thirty yards. What? It must be the empty booster shell; it's cutting off at an angle. No, no. From the way it looks here, it won't go into a separate orbit; not really. It should swing out at a hell of a tangent, though.

"Yeah, Goddard should be giving Cape Control the news on both of them. Wait a moment—we're picking up a couple more on the scope. The return is weak on those. It must be the interfacing clamps. Probably separated by explosive bolts or springs. Just some small junk. Yeah— affirmative on that, too. They're moving out pretty well from the main target.

"I'll say he is! From first indication, he's as clean on the Mercury track as though we put him up ourself. That must be one hell of a piece of machinery that guy has. . . ."

The electronic monitoring officer in the nuclear submarine was rock-still as he studied the instruments before him. On the submarine's rounded deck banks of antennas turned slowly, following with their electronic senses the flaming life high above the ocean. Slowly but surely he began to smile, and the officers watching *him* felt the tension easing, and they were quick to share the changing mood. The instruments ceased their steady movement and the recordographs ended their curving lines, continuing their inked path without a quiver.

The electronic officer removed the earphones from his head and visibly relaxed his body. He looked up at the captain.

"It is done. He has carried out every step with perfection. Send the short-wave signal code to Moscow at once. I am sure they will be most interested to—"

Alarm bells clanged painfully in the enclosed space. The electronic officer winced; the captain snapped around.

"Unidentified radar target. Approaching rapidly, approaching rapidly. Aircraft is in a dive, closing in rapidly."

A loud-speaker coughed. "Bridge to captain. Two aircraft in sight, approaching rapidly from the west. Both very low, from two-eight-zero degrees."

The captain laughed. He turned to the electronic officer who was his unaccustomed passenger in the submarine. "You will excuse my sudden reaction, Colonel," he said. He lifted an arm. "It is just that our instinct forces us to respond in such a manner. There is no need for concern; they are American planes. It is a little game of hide-and-seek that we play often."

He stepped to a bulkhead transmitter and leaned forward. "Captain to bridge."

"Sir?"

"How close are the American aircraft?"

"Range about one mile, sir. They have slowed down and are starting to come overhead. They are banking steeply; I can see the pilots."

"Good, good! Just don't stand there staring at them. Smile, wave at them, or something. . . ."

"Yes, *sir!*"

Laughter from the bridge. "Captain, they're not waving back. . . ."

At the moment of separation from the transstage, Vostok IX was in its new orbit. The weight of the spacecraft had been reduced to just under 12,000 pounds, and the ship was now in its final, "clean" working configuration.

Vostok IX and Mercury Seven orbited the earth along exactly the same inclination to the equator. The spectacular shift of the Russian spacecraft had blended and modified the forces acting upon it until it cut across the equator at 32.5 degrees, almost as if—as the radarman noted—it had been launched from the same Pad Fourteen that spawned the Mercury vehicle.

Once again the Vostok had moved closer to that planned goal of a convergence in space and time. The Russian vessel dipped in its perigee to within 101 statute miles of the earth's surface, almost exactly the same as Mercury Seven. But its apogee was *not* the same; in fact, it represented a major difference. Mercury Seven soared in its looping fall around the earth to a height of 177 miles. Vostok sailed much higher—nearly 130 miles above the apogee of the American spaceship.

This is exactly what the Russians planned. As Vostok IX slices over Cape Kennedy it is 127 miles above the earth, also well above the altitude at which Mercury Seven would pass over the Cape.

The stage, however, has been set with exquisite planning for a coming rendezvous. The movement of the two spacecraft toward one another is now a matter of orbital mechanics. The Russians have adhered to physical laws with splendid accuracy, and now they are prepared to have those laws work in their interest.

The factor of time has been shaped and modified to suit the purposes of the mission of Vostok IX. For all practical purposes—including the computation of the positions of the two spacecraft, and the growing chance for survival of the American still marooned in orbit—the clocks have been stopped, turned back to zero, and started anew.

The time hack of Vostok IX and Mercury Seven began at the instant that the Russian spaceship slipped into the Mercury orbital path. Whatever happens now will be related to that particular instant; whatever happened before is academic. Prior to moving into the Mercury orbit, Andrei Yakovlev could never have accomplished his planned rendezvous with the American capsule. At the moment of

254

insertion into the new orbit—the result of the plane change —he starts to move through space in such a manner that, following certain steps, the rendezvous is almost inevitable.

In the sprawling enclosure of Mercury Control at Cape Kennedy, in the semi-buried control room at Baikonur, and aboard Vostok IX and Mercury Seven, even the computation of time must change.

The period of each orbit, the time to circle the earth, must be judged while using the earth as a base reference. This is the earth-based orbit, which considers both the surface of the earth and the vital fact that this surface is rotating at a specific speed.

Thus the earth-based orbit requires exactly 93.78 minutes for Mercury Seven—this is the time it needs to swing about the planet, as computed by an observer on the surface of the globe.

Vostok IX, however, soars to a greater distance from the earth at its apogee than does the American spacecraft. Andrei Yakovlev, then, will spend exactly 95.78 minutes to complete his global passage.

The discrepancy in time is quite deliberate. . . .

Yakovlev pushes his finger against a button and watches the sweep hand of a chronometer begin to turn. He glances at the dial showing this total time from the moment of liftoff at Baikonur. The timer shows a total of 346 minutes. The second chronometer, just activated, began its movement from a reading of zero. From this point on the cosmonaut is interested only in the new reading, for it is his time-bridge to the American.

Exactly four minutes after Yakovlev starts the new timer, Vostok IX passes over the island of Bermuda. The height of the Russian spaceship is 101 miles.

Exactly six minutes after Yakovlev pushes the new timer, Mercury Seven passes over Bermuda. The height of the American spaceship is almost exactly 101 miles.

The two ships are separated in time by 120 seconds. The two minutes may also be expressed as the distance traveled in this time—almost 600 miles.

If the Soviets have prepared their blend of orbital mechanics with exacting thoroughness, the next swing around the earth will eliminate the difference of two minutes in their passage over the same point on the ground.

They rush away from Bermuda. Very rapidly the Russian and the American spacecraft begin to widen the distance between them. Vostok IX moves with greater speed and it pulls ahead of Mercury Seven.

Twenty minutes after the new time hack, the two spacecraft are high over Central Africa.

Approximately sixty minutes after the time hack, Australia is below. The two ships are far apart as Vostok IX loops more than 300 miles above the American tracking stations.

Andrei Yakovlev bides his time. Instinctively he scans his instruments. Everything is in readiness.

The cosmonaut looks down at the Pacific. A great storm has squatted over thousands of square miles, and he is awed by the sight of lightning among the upper clouds, a sight incredibly similar to anti-aircraft shells flaring in the distance. Then he has no more time for sight-seeing. He will be coming up on the Pacific tracking vessel, and he must report and, of course, receive any final instructions relayed from Baikonur.

The two spaceships plunge around the world. The inexorable laws of calculated orbital flight now begin to show their effect. On the tracking display in Cape Control, the effect is visible in the glowing dots that represent the American and the Soviet machines.

They near the end of the first *new* orbit. Both ships pass about one hundred miles south of Guaymas, Mexico.

Vostok IX has been rushing earthward along a different angle and with greater speed and acceleration as it swoops down from its higher apogee. South of Guaymas the Russian craft is slightly ahead of and above Mercury Seven.

Then his geographical coordinates lie between White Sands, New Mexico and Cape Kennedy. Once again Andrei Yakovlev is at a critical moment in his mission, and once again he prepares to modify the forces that sustain him in orbit.

They are beyond White Sands. . . . Mercury Seven races up to, matches the position of Vostok IX, and then moves ahead, passing the Russian.

"Seven to Eglin Cap Com. Okay, you're coming in five by. Can I see him? He's clear as a bell. I can make out the

256

details of the ship with straight eyeballs. Stand by. . . . I want to get the binocs on him.

"Christ, that thing is *big!* I can see the tail annulus clearly. He looks like he's about a mile away and—"

"You're close. Radar shows separation just under two thousand yards. What's happening with your friend up there?"

"Hard to tell. Nothing at the— *Damn!*"

"Dick? *What happened?*"

"Whooee . . . almost like a physical blow. That *hurt*. It's—"

"Are you all right, Dick?"

"Roger. No sweat. Our friend just turned on the house lights, that's all. I had the glasses on him when a line of lights, very, very brilliant, went on. It's a flashing arc light —Jesus, but they're *bright!*—a blue-white in color. They're going on and off very rapidly. That thing looks like something for opening night. There are four lights, apparently, and their on-off sequence is staggered. You can tell the boys to quit worrying about being able to see another ship up here when it's lit up. Over."

"Roger, Seven. You're starting to fade. Switch over to Cape Control. Eglin Cap Com out."

"Cape Cap Com, this is Mercury Seven. Over."

"Roger, Seven! Loud and clear. Over."

"Hello, Spence. I've still got my friend about a mile away. No change since the report on the lights to Eglin. No—hold it. I can see something reflected in the lights. It looks like—I'm sure of it; he's using his thrusters. They show up almost as a spray of flashing particles in those lights. He's changing attitude, now. There . . . he's pitched down and he's starting to come around in yaw.

"Same distance, it seems like. But he's stopped the attitude change. The lights are different now. He's . . . he seems to be pointing with his nose directly at me. The lights form a band right around the ship from this angle. It looks like he's getting ready to do something. . . . There go the thrusters again. Short bursts. Looks like he's trying to hold a new attitude.

"Wish to hell I could talk to that guy. From where I'm sitting, I like his company. . . ."

As the American spacecraft slides ahead, Yakovlev

works with extreme care to align his ship. For his attitude settings, he uses the normal references of his gyro instruments and visual scanning of the earth's horizon, as well as the infrared horizon scanners of the Vostok. There is, finally, the American machine itself—the single most important reference for this maneuver.

When Yakovlev completes his preparations, the Mercury capsule is at a greater distance, and still drifting away.

It is here and now—at this point in space and moment in time—that Yakovlev brings the Vostok's translational engine into play. This is his source of power for eliminating the discrepancies in time and apogee remaining between Vostok and Mercury.

He moves the black control handle to bring the spaceship around quickly to retrofire attitude. The engine points in the direction of flight. He studies the onboard computer, adjusts two control dials. He must reduce, *now,* his forward velocity by 150 feet per second.

The timer clicks; violet-green flame explodes silently in vacuum.

When the two spacecraft again pass over Bermuda, they are one right behind the other, Indian file.

On the radar scopes the two machines are only 1,600 yards apart.

Andrei Yakovlev has brought Vostok IX to a point where it leads the American machine. He sights visually on the small capsule. His right hand is firm about the grooved control handle and he makes steady, correcting attitude changes. With his left hand he moves a ridged bar forward and back. Each time he does so the flame erupts from the translational engine, and his velocity changes—slightly, very slightly.

Vostok IX is pushed and nudged like a wallowing creature of the sea, closer and closer to the Mercury spacecraft.

At a distance of 200 yards, Yakovlev switches to low-thrust power for his maneuvering rocket system.

He is prepared now to "creep in." He estimates that he will close the distance completely to the waiting American in only ten or fifteen minutes.

Flame stabs back from the Russian spaceship. . . .

Chapter XVIII

"CANARY CAP COM FROM MERCURY SEVEN. OVER."

"Roger, Seven. This is Canary. Cape Control says disregard on status report. Do you have anything different with Ivan? Over."

"Negative. He appears to be at the same distance, or maybe down to a hundred and fifty yards or so. The lights are still flashing, but even without them he's as big as a barn out there. And just as clear, also.

"I can see him thrusting. He's operating in short bursts with his maneuver engine and his attitude thrusters. He's playing it very cautious. No long bursts. Seems like he's taking his time and no chances. I don't mind telling you people that he looks very comforting out there. Seven over."

"Roger, Seven. Cape is asking for your oxygen supply at the present moment. Over."

"I knew you guys would turn to something unpleasant. It is not good. I estimate that there is remaining a maximum of six hours' oxygen. I repeat—estimate no more than six hours' oxygen remaining. Seven over."

"Understand, Seven. Six hours' oxygen remaining at the outside. We—"

"Canary, do you have Cape on direct tie-in? Over."

"That is affirmative, Seven."

"Then tell them for me that if they're going to do anything with Gemini, they'd better shake it a bit. I don't know how long this character is going to stick around up here. It's obvious he'll be knocking on my door pretty soon. And I'm ready to welcome the guy with wide-open arms. Over."

"Roger, Seven. Will pass your message to Cape Control. You're starting to fade out, Seven. Recommend you key in to Kano Cap Com. You should pick them up in just a few minutes. Over."

"Okay, Canary. Switching now. Seven out."

Andrei Yakovlev snaps out bursts from his maneuvering engine. The Russian is methodical. He takes no chances. He knows he cannot overshoot the American machine, for he may not have fuel sufficient to carry out any major corrections. The Mercury spacecraft is revealed clearly throught his viewport.

Yakovlev glances at the glowing miniature globe on his instrument panel. The small circle in the center of the crossing lines is moving up on the east coast of Africa. Yakovlev frowns.

He is behind his schedule for moving in close to the American spacecraft, to the point where he can begin the actual rescue operation. He glances at the second white plastic couch alongside his own, with the emergency oxygen hose and its connector carefully modified to fit the tri-lock adapter of the Mercury pressure suit.

He turns his head to study the onboard radar display.

He stares at the gleaming red numbers in their separate windows, and his eyes blink.

The figures in the three small windows stare back at him. They read *126*.

This should not be! He stares again at the glowing numbers and shakes his head slowly.

He has *lost* more than thirty meters in his closure maneuvers!

Something is wrong, *very* wrong. Even as he studies the radar indicator that shows his distance in yards from the American, the numbers flip again and the windows read *133*.

There can be only one answer. As the two spacecraft swing around the planet, Vostok still retains a slight superiority in perigee velocity. Now, pushing around the globe and soaring up toward apogee, the machines are naturally beginning to drift away from one another. And Vostok, Yakovlev knows, will continue to slide away from the target.

The American machine has a lower apogee; thus it will be moving faster through this part of the orbit. But once they are over Australia, both spacecraft will have reached their highest altitude. From that moment on, as the machines swoop down toward the earth's surface, Yakovlev knows also that he will begin again to close the distance between himself and the American. The Russian spacecraft will regain its advantage in speed, and with its increasing velocity it will push in closer to the other ship.

But what will be the separation? It is impossible for him to compute so complicated a series of events! It may be that he will reach an excessive distance, too far for the precise rendezvous maneuver.

Over the Indian Ocean, Andrei Yakovlev engages in a detailed conversation with the Russian tracking-communications vessel. The tracking radar will determine the separation between the two machines and will be able to work quickly on the problem.

Yakovlev is angry when he rushes past communications range. The tracking staff could not so quickly provide him with the information he needs; the shipboard computer needs more time to digest the raw tracking data. Yakovlev is instructed to contact Ocean Vessel *Ormsk* after he passes Australia. The Indian Ocean ship will contact the global communications center in Russia itself. There will be plenty of time for the reply to reach the *Ormsk* and the answer to be relayed to the spacecraft as it comes within range of the Pacific tracking vessel.

Yakovlev dismisses the matter from his mind until he can establish such contact. There is work to do in the meantime.

He glances at the radar display, and curses. The glowing numbers read *261*. He is still drifting away from the American machine. It is of little importance right now. He can see the small spacecraft with the naked eye. And the American cosmonaut, he knows, has no difficulty at all in seeing the big Vostok.

Yakovlev rolls Vostok IX and feeds in a yaw maneuver, then stops the spacecraft and switches to autopilot mode to hold his attitude. He leans forward and moves a small control. Now he has bypassed the circuit breaker of the arc lights on the exterior of his ship and transferred control of the lights to a telegraph key. Depressing the key to its contact position will flash the lights. Releasing finger pressure will allow a spring to bring the key free of contact and turn off the brilliant lights.

Suddenly he is angry with himself. He has made an error, and it might have been a bad one. Fortunately, he can correct in time. With scathing self-denunciation he notices that the maneuvering engine is still in *Manual Con-*

trol position. A sudden movement of his hand, and he might have wasted more fuel and added to the separation distance of the machines. Quickly he flicks the control to *Standby,* keeping the propulsion system pressurized and ready for use instantly.

He glances through his viewport. It is not good; he cannot tell visually whether or not the window of the Mercury spacecraft is facing toward his own machine. And the American has no periscope for viewing; he can see outside his vesscl only through the window.

The radar display reads *289.* Yakovlev mutters; if the separation continues like this . . . he is concerned about the distance. They are nearly 300 meters* apart at this moment.

Yakovlev peers through a viewport magnifier. Good! The American's window almost directly faces the Vostok. He is watching, then. Yakovlev has a message for the stranded spaceman.

He cannot talk to the American. Given sufficient time, it would have been an easy matter to match the radio frequencies. But there had not been that time, and one of the reasons, as much as any other, that Andrei Yakovlev is in this spacecraft is his command of the English language. It is too much, of course, to expect that the American could understand Russian.

But there is a solution to everything, it seems. . . . Yakovlev understands English, and all pilots—especially those who are cosmonauts—understand international Morse code. It is through this universal medium that Yakovlev will communicate with the American.

He presses down with his finger to activate the key and releases it quickly. He waits four seconds, then flashes on the lights. Several times he repeats the on-off signal, until it must be obvious to the other cosmonaut that he must pay the closest attention to the Russian spacecraft.

The Vostok winks out of existence.

"What the hell!"

Pruett lifts his hand to rub his eyes. The bang of his gloved hand against the helmet faceplate reminds him rudely that the plate is down and locked. Ruefully he

* 984 feet.

ignores the foolish action, and stares hard across the thousand feet of vacuum.

There it is. . . . *It's only the lights,* Pruett chides himself. *For some reason our boy has cut them off.*

But without that accustomed dazzling light, the spacecraft seems to vanish in the sudden dark.

Sudden, stabbing glare.

Darkness again.

Blazing light.

Darkness.

Ivan's getting chummy. I guess he wants to talk. Wish to hell I had something to respond with. Wait a moment! In the survival kit . . .

Still gazing through the window, Pruett digs quickly through the survival kit in his cabin and withdraws a small but powerful flashlight. *Never thought I'd be using this thing up here. . . .*

Vostok snaps back into darkness.

Pruett brings the flashlight lens against the capsule window. He feels clumsy with his gloves, but he is able to blink the light on and off rapidly several times.

This is hardly a signal flash for space work, but at this distance he should be able to see my response without any sweat. And here it comes. . . .

Pruett leaves the flashlight floating in mid-air as he grabs his clipboard.

Dot dash dash dot . . . dot dash dot . . . dot . . . dot dash dash dot . . .

Like a blazing neon sign, Vostok flashes on and off in hand-transmitted code. Pruett jots down the signals.

P * R * E * P * A * R * E

F * O * R

S * H * I * P

T * R * A * N * S * F * E * R

Pruett snatches the flashlight from where it hovers in the air and presses it against the window again.

O * K

W * H * E * N

He feels his body and mind coming alive. *Maybe I'm*

*going to make it, after all! And with only hours to go
before the lights go out for good.*

He studies the Russian spaceship. A dim spray flashes
from the nose thrusters as the autopilot corrects a drifting
motion of the Vostok.

*I'm ready to hug that boy like a long-lost brother the
moment he gets me into that big hunk of machinery. And
I'll gladly take the long way home!*

Relief spreads through him like a warm glow and
laughter spills excitedly from his lips. *Besides, I've always
wondered what their ships looked like from the inside. . . .*

> T * R * A * N * S * F * E * R
> I * N
> A * B * O * U * T
> T * H * R * E * E
> Z * E * R * O
> M * I * N * U * T * E * S

Pruett moves the flashlight switch back and forth.

> I
> A * M
> R * E * A * D * Y
> Y * O * U * R
> S * I * G * N * A * L

. . . and as an afterthought—

> C * O * M * R * A * D * E

*That should give him some idea of how glad I am to see
him and that big, beautiful lifeboat of his. . . .*

Vostok blazes on and off, an eerie, huge firefly of
vacuum.

> G * O * O * D
> S * T * A * N * D
> B * Y
> N * E * X * T
> M * E * S * S * A * G * E

```
          T * W * O
          Z * E * R * O
          M * I * N * U * T * E * S
```

He replies—

```
          O * K
```

But the Russian is not yet through—

```
          H * A * V * E
          Y * O * U
          F * R * E * E
          Z * E * R * O
          T * W * O
          F * L * A * S * K
          F * O * R
          T * R * A * N * S * F * E * R
```

Pruett tries to answer that and other questions relating to the portable oxygen bottle in his cabin—

```
          Y * E * S
          S * U * P * P * L * Y
          O * N * E
          F * I * V * E
          M * I * N * U * T * E * S
```

The space firefly flickers—

```
          G * O * O * D
          C * A * N
          Y * O * U
          R * E * L * E * A * S * E
          C * A * B * I * N
          H * A * T * C * H
```

He replies—

```
          Y * E * S
```

```
E * X * P * L * O * S * I * V * E
E * J * E * C * T
```

The lights flash again—

```
Y * O * U
W * I * L * L
T * R * A * N * S * F * E * R
H * O * L * D * I * N * G
M * Y
S * U * I * T
I
W * I * L * L *
U * S * E
B * O * D * Y
R * E * A * C * T * I * O * N
P * A * C * K
O * U * T
```

The lights blazed steady as the Russian ended the message.

Pruett's head was in a whirl. Apparently the cosmonaut —*damn! I should have at least asked his name*—was going to come in close, very close. According to his message, he would leave the Vostok, and use a bodypack propulsion system to push over to the capsule.

And then things can get sticky. . . . Obviously I'm supposed to hang on somehow while he uses that personal thruster to get both of us back to his ship. I sure hope that boy is good, because what with drifting rates and that limited oxy supply in the bottle . . . to hell with worrying about it; it's the ONLY chance I've got so far, and time is running out for me.

The Russian spacecraft seems to drift farther from Mercury Seven. Against the backdrop of the inky sky and stars, the curving horizon of earth below, it seems strange and alien, a machine not of earth, not spawned by man. . . .

And what if he—?

266

A faint burst of static in his helmet.

". . . in, come in, Mercury Seven. This is Muchea Cap Com. Muchea Cap Com calling Mercury Seven. Do you read, Seven? Over."

Hell, they must have been calling for a while.

"Roger, Muchea. Loud and clear. Over."

"Hello, Dick. How's the lung fuel holding? Over."

"I'm almost at five hours, and I can think of other things I'd rather be without. Repeat, down to almost five hours' oxygen supply."

"Ah, Roger, Seven. We're tracking you and Ivan clearly, and—"

"What's the separation between us right now?"

"Radar shows about four hundred yards. Over."

"*Goddamnit!* He's really drifting out. Do you have any estimates on closure between the Russian and myself? Anything in from Goddard? Over."

"That is affirmative, Dick. Goddard reports that from this point on you will start to pull in again as you make the downswing from apogee. As you come up on White Sands he will be very close. He will be drifting in as close as before, maybe a bit tighter. From this point on through Bermuda he will be in his best position to come in right next to you. We—"

"Hold it, Muchea. You better get some news to Cape. Ivan has been using the lights on his ship for Morse code communications. I was able to respond with the survival flashlight in the window."

"Roger, Seven. Go ahead."

"Okay. He seems prepared to come in close pretty soon, I guess as soon as we cut it over White Sands. His message asked whether I had portable oxygen—I told him a fifteen-minute supply—and if I could dump the hatch. I gave him affirmative on that one also.

"Got it so far?"

"Go ahead, Dick. We're taping."

"Roger. According to his message, he is prepared to get in close, leave the Vostok, and come over to me with a personal reaction maneuvering unit. I imagine it's like the bodypack we've been playing around with. I am to hang on to his suit—don't know if he has a brace or a line or what—and then he will use the personal thruster to take both of us back and into the spacecraft. Over."

"Okay, we've got it—"

"Oh, yes. One more thing. I expect to hear from him again by the lights. I'm holding attitude control to keep him in sight at all times. When—"

"You're starting to cut out, Seven. Recommend you pick up Woomera at this time. Over."

"Roger, Muchea. Switching Woomera. Out.

"Woomera Cap Com from Seven. Over."

"Mercury Seven, this is Woomera Cap Com, and you're coming in loud and clear.

"We have monitored your report by land line with Muchea. Understand you have additional data for Cape Control. Over."

"And how . . . I don't know what's happening with Dougherty and the Gemini, but make sure that Cape understands I've already had my formal invitation to ride in that big bus up here with me. And that I am most anxious to go along with it. I'm just at about five hours' oxygen now and that's cutting it too thin for comfort. Over."

"Understand, Seven. I—Stand by one, please."

"Roger."

"Seven from Woomera. Radar reports a definite start of closure between your spacecraft and the Soviet vehicle. I repeat, radar shows a definite start of closure between Mercury and Vostok. Separation range is definitely under four hundred yards at this moment. . . ."

So he's starting to move in again. Well, this looks like it, all right. C'mon, Ivan or whatever-your-name is, let's see you slide right in there in the groove. I'm sort of anxious to shake your hand, fella. . . .

". . . coming in garbled, Canton Cap Com. Say again your last message. Over."

"Roger, Seven. Repeat this is message direct from Cape. They are on final count for Gemini. I say again, they are on final count for Gemini, and expect to launch on this pass. Do you read? Over."

It can't be true! Things are looking up all over. . . .

"Right, Canton. Cape says that final count is under way on Gemini, for expected launch on this pass by me. Go ahead."

"Roger. Cape requests you stand by later for message

to be relayed through Guaymas Cap Com. Repeat that message will be relayed to you by Guaymas Cap Com. Over."

"Very good, Canton. You're fading on me, but I'll transmit in the hope you can pick me up. The Russian is definitely moving in closer now. Estimate between three and three hundred fifty yards. He's—hold it. Ivan is flashing his lights for a message. Seven out."

"Okay, Guaymas. What's the poop?"

"Roger, Seven. Count proceeding on schedule with Titan booster and Gemini. I repeat, everything is on the wire with the Gemini count. Cape says that your position will be over South Texas at Gemini liftoff. Do you read? Over."

"You're coming in sweet and loud, Guaymas. That's good news, very good *indeed.*"

"We thought it wouldn't make you unhappy, Seven. Cape has further details for you. Set your standby radio to VHF transceiver for direct communications between yourself and Gemini. That is VHF transceiver, standard channel, for direct communications between yourself and Gemini."

"Got it, Guaymas. Go ahead."

"Roger, Seven. We have a radar confirmation on separation distance between yourself and your friend up there. Radar shows separation less than two hundred yards and closing steadily. I repeat that separation is less than two hundred yards and closing steadily. Over."

"Roger, Guaymas. The Russian has signaled in Morse that he expects to effect his close-in maneuver beyond Bermuda. That is, after the pass over Bermuda. Over."

"Roger. Goddard reports his best chance of closing with fuel economy is to slide above you and move ahead on the run between White Sands and Bermuda. At that time he can cut his speed a bit and you will start to move in rapidly. That looks like the play for the money at that time. Mercury Seven, we have a request for you from Cape. Over."

"Okay, sound off."

"Cape is asking you to prepare to assist pilot of Gemini in visual identification and tracking of your spacecraft for attempted direct rendezvous by Gemini. Cape has opinion that Gemini pilot will experience difficulty in getting definite visual target. Radar display will be helped by transponder response your vehicle. But they are concerned about visual contact. They ask for effectiveness of flashlight with Soviet spacecraft. Over."

"I didn't ask Ivan, Guaymas. But we were at a separation of about one thousand feet as radar called it. He had no trouble getting my Morse signals. Over."

"Roger, Seven. We will pass that on to Cape."

"They seem pretty sure about getting that Titan off the pad on schedule, don't they?"

"Affirmative, affirmative. We're getting the count here direct. Everything is smack on the button. It looks very good."

"Guaymas from Seven. You're coming in weak. This is Mercury Seven, switching Cape Control. Seven out."

Ah—there is the west coast of America coming up now. And the closure rate is excellent! Thank the fates that Moscow came through in time with the coordinates for the translational maneuver. I would never have taken steps to change the orbit pattern here. So we will come close together past Bermuda—good!

I do not envy the American. If something goes wrong . . . He has so little oxygen left. I hope the mission goes well. I would like to meet that man. He is so calm in the face of certain disaster. Or almost certain, were it not for this machine coming to his aid.

I wonder what it would be like to orbit in such a small craft as the American flies. I take my hat off to the American cosmonauts. . . . It is like trying to cross the ocean on a raft.

The radar . . . very good! Only one hundred and thirty-six meters. We are closing nicely, like two trains converging to the same track. Now, the checklist for the maneuver . . .

Be patient, my Yankee friend. We shall be meeting very soon!

The two machines plunge in the grip of centrifugal force and gravity, swooping faster and faster over the surface of the earth. Coming around toward the end of their first and close to the beginning of their second orbit, they whisper over the planet almost one hundred miles south of San Diego. A red sun is sliding beyond the western horizon, and darkness is nuzzling its way across the surface. People in San Diego and the neighboring countryside look up, squint. Some stare through binoculars; many of them point. They feel on the edge of a great moment—a pause between miracle and tragedy. They look up and see a faint, faint dot in the heavens; that is poor Major Pruett. And the other light, so bright! That must be the Russian. . . .

". . . and he has been kind enough to be with us today for a special interview on the great drama in space going on at this very moment. Congressman Harrison W. Bloeth, Republican, has been deeply concerned for many years by our national space program. The Congressman has made his position very clear. He is opposed to much of our space effort, and he has many times stated that it is a politically inspired circus that wastes billions of dollars year—"

"That's absolutely right!" snapped the heavy-set man sitting across the table from the interviewer.

Bill Jackson, crack news correspondent for Washington's top television program, ignored the interruption and went on with his smooth, sure flow "—yearly. Because of Congressman Bloeth's active role behind the scenes, this station feels that he can contribute much to understanding the cause of the critical failure that has stranded Astronaut Richard Pruett in orbit. The latest report, just before we begin our interview, indicates that . . ."

The volume monitor seated in the control room nudged the engineer at his side. "That acid-tongued old bastard has been slavering for an opportunity like this one," he said. "I think we're going to be in for a beaut."

"Does he know his onions?"

"Hell, no! He wouldn't know a Titan if the thing fell on top of him."

"I don't get it; then what are we doing with him on this interview?"

"Mr. Bigmouth out there is a Name. He wields a lot of influence on the Hill, and he's been responsible for many of the roadblocks on space funding. Anything that makes us look less than superior to the Reds gets his dander up. That's why he's the darling of the right-wingers. We think he's a member of the Birch group, but no one has pinned it on him, and he sidesteps the issue neatly. There's the signal; okay, here we go. . . ."

"Congressman Bloeth, can you tell us anything about

Astronaut Pruett's position—aside from the latest report we just heard?"

The voice came out as a mixture of rasping honey; Bloeth was a crowd spieler from way back, and the television cameras were as warm to him as had been the uncounted faces.

"Yes, I can. I can do that, all right. His position, Mr. Jackson, is that he has been stupidly condemned. *Stupidly,* I say. He is in his grave situation because of the whole twisted approach to our space program, and—"

Jackson interrupted hastily. "What I mean, sir, was in reference to our possibly saving his life."

"Oh. Well! Now, that is only a direct result of what I have *been* saying. I don't think there is any hope—no, no real hope *at all* that we are going to be able to save that poor fellow's life. I think we must face facts, face the facts as they *really are,* Mr. Jackson, and not delude all those good people who are wondering and worrying about that young man. Yes! Those good people—" he assumed his most stately pose and looked straight at the unblinking red eye of the live camera—"cannot be misled any longer!"

"Misled, Congressman?"

"That's right, sir, I said mis-*led*. All this nonsense about our attempting to save his life with this new spaceship! Why, we haven't even completed the tests of this new machine with only remote equipment aboard. You were aware, I'm sure, Mr. Jackson—but perhaps our listeners were not—that we had not completed the unmanned tests?"

"Why, yes, I was. But—"

"How can there be any 'buts' about such a thing, Mr. Jackson! The space agency has told us in Congressional meetings that the rocket and the capsule would not be ready until October or November at the earliest. *At—the —earliest,*" he ground out with an expression of outraged morality. "The government is misleading our people when it tells them that we are going to perform a miracle and snatch our astronaut from the brink of death. After all, Mr. Jackson, this country has never performed a meeting of two ships in space. We don't know that much about it. And—"

He leaned forward in a move calculated to create the effect of joining his audience in a conspiratorial vein—

"And that new booster rocket, that Titan, is a *dangerous*

272

machine. Dangerous! It shakes like an old washing machine. It has too much vibration, Mr. Jackson, for us to risk a *second* man's life on this fool's errand!"

He knew his timing with perfection. He slumped back in his seat, the picture of sorrow.

And he caught the veteran Jackson by surprise. For several seconds there was silence. *You've still got it,* Bloeth smiled to himself. *Caught that young pup with his pants down. The audience will be crawling into their TV sets to hear the rest. Very, very good* . . . He seized the opportunity. Now, instead of the unseen audience, he struck against Jackson, using him as a focus for his attack. Anger must be vented, Congressman Bloeth knew well, but it must have an outlet instead of simmering around and going nowhere. This Jackson would do as well as any. . . .

Bloeth stabbed his finger through the air. "Have you ever thought, have—you—ever—*realized,* Mr. Jackson, that we are sending a man without any experience, without a *single moment's experience* in space, on this mission? If the national space agency *really* wanted to have us believe we could save young Pruett, then why—*why,* I ask you— are we not sending a man with *experience* to the rescue! Why do we not send our national hero, John Glenn, or Gordon Cooper, or those men who *know* what to do, what to expect in space?

"Oh, I'll tell *you* why, sir! It is because—" his voice mellowed and he looked again into the camera—"we dare not take the risk with a man who is well known to all our people. They would react with rising anger, they would be righteous in their condemnation of our space officials and our government, and *that* is why!"

My God, Jackson groaned to himself, *this is getting out of hand. I'm a fool for giving him this platform. Got to move in quick, try and get him off this, trip him up a bit.* . . .

"Congressman, can you tell us why we have a failure in Astronaut Pruett's capsule?" *Hit him with one he can't answer, then dog him with it, shunt him off.* . . .

"Yes, sir, I can. It's mismanagement, that's why. It's letting a bunch of people who are more interested in grabbing good, well-paying jobs handle such critical matters instead of—"

"Excuse me, Congressman," Jackson broke in, "I

meant with the capsule itself. Why the retrorockets failed to fire."

Young whippersnapper, he's come around to his senses; have to watch him now.

"Well, now, *young man,* if you had the advantage of experience in this field—" *Look at him; that grabbed him where it hurts*—"you would realize that we have had nothing with that Mercury thing except trouble. *Right from the very start* we have had trouble. We lost Shepard's capsule—"

"You mean Grissom's, don't you, Congressman?"

"Humph! Yes, yes, that's not important. We lost one capsule into the sea and nearly drowned our spaceman. It's a miracle that John Glenn is alive. And Carpenter— his family should pray every day that he survived being lost at sea; that was a terrible experience—"

The old windbag! Scott was "lost" for about an hour!

". . . and even Gordon Cooper, that splendid young man, survived only by another miracle. Why—"

"But, Congressman Bloeth, the Mercury program has had an absolutely perfect safety record. We have exceeded all the expectations from the beginnings of—"

"How can you call a whole line of miraculous escapes a 'perfect' record, Mr. Jackson?"

"With no disrespect to you, Congressman, the record stands clear. The capsule has fulfilled every mission, and the Atlas—"

"Oh, yes, that booster rocket!" Bloeth crowed. "That monstrosity. Why, that thing is a Rube Goldberg nightmare of plumbing. There's another miracle for you, that we haven't burned any of our *fine* young men to death aboard that thing."

"But it's worked almost perfectly every time, Congressman!"

"Ah! But you are mistaken, Mr. Jackson, you are very much mistaken, young man.

"It is the Atlas that is as much behind the inevitable loss of our splendid astronaut, right now seeing his life slowly ebb away, even as we sit here . . . It is the Atlas, sir, that has failed. Were it not for the fact that we could not control that machine better, Richard Pruett would be on his way home—safe and sound, yes! safe and sound—on his way home *right now!*"

"Congressman, the Atlas that sent Pruett into orbit gave

274

the best performance of any flight to date, and—"

Come, come, come, right into the trap, my fine young man. Wonderful . . .

A beefy hand slammed against the table, and Congressman Bloeth sat bolt upright in bristling indignation. He gave Jackson a pitying look.

"Your statement only shows, Mr. Jackson—although I cannot hold you to blame for this, of course—your statement only proves that you have been duped by the administration and their errand boys in the space agency. 'Best performance,' indeed! My dear sir, if the rocket worked as well as our administration wants our good public to believe, then why, *why* is Pruett in such trouble?"

He held up his hand as Jackson began to speak. "Do not interrupt me, sir. This is too important for side issues. . . ."

I've got the ball, and I'm running with it. . . .

"Are you aware of the *failure* of that Atlas, of the whole mission? Do you realize, young man, that we have sent a man into space on the basis of an unforgivable risk? How can we justify sending up a fine, outstanding individual like Richard Pruett *without enough oxygen to last him through his mission!* The Atlas has failed, Mr. Jackson, because our astronaut will not return to us until after he has been condemned by official stupidity, and by the bungling of engineers . . . condemned to die."

He dropped his voice, and the honeyed tones of releasing "secret" information came back. "Why did not the Atlas send Astronaut Pruett into a lower orbit? Why could we not control the rocket to do this? Why did we not plan to have his machine come back of its own accord, without those rockets, after four or five days in space?

"The Atlas can't do that for us!" he shouted. "We cannot control that stupid machine with any accuracy. And because we cannot do this, that is why Astronaut Pruett has been condemned! That wonderful Atlas of which you speak—" he brought contempt into his tone— "is so perfect that it sent our astronaut into too high an orbit. And so we are all witness to this terrible tragedy, this horrendous scene of a man who is condemned by official stupidity and incompetence to die slowly. My heart goes out to his parents, those helpless people. . . ."

His voice trailed off and he slumped in his seat, shaking his head slowly from side to side.

"Congressman Bloeth, the mission was as perfect as it could possibly be. The Atlas sent the Mercury Seven spacecraft into exactly the orbit that was planned for it and—"

Bloeth smiled coldly at him. "Yes, yes, indeed. Let me use your own words, Mr. Jackson. *Your own words.* You said, 'into exactly the orbit that was planned,' did you not? Ah, yes. And you do not find it strange, sir, that this orbit that was planned would cause the astronaut to use up all his oxygen *before he returned to earth?* That, Mr. Jackson, is criminal negligence, or stupidity, and I am convinced that both are involved. Yes, indeed, that is the kind of planning that frightens me. Would *you* care to do such a thing, Mr. Jackson? Would *you* care to go into space, knowing full well that you did not have enough air to breathe for your mission? *Would you do that willingly?*"

"Why, no—no—but—"

Very softly. "But what, Mr. Jackson?"

"But the problem, Congressman—and I do not agree with you at all about the Atlas—is not in the booster rocket. It is with the small rockets aboard the capsule. We've never had a failure before with the retros, and this is what is causing the present difficulty. Can you—?"

"Yes, I can," Bloeth snapped, breaking in suddenly. "The failure of the rockets aboard that spaceship is only one more in the continuing series of weaknesses we have been discussing. If the Atlas had worked properly—as I explained in some detail to you, young man—the retros would not even be needed. *But,* after placing Astronaut Pruett deliberately in a critical situation, and mark my words when I say *deliberately*—after we did that, we risked his life on those three little rockets, a risk we have come to regret deeply, although I dare say none of us will feel this tragedy so much as his poor mother and father.

"There has been not *one* failure, Mr. Jackson. There has been failure after failure after failure!"

The newsman reached out desperately. "Congressman, aren't you being premature? After all, there is that Russian spaceship up there with him in orbit. And as you know, the Russians have already had a rendezvous in space, and they are preparing to try and save Pruett for us and—"

The smile was like that of a snake. *"Go on."*

"You have listened to the reports with us, Congressman.

276

The Vostok is right now moving into position, and as a *second* means of aiding Major Pruett, there is the Gemini, which—"

"Do not change the subject," he said abruptly. His voice mellowed. "Let us stay with this Russian that you brought up."

"Well—"

"Never mind, Mr. Jackson. I will make it very clear. And I do appreciate your having brought us around to this matter; I appreciate it, as will all those good people who are listening to us right now. Oh, yes, this is a matter we must strip wide open, that we must expose for the sellout that it represents."

He moved in fast, dominating the conversation.

"Is it not strange—" he addressed the camera, completely ignoring the newsman—"that we have been placed in a position whereby we are forced to beg of the Soviet Union that it try to save an American life? Do you not find it sinister, yes—sinister!—that the whole world is witness to this spectacle of the United States of America, our great and powerful country, completely helpless to save one of its own? Are we not debased that we must lie to our own people, and to the people of the world, because of our weakness and our failures?"

Again his big hand crashed onto the table, and he was in command, his voice powerful and sure of the complete advantage he had gained. "I say to all of you that there are those in our government who have sold us—*all* of us, you and me and those whom we know—down an alley of perfidy. We have signed a pact with the tyrannical government of the Soviets whose record is stained with the blood of American airmen! We have asked the killers in their airplanes and aboard their ships to help us—we, the most powerful nation on earth—to help us. We are even now treated to a spectacle of the entire world watching the Soviet Union demonstrate that they may save the life of our astronaut, while we can only issue press releases and inane remarks!

"Where did this begin? Who sold us out? I ask all of you for the answer to such a grave question. . . ."

He turned to confront the newsman, his voice harsh and grating. "I will tell you, and all those good people out

277

there, Mr. Jackson, what I am going to do. I am going to demand that the House Committee on Unamerican Activities begin an *immediate investigation,* immediate, I say! into this whole sordid affair.

"For there is the true failure, the deadly weakness, that is the reason why the helpless parents of young Pruett can only suffer the waning hours until his last moment comes. . . ."

"Wilco. I will punch the backup clock at your count— on your call, that is—for Gemini liftoff. Over."

"Seven from Cap Com. Okay, Dick. Say again your control mode during Gemini flight? Over."

"Seven to Cape. Roger. I'll keep her on fly by wire low, ass end first, and pitched well over so that I can try to get visual sighting of the booster. How's the count going?"

"We're on the money, Seven. Coming up on three minutes. Over."

"Roger, Spence. My Russian friend is sliding past me now; looks like he's going along at a pretty good clip. How goes it with radar? Over."

"Cape to Seven. Radar confirms passage between you and Vostok at seven-zero yards. But he was moving too fast and was at too great a side angle to bring it in then. Goddard is convinced he must wait until you are both well past Bermuda before he can move in close to you and match up. Over."

"That's the way it looks with the eyeballs, Cape."

"Roger, Seven. We're coming up on two minutes to Gemini liftover. Everything is running right down the groove. No holds. A lot of fingers crossed for you, Buddy."

"Sounds good, Cape. I'll—"

"Mercury Seven—Dick—this is George Keith on. Over."

"Hello, Uncle George."

"Dick, we've only a minute or so. Now, listen carefully to me. No matter what happens with Dougherty, no matter *what,* I don't want you making the mistake of passing up a sure thing. If your Russian friend comes in close and knocks on your door—even if Dougherty looks good and is moving in tight and it looks like a guaranteed pickup—*I want you to go with the Russian.* Is that clear?"

"Sure, George, but—"

"No buts and no maybes. I am *ordering* you to go with the Russian if he gets into position to pick you up. You haven't any time to waste and little enough oxygen——"

"Don't I know it!"

"Okay, then. You go with Ivan if that's the way the thing turns out. I'm putting Spence back on. I——"

"God be with you, Dick."

Pruett's jaw sagged. George *Keith* said *that*. . . .

"Cap Com to Seven."

"Yeah . . . Go ahead, Spence."

"Seven, we're down on the final swing. I'm patching in the blockhouse line so you can hear the count directly. I will not break in unless it is absolutely necessary, and I will be ready for any call from you. Over."

"Okay, Spence."

"Roger. We're at minus twenty seconds and——"

The cry of *Liftoff!* crackling with static, tinny in his earphones, was the sweetest sound he had ever heard.

Chapter XIX

PRUETT ROLLED THE CAPSULE THROUGH 180 DEGREES. Inverted in relation to the earth, he pitched the neck of the spacecraft down until he could observe the extended lower half of the Florida peninsula. In this position on the ground, he would have been acutely uncomfortable. Here, in the eternal wafting of weightlessness, it did not matter.

The world below cringed in black. No, not quite. He could see dim glowing lights that should be . . . yes, that was Tampa, spilling its light weakly through low clouds. He fed in a few degrees of roll to the right, revealing the southern curve of the peninsula through his window. There was no mistake about it. Miami and Miami Beach and the shore communities formed a glowing orange necklace, diffused by distance and atmosphere, but unquestionable as to their identification.

He nudged the control stick and the capsule rolled back, holding the desired position. Pruett set the ship on autopilot and carefully scanned the area along the coastline, where the launch complex should be located. Impatient at the mixture of unrecognizable glows, he brought the binoculars to his eyes and quickly focused them on a bright star near the horizon. Then he swung his gaze down again—

There!

It was the thinnest line of pale violet fire. A long silken hair of pink, washed with . . . he couldn't tell if the flame spread a green glow outward, but it mattered little. There could be no doubt. He snapped a glance at the timer. It checked, neatly, right to the second. Far ahead of him, arcing out over the bottomless black of the ocean, the flame disappeared.

It came back again, an ethereal creature, an utterly silent liquid splash. He knew the sight for what it was without ever having seen it before. He knew it from his earphones as he heard Jim Dougherty cry out *BECO!* in a voice that seemed a million miles away, and immediately after, when ghosts of voices watching electronic whisperings on robot panels hissed their confirmation of the sequence of events. Even before he heard the words that cried jubilantly of ignition and flaming life in the upper stage of the Titan, he had seen the tenuous sign—flame washing back, splashing on the discarded shell of the empty and useless booster, an act of rejection, and a glowing bulb that spread farther and farther. In the growing absence of restrictive air, the stripped atoms and wildly agitated gases howled mutely in every direction, spreading in the form of a phantasmal spheroid, its surface and inner space rippling and turning with the light reflected from the blazing rocket.

Of all that he had seen in more than five days and five nights in the wonder of space, nothing had been even remotely like this incredible sight. It was as if he were witness to some creative process of life itself.

The flame behind the accelerating rocket stretched in what now was vacuum for many, many miles, a living comet pushing the still invisible rocket and its spacecraft to their slot in the efficiency of orbital mechanics.

He moved with tremendous speed toward the expanding blossom of flame, for his was full orbital velocity and the rocket in his sight still fought for that same speed. If the

Titan performed in the manner for which he hoped, if the flaming comet obeyed the whims of its electronic brain and the nudging of its gimbaled engine—if it did all these things and responded to the demands of its astronaut pilot —then Pruett would see the flame continue to expand. It would grow more and more until he was almost atop the onrushing booster, and then, slower and slower, he would reach and pass the fire. If it all went with that extraordinary precision which the simple matter of his life required, he would be able to tell the man seated at the head of the comet how truly beautiful had been his fiery leap away from the planet. If the precision were lacking, not only with the man he knew so well, but also with the nameless one in the big Russian spacecraft, then . . . well, then it wouldn't matter at all to him, would it?

He watched the fire now without the glasses, for he wished to judge distance and perspective. It was still below him as they crossed an invisible line in the heavens, and then, somehow, in the eeriness of staring down at lights swimming in a bowl of infinity, it was at his height and well back toward the Cape.

The flame disappeared. Anxiously he turned up the receiver volume, listening intently.

And his face broke out into a wide, splitting grin. . . .

Not even the fierce eyebrows and frosty, disapproving glare of George Keith could stem the outpouring of relief and tension in Mercury Control. *"He's done it! He's done it! Oh you beautiful bitch, you lovely, gorgeous bitch . . . she's slapped right through the middle of the keyhole! Oh, what a beautiful bitch of a rocket that Titan is! Man! He's right there in the center of the track. . . . !"* Two men had their arms clasped tightly around one another and were dancing wildly by their desks. Others were pounding backs and shoulders and spilling emotions as water bursts through a ruptured dam. Dougherty had threaded the eye of the space needle with the Titan upper stage as though he'd been doing this sort of thing all his life. Those yaw corrections *were the answer*. . . . Where the hell was that radar separation report from Goddard! He wanted facts. . . . George Keith grabbed the microphone on his desk and switched to the loudspeaker.

"Gentlemen . . . *GENTLEMEN!*"

281

He waited for the rush of quiet.

"If you are quite through with this exhibition . . ."

He saw abashed looks.

And plenty of grins.

"We haven't brought this in as a winner. Not yet. Not without a lot of skill and the kind of luck we can always use in this game. Let's get with it." He snapped the switch off.

"*George!* The board—*look!*"

There it was—confirmation from the computers, in big, glowing, wonderful numbers.

Jim Dougherty was within nine miles of Mercury Seven.

And George Keith couldn't help himself. He snatched up the desk microphone again.

"Would someone please give me a quiet cheer?"

The sprawling room lit up with the smiles.

"*East Nine to Ocean Vessel Victory. Come in, Victory.*"

"*This is Ocean Vessel Victory. Your transmission is clear, Comrade Yakovlev. Over.*"

"*Victory from East Nine. I have picked up two strange reports on my radar. In the direction of the American spacecraft, I have . . . two new targets. The Mercury vehicle I can still identify. But I have one target, strong, at a distance estimated at one seven kilometers, and at the same elevation as the Mercury. There is another target on the scope, but it is much weaker and at a greater distance. Also, it seems to be dropping away, almost moving back toward the earth. Do you have any explanation of this for me? Over.*"

"*Victory to East Nine. Our tracking radar confirms your observations. Do you wish azimuth and range readings at this time? Over.*"

"*East Nine to Victory. No! No! I am asking you for explanation of what these radar targets ARE. Obviously the Americans have fired something into orbit. Do you have any information in this regard? Over.*"

"*Stand by, East Nine. . . .*"

The Russian pilot felt anger building up within him. He glanced impatiently at his timer. In just a few more minutes he must commence the final maneuvers to close in with—

"*Victory to East Nine. How do you read? Over.*"

"Get on with it, man!"

"East Nine, we have monitored the radio broadcasts of the Americans. A special bulletin has just interrupted all programs. It—"

"Quickly, you fool!"

..."It says that the Americans have successfully placed into orbit a Gemini spacecraft, and that—"

"REPEAT THAT."

"The Americans are claiming, Comrade, that they have placed another spacecraft in orbit. They say, as well, that it will attempt to rescue the cosmonaut in the disabled Mercury and—"

"It is no idle claim. There is certainly something up here!"

"I understand, Comrade. Do you wish us to contact the Moscow Center by short wave? Over."

"That would be quite useless, I'm sure. And—no, wait. Send a communiqué that in, ah, . . . three minutes from now I will begin closing with the American cosmonaut. Over."

"As you say, Comrade. However, radar advises that you delay the start of maneuvers for another four minutes beyond your scheduled time. There has been a further refinement of tracking data. Your most economical fuel points will come in just under seven minutes from now. The next ocean vessel will be within your range in about five minutes, and they are prepared to assist you with the count. Over."

Angrily: *"East Nine is closing contact. Out."*

He scanned the instruments. The batteries! The lights on the outside of the spacecraft were drawing too much power. He pushed a switch and turned them off.

The chronometer hand swept around slowly.

"In six more minutes, then . . ."

He studied his radar scope. The second target—what they call the Gemini—it . . .

It was closing the range—fast!

The brilliant light suddenly winked out. Jim Dougherty ignored it. He wasn't interested in the Vostok. . . .

"Gemini to Mercury. How do you read me, Dick? Over."

"You're coming in like churchbells on a Sunday morning, Gemini. How does it look?"

283

"Don't hold your breath yet, Dick, but we look very good. Onboard radar shows about nine miles, and Bermuda has passed Goddard confirmation to me."

"Roger. I've been listening on the party line. What's your estimate on locking bumpers?"

"Don't bug me, space cadet. I got some work to do and, ah, I will have a better idea very shortly. Stand by one, Dick, we're coming up on Canary, and I need radar checks before I fire up this bird."

"Take your time and hurry up. I'm impatient to see your ugly face, carrot top."

"Knock it off. . . . Okay, stand by; wait for my call."

Pruett remained silent, listening.

"Gemini to Canary Cap Com. Come in, Canary. Over."

"This is Canary, Gemini. We have velocity and coordinates for you to copy from Goddard. Over."

"Roger, Canary. Let's have it."

"Roger, Gemini. Goddard wants you to correct a minor plane discrepancy. After that, they believe they can vector you for an immediate collision course with Mercury. Are you ready to copy?"

"Ready, Canary. Over."

"Roger. Plane correction maneuver is as follows. . . ."

He made sure not to rush, to commit the kind of small error that might sling the Gemini too far out of the orbital plane, too far, perhaps, for him to come back in enough time. So he did everything with exacting, triple-checking thoroughness.

Jim Dougherty was strapped into a spacecraft that looked like a throwback to a side-by-side fighter; it reminded him, in fact, of the TF-102A fighter-trainers he once flew—big in the cockpit, without the cramping isolation of the Mercury.

Dougherty sat in the left—the pilot's seat. Directly in front of him glowed the dials of his flight and timer instruments. To the other side of the low beam column by his right—the empty copilot seat—the panel was duplicated. The upward sloping front of the center column bristled with switches and controls, and a larger instrument console was mounted in the front center of the ship, between the seats. Directly in the center of the spacecraft, atop the pedestal, was the black control grip for the attitude control thrusters. To Dougherty's immediate left, on a small pedestal against the bulkhead, was a knobbed handle. This was the control for his maneuvering rocket engines.

That handle, keyed in the computer-autopilot system of the Gemini, was—*must*—be the salvation for his friend. It controlled the OAMS, the Orbital Attitude and Maneuvering System. . . . There were two engines, each of a hundred pounds thrust, for forward acceleration, and two engines, each of eighty-five pounds thrust, to decelerate the spacecraft. Besides these, he had at his command four additional engines, each of a hundred pounds thrust, that enabled him to move the spacecraft laterally. It wasn't enough simply to aim at a point where he could get close— could meet—the Mercury capsule. He had to maneuver within the confines of a great barrel, sliding down to the exact center of the barrel, not too much to the left or right, or above or below his target, where a man with too few hours of oxygen waited for him.

And then there were the attitude thrusters, eight more engines, each thrusting at twenty-five pounds, for his pitch, yaw, and roll control. All he needed to do was to use all that varied and variable power with consummate skill. The translational thrusters gave him the means of changing his velocity by a total of more than 700 feet per second. It was more than enough for the kind of rendezvous mission they had planned. But now there wasn't time to park Gemini into an orbit where they could spend a day or two waiting for the target vehicle to slide neatly into position. There was hardly any time at all.

But he had help. Inside the spacecraft with him was a small and unbelievably versatile digital computer. The computer itself functioned as the heart of a complex and inertial guidance system adapted particularly to the rendezvous and docking missions intended for the two-man ship. Until he had his visual cues to push and prod the Gemini manually in close to the Mercury capsule, that computer and its subsystems were the *only* hope for the rescue mission to achieve the success they all wanted so desperately.

A small and powerful radar scanned the emptiness of space ahead of Gemini. Finding a target in this huge blank can be extremely difficult for a small onboard radar, but the task was simplified greatly by keying in to the Mercury transponder. This small electronic voice sent out an almost constant signal from Pruett's ship during his orbit. It helped precision radar on the ground in finding and tracking the vehicle as it shot overhead in orbit.

With Gemini itself in orbit, and the transponder as an aid, Dougherty could get a solid radar contact with Mercury at a range of 250 nautical miles. But everything had worked so beautifully with the Titan stage that he had dropped right into the orbital slot, and when he separated from the booster the red light by the radar set was gleaming brightly at him, telling proof that he had a good acquisition of his target—Mercury Seven. But even Dougherty was surprised at the accuracy with which he had sailed into the orbital track. Originally they had estimated that immediate rendezvous methods would bring them within twenty or thirty miles of a target vehicle in orbit. This, however, was their first attempt, and for safety they had doubled the estimate to about fifty miles.

It was that sweet guidance correction in yaw, Dougherty thought. *Give me a set of rudder pedals on that bird, and I'll fly it right through the keyhole myself.*

Only nine miles away from Pruett in the smaller capsule, the radar return was strong and solid. Once Dougherty's radar signals came in—came back—they were fed into the digital computer. The electronic brain quickly translated the echoing microwave signals of the radar transmitter into data relevant to range, rate, and elevation. Almost as quickly as the computer ingested the radar signals, it chewed them up and presented them to Dougherty in windows that blinked glowing numbers at him. At the same time, it gave the same information in a different form on an indicator with three needles that referred to his X, Y, and Z axes of control movement for the powerful maneuvering engines.

The immediate obstacle to eliminate was the discrepancy between the plane of his orbit and that of Mercury. Their orbits were like two irregular hoops placed around the great ball that is earth. Each hoop was, figuratively, at an equal distance from the surface, but they weren't at exactly the same angle. It was as though the hoops were connected at top and bottom. While one hoop remained still, you could turn the other one until they were at a slight angle to one another. It was critical to eliminate that slight angle, and to slide the hoops together—until the

286

orbital planes came together, that is. To the eyes of an outside observer, the hoops would then mesh so perfectly they would seem as one.

There was no time to waste if Dougherty hoped to accomplish the immediate—direct—rendezvous. Otherwise the slight angle of the plane error would become magnified by the speed of their orbital travel.

The Gemini pilot adjusted the control of several gyros. A visual display on his instrument panel shifted until it read zero. He studied it for a moment. The degree of adjustment he had made to each gyro control was representative of the degree of correction he must accomplish with Gemini. But no man could quickly run through those calculations. . . .

Dougherty punched a button marked START COMPUTATION. Quickly the computer accepted the order, and came back with a visual number display. The display revealed to the pilot exactly what thrust he required from his translational maneuvering engines through the three velocity axes of Gemini in order to slide his orbital "hoop" dead center with that of Pruett.

In front of Dougherty there was a small manual data keyboard with ten numbered keys. Dougherty checked the computer display and tapped in the requirements on the keyboard. Again he rechecked his figures. Each time he had punched in a maneuver order to the computer, a separate data readout panel came alive, duplicating faithfully his own orders. There could be no question of a slipped finger or an error of this sort.

Satisfied with the cross-check, Dougherty nudged the autopilot control. The electronic robotry of Gemini responded instantly. Operating under the orders of the electronic brain, itself slaved to the computer, and the computer observing both the inertial guidance system readings and the subtly shifting radar echoes, Gemini fired its maneuvering rockets. The engines boomed silent within seconds.

He studied the visual display of the computer memory banks, glanced at the elapsed time indicator. Everything fitted in. Quickly he moved the gyros again to check the magnitude of the plane error.

There wasn't any—he was neatly in the slot.

And what also was vital information came in the radar readout. They were closer—down to just above eight miles separation. *That* could be a tremendous help. The plane correction maneuver had subtly shifted their orbital relationship. Mercury Seven was moving on the upswing of its orbit just a hair's breadth ahead of Gemini. If Dougherty could make his move *now,* without wasting time, he could take advantage of that break. Otherwise, he would have to fly Gemini through a constant-correction pursuit which would gulp both time and maneuvering fuel with abandon.

And there was also the matter of that Vostok out there. . . .

"I don't give a damn what old Keith wants," Dougherty muttered. "Pruett's coming home in this baby, and *not* by way of Moscow, if I have anything to say about it!"

He glanced ahead through the pilot window . . . nothing; too far yet for any really good visual identification, and he couldn't afford to waste time playing eyeball games. He—

"Gemini from Mercury. How you doing, boy?"

"You sound impatient, space cadet. Just tighten up your jockstrap and relax. Just completed the plane change. Radar shows eight miles separation. I'm punching in the keyboard now. . . We're going to give it a whirl for direct collision course. We'll never have a better chance than right now, and—"

"Hate to bust up your pretty words, carrot top, but you better kick that horse of yours quick."

Dougherty froze. *"Why?"*

"Well, Ivan seems like he's trying to cut into your routine of the cavalry troop to the rescue. I've just rolled around to take a look, and he is definitely thrusting again."

"How far out?"

"Hard to tell. I'm estimating maybe hundred, hundred and ten yards. He seems to be having some trouble with his yaw. The nose thrusters keep kicking in and out."

"Any more signals?"

"Negative. I think he must have drained a lot of his battery juice with those lights and he's playing it cool on those. Say, do you have visual contact with us yet?"

"No. I haven't been looking too hard. How you?"

"Negative. I've come around again to look through the window at where you should be, but I am not getting anything I can be sure of."

"Roger. Stand by, Dick. I've got to get this thing cranked in."

"Okay. Wind it up, carrot top."

Dougherty didn't answer. He would have been a lot happier if the Gemini tracking net had been operational, but they were still shifting equipment and modifying the system around the world stations when the decision came to go with the last Mercury shot. Had the Gemini system been GO, he would have had ground radar giving him constant corrections. Bermuda had helped, but that was the last of it for a while.

Everything depended now on the onboard computer. If he could make his move to slice a bit out of the belly curve of the orbit, he'd come up fast and sure. He grinned; just like the horse cavalry coming over the hill instead of chasing the Indians all the way around.

He read the computer display with a small cry of joy. He would never have it better than now. Quickly he tapped out the code on the keyboard. In effect he was ordering the computer to tell him exactly what changes in velocity and angular displacement were necessary to effect that vital collision-course move.

The computer chewed the instructions. While Dougherty fretted and waited . . . *Good Lord, I've never even thought about the fact that I'm weightless . . . and look at that sight! . . . all those incredible stars, and I never realized what . . . no time for that now. . . . C'mon, my robot friend, let's have the poop. . . .*

"How's it coming, Jim?" Pruett's voice was too calm, almost a monotone. *The poor bastard, he must be going through the ups and down of sweating this out. . . .*

"Doing fine, Dick. Charlie the robot is about to give me the word, and I'll punch in the commands. What's with Ivan?"

"About seventy yards. He's closing, but not too fast. No question about his yaw thrusters giving him trouble. That boy is good, though. He's compensating beautifully."

There was a pause.

"He's still too far out, I think, to try the maneuver of crossing to me. He'd have to be sure he wouldn't drift out once he shut everything down. He—"

"Christ, *hurry up*, Jim."

"Be there soon. . . . Stand by."

The computer lights gleamed. There they were—the changes represented on the X Y Z axes indicators.

Okay, now . . . let's get this bird around on the point, and ready to run. Dougherty gripped the attitude control and fired the thrusters to match the exact angles demanded by the computer in pitch, yaw, and roll. To be absolutely certain he punched in the Horizon Scan Mode. The autopilot immediately linked to the Gemini infrared horizon scanners, and took over control in pitch and roll. Dougherty nudged the stick until yaw was perfect, and switched control modes again, back to Direct.

Again he punched the keyboard. He cross-checked the computer readout with the command system, cross-checked again the display of the message he had punched for the autopilot.

"Okay, chum. We're firing up now. Try to get a visual track on me if you can."

"Roger, Gemini." *Pruett's voice . . . he didn't like it. He was on the emotional downswing again.*

Dougherty brought in the maneuvering engines, for full power. The two hundred pounds thrust shoved the capsule forward with a gentle but definite surge. Muted thunder vibrated through the cabin. He kept his hand poised over the manual cutoff control, watching the timer, scanning the gyros, being absolutely certain everything moved exactly on point.

"The cavalry troop is on its way, Mercury. . . ."

"Roger . . . I've got a definite visual on you, Jim. Or rather on your engines. They flare out beautifully. Unmistakable. Whip that hoss, boy."

No question, he was out of the mental hole. . . .

"Stand by one, Dick. . . . Okay! Engines just cut out. We've got a correction increment of one-six-eight feet per second and—hey!" His voice rose. "Radar shows less than one mile separation! Can you see me? Over."

Pruett laughed, excitement in his voice. "Eyeballs in and locked, Gemini. No question about it. You appear as a dim light at this time, but I can see you moving against the star field. Got the glasses on you for a few moments, and you sure do look good from here!"

"Roger, Dick. I have a visual sighting through the pilot window, but I can't tell whether it's you or Ivan. What's our friend doing?"

"Just a minute . . . I'm rolling around. Estimate about five zero yards. I don't see anything happening with his thrusters—no, they're on again. He seems to be having fits with that yaw. He's trying to make up some angular displacement, I think. He's still nudging in and—"

"Dick—"

"Yeah, Jim."

"If Ivan comes in—you go with him. Understand?"

"Screw you, carrot top. Just get your ass over here *quick*."

"Don't be a fool—"

"Knock off with the mouth and punch those buttons."

"Sure, sure. . . ."

He flicked the maneuvering system to *Standby* and studied the readout displays. The computer was chewing the new radar information and recomputing. The answer came out for a direct velocity increment of nineteen feet per second.

Dougherty wracked his brains. *To hell with that,* he thought. *If I know this system as well as I do, that means inching my way in. I'm going to chance it. . . .*

He punched in the orders for a velocity increment of forty feet per second, and set up the autopilot. He moved his hand and hesitated. . . .

"Seven—come in."

"Right here, Jim."

"Okay—now listen carefully. I'm going to exceed the computer recommendation for the next increment, about twice as much. The computer works things out on fuel economy. If I come in with forty fps, I should come sliding right on in toward you, and then I'll hit the forward engines to brake. We can afford the fuel.

"But—I should have, I need a better eyeball reference. Radar isn't that hot close in, and I don't want to go sliding past you. Any ideas?"

"Yeah—I've been thinking that one over also, and I've got the answer—the flares in the survival kit. I'm going to pitch around facing your direction of approach and go on auto mode. Then I'm going to blow the hatch and—"

"*What?*"

"Shut up! I've already dumped cabin pressure. A bit rough doing anything in this suit, constricted as hell. But I've dropped the suit pressure a bit and it helps. I'll blow the hatch and hope the auto will keep me locked this way; it should. Then I'll fire one flare on a vertical reference, about forty-five degrees up, and another one immediately after, forty-five down. You can't miss those things—and, well, just aim down the middle of the hole, and here I'll be.

"Okay—here goes the hatch—"

Pruett strained against the binding pressure of the suit to reach up for a cable. He got three fingers around the cable and yanked hard.

The capsule rocked sharply. Vapors appeared and instantly froze. He stared, eyes wide, as the hatch cover blew straight away from the ship, and he looked out into the yawning abyss. . . .

Suddenly he felt a touch of alien cold. *Just my imagination, damnit. I'm getting the shakes from all this. Grab tight of yourself, Pruett. You can't afford to start coming apart now.* . . .

He held the flare gun with both hands and aimed upward through the hatch, and squeezed. . . .

What happened? . . . Something is going on with the American. . . . I do not understand. It must be; yes—he has ejected his hatch. Curse that infernal yaw thruster! I am still at about fifty or sixty meters. It is too much of a risk yet to chance a free crossing to the American unless he also has maneuver control. And the other one is coming in. Ah, that cosmonaut is like an artist with that ship the way he is closing! What is that now! Flares!

Andrei Yakovlev smiled in grudging admiration. *Unless I close in at once, I think the other American is really going to come right on in. General Karpenko will not like this. But it does not matter. . . . I would like that man out there to live. . . .* He flexed his wrist, eased in the power. The Vostok slid in closer, and then its nose swung sharply from the erratic yaw control, and Yakovlev cursed bitterly. . . .

Dougherty punched the ignition control. He tensed as the spacecraft rumbled through its structure and pushed ahead. He strained to see a definite sign of the capsule. Directly ahead of Dougherty was a teardrop-shaped observation window. He looked down a scoop five inches deep and twenty inches long, a scalloped trough that gave him excellent sighting reference and—

292

There!

A searing ball of red flame appeared magically in the blackness and shot upward, directly toward him, but climbing at an angle, straight out, like a fiery arrow. *Of course! Zero g and the flare will shoot straight with no curve for a while. . . . There's the second flare; now, let's drop it in right where that flare started. I think I can make him out; damnit, he's still too dim. . . .*

"Seven! Fire another!"

Dougherty cut the autopilot control and went immediately to manual. It was like being in a fighter again. . . . He pulled the maneuvering engines to off and prepared to decelerate and—

Brilliant, dazzling light exploded silently ahead of him. *What in the—*

Vostok shone with intense light, and in that blue-white radiance Dougherty saw the Mercury capsule with absolute clarity, one-half of its surface reflecting the light from the Russian spacecraft.

"Hold the flare. . . . Ivan's giving us some help; he's turned on his lights and you're clear as a bell! Coming right on in. . . ."

God bless you, whoever you are in that ship. . . . He's saving the day for us . . . and maybe Pruett's life.

Andrei Yakovlev had realized at once what the second cosmonaut was attempting. Watching the other spaceship closing in rapidly, he knew also that the American was in the best position at the moment. And he could help. He grinned broadly; the Americans would not expect this, but it should help ease their task.

The big Russian spaceship eased around and locked to a new attitude, broadside to the Mercury spacecraft. Yakovlev glanced through a port, judged his distance correct, and switched on the lights. Instantly the American vehicle leaped into garish prominence.

There! There you are, my American comrades. Now you will have no problem to see one another. And I will remain here, watching. Still I may be of some assistance to you. It is interesting to think of this rescue mission, with still another ship, my Vostok, standing by. . . .

He pulled back on the knobbed handle. Thin flame spat forward, and his body pushed against the straps. Again the rumble as the engines fired. Gemini decelerated steadily.

Slightly off to the right . . . okay, feed in some yaw and pitch; there—now, just a bit of roll. Good! She's as sensitive as a cat on ice . . . and there he is, waiting. Goddamn, but we're slicing this one beautifully. . . . Maneuver engines off . . . one more short burst. Very, very good. . . . Okay, in with the attitude thrusters now. . . .

Gemini rolled gently, obeying the thrusters, and eased to a stop in relationship to the Mercury spacecraft; their orbital sweep around the planet was meaningless in reference to one another, just as a man standing on the earth can't sense the earth swinging around the sun, orbiting at nearly nineteen miles a second.

"Carrot top, but you do look *good!*"

"Nice to see you, too, space cadet. Ah, Dick, I've got the thrusters off. Look carefully. Do you see . . . can you tell if we've got any drift?"

"Stand by . . . negative. Nothing I can tell by looking. Hell, you're sitting right on top of me."

"Okay, fella. Now we make the big play. Let's get this over with. Ivan is sure a help with those lights." .

"And how! . . ."

"Let's get with it. Are you unstrapped?"

"Roger. All straps free. Hatch is gone. Thrusters are off. Powered down almost everywhere; no sweat from anything kicking in. Just a second—

"There. I've got the oxy bottle all set, strapped to my leg. I've already checked out the trilock. Pulled out the hose for a moment and no leakage. Plug snapped right in and sealed the suit port. Exhaust valve staying open, of course. I won't plug in the bottle. . . . I'll wait until you're here before I unplug the cabin hose and go to the bottle.

"I'll watch your movements. When you sign off on the radio, I'll start to pull the wires, and be ready for you when you get here."

"Roger."

"No—hold it. When you get here, I'll push the panel as far up as it will go. But I'm still going to need some help getting out of this bird. With this suit grabbing the way it is, working out of that hatch could be a problem."

"No sweat. Okay, now here's what I'm going to do. . . ."

Chapter XX

JIM DOUGHERTY moved quickly. From the gear locker, he withdrew a long, thin safety line that could withstand temperature extremes without losing pliability or strength. He leaned down and snapped a steel hook to the bar that ran across his seat, beneath his thighs. He yanked as hard as he could; the hook didn't move.

He checked the line to be sure it was free of snags, and then ran it through two rings on the harness strapped to his body around the pressure suit. He pulled through an additional dozen feet of line beyond the last ring, and secured the line to his harness with the snaphooks.

With the cabin pressure still full, he adjusted and tightened the strap clamps that held the oxygen bottle to his left leg. He released the cabin hose and turned the connection to its off position. Next he snapped the bottle connection to the suit inlet, twisting it sharply until he felt it snap home. He tugged and met full resistance, then pulled the T-handle until oxygen flowed from the bottle into the suit. It took only a moment to check the pressure readings.

He took a deep breath and forced himself to act coldly, efficiently. A mistake now could be fatal. . . .

He rechecked the instruments. All maneuvering engines and thrusters to *Off*. He glanced through the pilot window; the capsule seemed to be exactly where it had been before. *Thank God for that—no drifting we can see. It looks good, real good. . . .*

He released his straps until his body floated free of the seat. *Okay, here we go. . . .*

"Breaking contact now."

He did not wait for the answer, but unplugged the electrical cable connection to the suit. He reached up and slowly pulled on a handle. A hollow sound, a hissing roar that faded rapidly, came to him as the cabin pressure began to vent into vacuum. As quickly as the pressure level dropped, he felt his suit inflating, squeezing his body. He glanced down at his wrist cuff. The needle came around to read 4.4.

He looked up. Cabin pressure read *zero*.

Bracing his body with his feet and back, he reached up to grasp a small ratchet wheel. He turned steadily to the left. Ten locking dogs began to release their grip that clasped the hatch to the spacecraft cabin. He looked straight ahead at the hatch perimeter. The ratchet wheel stopped turning beneath his hand. With steady pressure he pushed. Ahead of him he saw the bottom line of the hatch move. The sealed groove of the hatch lifted slightly and he saw the hatch edge itself. He pushed some more, and gazed out at the thin line of black and . . . empty space.

The hatch kept moving. Dougherty brought his legs beneath his body, felt contact with the seat. He rose slowly, still keeping pressure against the hatch.

Moments later the hatch jutted up from the Gemini cabin. Jim Dougherty stood straight . . .

. . . *no; that's wrong. There's nothing against your feet but emptiness.* He hung, suspended, his feet an inch above the seat. He looked ahead, then turned his body . . . *slowly, carefully; you can't make any wrong moves under zero-g. . . . You must remember action and reaction. . . . Don't do anything sudden or you'll whirl around in the opposite direction. . . . Careful!*

He looked out into space. . . . His head roared.

It's—it's unbelievable!

Billions of stars gazed nakedly upon him. . . . He felt a sudden, deep humility. . . . *Good Lord!* he whispered.

He shook off the feeling, fought his mind back to the critical move he must now make.

Very, very carefully he grasped the hatch cover and worked his gloved hands to the edge. With the slightest of pressure he moved his body until his feet were planted firmly on the Gemini structure. *Keep a down pressure with your hands; that's it. Good. Move carefully, very carefully, or you'll spin off away from the ship, and you haven't got enough time to waste trying this several times. . . .*

He flexed his knees slightly, still pressing down with both hands. *Not good enough yet. . . .* He moved his feet two inches forward. . . . *There; that should do it. . . .*

He released his handgrip on the hatch, held his breath, and straightened out his legs.

He . . . floated.

Slowly, unmistakably, he floated.

His body drifted toward the Mercury spacecraft, only twenty feet away across an infinity of nothingness. . . .

He heard his breath wheezing, the air moving through his suit, trembling from the exhaust port.

He *seemed* to be absolutely unmoving. The capsule drifted slowly, drifted toward him.

It was drifting up . . . it would come up by his head. He fought the impulse to move his arms, to try to swing his body. He was afraid he would simply roll or tumble. He forced himself to wait. . . . He could almost hear the seconds ticking away.

Now . . . almost there. Don't grab at it! Do it easy, slow, gentle. . . .

His gloves brushed the surface of the capsule. He forced himself not to push; he tried to brake his motion with his fingers. The capsule still had its mass of 3,000 pounds, and he could rebound off. He held the gentle pressure with his fingers, then his hands, and let his body come around, his feet swinging down to the spacecraft.

The hatch . . . he grasped the open edge of the capsule hatchway and gripped hard. With his other hand he pulled in the loose safety line. There . . . he swung the end of the hook—*slowly, slowly!*—into the open space.

A moment later he felt the line tug sharply. Pruett had it! His breath came out in an explosive gasp.

The worst of it was done.

Inside the capsule, Dick Pruett slipped the line around his body. It was hellishly awkward in the pressure suit, but the floating line helped. He looped it between his legs, twining it around one of the suit harness straps. Then he brought it twice around his waist, slipped it again through his suit straps. His hands fumbled awkwardly, but he managed a simple knot, and tugged as hard as he could. *There . . . that does it. It may be clumsy, but it won't pull free.*

He heard three sharp rapping sounds. He grinned; Dougherty said he would come knocking at his door. . . .

Now to get out of this thing . . .

He had to keep reminding himself to brace against the

seat or the bulkhead, or to grasp something when he moved. But he had been weightless for more than five days, and it went much easier than he had expected. He raised one arm and pushed it through the hatch space. With his other arm he held fast to a support bar. Slowly he began to ease his way out.

He got his head clear—and received a close-up look at a boot. *Hell of a way to see Dougherty, but that's the best goddamned boot I've ever seen.*

It took almost all his strength to bring his other arm down against his body, fighting the suit pressure. He pressed against his midriff to keep the arm from jerking out awkwardly. Gently, he pushed with his feet.

He felt pressure beneath his left arm. Slowly he turned. Dougherty was gripping the hatch sill with one hand and helping to pull him through the hatch.

They looked face to face and grinned widely.

Dougherty leaned forward until his faceplate touched that of the other pilot. He applied a gentle pressure to keep the helmets in contact. They didn't need radio to talk this way; the sound would transmit directly through the helmets.

Dougherty almost laughed when he heard Pruett's voice, vibrating its way to him.

"You know you're the most beautiful looking son of a bitch I ever saw in my life?"

"Okay, space cadet. Daddy's come to take you home."

Pruett grinned at him like a delirious idiot.

Dougherty tugged gently; Pruett got his fingertips against the hatch sill and pushed. A moment later the two men floated free, drifting off at an angle from the spacecraft. The capsule was rolling very slowly.

Dougherty grasped Pruett's arm. He brought their helmets together.

"No time to waste. You've got only about ten minutes of oxygen left. Let's move."

"I'm with you, friend."

"Okay. Your line secured well?"

"Right.'

"Slide down and hang on to both my legs. It will be easier in that suit. Try to keep a steady pressure if you can; otherwise we'll be flopping around out here. I'm going to pull the line taut, and start easing us back to the ship. Ready?"

"Go."

Pruett pushed his way down and crawled around until he faced Dougherty's back. He circled Dougherty's hips with his arms, applying as much pressure as he could through the suit.

He felt a sudden tug. *Jim must have the line tight and is starting in. . . . Keep going, friend, keep going. . . .*

Andrei Yakovlev stared in wonder at the sight of the two figures, stiff and awkward in their movements, pressure suits shining brilliantly in his lights. *Good, good,* he whispered, *they are almost there.*

Dougherty reeled in the line, sliding his hands along in a clumsy pulling motion, drawing them closer to the ship. Then his hands touched.

You stupid bastard! he raged to himself. He had forgotten to release the copilot hatch! It was still dogged tight. And time—in the form of the vanishing oxygen in Pruett's bottle—was running out.

He bent his body to turn. He reached down and slapped Pruett's arm. The other man released his grip and floated awkwardly. *He must have realized almost as quickly as I did about the hatch. . . . Move, Dougherty, move!*

He loosened the line connecting him to Pruett. Grasping the hatch sill, he swung himself around and worked his way in, feet first, to the cabin. He pushed his body to a sitting position and grasped the overhead edge of a control switch panel. Awkwardly, perspiring freely in the suit, he pushed his head and shoulders across the space to the other seat. A few moments later the ratchet wheel ended its movement, and he shoved against the hatch.

He felt the line tug. Pruett was pulling himself in now, clumsy but sure of his movements. The hatch extended all the way out. He saw Pruett's gloves on the upper sill, and a moment later his boots came into sight.

Dougherty reached out and grasped his left leg and began to maneuver Pruett into the cabin. Slowly his body came down and his feet touched the floorboards. Dougherty helped to bend the knees of the other man until he could bring his body lower. Quickly he pulled the seat strap around tight on Pruett, securing him to the seat.

Pruett nodded his thanks and pulled the hatch cover

down. Dougherty signaled frantically with his arm and pointed to the line.

It took another two minutes to untie the safety line and push it away from the hatch. Dougherty signaled, pointing to the ratchet wheel. Pruett closed the hatch and began to turn the wheel, dogging and sealing the hatch.

Dougherty hauled in quickly on the line to bring it within the ship and clear his own hatch space. He pulled in the last of the line and left it dangling in mid-air.

Quickly, quickly!

He dogged the hatch, checked the seals, and pushed hard against the handle marked REPRESS.

Oxygen poured into the cabin. Moments later the dial came around to stop at exactly 5.1 pounds per square inch. Dougherty quickly powered up the environmental control system. He glanced to his side. Pruett had just completed hooking up his hose line.

With sweet, sweet relief the two men opened their faceplates. Both pilots dripped perspiration.

Pruett released the oxygen bottle and handed it silently to Dougherty.

The pilot stared at the gauge and felt a chill shudder through his body.

There was just over one minute of oxygen left in the cylinder.

Outside the cabin, the dazzling lights winked out.

Dougherty rolled the Gemini around until they could see the Russian.

The lights blinked rapidly on and off three times, and went out for good.

The three spaceships rushed around the planet. Two of them contained life; the third was an abandoned derelict.

Far below, the tidal wave of night-day rolled across the world. Dougherty pitched the spacecraft down. He stared in awe at the intense colors as they hurtled into the night, colors glowing deeply from within, unbelievably clear, and set against the backdrop of utter blackness that went on black forever and ever.

"I had no idea it could be like this," he whispered to Pruett.

"Watch."

The earth dissolved into a mass of stygian black. Just

300

below the curving rim there burned a deep, deep pit of nuclear fire. It was unbelievably *hot;* it was orange and red and white and yellow and it was heat like none other, as though they had peered deeply within the fires that burn inside the atom. The earth had become hard and impenetrable in its blackness, and the blazing nuclear globule seemed to permeate the black and to sink slowly into its mass.

Between the lower blackness and the great void that was space there ran a thin line of demarcation. This was the border visible only to the spaceman, a rim that hung suspended in nothingness and that separated black from black. At the very top of the rim, the onionskin of a planetary atmosphere, the colors blended into a spectrum that tantalized the eyes but refused distinction. Here there was a shifting green and yellow and a blue that was really an almost-blue . . . and a deep red, all of it swirling together. It had the thinnest crown—a crown flattened into a still thinner sheet, extending on either side, for hundreds and hundreds of miles to each side of that slowly vanishing globule of blazing fire.

They stared in wonder. . . . They looked just above the flattened crown where there was displayed a literally unearthly blue, glowing richly from within. They spoke no longer, swept up in the fantasy of space, and saw where the blue terminated suddenly, marking the final vestige of the skin of air which harbored the human race—the bulwark against vacuum.

The nuclear fire vanished. Thin tendrils glowed briefly around the curving edge of the planet, and then night was truly upon them.

Soon after, far off in the distance, they saw a sudden flash of fire. It lasted for ten seconds, and night reigned again.

"His retros," Pruett said. "Our friend is going home."

Eighteen minutes after that, Jim Dougherty flicked the switch to the Gemini retrosequence controller.

The seconds passed in silence. Then the retros thudded into life, and stopped.

Jim Dougherty turned to Pruett.

"And so are we," he said very softly.

"And so are we. . . ."

Acknowledgments

The story told in *Marooned* has been assembled with great care about a framework of technological actuality—the authenticity of programs and hardware, the reality of situations, and the rigid requirements of orbital laws and mechanics. Much of this is the result of my long association with Projects Mercury and Gemini, and related programs, in various capacities as a government consultant, newsman, and broadcaster. Close association with activities since 1950 at Cape Kennedy, active participation through a wide spectrum of actual flight—these and similar events were all vital to this story. I have taken no liberties with the technicalities of the American and Soviet manned space flight program which form the basic factual framework in *Marooned*, but have carefully remained within the restrictions of actuality. I am grateful to many people for their assistance in making the background and technical details in this novel very real. Thomas F. Heinsheimer, a brilliant young scientist, one of the designers of the Mercury-Atlas abort system, and a member of the design team for Apollo guidance at the Massachusetts Institute of Technology worked many hours with me to establish the accuracy of actual and created orbital events in the novel; the results of our labors were subjected to the scrutiny of top engineers and to electronic computers. My gratitude goes also to the personnel of the following offices of the National Aeronautics and Space Administration: the Goddard Space Flight Center in Maryland, the Launch Operations Center at Cape Kennedy, the Office of Information Services in Washington, and the Office of Public Affairs of the Manned Spacecraft Center in Houston. I am indebted to the McDonnell Aircraft Corporation (Mercury and Gemini spacecraft) for invaluable assistance; to friends at the many schools and research centers for aerospace medicine within the United States Air Force; and to Ed Lyons—close friend, tutor, and brilliant airman. All these people and many more, have provided the substance out of which came this book.

For those who care to study and check them further, the chief technical data pertaining to booster flight and orbital mechanics used in writing the novel will be found in the appendices that follow.

MARTIN CAIDIN

302

Appendices

Mercury-Atlas Launch Vehicle and Guidance System

Height of the Atlas-D booster for the manned Mercury orbital missions is 65 feet from the base of the booster to the adapter section for the Mercury spacecraft. Height of the entire Mercury-Atlas system from the booster base to the top of the spacecraft escape tower is 93 feet. The Atlas-D booster at launch weighs approximately 265,000 pounds. Atlas booster base diameter is 16 feet and tank diameter is 10 feet. The Atlas propulsion system consists of five engines. The main booster is in the form of a flared chamber skirt that surrounds the entire lower end of the vehicle. The booster consists of two main engines, each of which develops 150,000 pounds thrust for a sea-level rating of 300,000 pounds thrust (this thrust rating increases as the rocket ascends and air pressure diminishes). A single sustainer engine in the centerline of Atlas-D develops a sea-level rating of 60,000 pounds thrust (near SECO thrust has increased to 80,000 pounds). Two vernier engines for sensitive roll control and fine velocity adjustments each develop 1,000 pounds thrust. Launch thrust rating, then, is 362,000 pounds. Flight burning time extends from 300 to 320 seconds, depending upon mission.

Guidance System: The MA booster for earth orbital missions is controlled by a radio-inertial guidance system, a refinement of Azusa guidance from the Atlas ICBM system. Radio signals are broadcast from a transponder (amplifier for radio or radar transmission and/or responses) aboard the rocket as it climbs. The signals are measured by a powerful ground-based radar system. The flight data as determined by the radar-system controls are fed into an electronic computer. The computer immediately checks all the information it receives against the flight plan that was programmed before the flight. The computer notes any deviations from this plan. At once it transmits by radio signal flight corrections to the climbing rocket. These signals are picked up by a robot brain within the Atlas-D. The robot brain (also known as *internal programmer* or *autopilot*) gimbals the main booster and smaller vernier engine of the Atlas to modify its course as it ascends. This is the *radio portion* of the radio-inertial system. To complete the guidance system are the *inertial elements*—the gyroscopes that react to any changes of the Atlas-D through the three fundamental axes of flight: pitch, yaw, and roll. Any deviations from the flight path that were programmed before launch are noted and corrected.

In addition, there is an accelerometer to measure the rate of acceleration of the Atlas-D in terms of g-forces and time—a measure of the continuing increase in the velocity of the Atlas-D. "Reading" the guidance system and the performance of the Atlas-D at all times from the ground is the *impact predictor system*. This electronic system follows the powered flight of the ascending booster and predicts, at regular intervals measured in fractions of a second, where the booster would impact if its thrust failed at that instant. The system consists of a transponder carried in the booster that receives signals from ground antennas, then sends signals to the impact predictor station where they are analyzed for the computer which, in turn, plots the course on a board. As used in Mercury, the impact predictor system at Cape Kennedy, Florida, includes (1) the Azusa tracking system, (2) an IBM 704 high-speed digital computer, and (3) a plotting board in the main control room of Central Control, where the Range Safety Officer (who can order destruction of the booster) is located.

Appendix II

The Computer Operation

Four IBM 7090 electronic computers constitute the brain core of the Mercury mission. One 7090 operates at Cape Kennedy, the second at Bermuda (which has emergency secondary command operation capabilities), and the remaining two at the Goddard Space Flight Center in Maryland.

The Goddard-center role is considered one of the "miracles" of space-age operations. Built into the computers are special information channels that permit the astronaut flight to be conducted on a *real-time basis*. During the most critical parts of the orbital mission, the real-time channel is brought into maximum operation. It allows command personnel to read their information displays on the basis not of what happened several minutes in the past, but *now*, and in the immediate future.

Critical time-elements, as applied to the Mercury orbital flight, include the launch, ascent, and moment of insertion of the spacecraft into orbit. During the later minutes of flight, critical time exists for the period of re-entry, commencing from that moment that Cape Control institutes retrosequence and subsequent events.

From the moment that the Atlas booster lifts from Pad Fourteen to initiate the ascent, the Goddard 7090 computers move instantly onto a preprogrammed operational basis. The mechanics of the flight have been programmed into the computer operation to take

305

into consideration not merely the events that are scheduled, but also any possible combination of events. The moment that Atlas initiates first motion, the computers function on real-time. They receive information from the spacecraft and extensive data from the programming devices of the Atlas, such as accelerometers, attitude indicators, and other performance-reading instruments that portray a complete running flight picture measured down to a tolerance of one-half second.

The information is transmitted to Cape Kennedy and is almost instantaneously relayed to Goddard. Flight-performance readings continue to Goddard until the moment that the Atlas SECO takes place to end powered flight.

There is a period of some 30 seconds after capsule separation from the booster which is considered as *extremely critical* time. In this period the Goddard computers must digest the final bits of data on the booster phase of the mission, and they must make— still within the frame of 30 seconds or less—a positive *GO–NO GO* recommendation. The computers display simultaneously at Goddard and at Cape Control in Florida data pertinent to the orbital parameters and events that will exist as dictated by orbital conditions at the moment of separation.

Subsequent to this phase of the mission, tracking data from all world stations are computed at the rate of "1,000 data bits" per second.

Appendix III

Comparisons of Three Mercury Orbital Missions

	MA-6/Glenn	MA-9/Cooper	MA-10/Pruett
Maximum Velocity .	17,544 MPH	17,547 MPH	17,548 MPH
Orbital Inclination .	32.5°	32.5°	32.5°
Perigee [1]	97.6 mi.	100 mi.	101 mi.
Apogee [1]	162.1 mi.	165.9 mi.	177 mi.
Orbital Period [2] . .	88.2 min.	88.7 min.	88.78 min.
Capsule Launch Weight	4,100 lbs.	4,000 lbs.	4,266 lbs.
Capsule Orbital Weight	2,987 lbs.	3,000 lbs.	3,089 lbs.
Capsule Landing Weight	2,400 lbs.	2,460 lbs.	N/A

[1] Statute Miles
[2] Earth Referenced

Appendix IV

Vostok IX Booster: Launch—Staging—Specifications

Baikonur launch site is at 47°22′ North latitude. Normal launch azimuth is at approximately 48° to obtain orbital inclination of 65°. Vostok IX cannot be launched on ascending dogleg basis to reach Mercury orbit at inclination of 32.5°. Distance from Baikonur to intersection of Mercury orbit is approximately 2,500 miles, and the dogleg would have to occur approximately over Nanyang, China. Long before this was reached all propellants would be exhausted. Thus Vostok IX launches on azimuth of 90° from launch site, swinging into the Baikonur latitude, or orbital inclination of 47.3°.

At liftoff +368 seconds, Vostok IX is in 47.3° inclination orbit with payload of 30,400 pounds. Perigee of 101 statute miles approximately that of Mercury Seven; apogee, yet undetermined, above 260 statute miles.

Vostok IX 47.3° Orbit Payload

Vostok weight/dry . . . . 9,800 lbs.
Vostok translational fuel on board . . . . 2,000 lbs.
Empty transstage . . . . 2,000 lbs.
Fuel requirement for Vostok IX orbital transfer . . 12,600 lbs.
Stage II empty weight . . . . 4,000 lbs.
Total weight injected into original 47.3° orbit, including transstage booster and fuel . . . . . 30,400 lbs.

Vostok IX Booster—Stage I

Thrust (4 engines x 500,000 lbs.) . . . 2,000,000 lbs.
Stage I tank diameter . . . . 19.6 ft.
Stage I structural weight/dry . . . . . 75,000 lbs.
Stage I fuel/oxidizer weight . . . . . 1,303,000 lbs.
Stage I fuel consumption . . . . . . 2,200 lbs. per sec.
per engine

Stage I Burning Times/g-Factors

Engines 1 and 3 . 137 seconds . . . . burnout = 7.75g
Engines 2 and 4 . 160.5 seconds . . . . burnout = 5.7g
(Lessened final cutoff g-factor to reduce structural rebound.)

Launch factor g 1.33
Stage I maximum g 7.75
Stage I BECO g 5.7

Vostok IX Programming and Specifications—Phase I

Vostok booster liftoff weight/complete .	1,510,000 lbs.
Stage I mass ratio	7.29
Stage I performance yield (includes consideration for velocity/thrust gained, and drag/gravity losses)	16,000 ft. per sec.
Stage I average specific impulse	250 secs.
Stage I maximum thrust/immediately prior to cutoff of Engines 1 and 3 at liftoff + 137 seconds	2,400,000 lbs.
Total weight at Stage I cutoff	207,000 lbs.
Weight of Vehicle Assembly remaining after Stage I cutoff and separation (jettison) of Stage I	132,000 lbs.
Weight of remaining Vehicle Assembly at ignition of Stage II (ullage rockets weight loss = 300 lbs.)	131,700 lbs.
Stage I retros (4 solid-propellant rockets each burning 1 second) fire at litfoff +	161 secs.
Stage II ullage rockets (4 hypergolics each burning 4 seconds) fire at liftoff + .	162 secs.
Stage II ignition (+ 3 seconds ullages burn)	165 secs.

Vostok IX Booster—Stage II

Thrust (2 engines x 75,000 lbs.) . . . . 150,000 lbs.
Total fuel/Stage II . . . . 101,300 lbs.
Average specific impulse/Stage II . . . 300 secs.
Fuel consumption rate/Stage II . . . . 500 lbs. per sec.
Total burning time/Stage II . . . . . 202.6 secs.
Stage II SECO/Liftoff + ... 368 secs.
Stage II total velocity delivered (includes velocity/thrust gained and small gravity loss) . . . . 14,500 ft. per sec.
Stage II mass ratio 4.4
Stage II ignition g-factor 1.14
Stage II cutoff g-factor 4.95

Vostok IX Transfer Maneuver/Liftoff + 343 Minutes

Azimuth . . . . 130.5°
Deviation from orbital inclination . . . . 83.2°

Ullage rocket burn time . . . . 4 secs.
Transstage engine burn time (ignition comes at ullage ignition + 3 seconds) . . . . 50.5 secs.
Transstage engine thrust . . . . . . 75,000 lbs.
Mass ratio 1.9
Fuel (hypergolic) consumption . . . . . 250 lbs. per sec.
Total transstage fuel burned . . . . . 12,600 lbs.
Ignition g-factor 2.88
Burnout/cutoff g-factor 5.43
Velocity change accomplished in transstage maneuver . . . . 6,500 ft. per sec.

Appendix V

Notes on Orbital Times

Reference: Mercury Seven and Vostok IX, after the Vostok orbital plane change, both spacecraft in 32.5° orbit.

Using the earth as a base reference, the earth-based orbit, which is computed with consideration of the rotating surface of the earth, produces an orbital period of:

Mercury Seven . . . . 93.78 minutes
Vostok IX . . . . 95.78 minutes

The Keplerian Orbit is *not* earth-based, but is space-referenced. It does not consider the rotational movement of the earth, and produces an orbital period of:

Mercury Seven . . . . 88.78 minutes
Vostok IX . . . . 90.78 minutes

As considered by a tracking station at any one point on the surface of the earth, the earth-based orbit with the longer orbital period must be used.

Appendix VI

Notes on Gemini and Gemini Systems

(1) *Excerpts on Gemini Launch Simulation Problem: Source—NASA* A launch simulation was conducted to evaluate the launch vehicle displays and to confirm that the crew could assess the status of the launch vehicle and take abort action if required. . . . Three degrees of angular freedom were available in the moving base cockpit with adequate displacement and washout capabilities to simulate small perturbations of the normal vehicle accelerations. In addition, a pitch rotation of plus or minus 100 degrees from the

horizontal permitted a partial simulation of the direction and magnitude (up to 1g) of axial accelerations. The cockpit motions were accomplished with hydraulic servo mechanisms driven by analog signals. The cockpit was rotated in pitch to 57 degrees from the horizontal for the launch position. At liftoff the cockpit was rotated from 57 to 75 degrees, producing the sensation of liftoff thrust to the pilot. The cockpit then continued to rotate up to 90 degrees, representing the first few seconds of acceleration after launch. For abrupt changes in axial acceleration such as staging and loss of thrust, the cockpit was rotated rapidly downward.

. . . The simulation program involved 51-malfunction runs representing nine major types of malfunctions. . . . Selected malfunctions were based on failure analysis data for the Titan II launch vehicle.

The NASA astronauts who participated in the simulation were given only one day of indoctrination. Each pilot was scheduled for approximately 75 runs, 65 runs having malfunctions and 10 being normal. Each of the 51-malfunction runs was presented to the pilots at least once, and the 13 most difficult runs were presented twice to each pilot. . . . It becomes readily apparent to the pilots that the most critical malfunctions were engine failures or tank pressure losses immediately after liftoff or immediately after staging. The critical engine failures were readily detectable through redundant cues, including decrease in sound level, decrease in acceleration, and illumination of the combustion chamber pressure light. Pilot reaction time to this failure was as low as four-tenths of a second. Reaction time requirements varied from approximately one second to 2.5 minutes, depending upon the type and time of malfunction. Several of the malfunctions . . . were noncritical and required no abort action.

(2) *Excerpts on Gemini Mission Control: Source—NASA* The Flight Director will . . . receive inputs concerning the performance of the spacecraft and its systems, the launch vehicle, and the flight crew from flight control personnel; and on the basis of their analysis, and by correlation with the detailed mission rules, he will direct continuation or abort of the mission.

The basic objective of the Gemini mission is to place a target vehicle in orbit and follow it with a manned vehicle which is to rendezvous wth the target vehicle with a minimum of fuel usage and in the shortest time . . . the countdown of both vehicles must be conducted in the same period . . . the launch time and launch azimuth of the second vehicle are extremely critical if the objectives are to be met.

There is about a 20-minute period each day when launch can occur into the correct orbital plane and with an acceptable phase difference. This time period corresponds to a plane error of 0.4 degrees and a phase difference of 70 degrees. . . .

The launch phase remains the most critical period of the flight.

However, a redundant guidance system with automatic and manual switchover has been provided in the Gemini-Titan configuration.
. . . Preplanned mission documentation and computer programs will again be used to assist in determining the course of action in the case of contingency situations. One point which should be mentioned is that, in the case of Gemini, the crew has a much greater onboard capability than before. The computer controlled guidance and navigation system together with the propulsion system provide the crew with the capability to complete a normal mission without further trajectory assistance once the initial ephemeris of the two vehicles has been properly established by the ground systems.

(3) *Excerpts on Gemini Rendezvous Mission Launch and Terminal Rendezvous Phase Maneuvers: Source—NASA* [One] variable-azimuth launch technique makes use of *launch-vehicle guidance in yaw during the latter phases of powered flight to minimize or steer out plane errors.* Guidance is accomplished by varying the launch azimuth of the spacecraft so that the azimuth is an optimum angle directed toward the target's plane. This will reduce the out-of-plane distance prior to initiation of yaw guidance. . . .
. . . appreciable performance margins may not be available. Therefore, the Gemini parameters are being selected on the basis of a parallel-launch variable technique. However, provision is being made for the variable-azimuth yaw steering technique so that it could be used should a sufficient performance margin be available. The variable-azimuth launch techniques will provide biases to offset relative nodal regression effects of the two orbits so that a minimum out-of-plane error is provided at the start of the terminal phase rather than at insertion of the spacecraft in its initial plane. . . .

In the terminal phase of the mission, Gemini will develop terminal maneuver techniques in which an orbital mechanics guidance method and an optical guidance method are used. An interferometer-type radar with both angular and range measuring capability, together with the onboard computer, will provide the hardware system necessary to compute an optimum orbital mechanics solution. The onboard computer will be programmed with a set of equations which describe the motion of the spacecraft with respect to a rotating coordinate frame centered in the target vehicle. These equations will be "modified Clohessy-Wiltshire" . . . linearized equations of motion.

The spacecraft will acquire the . . . target vehicle with its radar at a range of approximately 250 nautical miles. Upon acquisition, the radar will provide range, range-rate, and angular-displacement information. Range and range-rate information will be displayed to the astronauts while range and angular-displacement data are introduced into the computer. With these raw data, the computer will calculate the relative velocity components along the three axes. From these velocity components, the relative motion equations will be used to determine the velocity increment and direction required in real time to establish the spacecraft on the optimum intercept course. This information will be displayed to the astronauts who will monitor the changing velocity and position requirements. . . .

There are two primary methods of conducting a terminal maneuver. One method uses orbital mechanics to optimize the intercept course of the chaser vehicle. This method requires the use of a radar with angular measuring capability and an onboard computer. The method minimizes the fuel required for the maneuver, and thus allows relatively large initiation ranges between the target and chase vehicle. Approximately 30 to 330 degrees of orbital travel would be required to complete the maneuver, depending on the accuracy of the launch and midcourse maneuvers.

A second method for conducting the terminal maneuver would use optical guidance for establishing the intercept course. This method is more expensive from a fuel consideration since it does not use orbital mechanics as such to optimize the hardware. The initiation ranges would be more restricted but the hardware requirements would be minimized. In order to use an optical guidance method, ranging information would be provided to the astronauts. This information can be provided by a radar with range and range-rate capability or by cruder optical measuring devices such as reference guide or simple sextant.